MANHANDLED

ROCKSTAR ROMANTIC COMEDY

CARI QUINN
TARYN ELLIOTT

MANHANDLED

© 2017 Taryn Elliott & Cari Quinn

Rainbow Rage Publishing

Cover by LateNite Designs

ISBN: 978-1-940346-48-9

First print edition: July 2017

ACKNOWLEDGEMENTS

Sometimes we make up fictional places that end up having the same names as actual places. These are our fictional interpretations only. Please grant us leeway if our creative vision isn't true to reality.

For all those who live with songs in their head at all times.
You are our people.

1

KEYS

"DUM-DUM-DA-DUM, DUM-DUM-DA-DUM." I HUMMED UNDER MY breath as I fluffed out my skirts.

"Keys, if you don't stop humming that, I'm going to strangle you."

I stuck out my tongue at the all-around pain in the ass I usually called friend. Hudson Wyatt, our drummer, had been a bear lately. Actually, everyone in the band had been.

Well, except Hunter. He was wearing googly-eyes with hearts for irises. Our lead singer was whipped in a serious way. Don't get me wrong, it was adorable as hell. I just never thought I'd see the day that a woman—and a pair of dogs—would wrap him around their fingers —and paws—so tightly.

"Why are you so bitchy?"

"Because this wedding has fiasco written all over it. Who the fuck has three dogs in a wedding?"

"People who love animals."

"Love animals on your own time. I'm the one who has to try and keep white hair off my tux." Wyatt pulled a mini lint roller out of his breast pocket and started attacking the four hairs that dared mar his lapel. "Armani should not have fluffy white fur on it. Ever."

"Not your wedding," I said in a singsong voice. It was a refrain I'd been singing for three weeks.

"I hate you."

"Nah. You love me." I had to tip my head back to meet his arctic gaze. I was still in my stocking feet, because I refused to put on the stupid ankle breakers that I had to wear with my dress until the last possible moment.

In fact, I wondered if Kennedy would notice if I wore my Chucks down the aisle. I had cute lilac ones that would coordinate well with the deep purple dress. I didn't really do heels unless there were boots involved. I could rock a pair of boots.

I was actually looking forward to boots weather. It was late August and I was bored with sundresses and shorts. I was a fall girl. Not that there was much of a fall in Los Angeles, but enough that I didn't sweat my butt off when I was wearing cute sweaters or jackets with my jeans.

Man.

Jeans.

Can I explain how sick I am of shaving my legs?

But alas, that wasn't the topic of conversation today. Wyatt stomped off, muttering about crazy animal people. I wasn't going to let him ruin my good mood. Today was all about wedding rings, the wedding march, and a kickass end to the whirlwind courtship of one Kennedy McManus and Hunter Jordan.

Our lead singer and the PR princess who loved him to pieces. Kenny had been the one to save our bacon when Hunter had gone a little bananas with the infamous *Rolling Stone* cover.

I couldn't really blame him. Personally, I thought it was pretty hilarious that he got a taste of what women dealt with on a daily basis. I couldn't count the number of times men stared at my girls instead of into my eyes when we were at fan events.

Actually, scratch that—*any* event. The suits—aka record execs and marketing people—were worse than any fan. Since I was the one and only female in the band, they thought I was pretty much party central. I disabused them of that fact quickly, but it was a never-ending battle.

Long story short, I had to force myself to feel sorry for Hunter. Especially since that cover shot our careers back into gear. Our careers had been languishing for a long damn time. Now, we had a sold-out tour to get ready for and a triple platinum album.

And not all of it had been because of Hunter's goods outlined in a tight pair of jeans. Who knew a male appendage held this much power? I mean they all believed it did, but the actuality was mind-boggling.

Hammered, our band, was in a really good place right now, so I tried not to focus on the pissy nature of half my friends. There was something more than dog fur up Wyatt's ass, Hunter waffled between basket case and sickeningly happy, and Bats was either silent or missing in action.

Owen was my rock lately, and Zach was his usual brand of crazy. Zach was our co-lead guitarist with Bats. We usually called them the Terror Twins for a reason. And the fact that Bats was MIA so much was definitely messing with the band mojo.

I was hoping this wedding would put us all back on an even keel. No one could duck out of the festivities. There were enough bottles of bourbon on the bar of the suite we were in to lubricate a good mood, at the very least.

We were back where it all began. The Ace Hotel had been the scene of the crime, so to speak. It was where Hunter and Kenny met, so it was only fitting to have the wedding here. It sure didn't hurt that Hunter's famous chef bestie, Tristan, also had a lot of pull at the hotel.

Hunter paced up and down the length of the room. Noah, Hunter's brother, had left to make sure everything was running smoothly. I went over to the bar and cracked open the bottle of Belle Meade Tristan had sent up.

I splashed some into a glass for myself and sipped. Smoke and the sweet bloom of caramel and cherry notes pulled out a low moan from me.

"You're sharing that, right?" Bats asked from the far side of the room. His knee was still bouncing as he gripped his phone.

I pulled down five other glasses and dealt them out around the bar top. "You know it." I dumped bow-tie shaped ice cubes into each one.

All the important men in my life came forward in various levels of suited-up status. Zach had his tie around his forehead like an '80s video reject, Owen was almost as impeccable as Wyatt, Bats had his tie askew and his sleeves rolled up.

Hunter drummed his fingers against the bar, sweat rolling down his temple.

I slid the glass in front of him. "Relax. The wedding is going to be beautiful."

"I just want it over with."

I arched a brow at him.

Hunter flushed. "Not like that. I just want her mine, then I can breathe and know nothing is going to happen. Right now, all I can think of are reasons for her to turn around and say she changed her mind."

"If she didn't change her mind after you got arrested—almost twice, mind you—then I think you're golden."

Bats's ears went red. He dug out his phone and flipped it around and around in the palm of his hand. When the screen lit up, he quickly flicked a message away.

I managed to cut the growl growing in my throat to a purr. Bats glanced at me and shoved his phone back into his pocket.

Today was not the day for him to pull his bullshit with Victoria like he had been for the last few months. We'd been on tour for the last eleven weeks, and Bats's regular sightings with Hunter's ex-fiancée were wearing on everyone.

If she showed up today, there would likely be bloodshed. And if Hunter did strangle Bats or Victoria, then there really wouldn't be a wedding. I wasn't sure there was enough subtext in the universe for me to relay all of that in one look at Bats, but I was going all in.

He downed his glass and poured another.

Point made, me thinks.

I splashed refills in everyone's glasses. "To Hunter and his beautiful bride. Today is going to be perfect."

All my guys raised their glasses. "To Hunter," everyone said.

2

KEYS

"COME ON, CUJO. GIVE ME A BREAK HERE." I SETTLED THE LITTLE Morkie on my lap out of the sun. There was a light murmur of people talking as the wedding party made their way down the aisle.

"Look at Daddy right down there waiting for you. You have a very important job today."

Cujo's little pink tongue lolled out the side of his mouth. A purple bow wove through his studded black collar, and two wedding rings clinked together with each hiccup the dog made.

"Here."

I looked up to find Tristan standing beside me with a Dixie cup full of peanut butter. "Really?"

"Works for humans," he said with a shrug. He had on a plum-colored chef's jacket with tight black jeans and motorcycle boots. He was Hunter's best friend, but had deferred to Hunter's brother for best man status so he could cook for us instead. He was the head chef here at the Ace Hotel.

I took the cup and held it out to Cujo. He happily inhaled the peanut butter then licked my face.

"Oh, man. All right."

Hunter shot out his cuffs again and rolled his shoulders.

"Okay, Daddy really is going to have a heart attack. And you know you want to see Mommy with her pretty dress, right?"

Cujo yipped.

"See?" I set him on the floor and the little dog danced around my ankles. "If you trip me, I'll take away the huge pack of rawhide I smuggled into my hotel room."

He plopped his butt down and lifted both his front paws.

"Yeah, yeah. You're cute."

Sammy popped up from his seated position. The Australian Border Collie was dapper in his purple bandana with the single platinum ring hanging from his neck.

Tank, Kennedy's childhood dog, was sitting pretty next to Hunter at the end of the long white-silk runner that bisected the one hundred white chairs that made up the intimate ceremony. Lilacs and white lilies were tied to every other row, and Los Angeles had blessed us with a serene afternoon with only a touch of smog.

"Okay, we can do this, right, boys?"

Cujo pranced and Sammy wagged his tail.

"Of course we can." I patted both dogs and straightened as the last bridesmaid made her way down the aisle accompanied by Zach.

I grabbed my bouquet and gave the dogs their signal. Kenny had been working with them both for weeks.

"Nice and easy," I said quietly. The dogs stopped at the end of the runner and barked. The guests laughed, as they should. Cujo—Hunter's dog, of course—changed his mind about following directions, and went up on his back paws and danced down the aisle.

"Stealing the show," I said out of the side of my mouth at Sammy, who walked patiently at my side.

He leapt into Hunter's arms for praise. Wyatt rolled his eyes and stared up at the sky.

The priest patted Cujo's head before he was set down to stand between Noah and Hunter. I moved to the bride's side and Sammy sat beside Carter, Kenny's best man/maid of honor—because why would any part of this wedding be traditional? It so wasn't them.

When everyone was settled, the wedding march started. Instead of an organ and strings, Bats played a twelve-string acoustic guitar for Kennedy's walk down the aisle.

He'd slowed down the song and spun it out until it was a beautiful version that immediately put tears in my eyes. Things had been so strained between Reed and Hunter, but the fact that he'd obviously put so much thought into the traditional song gave me the first burst of hope in a long damn time.

Kenny paused at the end of the runner, her simple off-shoulder dress falling in a swish of white silk that trailed behind her with a short train. She was radiant and perfect, with just a touch of amethyst at the gathered silk at her midsection that left the rest of the silk flowing behind her in perfect folds. A matching cluster of amethyst fastened her veil into her sweep of auburn curls.

She walked up the aisle with her father, but her eyes were for Hunter. No hesitation, no trembles, just a woman walking down the aisle to the man she loved. Down to her future.

Hunter's gray eyes were shiny. A huge smile lit his face when he saw her.

My eyes misted again.

I wanted a man to look at me like that.

I couldn't remember *anyone* looking at me like that, to be honest. Pride and love shining brighter than any jewel, or sun, or light.

That was them.

It may have been a whirlwind romance, but there was no way anyone could deny the love between them. When Kenny's father handed her off with a kiss, Hunter clasped their hands and didn't let go.

The vows were said with very little preamble. Kenny sniffed a little during the embellished vows that Hunter had added to his side of the deal.

Never in all her life had I thought Hunter was secretly a big ol' smushball, but he was. At least for Kenny. Anyone else would probably see the receiving end of his fist if they called him on the sensitivity thing.

It was refreshing, and jealousy-inducing.

I'd had a few dozen boyfriends in my twenty-nine years, but none had ever looked at me like that. Not even a hint of it. A few friends and family members had gotten married over the years, and none of them had choked me up like this either.

Man, what the heck was wrong with me?

I wasn't the girl who pined for suits and lace. I'd rather have a guy who could party with me in a mosh pit at a show, drive two hours for a hamburger, or backpack around the mountains. Even Hunter and Kenny were way more conventional than I was, and that was saying something.

But as Noah crouched down for the rings from Cujo, and Carter unfastened the ring from Sammy's collar, I had to blink away tears. This was the perfect ceremony for them.

Some of the traditional touches with a twist of animal crazy.

When the rings were exchanged and the slightly inappropriate kiss signaled the end of the ceremony, I was happy to get my bearings again.

I laughed and clapped with everyone as Hunter swept her up into his arms and stalked down the aisle. Instead of going into the covered areas for the reception, he stalked off to a door along the edge of the pool.

Where the heck was he going?

Hunter looked over his shoulder at the wedding guests and waved as he ducked inside the "Employees Only" door.

I rolled my eyes. He probably had some ridiculously fun version of a scavenger hunt in store for her. The tunnels of the Ace Hotel were their particular playground. Or they were going to do things I didn't want to think about. Possibly a few I saw on YouTube, from the dozens of videos that caught the two of them on more than one occasion.

Hunter was quite the exhibitionist for someone who wanted to keep his life private.

And that was enough of that thought train. I linked my arm through Noah's. "Good job, best man."

"Not so bad yourself, dog wrangler." He grinned down at me with those ridiculous dimples. If the idea of hooking up with Hunter's brother didn't feel so incestuous, I'd be on him like a rash.

"Care to join me for a drink?" I asked.

He nodded and we headed into the covered area of the reception. He was good at casual conversation, and was unusually good at listening.

He was light where Hunter was dark. Golden-toned skin and light eyes that bled more into blue than Hunter's gray-washed green. The two men also couldn't be any more different in temperament.

Probably why I had to talk myself out of a crush a few times a day when he came to visit. I'd kill Hunter if he was my significant other, but Noah was a bit aloof and had an air of badass that seemed to permeate the room when he was in it.

He was only alluring because I saw him for approximately fourteen hours total every few months. Oh, and he smelled like leather and sin even when he was wearing a suit.

Hunter and Kennedy didn't want a formal affair for the reception, so a buffet was set up on either end, with open bars available at a few different stations around the rooftop.

Noah waded into the fray for a tumbler of bourbon for me.

Fat white lights were strung along the rafters of the covered areas. A large dance floor was set up with a band that could play every cover song under the sun. The four corners had towering spires that crisscrossed with lights for when the sun went down.

I smiled and nodded at people I knew, feigned a polite half-smile for those I didn't. When I spotted my sister, my heart sank.

I'd hoped she and my parents would disappear after the ceremony. They were only here because it was proper. And they'd leave an equally proper card in the large white wrapped box at the bride and groom table.

Hope Driscoll sailed across the sea of people, her fingers loosely linked with my brother-in-law's. She was wearing a slim rose-colored dress that emphasized her bump just enough to ensure people knew she was expecting prodigy number two, and not carrying baby weight from el numero uno.

Hope reached me and pressed an air kiss to my cheek. "You look beautiful, Faith." She clutched my fingers quickly before backing up to stand beside the hubs.

Andrew nodded at me. "Hey, sis."

"Aren't you two all glowy?"

Hope twisted her fingers with Andrew's and looked up at him with adoring eyes. "We're having another girl."

A small twinge hit me low. I wasn't even close to ready for the baby train my sister was on, but again—someone in my life with stars in their eyes for a man. It seemed so foreign to me.

Would Hunter and Kenny be just like them this time next year?

Perish the thought.

"Mom and Dad were looking for you as well."

"They're still here?"

"Yes. Dad ran into a few clients, so they decided to stay for the reception."

Fabulous.

Noah came up beside me, and I practically snatched the glass out of his fingers. He gave me that Noah arched brow he'd perfected when I downed it and relieved him of his own. Today was going to require far more alcohol than I'd first thought.

Hope eyed Noah before slanting a look at me. "Who's your friend?"

Oh, no. I could see the matchmaker gleam in my sister's eye. She wanted me as blissfully attached as she was.

My family didn't understand any part of my lifestyle. From the full ride at Berkeley that I'd turned down to go on tour with

Hammered, to the trust fund I'd created with my fame. None of it made any sense to my high-powered, very rich family.

I may have grown up with a silver spoon—literally—in my mouth, but I'd never really cared about the huge house and labels, unless I counted my Chucks. There were no other shoes that would do as far as I was concerned. Probably why I had a good twenty-seven pairs at last count. Nor did I like the list of acceptable men that my father seemed to have for his girls.

Hope had fallen in line quickly, but then again, she liked the Santa Barbara country club set. She'd grown up playing tennis and "doing lunch" with my mother. I'd been too busy sneaking into bars. Not to drink—okay, well, not only to drink. I loved music. I learned how to play the blues and hard rock on the Strip. Any kind of music I wanted to experience, it was there.

Consequently, I'd never really been all that close to my mother or sister. Didn't stop them from trying to get me to turn my life around—their words, definitely not mine.

"This is Noah Jordan, Hunter's brother."

Hope's eyes sparkled as she held out a very dainty hand with its perfect sheen of pearl polish to accentuate the platinum and diamonds she wore. "What is it that you do, Mr. Jordan?"

"I'm in a security firm."

"Oh." Hope's blue eyes widened. "What exactly does that mean?"

I slurped down the last of Noah's drink. "It means he carries a gun and shoots people."

"Faith," Hope gasped.

I shrugged.

Noah slid his hand along my lower back and thwacked my zipper. I just smiled wider and plucked out an ice cube and crunched loudly.

"I handle some bodyguard duty, but mostly just a lot of babysitting. Kind of like what your sister needs on occasion."

I squinted my eyes at our personal bodyguard. "I have Patrick." I craned my neck and pointed at the hulking redhead with his arms folded in perpetual pissed off-ness. His hair was buzzed tight to his head and he wore aviators so people didn't know he was constantly skimming the room for trouble.

Whether it was from the band members, or outside trouble, was always a crapshoot.

"He takes care of us on tour. Makes sure the handful of crazy fans stay at a distance."

Hope frowned. "What do you mean, 'crazy'?"

I glanced down at my short bronze nails and dozen rings stacked on my long fingers. It wasn't exactly my favorite conversation. For the most part, being a musician was amazing. The tours could be grueling, but the fans were awe-inspiring. Mostly. "Not a big deal. Just some fans get a little overzealous in their love."

"Like men?" Hope whispered.

I glanced up. "Sometimes."

"Women?" she squeaked.

I grinned. "Sometimes."

"Wow." Hope's eyes were the definition of owlish. A tiny wrinkle formed between her brows, then she chewed on her bottom lip.

If she actually asked the question brewing in that good-girl brain of hers, I'd eat my favorite pair of *Dr. Who* Chucks.

I hadn't been with a guy in a while, and I resisted any and all fix-ups from her and our mother. She glanced at Noah, then back at me, then finally made a "hmm" sound.

"Patrick keeps me safe. Not to worry." I had to bite the inside of my cheek to stop the smile. Hope was just too easy to tease.

She opened her mouth as if to say more, but snapped it shut when our parents waved and made their way over.

On second thought, maybe I could bribe Noah into playing my boyfriend for the night. It was better to get a disapproving look from my father than to endure the list of eligible bachelors my mother probably had in her iPhone.

My mother was wearing a baby-blue dress with a slim black belt that was a throwback to Jackie O's style. Her hair was a perfect champagne blonde and swung in a knife-blade sweep of straight hair just above her shoulders. My father wore a sand-colored suit with a matching blue tie.

Prom.

How sweet.

I beat down the snark with my internal bat. It was always at the ready.

My parents weren't bad people. Actually they were the nicest people on the planet, as far as I was concerned. The problem wasn't them. It was me. I didn't belong in their country-club lifestyle.

I was dark-washed denim and a rude T-shirt to my mom's silk and pearls.

I was seedy bars with a battered upright piano jammed in the corner screaming my name. They were a baby grand on glossy marble floors with Beethoven's 5th playing in the background at a party.

I was rock and roll, and they were classical.

Noah must have read my mind, because his pinkie brushed mine. He'd play the boyfriend if I really wanted him to. We'd done a similar role play at a party in Hollywood. Noah might be the quiet brother, but he was far more intuitive than people gave him credit for.

I lifted both glasses. "Refill?" I asked him.

His dimples flashed. "Sure."

"Thanks."

I let my mother envelop me into her Dior signature scent. She didn't give air kisses like Hope. She squeezed and didn't worry about wrinkles. She tucked a few strands of my hair around my ear. "So nice to see it back to blonde."

"Mom."

She sighed. "Hair isn't meant to be blue."

The only reason mine was back to my natural color was because everyone and their dog had rainbow hair these days. Going back to my pale blonde was actually being rebellious.

She cupped my cheeks. "You're beautiful. I'm so glad this was a traditional wedding."

I rolled my eyes.

If I ever got married, I'd have to come down the aisle in tartan plaid with Converse sneakers just to freak her out. Maybe black lace with a red bodice.

Hmm.

That could work. Might be cute, actually. I blinked back into the conversation as she rattled off names of the people she knew at the party. When she mentioned Donovan Lewis, my ears perked up.

"How do you know Donovan?"

"He's on the board at the Children's Hospital with your father."

My eyebrows shot up. "Really?"

She nodded. "Why do you think we were so thrilled when you signed with his little company?"

Little?

I frowned. A multi-billion-dollar company wasn't chump change, but I refrained from commenting on that one. Ripper Records might be a smaller subsidiary of the Lewis fortune, but there was nothing little about the label.

In fact, his name was another reason we were climbing back up the charts. Ripper Records was synonymous with incredible talent. We'd been languishing on a larger New York City label, and when our contract had come up, Lila had pounced on us to sign with them.

Best decision ever.

Between their marketing, and Hunter's crazy *Rolling Stone* cover, we were climbing higher than ever. The tour was amazing, the videos were stacking up, and the merchandise was overflowing.

We were in our element, but as far as my mother was concerned, I was going to grow out of the music phase. It was her job to worry about me on a constant basis, but she had nothing on my father.

Isaac Keystone might be a stone cold-businessman when he was in the office, but when he was around me, he was Mr. Overprotective.

"Move over, Meredith."

The comforting scent of Aramis surrounded me as my father drew me up off my toes. "You were beautiful, sweetheart."

I patted his shoulders. "Okay, down boy."

"Right." My dad put me down. "You haven't been around much, Faith."

"I know. Touring has been insane."

Noah came back with a waitress and a tray of wine, bourbon, and a single glass of seltzer with lime. The man was beyond detail orientated. And a savior.

"Faith, I wanted to introduce you to Derek Burlington." My dad held out his arm to a guy in his early thirties with shellacked blond hair and a suit that definitely was not off the rack.

I stole Noah's glass again.

I definitely needed more bourbon to get through this conversation.

3

KEYS

I DESERVE ALL OF THE AWARDS—ESPECIALLY ACADEMY ONES—FOR my portrayal of the indulgent daughter. Maybe it was the bourbon talking, but I was a friggin' saint for listening to Dick—or was it Derek? Hmm.

No real difference.

The dude was full of himself and kept twitching his hips forward. So much so that even Noah gave him a steady stare that said, "step back, son".

Of course my mother and father were blissfully unaware. They kept pumping him for information on his partnership in some law firm. Probably why his hips were twitching.

I giggled.

Noah arched a brow at me.

The soft tones of an acoustic guitar saved me. We all turned to see Hunter drawing a decidedly flushed Kennedy into the center of the dance floor.

The reception crowd spread out to get a good view of them. I kissed my mother's cheek. "That's my cue to split."

"Oh, Faith."

"The band is doing their first dance song."

"Oh." She looked crestfallen. "All right, but don't disappear afterward."

I swallowed a sigh, but nodded. I slipped through the crowd and climbed onto the dais where my band was settling in. Bats had his jacket off, Wyatt did not, and Zach and Owen were already down to band T-shirts that had been under their tuxedo shirts.

I grinned.

These were my people.

I rushed around the keyboards from the band Hunter had hired. Definitely not my setup, but I could pretty much play anything. I resisted the urge to move things and change settings. Instead, I familiarized my fingers with the worn keys.

The intro was mine. The song Hunter had written for her was embedded into my brain. We'd been practicing it daily for a month.

Owen stepped forward from his usual station in the back. His Irish flowed sweet and soft into the microphone. It was a mashup to start. Peter Gabriel's "In Your Eyes" made Kennedy throw her arms around Hunter and laugh.

Her eyes were only for him, a sheen of tears bright and sparkling as they finally settled into a slow sway. Bats gently eased into Hunter's song.

The acoustic sweep was everything my band could be when the artifice and lights were stripped away. This was my favorite sound for Hammered. I loved the anthems, adored the hard-hitting beats that Wyatt poured into an arena, and lived for the growls that Hunter brought to songs—but this?

This was the heart of us.

Owen stayed at the microphone, his bass switched out for a worn Taylor acoustic that sweetened Zach's and Bats's dueling twelve-strings.

Wyatt used the padded sticks to soften the beat, and the words carried.

A stolen kiss
  A broken man
  A heart that was lost
  A man who's been longing to be found

In your eyes I found the light
  With your love
  I found the courage to change
  In your eyes I saw the reason to fight
  With your hand in mine
  I found pleasure beyond the pain

They twirled and laughed, they slowed and swayed. His forehead to hers, Hunter whispered the words in her ear. A lump grew in my throat as I watched them press cheek to cheek.

I'd resigned myself to being too busy for love for a long time. And mostly I was okay with that. Until these moments, when the kick to belong to someone—with someone—was too hard to ignore.

As we finished the song and the happy couple drew people onto the dance floor, we jammed on stage with the hired band for a few songs. More bourbon was passed around, along with flutes of champagne as Noah and Wyatt took turns toasting and roasting Hunter.

I escaped back into the crowd. The boys didn't seem inclined to stop playing, but I needed a drink that wasn't laced with alcohol, and to find my bag so I could get out of these stinking heels.

Lilac Chucks, how I need you.

A waitress ambushed me as I jumped off the stage.

"Miss Keystone, can I offer you some water?"

"Bless you, girlfriend." I accepted the bottled water and drank greedily. When she didn't move off, as most of the waitstaff usually did, I put on a polite smile.

The help wasn't supposed to come at us with the fame game, but I didn't mind. In fact, I tilted my head. The young girl could have been my twin on a first look.

She had the same purple streaks I usually wore. Hell, she even had the little trio of crystals on the apple of her left cheek like I wore for photo shoots.

Definitely a fan.

"Hi, what's your name?"

She blinked at me. "My name?"

I nodded. "Yes, sweetie. I have to know the name of the girl who borrowed my look."

She touched her cheek. "Oh, gosh. I forgot to take these off before work. I was just so excited to get this job." She frowned. "You changed your hair."

I took another swig from the bottle and nodded. The room swam a bit. Wow. Way too much bourbon. Damn those behemoth men and their ability to outdrink me.

Five feet three and a buck seventeen was no match for the six-feet-and-over club with lots of muscles. Well, except for Owen. He was whip-lean, but could outdrink us all. Damn Irish blood.

I really needed to go sit down in the shade for a bit.

"Are you all right?"

I blinked at the girl. My mouth didn't seem to work, and my fingers were tingling. Were my lips numb?

"I'm going to take good care of you. I promise." The girl gathered me close, hooking her arm around my back.

I frowned and pushed at her. At least I thought I did. I wasn't sure my arms were working.

My head fell to her shoulder. I looked up at her. Blue eyes like mine. I frowned. No—not like mine. Fake. All of her was fake.

She wasn't me.

My ankles wobbled. I couldn't walk in the heels like this. Actually, I couldn't feel my feet.

"Wow, you must have had more to drink than I thought," the girl said.

Why would she say that?

"Guess I should have done a drop or two less in the bottle, huh?"

I tried to pull away. The wrongness of the situation finally dented the hazy bubble I was in.

"I'm going to make sure you have everything you need. No one cares about you like I do. We're sisters."

I had a sister already.

The skyline dimmed.

It wasn't sunset yet, was it?

She led me around the back of the stage. The voices around me faded. My feet wouldn't work, but the girl didn't seem to notice. She was dragging me along.

"Come on, Keys, help me out here."

Hell no, I wasn't going to help her.

I tried to speak. I tried to get someone to notice me.

"She's had a little too much to drink. Just going to get her…"

Words didn't work.

Ears didn't work.

I shook my head as a few people laughed.

No.

Can't you tell I'm not drunk?

Was I?

No.

No, I wasn't.

"Hey."

I was getting dragged along faster.

"Hey!"

"No, no, no," the girl said. "You ruined everything. Why did you have to drink so much?"

I didn't.

It wasn't my fault.

Suddenly the ground was rushing up to meet me. I dropped like a rag doll. So many shoes around me. Heels, dress shoes, ballerina flats —Chucks.

I frowned.

Purple and pink Chucks.

Just like mine.

"Keys!"

Someone shook me, then someone was lifting me.

I struggled. "Just like mine," I mumbled. "No."

No.

"Keys."

The voice was male. Not her.

I relaxed.

Not her.

Not her.

Then the sun set on me. Where were the stars?

Why weren't there any stars?

4
KEYS

"REMIND ME ABOUT THAT NO-MORE-BOURBON CLAUSE," I MOANED.

"It wasn't bourbon that put you on your ass."

I frowned at the male voice. Who was in my room? I took a deep breath and tried to move. Worst hotel room ever. The bed sucked.

I peeled my eyes open. Way too much bourbon. I tried to sit up, but a firm hand held me down. Beige walls, white curtains, and mint vinyl chairs were in my line of sight.

Definitely not hotel. Hospital?

"How are you feeling, sweetheart?"

"Mom?" I turned my head and winced. She stood over me, her blue eyes bloodshot and makeup free. "Oh, my head." I lifted my hand, but found an IV attached to my arm. "What the hell?"

I tried to blink away the fuzzy edges, but my head had been replaced with Wyatt's kick drum.

"Can you turn down the lights?"

"Sure, baby." My mother reached above the bed and pulled on a string. The overhead light went out. "Better?"

"Yeah." I looked around. My father was pacing at the end of my bed. "Wow, what's with the long faces?"

"What do you remember?" Noah asked.

I swiveled toward his voice slowly. Nausea swam up and I had to close my eyes and breathe. When I opened my eyes, he was still there. His arms were crossed and his shoulders stiff. No dimples this time around, just his work face.

That wasn't good.

I frowned. Everything was jumbled. I tried to swallow, but my tongue felt like it was two sizes too big and made of sand. "Can I have a drink?" Why the hell was my throat on fire?

Worst flu ever?

My mother held a cup with a straw to my lips. I took a sip, but had to lay back down when the nausea rolled over me again. I was pretty sure I got hit by our tour bus, then the driver backed up and went for another joy ride.

I used my other hand to wipe my eyes. It was as if an impermeable film was over them. Finally I noticed the other people in the room.

Hunter and Kenny were clustered together at the edge of the privacy curtain. She was still in her wedding dress, for God's sake. Hunter's bowtie dangled on either side of his unbuttoned collar.

Wyatt, Owen, and Bats were along the wall looking worried. Bats gnawed on his thumbnail, his eyes deeply shadowed. Zach sat in a chair beside Bats, his knee bouncing.

"Hi, guys."

That's all it took. All of them came forward and surrounded my bed, talking at the same time.

I held up my untethered hand. "Guys."

Hunter clamped a hand on Noah's shoulder. "We don't know what we would've done if Noah hadn't been there."

"And we're not going to find out."

I sighed at my dad's terse voice. "Let's talk about this."

"What's to talk about?" My dad stopped pacing and gripped the bottom of my hospital bed. "Some...person tried to drug you and do God knows what to you."

Bits and pieces started to fill in. "I think there was something in a water bottle." I closed my eyes and tried to shuffle the flashes of memory together. "She was dressed like one of the waitstaff."

"Just take it slow," Noah said.

"Right." I swallowed down the nerves that jumped in my belly. "I thought it was the bourbon at first. I'd had more than my share with everyone toasting. Then there was champagne..." I trailed off.

I sounded like a lush, but I knew they wouldn't judge me. If anyone was a lightweight on the drinking scene, it was me. I could hold my own, but I didn't need booze to have fun.

Not to mention I got a little too mouthy when I had too much to drink.

"Your blood alcohol wasn't terrible, but they found ketamine in your system."

My eyes flew open at Noah's words. "What?"

Noah nodded. "We're keeping it in house right now, but we really need to bring the cops into this."

I ran my middle fingernail across my forehead lightly. We dealt with overzealous fans more often than I really wanted to let on with my parents in the room.

It was just part of being famous. And since the surge in our band profile, it was only getting worse. We didn't closet ourselves away like some artists in the industry.

We didn't have an entourage of bodyguards with us.

We had Patrick. And he was usually enough.

But ever since our *Tonight Show* appearance, and subsequent appearances on a handful of daytime talk shows, there was definitely a bit more of a security issue at play.

We handled it.

We added extra security when necessary, but this felt different.

I didn't like the ribbon of fear that was trapped in my chest. I really didn't want to worry my parents, but it wasn't like they were going to leave the room while we had a band meeting.

Hmm.

Maybe. I opened my mouth to try it, but my dad's face was mutinous and my mother was shredding a tissue.

I dropped my head back on the pillow. There was a frustrating level of details that I couldn't quite capture. Like her face.

All I could picture was my own face.

But that wasn't right.

I crossed my arms and the IV pulled. I growled. "Do I really need this?"

"Yes," everyone said together.

"Who made you all doctors?" I groused.

Noah moved up to the head of my bed, across from my mother. "Look. This is what I do, okay? And this is way more than your run-of-the-mill fan. This woman went out of her way to get a drug that would scramble your memory. That's concerning."

I glanced away from Noah to my father, who had resumed pacing. So not helping my situation. "Can't any kid on a college campus get this stuff though?"

"It's not quite as easy as you'd think."

"This is LA, Noah," Bats said quietly.

Noah sighed. "All right, I'll concede that this is definitely an easier town to get it in, but I still don't like it. We need to make a report to the cops. We need to have this sort of thing on the record."

"Even if I can't even tell you her name? Or what she looks like?"

"Yes."

I crossed my free arm over my middle. "All right. They aren't going to do anything."

"I know."

"What the hell?" Hunter sputtered.

Noah held up a hand. "You know better than anyone that stalking cases are hard to prove."

"This isn't just stalking. This bitch— Sorry, Mrs. Keystone."

My mom gave Hunter a tight smile. "It's quite all right, Hunter. I've heard worse."

His lips flattened into a thin line. "This girl got through security, which was top shelf, I might add."

Noah nodded. "The hotel has a good staff. They deal with a lot of celebrities. I also vetted the waitstaff list through my own databases at Roth Defense."

"She was dressed like a waitress, but didn't have one of those little gold name pins." I gestured to my chest.

"That's good." Noah pulled a notebook out of his pocket and scribbled into it.

At least I remembered that. "And she was wearing my shoes."

Noah's eyebrow spiked.

I rolled my eyes. "Not my shoes, but ones that I wear a lot." I shrugged. "It's not like I'm Gwen Stefani or anything. People don't copy my look—"

"Sure they do," Kennedy said. She came up alongside Hunter and linked her fingers with his. "That stuff is my job, and I know for sure there are message boards dedicated to your style, Keys."

"Really?" I was honestly shocked. I didn't exactly have a style. Well, unless you wanted to call British punk rock with an LA flair a style. Sort of.

"Yeah. When I was researching you guys as a client, I dug around a bit. There's a Reddit with everything from the T-shirts you wear to the colors of your Converse sneakers."

I rubbed at the goose bumps that suddenly flared on my arm. "Wow."

Noah nodded. "We live in a digital age that makes stalking pretty easy."

My dad growled.

I gave Noah a look, but he ignored me and kept on talking. Actually, to be honest, this was probably the most I'd ever seen Noah's lips flap in all the years I'd known him.

Noah rattled on about all the scary things that made my mother's eyes shrink farther into her sockets, for freaking shit's sake. I didn't want them to hear this.

I liked keeping my life separate from theirs. Sure, sometimes I felt a little lonely at family functions, but at least they didn't worry about me. Now, I'd have my mom crawling up my butt and my dad losing his freaking mind.

"Enough," I finally said.

Noah patted my arm. "I know it's a lot. It might be a situational thing. There are a million different stalkers active in this region alone. They don't call it Hollyweird for nothing, Keys."

Hope flared. I tried to beat back the uneasiness. Honestly I did. But the creepy way I couldn't remember the girl's face was really messing with my head.

I wanted to keep the details to myself. Each one was more damning than the last. But it wasn't fair to my family, and it surely wasn't fair to my band.

And dammit, it scared me.

I didn't like being scared. I loved my fans. I loved reaching out to soothe a fan who was excited to meet me. I wanted to be able to still hug a stranger.

I gritted my teeth.

No one was going to take that away from me, dammit.

"She was dressed like me." I swallowed and gestured to my hair. "How I wore my hair even just a few weeks ago. The same strips of purple. The same way I wear my long layers. If I had to actually say it, she probably had the same base color for my hair before I added the temporary dyes."

Noah started scribbling again. "So, she had the same shoes and look?"

I fisted my fingers. "Even the same crystals I wear on stage."

"Jesus, Keys," Bats said, and broke through Hunter and his brother to get to me. He pressed his forehead to mine, his huge hand curling around the back of my neck.

I patted his cheek. "I'm fine."

Reed Mason was the most volatile of all of us. From anger to love, and all the emotions in between. We fought as much as we loved in this band.

Not romantic love.

They honestly were my brothers. I'd never felt the need to get my Stevie-Nicks-and-Lindsey-Buckingham style love story on. The guys were hard enough to deal with as brothers without getting a dick involved.

Besides, I knew way too much about them and their habits. I'd kill all of them inside of a month if I dated any one of them.

After ten years, that was so off the table that it was dust in the far corners of our history.

It didn't stop my eyes from prickling with tears as Bats brushed a kiss over my temple before he rushed out of the room.

I sighed. "I'll stick close to Patrick."

"That's not enough," my father said.

"Dad."

"No. If Mr. Jordan is right about the police's lack of help in this situation then I'm hiring you a bodyguard."

"Over my dead body." I winced. Okay, so that wasn't the best choice of words in this particular instance. "Dad. Patrick is amazing—"

"Where was he when this happened?"

I opened my mouth to answer, but couldn't. I remembered seeing Patrick at the reception.

"I was seeing to an issue with another fan who crashed the party."

I craned my neck to see Patrick hovering just outside the room. Was he guarding my door?

This was way out of control.

He came inside and stood beside Noah. His usually clean-shaven jaw was shadowed with auburn stubble. Patrick had been with us since the beginning. We'd never needed more than him unless it was a special occasion.

He clasped his hands in front of his belt, his fingers clenched. "Three people had been at the wedding off our no-fly list."

"This girl?" I asked hopefully.

He gave a curt shake of his head. "Two of Hunter's and one of Owen's."

My father's eyes went arctic and his dark blond brows snapped even lower. "You have a list of these people?"

"Aww hell," I muttered.

This so wasn't going to end well.

5

KEYS

"OUT!"

I nearly slumped against the crinkly POS pillow when a nurse bustled into the room.

"Visitation is long over, and we're keeping Ms. Keystone for the night just to be safe. You can return in the morning for visiting hours, but she needs her rest."

My dad started blustering, but my mother caught his hand. "Isaac," she said in her quiet way.

He immediately went into protective mode. For once it wasn't aimed in my direction. He gathered my mom into him and pressed a kiss to her temple. "I'm sorry, Mere." He looked over her head at Patrick, then at Noah. "I want a protective detail hired. Money isn't an option."

I closed my eyes. I knew he was worried, but the idea of someone following me around at all times was even more daunting than having an active stalker. I was used to people getting fixated on me. I was the only female in our band. There were just as many male fans, thanks to Hunter's growly singing style and our heavy guitars that were tempered only slightly by my keyboards.

We were definitely in the hard rock category, and brought the rougher element to our shows sometimes. We'd made it through the crazy shift in music in the 2000s, and had come out even better as we were firmly heading to the other side of another decade.

But this was different.

This wasn't just a guy who thought I was an easy lay.

This wasn't a guy at all.

And somehow that made it all the more incredible to me.

Was this woman just fixated on my public persona? Or had she been trying to drag me off to her creepy basement to keep like a pet?

There was absolutely no reason for her to try to drug me.

The fact that I couldn't remember everything that had happened was even more frustrating. I just wanted my life back.

I wanted to go on tour, and play music for my fans.

I didn't want this.

But what exactly could I say? So I said nothing, and tried not to snarl and seethe at the people who loved me best. Wyatt and Owen came forward and gave me quick kisses on the cheek.

"I'll be back tomorrow," Owen said. His Irish was thick, worry etched in every word. He twisted his fingers with mine. The familiar scars webbing across his fingers made my eyes prickle.

I should be with my friends, celebrating at the wedding. At most parties, we usually ended up jamming on our acoustics to the drunken fight songs that Owen loved to pull out.

I shouldn't be in this freaking bed. I shouldn't be worrying my parents.

I shouldn't have any of these problems, dammit.

Kennedy came forward with Hunter behind her. "Get better, okay?"

"I'll be fine. The doctors are just being a pain in the ass." The nurse made a humming sound, but I ignored her. "I want you guys to go on your honeymoon."

Hunter shook his head. "Hell no."

"There's nothing you can do. Noah will be here until we figure out what to do. Heck, maybe I can hire him." I spared him a glance. He was speaking with Patrick in hushed tones. Probably figuring out some sort of schedule to babysit me on the overnight.

"I already asked him to handle this," Hunter said.

"Hunter—"

He moved around Kennedy and sat on the edge of my bed. "If I could get him out of his contract, he'd be hired right now."

Disappointment hit me harder than I thought it would. I didn't want to break in someone else. Noah might be a pain when it came to his rules, but at least I understood him. I knew him and was comfortable with him.

I didn't want some stranger hovering around me at all times of the day.

"I understand. He's always in high demand." I knew he wasn't just a bodyguard from the stories Hunter had told me. Noah was always going overseas or into some strange town in the middle of nowhere. I didn't exactly know what he did, but I knew there was a lot more danger involved than a babysitting detail like mine.

Patrick walked to the middle of my room. "I'll be right outside, all right?"

I sighed. It just wasn't worth arguing about. At least not tonight. I smiled. "Thanks."

He nodded and left.

My mother came up beside my bed and smoothed my hair back.

Hunter smiled at my mom then stood.

Noah came up beside them both. "I'm going to check in with a buddy of mine. He's just finishing up a long-term job, so I'm going to see if he's interested."

Hunter frowned. "Who?"

"Quinn."

Hunter's eyebrows shot up. "Alexander?"

Noah nodded. "He's one of the best I know in this business."

"For Keys, though?"

I looked between the two men. "What the hell does that mean?"

"Nothing," Hunter said quickly.

My mom's hand came down on my shoulder. "All I care about is that he's good at his job. Does he work with you, Noah?"

He nodded. "He works for Roth with me. He only does long-term assignments. People don't ever want to give him up."

"So, why is this job ending?" I asked.

"Because the client is moving overseas. Q likes to stay stateside. Believe me, the ambassador tried to get Quinn to relocate with him."

Ambassador? I didn't want to be impressed, but really? How could I not be?

"If he can protect a diplomat, he can protect my daughter," my father said firmly.

"Dad, I don't think he's going to want to take on my job after he's done something so important."

"You're important," my mother said briskly.

If I rolled my eyes any harder, they would actually land on the floor. "You know what I mean."

"If Quinn isn't available, I have two others I can use, but he's my first choice. He's my best friend and I trust him with my life. Seems good enough for you, blondie."

My lips twitched. "Smooth talker."

Noah grinned and I relaxed a little. The dimples were back.

After Hunter glanced at his watch, Noah nodded at his brother. They were all fidgeting as if they were on the verge of taking off. But no one moved.

"Honestly guys, go. We're going back on the road in two weeks, so I'll just be hanging out at my house. I'll be fine."

"Like we'll be able to eat, drink and be merry."

"I'm sure you'll think of something to distract yourselves."

Kennedy flushed. "It still wouldn't be right."

"Go. There's nothing you can do here. Noah will take care of it, right?" I glanced at him.

Noah nodded. "Absolutely."

"Then it's decided."

Hunter's brow was still furrowed, but he nodded. "Get some rest. We'll check in on you tomorrow before we leave. How's that?"

"Sounds perfect."

Now I just had to get rid of my parents. My mom dragged over the chair and sat down. "Now, it's time for you to go to sleep, my darling."

"Mom, you need to go home."

She shook her head. "No way."

The nurse was reviewing the bags hanging beside my bed and checking my IV. I looked up at her. "She should really go home, right?"

The nurse glanced from me to my mom, and opened her mouth. When my mom gave her a mutinous look, I knew I was toast.

Guess I was having a sleepover with my parents after all.

Lucky me.

6

QUINN

I PULLED THE BOOKS OFF THE SMALL BOOKCASE IN MY QUARTERS AND loaded them into my ancient footlocker with the rest of my belongings. I'd been on this detail for close to eight months. One of my longer assignments to date.

It was my preference to live with my clients, or on the property close by so they could reach me easily. Aidan Roth, my boss, never seemed to have a shortage of these types of jobs lined up for me. Probably because I was the exact opposite of most of his operatives.

The bodyguard unit of Roth Defense was made up of a lot of retired or former military, and a few civilians with similar training. Aidan and Marcus Roth had created a very lucrative security agency based in New York City. When I'd left the Army Rangers, I'd been at loose ends.

Aidan had hired my best friend, Noah, and when he'd put feelers out for more people to add to the team, it had been a no-brainer. I trusted Noah more than anyone on this planet. The best part? Aidan wasn't the micromanaging type. He left me the hell alone.

I took the shit assignments that the others didn't want.

Gladly.

Most of the security team wanted action. I was the exact opposite. I liked order, and to keep order. The French ambassador was an older gentleman who liked routine as much as I did. He only entertained when absolutely necessary.

He preferred quiet nights with his family, and never gave me much trouble. His kids required a little more effort to keep in line, but for the most part it was exactly the kind of job I loved.

Orderly.

Structured.

No surprises.

I'd been tempted to go back with him to France and continue as his personal security, but I was tired of the politics. And without the ambassador, I sure as shit didn't want to stay in Washington any longer than I had to. Security was a nightmare on Dupont Circle. I definitely wouldn't miss that.

For the first time, I didn't have another assignment lined up. I usually had at least a half-dozen people on the waiting list for me.

A soft hiss had me instantly reaching for the firearm that was never far away from my side. I slid my Glock out of my holster and pointed it toward the floor.

"Hey, old man."

My shoulders relaxed. "Jesus, Noah."

My best friend leaned against the doorjamb to my room, his eyebrows waggling in unapologetic glee that he got in without me noticing. Maybe it was a good thing I didn't have another client in the wings. Obviously I wasn't on my game.

Or I'd gotten too used to the easy nature of this job. Neither was a comfort.

I tucked my gun back into the holster under my arm. "What the hell are you doing in D.C.?"

"Looking for you."

It was my turn to raise my eyebrows. "Is this why I don't have an email waiting for me from Aidan?"

He shrugged. "Maybe."

I'd worked with Noah more than a few times, but not in the last five years. He worked the more chaotic posts that usually included a few off-the-books operations. I had a greater chance of getting shot, usually. Even when I was a better shot than he was.

"Not like you to be cagey." Again with an eyebrow response. "All right, not cagey with me."

He grinned. "Truth."

I resumed my packing. I wanted to get out of the house before the movers took over. I'd already handed the family off to their new detail, and did the goodbyes. I hated them. Avoided them at all costs, but the ambassador's daughter was young and had grown very attached to me.

Probably why I was out of sorts. There was no other reason that Noah should have been able to sneak up on me.

I held up my dog-eared copy of *The Stand*. "I'm not going some-where sandy and hot, am I?" A little Stephen King was good for a long, boring flight.

"Depends on your definition of sandy and hot."

"Desert?"

"Then, no."

I tossed the book into my bag, then crossed my arms. "Again, what's with the lack of detail?"

"I know you're not going to like it."

"'Not like it' like when you dragged me to Fallujah for twenty-four days? Or 'not like it' because you're passing off a pain-in-the-ass client?"

He drew air between his teeth. "Pain in the ass isn't exactly right. I love this girl like a sister."

My chest tightened. "Girl?"

Noah rolled his eyes. "Okay, not a girl. She's almost thirty, for Christ's sake."

I frowned. Noah didn't talk about too many people. One of the reasons we got along so well was because we didn't push each other for a lot of discussion about our personal lives or pasts. The stickler for me? Family wasn't a word he threw around lightly. "How much like a sister?"

His other dimple came out.

"No." I backed up and slammed the top of my trunk closed and locked it. Before I could heft it up by the handles, he grabbed one side.

I was not working with his brother. Probably one of the band members' girlfriends were... I frowned. No, he said family.

A flash of memory drifted in. Noah had a cigar box that he kept with him. It had a handful of photos, a sniper shell, and a cross. One of the photos—an old one that curled at the edges—was of him and Hunter with a girl hanging between them.

All smiles.

Blonde.

Trouble.

Like a sister.

"Come on. It'll be a cake job."

I pushed him through the doorway, not caring when his elbow clipped the doorjamb. "No, it won't. Nothing involving *that* band is a cake job."

He swore and shook out his arm. "Hammered isn't dog shit on your shoe, Quinn."

"Close enough." One of the reasons I stayed away from the fame end of the bodyguard game was the pure lack of control. Venues, fans, entourages—all security nightmares.

He sighed. "I wouldn't ask if it wasn't important."

I stopped the trunk midway through the doorway. The dimple was gone, and his face was a little too bleak for my peace of mind. Noah didn't ask for favors. I owed him about four by my last count, which meant my chances of saying no to this job were between none and zilch. "You're a son of a bitch."

"I beg your pardon? My mother is an angel, fuckface."

I tried not to laugh, or even smile. For anyone else, I could manage it. "Yes, she is. I have no idea how you came from such a wonderful woman."

"She says three rosaries for me daily. Says it's the only way my soul will have a chance in getting to heaven."

I started walking again. "That makes sense."

"Did I mention you're a shit?"

I nodded. "And yet you're still here asking for a favor."

"I'd do it if I could, but I was only in town for my brother's wedding. I've got to report back to my client tomorrow night. I got Sarah to cover me, and she's already bitching for me to get my ass back to Louisiana."

I backed Noah through the living room in my small apartment, then we set the trunk by the door. I moved to the fridge and grabbed two bottles of water, offering one to him.

This August in D.C. was hideously humid. My T-shirt stuck to my back and I'd barely had anything to pack. I sat on the edge of my couch. "All right. Give me a rundown."

Noah leaned against the doorway between the living room and vestibule, and downed the bottle in thirty seconds. He tapped the bottle against his thigh, not saying a word.

I waited him out.

Either this was going to be one helluva whopping lie, or the job was a shitshow. I had a feeling it was the latter.

"Someone drugged Faith Keystone at the wedding."

I slumped back on the cushion. "Not exactly what I was expecting."

"Yeah. We were damn lucky I was about twenty feet from her when it was going down."

"Was the guy caught?"

"Negative. Get this—not a guy."

My eyebrows shot up. "All right. You got me twice."

"She was dressed as the waitstaff and melted into the crowd as soon as I yelled. I didn't even get a look at her. Just that she was blonde, five-three, and built like Keys. Also part of the problem—

she's got herself dressed up like Keys. Hair, clothes, hell…even her shoes."

"Police?"

"Questioned her this morning before I left. Ketamine," he said simply.

I sighed. "Swiss cheese for memory, huh?"

"Pretty much. The cops filed a report, but there's not much they can do. There was intent obviously, but they can't put a detail on her. The band has security, but Patrick O'Connor is more of an all-around babysitter. He'd punch me dead in the mouth for saying that."

"And I get to work with this joyful person?"

Noah shrugged. "You'd probably get along with Patrick. He's about as much of a conversationalist as you are."

"Trying on that comedian hat again?"

"I hung out with the guys for a weekend. It happens." Noah moved forward and leaned his hip against one of the club chairs. "Honestly, for the most part, these guys don't have a lot of trouble."

"I don't believe you."

He snorted. "I've known Keys since before she could legally buy a shot. She's a good kid."

"You're thirty-six, Noah."

"Yeah, well as I said—sister." He folded his arms. "If something happened to her, Hunter would probably be arrested for murder. I might get away with it, but he's dumb and passionate."

I sighed. "Does she know you're siccing me on her?"

"Yes."

"You're still not telling me everything."

Noah paced away. "Look, I know you've got issues with the weirdness of LA—"

"I like LA fine. Great Mexican and sushi. Best I've ever had without being in the actual countries of origin. What I have a problem with is the absolute lack of security protocols followed. D.C. might be a pain in the ass, but people here know how to deal with security. Fans are worse than suicide bombers. You never know what the hell they're going to do."

"Yeah, well—full disclosure—they got nothing on Keys."

"This kills two favors." I leaned forward, the bottle dangling between my knees. "Two."

"I saved your life three times, and dragged your ass out of Paris when that bitch tried to skewer you with a saber."

I flushed. "You were the one who came up with the harebrained scheme to seduce a fencing champion at the embassy, you ass."

"Can I help it that you suck at seduction?"

I opened my mouth to argue, and closed it again. It really wasn't worth it. There was no way that I was going to win this argument. And there was no way I was saying no.

"When do we leave?"

"Let me help you with that trunk."

"Crap."

"It's good for you to get out in the world."

I hauled myself off the couch that had always been too short for me. "I hate you."

"Nah. You hate rockstars."

"Truth."

7

KEYS

"MOM, I SWEAR IF YOU KEEP PACING, I'M THROWING YOU OUT."

She stopped at the window. "How can you just lie there reading?"

"Patrick vetoed going outside, and my wrists actually hurt from practicing the piano." If I didn't find something to catch my interest, I was going to go insane.

My mother pacing all over the house wasn't helping.

Wringing her hands and staring at her phone wasn't helping.

Nothing was helping.

It had been one day since the attack and the cops hadn't even pretended they were going to offer much assistance. The Special K part of the equation had given them pause, but since I couldn't remember a damn thing about her—and no one else had seen her—well, it was pretty much the definition of moot.

So, I was under house arrest with Patrick turning my place into a security nightmare. Noah had sent equipment ahead and was en route with his friend.

Just the thought of someone shadowing me for the foreseeable future was mind-boggling. Why the hell would anyone care about me to this level?

That was the worst part. Wouldn't this be an escalation kind of deal? Uber fan to Crazytown? Not just straight into Kidnap-Keys-to-keep-as-my-very-own? I didn't even know if that's what it was.

I slammed down the book I was reading. And this book—*1001 Rockstar Deaths*—wasn't exactly the best reading material. Even if they were fascinating in a completely masochistic way.

My mother sat next to me and picked up the book. "Oh, Faith."

I snatched the book and lifted the top of my coffee table and shoved it in the storage space. "It was something Owen gave me as a joke last Christmas."

"This is no laughing matter." She sniffled.

"I know." *Oh, here we go with the waterworks.* "Mom, don't start."

"How can you be so calm?" she wailed.

I pulled her into a hug and fought back my own wash of tears. I wasn't calm. I was going nuts, but crying about it wasn't going to help anyone. But I also had a tendency toward sympathy tears. If she started, I would probably dissolve into a full-fledged sobfest myself.

Not good.

I stood up and dragged her over to the sideboard. I opened the tall crystal decanter with bourbon in it.

"Faith…"

"Don't argue with me."

"It's too early to drink."

"It's never too early for a good bourbon." I splashed a mouthful into two tumblers. I slung a glass over to her.

She wrapped her shaking fingers around the glass and slowly sipped. Her eyebrows went up.

"I know. It's like chocolate had sex with alcohol."

My mom huffed out a small laugh. "I don't know if it's more horrifying that you talk like your band, or that I find it funny." She took another drink. "Don't tell your father."

I lifted my glass to clink with hers. "Secrets to the grave."

"I don't really appreciate this dark sense of humor you have."

I finished off the glass. "You never did, but if I don't joke then what the hell am I going to do?"

"Take it seriously?"

I whirled on her. "Of course I am." I held my arms out. "I have a huge house and it's never felt so small in my life," I shouted. My mom's eyes filled again and I tipped my head back. "Dammit."

"Keys?"

I jumped at Patrick's voice and spun around.

"Sorry." Patrick stood at the entry of the hallway down to the front door with Noah and another man. His lantern jaw was locked and a scruff of red hair covered his cheeks. His eyes were exhausted, under the worry.

I rushed over to the men and gave Patrick a quick pat on the arm.

He stiffened and backed up. "I'm going to check the perimeter."

I sighed, waiting until his boots echoed and the door slammed behind him. "He's just worried," I said to Noah.

He dragged me in for a tight hug. "How're you holding up?"

I pulled away and looked over my shoulder at my mother staring out the window at the mountains. "We're doing okay."

Noah frowned down at me. "No, how are you doing?"

I gave him a wry grin. "Going stir-crazy."

"That's what I thought."

I peeked over at his friend. He wore a crisp white shirt and black suit. His hair was military short, but his skin was tanner than I'd have expected for someone so…suit-ish.

But man, his eyes.

Arctic blue and assessing.

His gaze surveyed every corner of my living room, and he frowned at every damn thing. Before I could open my mouth and introduce myself, he walked away and checked my dining room, then walked into the kitchen.

I stood in my living room watching him, my hands on my hips.

Really?

Not even a "Hi, my name is"?

"Don't mind Quinn. He's just thorough. He's been studying your blueprints on the flight."

I turned to Noah. "How the hell did you get my blueprints?"

"You don't really want to know."

I crossed my arms over my middle and followed Quinn down the hall and up the stairs to the second level.

"Keys," Noah called after me.

I ignored him and trailed Quinn into a guest bedroom. "Make yourself at home."

He glanced over his shoulder at me. "Your house is a nightmare."

"Why, thank you. So glad you could share your opinion." My house was the one thing I was incredibly proud of, besides my collection of instruments. It was the first thing I'd bought on my own, without anyone's help.

Okay, so the bank helped, but no one had co-signed with me and the payment came out of my personal account every damn month.

And I loved my house.

He ran his hand along the sill of the huge window in the second bedroom. "These will need to be replaced."

"Hell no."

He looked down at me. "So, you don't mind that anyone could look into your windows from that mountain range across the way?"

I looked out the window at my favorite view. It was the Hollywood Hills, for God's sake. I could see the Silver Lake Reservoir from my freaking living room.

Suddenly the perfect view seemed a little ominous.

Every window was huge and had a view.

I'd had them lightly tinted against the relentless Los Angeles sun, but that didn't mean people couldn't see in.

I backed out of the room and down to my bedroom with my huge sliding door. I'd never wanted to put curtains up, because I loved the natural light that seemed to infiltrate every corner.

This was my house.

My sanctuary.

I loved the road. I loved the venues, and the different places we visited. I loved finding hole-in-the-wall dives with their bar bands, and their seas of strangers who didn't give a shit who I was.

But when I was home, I loved this house.

Loved the peace.

Loved the space.

Now it felt like a glass box leaving me on display.

I backed away from my huge patio that I'd spent months getting just right. The patio I spent late nights on with my notebook and a guitar. The ancient upright piano I had in the corner of my bedroom that I played with the door wide open so I could hear the night sounds blending with my music.

I turned to the doorway and he was there.

The sunshine lit his blue eyes and accentuated the crow's feet at the corners as he squinted a bit. His face was a little softer. "I didn't mean to scare you." His voice was deep and calm.

"Yeah, well, too late."

He dipped one hand into his pocket and jangled something. "I know of a company that can give you privacy and let you keep your views." He walked up to the slider and opened it. He held out his arm. "Come on. Come out here."

"What, so someone can watch me with binoculars?" Or worse? I shivered even though the sun was flooding my room.

He sighed. "I'm sorry. That was uncalled for. I'm trained to look for problems." He shrugged. "I worked for an ambassador before this."

Like that was supposed to be the entire reason behind why he was so rude? I crossed my arms and followed him outside. There were a half dozen lemon trees growing around my patio, providing a lot of privacy.

Instead of improving Mr. Brooding's mood, it only seemed to make him more pensive. He looked over the waist-high fencing to the valley below. One of the best features of my house was the lack of neighbors behind me, just the view.

He frowned at the rough walking path that wound around my property. "Where does this lead?"

"Down to a small park then out to the main road."

"How long is the trail?"

I shrugged. "Takes me about an hour to walk it."

He looked me up and down. "Three miles?"

"I have no clue. I gave up on wearing a Fitbit last year."

He made a humming sound. "And we have two weeks before you start the tour again?"

I nodded. "We're heading to the East Coast and into the Finger Lakes region for some summer spots, then inside venues through the third week of October."

"What happens then?"

"We have our annual charity masquerade for Halloween, then break through the holidays. Start again after the New Year."

He unearthed his phone and skimmed his finger down the face.

Long fingers.

Blunt ends.

Nails clipped short, a few calluses and a busted knuckle on his right forefinger. He looked down at his finger then at me. "Gun jammed."

My eyebrows shot up. "Happen a lot?"

He tilted his head. "Never."

"Well, I guess you can't say never."

His nostrils flared. "Wasn't my gun. *My* gun doesn't jam."

I trailed my fingers over the heated metal of the fencing. "You always carry?"

"Always."

"Then why did you have to use someone else's gun?"

A muscle in his jaw flexed. "Because I had to surrender my gun for a political dinner."

"Of course you did." I leaned my hip on the post at the corner of my patio. "Noah said you like boring jobs."

His brows furrowed. "I like order."

I smiled for the first time since he'd arrived. "Oh, honey…you're going to hate me."

That jaw thingie flexed again and he tipped his chin up, peering down at me like I was a puzzle to solve.

I held out my hand. "Faith Keystone, by the way."

He tucked his phone back into his pocket and took my hand. "Quinn Alexander."

8

QUINN

I dropped her hand as soon as I could without being rude. Her grip was surprisingly strong and warm, with multiple rings on every finger. But not all at the base of her knuckles. Some at the top joints, some in the middle, some traditionally set.

All of them slim and gold in an array of symbols. Her nails were short, and painted a deep red that reminded me of my favorite California merlot.

She wore white cutoffs that barely grazed her thighs. A red tank top hugged her body, covering the shorts so only a few inches at her legs showed. She wore a purple shirt that fell off one shoulder and skimmed a few inches below her breasts. Her feet were bare, with more flashes of gold there too. Gold hair was piled at the top of her head in that magical way that women had.

She didn't look twenty-nine, thanks to her lack of make-up.

Oh, and she was stunning.

As if this job didn't suck enough.

I'd seen photos during my research on the plane. Objectively beautiful in every damn one of them, but in person? Photos had nothing on Faith Keystone in the flesh.

I'd already decided she was going to be nothing but trouble the moment I'd walked through the door—her house was a security nightmare. Five egress points from my quick count on the exterior of her house, not to mention a shit-ton of windows that I could climb through without even ducking my head.

Inside was even worse.

Anyone with a couple hundred dollars could watch from across the hills. Binoculars, a high-powered rifle scope, hell...even a telescope from a bordering house could do the job.

Security hell.

I'd tried to ignore her as I'd gone through the house. She just kept following me. Noah couldn't keep her busy, for fuck's sake?

And now I was the one trailing after her.

I'd checked out the last of the guest bedrooms, saving her sanctuary for last. I understood that everything about me was intrusive— necessary, but ultimately I was going to have a hand in changing her life. Usually not for the better, in a client's eyes.

I'd walked into her domain and swallowed hard. I'd caught it earlier, but now her scent wrapped around me. Peaches—fresh peaches. The kind my mother cut up to jar this time of year.

Christ, where had that thought come from?

It had been ages since I'd helped her with canning. Not since I was a boy. It was a scent that meant summer was ending and cool nights were on their way.

I pushed those thoughts back. I needed to concentrate and get the lay of the land—make sure she understood just how things were going to be from now on.

Out here on her patio was much better.

The lemons and the fresh air from the trees helped. The skyline had the familiar haze of California smog that was prevalent this time of year. All of it grounded me again.

Protection detail was my specialty, but it had been a very long time since I'd had a woman as a client. The fact that she was so important to Noah was another layer I had to come to terms with.

I met her gaze. She didn't break the stare—in fact her shoulders straightened and she stood a little taller. There was an innocence in her huge eyes that didn't belong to someone who had been in the music industry for over ten years. There was fear too—probably because of me more than anything—but, she needed to hear the hard truths.

Maybe if she was afraid, she'd actually make my job easier.

I sat on the bench. "Can you sit for a minute?"

She licked her lips as she twisted a slim ring on her thumb. "All right."

"I'd like to call my contact over at Carson Covenant. They have specialty glass that I think you'd like."

"I don't want my house dark with tinted glass."

I shook my head. "This is special. It's just like the kind you have from your point of view inside. Outside? Opaque."

She pulled her knees together and turned toward me. She rubbed her palms down her legs. "If you could give me the details, I'll look into it."

"I can do it."

"My house, I'll research it."

No winning this one. And I had a feeling I was going to need to pick my battles. "Fair enough."

"All I know about you is that you're Noah's friend. Were you a Ranger too?"

I nodded. "I've been in the private sector for five years."

Her knee bounced and her ring kept going round and round. "Have you ever lost anyone?"

Well, fuck. Right down to brass tacks. "Not while I've been in the private sector."

She stopped spinning her ring. "But you have lost people?"

I inclined my head. "Being a Ranger isn't a walk in the park. We get sent to the worst places on the planet. I've lost people in my unit."

And Lissa. I lost Lissa, too.

Shut it down.

It seemed like she was going to ask more questions, instead she sat back against the cushion. "I'm sorry."

I nodded.

There really wasn't much to say on that. I didn't like thinking about that time in my life. Wars would always be waging, and there would always be someone there to fight. It just wasn't going to be me anymore.

I'd served my time, and watched dozens of friends die in the name of fighting for peace.

"So, what happens now?" Her lips tipped up at one corner. "You watch me read books for the next two weeks while I wait for the tour?"

I pressed my lips together. "Somehow I doubt there's even an ounce of truth in that statement."

"Well, there was a drop. I was actually reading a book when you came in." She stood up. "In fact, you should probably meet my mom before she busts in here. Noah probably had to sit on her to keep her out of our hair this long."

"That's it?"

She shrugged. "Why explain it twice? My mom's going to ask the same questions plus twenty more."

I opened my mouth, and shut it again when she rushed on.

"If you say you're shocked I'm not peppering you with questions like most women would, I'll slug you. Even if you're some hot-shot Ranger."

"I was going to say you're pragmatic. Nothing about your gender."

"I'll take it." She swept by me and the wash of peaches made me suck back a groan.

Had to be peaches. Couldn't be some fancy French perfume that I could ignore.

Son of a bitch.

I followed her out into the living room. A blonde that had to be her mother was pacing in front of the kitchen counter. Evidently

Noah had given her a similar pep talk about being near the windows.

"There you are. You were gone forever." Mrs. Keystone rushed up to her daughter.

"Mom. We just had to talk. And he needed to look around."

"Right, of course." She dragged Faith into her arms. They were similar in height, save for the extra three inches her mother had with the ice-pick heels.

Faith rolled her eyes. "Mom."

"Just a minute longer."

She sighed, and looped her arms around her mother's waist. "We've got two Super-Rangers here. The cavalry has officially arrived."

Mrs. Keystone gave a watery laugh. "Must you make light of everything?" She looked up at me. "You should have seen what she was reading before you got here."

I quirked a brow in Faith's direction.

"What? Who knew there were one-thousand-one ways to kill a rockstar?"

Noah stood up with the book in hand. "Some of them are pretty entertaining. Not shockingly there are far too many..." He trailed off and cleared his throat. "Never mind."

"Could you dog-ear that chapter?" Faith asked.

"Cheeky girl," he said, and shoved a piece of paper in the book with a wink.

"Can we be serious here?" Faith's mother asked.

I nodded and crossed the room to her. "I'm Quinn Alexander. I work with Roth Defense out of New York City."

"And you came all the way out here?"

"We go where the work is, ma'am."

"Meredith."

I inclined my head. "My specialty is home and personal security. Some of my clients have included the French Ambassador, a council-man, and a billionaire from Nebraska."

Mrs. Keystone stood up straighter. "Well, then."

"I don't say that to brag."

"Liar," Noah quipped.

I gave him a side-eye. "I just want you to believe that I'm well qualified to make sure your daughter stays safe. That is, if she cooperates."

"Oh, she'll cooperate," Mrs. Keystone said.

From the smart remark in our first five minutes, I doubted that, but I would reserve judgment until we went over the rules. "Why don't we sit down? I'll explain how things are going to be for the foreseeable future."

"I should probably get the bourbon now," Faith said.

"I'd prefer you kept a level head. And a clear one."

"Yeah, water definitely isn't going to cut it with this conversation."

"Faith, please." Mrs. Keystone twirled her wedding ring. A Keystone women thing?

I walked over to the dining room table and pulled out two chairs. "Ladies, please sit."

Mrs. Keystone sat in the chair I was clutching.

Faith went to the sideboard, dropped a fat spherical ice cube into the glass, then splashed two fingers of bourbon over it.

Oh, yeah. She was going to be a cakewalk.

9

KEYS

I TWISTED MY GLASS AROUND AND AROUND AS QUINN DRONED ON about every rule known to man. I essentially was going to be a prisoner in my own home for the next two weeks. After that, I was simply going to have a leash.

That this six-foot-two goon was going to own.

The longer the list of rules, the more I had to hold back a snarl.

Noah watched from the other end of the table. His fingers were folded over his belly as he tipped back his chair. He didn't look as though he was listening, but I was pretty sure he heard every word. Especially when his lips twitched a few times.

Most notably when Quinn explained that there were going to be no unnecessary trips into the city.

Noah knew I was going to lose my damn mind.

When Quinn went into another round of rules—these about my car and how I wasn't going to be driving myself anywhere for the foreseeable future—I stood up. "Enough."

He looked up from the legal pad he was flipping through. "Do you have a question?"

"I thought you were a badass Ranger, not a jailer."

Quinn put his pen down. "I'm not your jailer, Faith."

"News to me." I snatched his pad. "Rule one—no leaving the premises alone. Rule two—no driving. Rule three—all outings must be scheduled in advance. Rule four—no fun."

Noah's lips twitched again and his feet on the chair thumped back onto the floor.

I pointed at him. "Don't you laugh."

Noah held up his hands. "Wouldn't dream of it."

Quinn took the pad from me. "I'm not here for fun, Faith."

I crossed my arms. "No freaking kidding." I tempered my rage before the room was washed in red. I could feel it happening, but I wouldn't do it in front of my mother. I took a long, slow breath. "I have two weeks off before we're touring hardcore for two solid months."

"And you'll be able to relax here, in the house."

Relax? I was going to go out of my ever-loving mind. I wasn't a homebody. I went out and saw shows when I was off. Most importantly, I took in what was hot and kept the ideas fresh for new songs. These two weeks were supposed to include me getting reacquainted with the LA scene.

Now, everything was ruined because some nutjob wanted to play *Misery* with me as their co-lead in some freakish fantasy. Or whatever she was trying to do.

Frustration welled up because I still couldn't remember exactly what she'd wanted from me.

"We're sisters."

I fisted my hands. A new memory? Or was it me overlapping with the craziness of the night. I hadn't seen Hope in so long. We'd actually spoken like sisters for the first time in a very long time. And then she'd been gone again.

Hope hadn't even come to the hospital.

I swallowed hard.

I was sure it was because of the baby—being pregnant, she had to worry about herself. She'd texted me. She'd even called me at the hospital, but she was back to her distant self.

And on the flip side, I had a stranger who wanted to be so close to me that she'd snuck into Hunter's wedding?

Why?

What could she want with me?

Quinn stood up, then pushed his chair in. I snapped back into my surroundings and crossed my arms.

"Everything all right?"

I nodded. "Fine."

He studied me for another moment then seemed to come to a decision. "I need to go out and get my things. Why don't I walk you out, Mrs. Keystone? Noah is going to take you home."

"I am?" A look passed between him and Quinn. "Right."

"I want to stay with my daughter."

"I understand your husband needs to get updated. He had a meeting he couldn't reschedule?"

My mom's eyes widened. "Yes. How did you know?"

Quinn gave her a soft smile. "It's my job to have everyone's schedule. I spoke to Mr. Keystone's secretary this morning."

"Okay." She looked at Noah, then at me.

"It's okay, Mom. I'm beat. I'm just going to curl up on the couch and veg out."

She tucked a lock of hair behind her ear, showing just how worried she was. My mom's hair was nothing if not perfectly coiffed at all times. She didn't fuss with her hair or her clothes.

I crossed to her. "Honestly. I'm just really tired."

She frowned. "Are you sure?"

I hugged her tight. "I've got Warden Alexander to take care of me."

Quinn's jaw did the flex thingie. "Your daughter will be very safe." Another look passed between him and Noah, then he led my mother to the door.

She stopped at the edge of the hallway. "I'll call you later to check in."

"Thanks, Mom."

She rushed back over and hugged me again. "I can't guarantee that me and your dad won't come back here when he returns from work."

"Save it for tomorrow, huh? I'm really just going to pass out. The hospital was too busy last night. I didn't really get any sleep." That was the truth, but I'd survived on much less sleep most nights.

I needed to decompress, and I wasn't going to do it with my mother there.

Not when she was staring at me every three minutes waiting for me to breakdown.

"Come on, Mrs. Keystone," Quinn said, and herded her down the hall.

Noah waited for the door to close before crossing to me.

I held my hands up. "If you hug me, too, I'm definitely crying. And then you have to deal with girl tears and I know you hate them."

Noah rolled his eyes and tugged me close. "Shut up."

I buried my nose into his chest and drew in his Irish Spring scent. I looped my arms around his waist and drew in a shaky breath. "Dammit."

He drew his hand down my hair. "You're gonna be okay, kiddo. I know Quinn seems a bit...intense."

I pulled back. "Intense? There are twenty-four rules on his list. I have to schedule a shit, for God's sake."

He laughed. "It's not that bad. You're just used to doing your own thing."

"You're damn right."

"He'll calm down. He just doesn't like when there's no schedule to follow."

I frowned. "Isn't a schedule bad though? I've been reading up on stalkers and they like to figure out your schedule and you know... attack because they know where you're going to be."

"Holy Christ." He hauled me back into him and kissed the top of my head. "No reading up on this shit. All right?"

I sighed and squeezed back a prickle of tears. There were far too many articles about fans going off the deep end. Not just the famous ones who'd killed Lennon and Selena. But insane home invasions and others being shot down in their cars.

"He knows what he's doing. And yes, he'll make sure you don't do the same thing every time you guys go out, but until he figures you out—hell, until you figure each other out—how about cutting him some slack?"

A voice cleared behind us. "Mrs. Keystone is loaded into your truck."

I pulled away from Noah. "She's not luggage."

Quinn's face went blank. "Of course not, I'm sorry." He glanced at Noah. "Are you heading out after you drop Mrs. Keystone off?"

Noah rubbed my arms, then hooked his arm around my shoulders. "Yeah. I have a flight at seven."

Quinn nodded.

I squeezed Noah around the waist. "I wish you were doing this."

"I know, kiddo."

I winced. "Enough with the kiddo."

"Brat?"

I pushed him away. "Just get out of here."

His smile slid away, and he dropped his hands on my shoulders to hold me still. "You're going to be fine. There's no one on this planet that I trust more than Quinn."

"Right." I glanced over at the warden. His shoulders were stiff under the jacket, and the sun glinted off a few silvery hairs at his temples. His jawline was as stiff as the rest of him.

Yeah, we were going to have a ton of fun.

Noah kissed my forehead. "I'll check in when I can."

"Where are you off to?"

"Albany."

"Georgia?"

He grinned. "New York." He met Quinn's gaze. "Your parents' stomping grounds."

"Yeah? Ma will kill you if you don't stop in sometime while you're there."

"Peach pie." Noah groaned. "Yeah, I'll have to make some time."

Quinn's nostrils flared. "She makes a mean peach pie."

"Yeah she does."

I hugged him one more time. "All right. Safe flight. I'll see you soon?"

"I'll do my best."

Which meant probably not, but I took the comforting gesture for what it was. "I'm going to go take a shower." I drew back. "If that's all right, Warden?"

Jaw tick again. I was going to start counting them. "Yes, that's fine. How long?"

"Well, I don't have to shave my legs since I'm never getting laid again…"

Noah snorted. "Keys," he said with a warning voice.

I sighed. "Fifteen minutes."

Quinn nodded. "Sounds good."

"Bye, pita," I said.

"Love you too, Brat."

I fought back the prick of tears—again. Honestly, I hadn't cried in years and now I was ready for the waterworks every time someone said something nice to me. I took the stairs two at a time, slamming the door to my bedroom.

I flipped my favorite shirt over my head and peeled off my tank top. I was clammy with fatigue and nerves. Sunlight poured into my bedroom.

My favorite room.

But all I could focus on was how many windows were in my room. I rushed into the bathroom, but there were an equal number of windows in there too. At least they were higher up over the lip of iridescent gray tiles. I'd chosen them because they looked like the inside of an oyster.

Swirls of pearl color glinted in the light.

So much light.

I cowered into the corner of my shower were there was no line of sight. Was she watching now?

Was it someone else?

Did she have an accomplice watching out for me?

Did she even know where I lived?

I slid down and hugged my knees. I don't know how long I was like that. The water was barely a mist from this angle and my teeth were starting to chatter.

I forced myself to stand under the water and put conditioner in my hair at the very least. I washed quickly, then shut off the water and wrapped myself in two towels.

No way was I going to do this.

My house.

My privacy.

I sat on my bed and opened my laptop. I typed in Carson Covenant and picked up my phone.

My fucking house.

10

QUINN

I STOWED MY FOOTLOCKER INTO THE LARGE CLOSET. I TOOK THE ROOM next to Faith's so I could hear her if there was trouble. I was pretty sure she'd be ecstatic about my choice of rooms, but she'd get used to it.

Or it was going to be a long damn two weeks.

I checked my watch when the water finally shut off. Talk about taking her time in the shower. She'd said fifteen, but it had been more like forty.

I stashed two weeks' worth of clothes and hung up my suit jacket. I changed out of my my suit pants to a pair of cargos and a T-shirt. It was going on six and I'd barely eaten.

I needed to stay sharp, and that required balanced meals.

I paused at Faith's door. The clicking of keys was loud and clear. "Faith?"

"Yes?"

"I'm going to fix some dinner."

She opened the door and her scent swirled out the door. "Good luck finding something in my kitchen." She squeezed water out of the ends of her hair. The collar of her T-shirt was damp and her breasts moved unencumbered with each fluff of the towel in her long hair.

Sweet fuck.

I was never going to look at Ziggy Stardust the same again.

"I brought a bag of food."

She crossed the room and hung her towel on the door to the bathroom. The ancient T-shirt barely skimmed the soft pants that hugged her from ass to knee. There was a very thin strip of skin showing with each sway of her hips.

She was perfectly covered.

And still my chest tightened in reaction.

Was she doing this on purpose? I forced my eyes up to her shoulders and the tumble of tangled waves that darkened the back of her faded concert shirt.

She lifted her arms and quickly plaited her hair in a high braid that was endearingly lopsided. Not an ounce of seduction in the action. Instead, she shrugged on a sweater that looked like a cat had attacked it and turned back to me.

She was distractingly beautiful. Not the come-on kind that I could ignore—no, she had to be guileless.

Because that was my lot in life.

She gave me a tentative smile. "Much better."

"The shower helped?"

She shrugged. "A little. I was talking about the…what do they call regular clothes in Ranger speak?"

I sighed. I couldn't even say I wasn't a Ranger anymore, because once a Ranger, always a Ranger—but it had been a long time since I'd thought about that part of my life. "Civvies."

"Ahh. Yeah, heard that on NCIS."

"I was Army, Faith."

She snapped her fingers. "Right. Navy boys and Army boys like that distinction."

I stiffened. I had plenty of Navy friends, but there was and always would be a level of one-upmanship between us. Instead of arguing, I inclined my head. "Do you want to help me? Or I can just cook and let you know when it's ready."

"Does cooking come with your crazy price tag?"

"Bonus," I said drily.

She curled her toes into the thick area rug that flowed from under her bed. "I'm a decent sous chef. At least that's what Tristan tells me."

I quickly shuffled names in my head from the files I'd read on the way over. Friends, family, friends of friends. Noah had done a quick search on all of them, and I'd done my own on the plane ride into Los Angeles.

"Tristan Eves?"

She crossed her arms under her breasts. "Wow. Does that brain come with a USB cord for downloads?"

A light breeze came in from her patio. I tried not to notice the way her nipples tightened. Couldn't she close that sweater—cover them up? Hell, wear a bra?

It was going to be a long assignment if I didn't get myself in check.

I crossed to the door that was still cracked and closed it, snicking the lock before I faced her, and her magnificent breasts, again.

Now, she had herself covered. The bulky sweater wrapped tight under her crossed arms. "I forgot to close that earlier."

"You'll get into the habit," I said quietly.

"I don't want to get into the habit."

Damn she was stubborn. "It doesn't have to be out of fear. These things are common sense for a woman living alone."

"I have a security system."

"Well, it won't work if the door is open, now will it?"

She stiffened. "The screen was closed."

"A screen wouldn't stop someone from hopping that fence and coming inside." When she flinched, I wished I could take back the words.

"You're right," she said in a small voice.

These were the lessons she needed. It sucked, and I hated to be the bad guy, but if that stopped her from getting hurt, then bad guy it would be.

"Come down when you're ready," I said and strode out.

When I got to the bottom of the stairs, I heard her moving around and then the pounding of notes flowing through the ceiling. Her piano. The song was angry and passionate.

I wasn't a music guy, so I didn't know what the song was, but it was definitely preferable to a temper tantrum.

I took out the white-paper-wrapped chicken from the market we'd stopped at on the way over. It was pre-marinated in a rich balsamic and rosemary oil. She hadn't been kidding about her fridge. There was a six pack of flavored water, two bottles of white wine, and a tub of hummus among the handful of condiments.

I grabbed the smaller bottle of white and made a vinaigrette for the simple salad fixings with the herbs I found in her cabinet.

Finally the music stopped and she came down the stairs. She said nothing, and I was all right with that.

She drummed her fingers on the kitchen island. "What can I do?"

"Chop up those vegetables."

She pulled out a drawer and there was a knife and slicing board at the ready. I must have shown my surprise because she shrugged. "Tristan designed my kitchen."

"Even though you don't cook?"

She shrugged. "I do sometimes. But my roommate—"

My hand hovered over the baking rack I'd tucked into a heavy stoneware pan. "Pardon me?"

Her wide blue eyes got even bigger. "Oh, wow. Yeah, I suppose I should have mentioned that."

"I had nothing about a roommate in any of my files."

"She's backpacking around Ireland right now. She comes in Tuesday."

I ground my teeth together. "That would have been important information to have."

She sighed. "She needed someplace to stay and I needed someone to watch my house when I'm on tour."

"How long have you known this person? Woman?"

"Forever. She's one of my best friends from high school."

"Name?" I'd gotten a lot of her friends from her social media accounts. Maybe she wasn't a complete stranger.

"Devon Murphy."

The bands that had tightened around my chest lessened. I'd researched her. Best friend, redhead, artist, and single. Still, this female best friend most likely would not be staying alone in the house while Keys was away. Not while I was in charge. "I noticed one of the bedrooms had an easel."

She nodded. "Yes, she's a painter. I'm sure I'll have to drag her out of the room when she gets back. She'll have sketches galore. She has a special cabinet on the deck that has her supplies in it. That's where she usually is. When she's not out getting inspired."

"So, she watches this place when you're out of town?"

"Yeah. It seemed stupid for me to pay for someone to check in on the place. My house is huge and we're best friends."

That didn't mean Devon should stay there alone. Female or not, she hadn't been trained on what she should watch out for, and she probably didn't have means of self-defense, either through classes or a weapon. But I didn't have any intention of putting a firearm into her hands.

Instead I would make sure she was being discreetly monitored at all times. Whether or not I would inform Keys of that remained to be seen.

"How long has she been living here?"

"It's a new thing."

I shook my head and slid the meat into the oven. "Please keep me informed of all situations."

"I meant to—"

"Are there any other surprises? A man in your life? I don't want to shoot him in the middle of the night."

She snapped the knife down on the plastic cutting board. "No. Remember that remark earlier? No sex for me with you around."

I gripped the edge of the island. "If you have a personal relationship that I'm not aware of, we can work around it."

Her laugh was strained. "Don't worry, Warden. No boys after curfew."

"This isn't a joke."

"Oh, I know it's not. You don't hear me laughing, do you?"

No, I didn't. Just bitching. I tipped my head back and counted to five. This job was a bad situation in the making, but I couldn't walk away. Not when Noah had asked me for help. Especially Noah.

She resumed chopping and scraping the cherry tomatoes into the bowl with the spring greens. I went to the fridge and pulled out the snap peas. The methodical job of using the paring knife to clean them centered me.

We didn't say anything else as we chopped mushrooms, snap peas, and onions.

"What are you cooking anyway?" she finally asked.

"Chicken."

"Fried?"

"No."

She wrinkled her nose. "I don't like dry chicken."

"It's not dry. It's marinated, then cooked slow."

She sniffed the air. "It smells herb-ish."

"Rosemary and balsamic."

"Hmm." She went to the fridge and opened the door, then to the slim pantry beside it. She pulled out bottles. "Ranch, bleu cheese, or Thousand Island?"

"I made dressing."

Her eyebrows went up.

"It's a wine vinaigrette." Again with the wrinkled nose. "Problem with that too?"

"You're one of those health-conscious people, huh?"

"Healthy body, healthy mind."

"Oh, crap. You don't do yoga or something do you?"

"No. Tai Chi."

She leaned against the island. "Is that like the hot martial arts thing that Patrick Swayze does in Roadhouse?"

I wasn't sure how to respond to that one. "You watch Roadhouse?"

"Oh, yeah. I'm a huge Patrick fan. I love action movies of all kinds. I hang with guys twenty-four seven mostly. We actually watch Roadhouse whenever it's on in the hotels. It's a thing. If one of us finds it, we call around and everyone gathers in one room." She smiled broadly. "We even live Tweet it."

"Live Tweet?"

She pulled her phone out of her sweater. "Yeah." She flicked her thumb down the screen, typed something fast, and then handed me her phone. "See?"

I sighed and wiped my hands on a towel before taking her iPhone.

There was a play-by-play of the way the actor jumped out of the barn and down to help the old man in the movie. I'd seen it a number of times myself. Her reactions were lively and funny.

So much so that I kept scrolling to follow her series of Tweets.

"You definitely know the movie."

"Right? Man, now I want to watch it. I have it on my Amazon account. How about we watch it as we're eating? If I have to eat healthy, at least I can watch Patrick's perfect ass."

"Acceptable." Not that I was interested in his ass, but the movie was entertaining.

"You can eat the vinegar stuff though. There's only so far that I'm going to go with the health crap."

"They're your arteries."

"Damn right."

11

KEYS

LIVING WITH A MAN WAS A NEW EXPERIENCE. OF COURSE, I'D LIVED with my parents, but that was far different from my current situation.

He didn't make a lot of noise. Actually, almost none to be truthful. We'd enjoyed our dinner and whipping-fest that was *Roadhouse*. I didn't want to think about just how hard my heart had kicked at the love scene in the movie as we sat across from each other in my great room.

Both of us had bowls of salad cupped in our hands as we watched. Instead of trying for a full-blown meal, we'd ended up slicing the chicken and putting it over the greens.

He was a good cook. The chicken had been tangy and moist—shockingly—and when I dumped enough Thousand Island dressing on it, I'd been delightfully surprised how filling it had been.

But it had been a little weird to have Dalton banging the hell out of Doc against the barn wall with Quinn across from me. His eyes didn't move from the screen, even if a slight wash of red had blazed strips along his cheeks.

Was kind of cute really.

Big tough guy a bit embarrassed about watching a love scene with a near stranger.

Me?

I was more worried about the fact that I wondered if he could do the same hoist-her-up-against-the-wall thing that Patrick had done.

Not at all what I should have been thinking.

My only saving grace was that he was hot and it had been a damn long time since anyone had hoisted me onto anything, let alone a bed. So, I was human.

That was my freaking story, and I was sticking to it.

The next few days had been the same. Quinn trying to feed me healthy food, Quinn vetoing any sort of outside trips—even walking the trails—Quinn putting the kibosh on visitors and, oh…doing anything fun.

I was about to go out of my damn mind.

If I watched one more episode of *Dr. Who* on my Netflix account, I was going to scream. Even David Tennant couldn't soothe me. The tenth doctor could always soothe me, dammit.

I spun around on the couch and hooked my knees over the back so my head could dangle off the edge of the cushion.

This was my vacation before we started tour and I was holding my ass because some crackpot might do something. How was this my life? The fear I'd been holding the last four days had slowly burned to anger.

I needed to get out of this house.

I needed to do something.

Devon was coming home Tuesday, but that was still days away.

"Hey, Siri."

"Yes, Keys."

"Play my Dance Around the House Mix."

"Playing Dance Around the House Mix."

I put my hands on the floor and did a backbend off the couch as Taylor Swift blasted out of the house-wide speakers. I jogged through the great room into the kitchen as I shouted along with the words to, "Shake it Off".

Bare feet slapping on the tile as I shook my booty for the pleasure of the fridge before opening both doors with a dramatic turn. I pulled down a peach-flavored water and closed the door and shrieked.

Quinn stood directly behind the door. "Can you turn it down?"

I uncapped the water. "Nope." Then did a bastardized version of the mamba out of the kitchen to the dining room. I grabbed a peach from the fruit bowl in the center of the table.

The song changed to a wild Frank Turner one and my dancing turned into a ska-like punk jumping as I shook my arms and tried to get the tension out of my limbs.

I'd been lying around for days. Quinn liked things quiet. I needed music. I needed life and sound around me. I needed people.

He kept to himself and did a "sweep of the perimeter"—his words —every other hour. Otherwise he was always on his computer. He'd taken over my office, usually closing the door so I had no idea what he was doing. On the phone, with hushed tones. Again, I had no idea who he checked in with, or who he was talking to—I'd tried to eavesdrop—nada.

He was like a freaking covert spy.

"Faith," he shouted.

I ran up the stairs as another of my favorite songs came on. I went straight to my upright and played with Frank Turner.

He followed me up the stairs and I pounded on the keys as the song burst into drums and guitars with crashing pianos. I screamed that I wanted to dance and to romance, though the words went so fast in this song that I had a hard time keeping up. I laughed as he laughed in the song, and the British pub song spiraled out about how he was no good at dancing but was going to do it anyway.

The song was exactly me.

I needed that life.

I knew every word of the song. I turned around and played behind my back as Quinn stood in the doorway with his hands on his hips.

I left the piano and crossed to him and dragged him inside and jumped around him. Every word screamed into his face. His expression was deadpan and stiff until I opened my arms at the end of the song where it was light and airy.

I sang the lyrics sweetly to the almost carnival tones of the song. His lips twitched and I ran over to my piano to play out the rest of the song until my heart was slamming and my breath couldn't keep up with the words.

I stepped away from the piano, my shoulders heaving as I laughed. "Better."

"Can you turn it down now?"

Miranda Lambert came on and I shook my head. "I can't turn off my girlfriend." I jogged past him and down the stairs again. The song was country and spice with a whole lot of rock.

It made me want to tug on my boots and two-step. But I settled for jumping around my living room. Just as I was singing along to her lyrics about gunpowder and lace, the song cut off.

"Hey!"

He came down the stairs, a smile on his usually staid face.

"What did you do?"

"Turned off the damn Bluetooth."

"You have no right."

"I can't hear myself think. Not to mention you're telegraphing that you're here for anyone to notice."

"Of course I'm here. The warden doesn't let me out of this place. You won't even let me go to my parents' house, for God's sake."

"Until we know what we're dealing with this is far safer."

I held out my arms. "I'm going nuts. Do you understand that?"

He tilted his head. "Find a hobby."

"Do you honestly think I'm going to sit here and break out the decoupage and scrap books?" I asked incredulously.

"Maybe. Or how about read a book. Or watch a movie. Or hey, write a song if that works for you."

"I've tried. I can't find a song. It's quiet as a freaking tomb in here because you don't like music, you freak."

"I don't hate music."

"You don't like it." I put my hands on my hips. "Who doesn't like music? It's just...wrong."

"It's just not part of my life like it is for you, Faith. I have to pay attention to my surroundings. I can't be distracted if someone comes up to the house and tries to break in. I have to be able to protect you, dammit. And I can't do that if you're broadcasting the entire Dance Party USA catalog through your fucking house."

I blinked at him.

He'd actually yelled.

His icy-blue eyes were wide and there was a vein popping along his neck.

I pressed my lips together. I should probably be horrified, but I couldn't stop laughing.

"Unbelievable." Quinn turned on his heel and stalked to the office and slammed the door.

"Oh, come on. I'm sorry!" I chased after him and stood outside the door. "Warden, open up." He didn't answer me. I pressed my forehead to the door. "Quinn. I was just trying to have a little fun. You can't fault me for that, can you?"

Still nothing.

I pressed my hand to the door. "Dammit, Quinn."

The door swung open and he was right there in front of me. I stumbled back, my heart skipping. I'd just stuck my face in his space fifteen minutes ago, but it was different now.

There was no playful banter, just a waft of spearmint and soap.

He fisted his hands under his arms as he crossed them. "Call one of your friends. Keep it a close friend."

"Owen," I said quickly.

He nodded. "Acceptable."

I frowned. "He better be. He's in my band, for God's sake."

Quinn said nothing, just arched a brow at me.

"He's one of my best friends."

"I said he could come, didn't I?"

"Right." My gaze dropped to his chest where his Henley pulled tight, then back up to his eyes. "Thanks."

Not that I should thank him for deigning to let one of my friends come over, but I wasn't going there right now. I'd won, and I needed to be good with that.

I skidded into the living room and swiped my phone off the couch. I didn't want to wait on a text. Not when Owen was famous for forgetting to actually check his phone.

The call went to voicemail. "Pick up, you lazy sod." A minute later my phone blasted out the *Boondock Saints* theme song. "What are you doing?"

"Waiting for you as always, darlin'."

I grinned. "My warden said I could have a friend over."

"What are ya, twelve?"

"I feel like it." I dropped onto the couch. "Are you busy?"

He paused and I heard him shuffling the phone to his other ear. "I've been begging to come over to see my favorite girl. Of course I'm not busy."

"You have someone there."

"No, of course not."

I drew my feet up to sit cross-legged. "Is she a blonde? Blondes always get you in trouble."

"You're a blonde, sweetheart."

"I don't count."

"You're trouble enough for a whole city."

Owen's Irish accent was music in itself, and instantly soothed me. "As far as my new bodyguard is concerned, I'm even more trouble than that. Come save me."

"Am I bringing movies and pop, or are we doing the other?"

My grin broadened. "Definitely the other." I heard a girl's voice. "You do have someone there."

"I'm on vacation, darlin'. Of course I do, but you're my mate and I'll be there within the hour, yeah?"

"Thanks, Owen."

"Just make sure you've got plenty of crisps."

"Ten years out of Ireland and you still can't say potato chips."

"Crisps. I can't help it if you people say it wrong."

I laughed again. "See you soon." I hung up and bounded off the couch. I took a quick shower and put on my favorite hoodie with a pair of yoga pants.

I needed to be limber for our marathon.

Fifty-eight minutes later I was pacing the kitchen.

"Would you stop slamming around out there," Quinn yelled from the office.

"Why isn't he here?"

"Because the traffic in LA is atrocious."

"Right." I cracked my knuckles and spun my jade ring. "You're right." Owen's place was a few streets over from the Strip. I didn't even know what day it was. Not that it mattered in this city. Every night was a show, or party, or premiere.

My phone buzzed in my hand. I frowned as a text came in twice. Same text.

"Stupid cell towers." I ran for the door and was jerked back by my hood.

"Really? How many times are we going to go through this?"

"Forgot. But it's Owen."

"You don't know that."

I jerked out of his hold. "He just texted me."

"Get back into the kitchen."

I growled and stomped back into the dining room. I fixed the stack of boxes on the table and moved the bowl of chips a little left of center as they talked.

"I thought you'd be bigger," Owen said.

I snickered and shot down the hall.

Quinn sighed. "Faith. Get away from the door."

I pushed by Quinn and flung myself into Owen's arms.

"There's a love." He put his arms around me and kissed the top of my head. "How's my favorite keyboardist?"

"Better now." I squeezed him hard. "So much better."

Quinn cleared his throat. "I've got some paperwork to do. You guys have a nice visit."

I looked up from the many layers of jewelry and cotton that was an Owen Blackwell ensemble and pulled way. I linked my fingers with his and gave Quinn a tight smile. "Thanks."

"Sure."

"Wow. He's intense, yeah?"

"He takes his job very seriously." I dragged him down the hall to the dining room. "So seriously that I require at least three games of *Hungry, Hungry Hippos* to help put me in a good mood."

Owen shrugged out of his denim jacket and hooked it around the back of the chair, then rubbed his hands together. "That's what I'm talking 'bout." He lifted the top of the box off the game and lifted out the board. "Prepare for domination."

"You're so going down."

Owen snagged a chip from the bowl and chomped. "Where's the beer?"

I winced. "I have soda, but not beer."

Owen wandered into the kitchen. "You wound me."

"My house is kinda like a dry campus at the moment. The warden is pretty strict on keeping all the faculties clear."

"Warden, huh?" He swung open the door to the fridge. "Wine will do, though."

I shrugged. "I could do wine."

"Beautiful." He grabbed the corkscrew magnetized to the side of the fridge, and went to uncorking. "How are you doing?"

I spun my ring. "Going stir-crazy."

"We're all worried about you."

"I know." I hopped up onto the counter and swung my feet as he poured two glasses. "I'm just sitting here twiddling my freaking thumbs. Thanks." I took the glass when he offered it.

"Has anything…you know, happened?"

I shook my head. "Nope. But then again, I'm trapped here, so who knows if it would or not."

"There's no need to take chances though."

I knew that, but it didn't make the whole situation any less shitty. I didn't want to get all depressing. Not when I finally had someone here that I actually wanted to spend time with.

I hopped down. "I'll just take all my aggressions out on your hippo."

Owen slung his arm around my neck. "Cheers to that."

12

QUINN

I SLUMPED BACK IN FAITH'S OFFICE CHAIR. IT WAS TOO SMALL FOR me, so my head tipped back before hitting the headrest. I stared at the beams above my head that made up a grid.

"I don't know what to tell you, Q."

"I know," I said into my earpiece. "I was hoping to find some sort of lead."

Aidan Roth sighed. "We have less than nothing to go on. I had two different people scour the footage. The only thing we found was a flash of blonde hair at one of the cameras on the south side of the building, but it could have been anyone."

"Yeah." I'd also gone through the hours of video and came up with one other Hail Mary shot of a woman near the stage at about the time Faith had been drugged.

Noah was in frame. The look on his face made my gut drop into my boots. I'd seen that face before.

"Q?"

"Yeah, here."

"You can take her out—"

"No."

Aidan sighed. "You know how to keep a client close and keep the danger to a minimum."

"Too many variables. And I don't trust her to stay close."

"Noah didn't say she was a flight risk. She understands how serious this is, right?"

"I don't know. It's been five days and there hasn't even been chatter in the fandom. That worries me. The ones who are harmless and exuberant can't keep their mouth shut. Quiet ones —patient ones—they're the ones who go into the history books."

They were out there slamming something plastic and...balls? No —marbles were scattering. Faith's raucous laughter drifted from the dining room, followed by the deeper male voice.

I curled my fingers into a fist and crossed the room to close the door. My nature wasn't to trust anyone, even if there was no reason to think Owen Blackwell would hurt Faith.

"What's going on over there?" Aidan asked.

"I think they're playing board games."

"Huh."

"Yeah, I don't know what to say to that, but at least she's not streaming her music at top volume." Just medium volume. Damn woman figured out how to get the speakers working again.

"Wishing you'd gone to France with Pierre?"

"Yes."

Aidan laughed. "You hate French food."

"I'd make do. At least the French *have* decent food. Faith eats like a fourteen-year-old boy."

"Faith, huh?"

"That's her name."

"All the reports I have show Keys is the name she goes by most often."

"When's the last time you heard me use a nickname?"

"Third of Never." There was a hint of a burr reminiscent of Owen's accent. My boss had spent a lot of time in Northern Ireland when he'd been a SEAL, and it slipped out when he was tired or super amused.

I had a feeling amused was the reason behind the current slip.

Why the hell was everyone so damn tickled about me and this assignment?

I cleared my throat to get back on track. "I've been researching the band and working with Patrick on the more problematic fans that have been on their radar."

"Take her out of the house, Q."

I gripped the back of the chair and spun it. "Why?"

"Because you need to see if someone's following her. You need to do some recon."

"I don't like it."

"I know you don't, but at least you can control the outcome here while you guys are in the city. When the tour starts, the fans and security will be even harder to control."

"Don't remind me." I paced to the windows as dusk washed the hills in a slate blue. "I wish they'd call off the tour."

"You know people can't live like that."

"I don't know what the true threat level is."

"And it might have been a one-time thing."

"Could be," I said, but I didn't mean it. No one used Ketamine when they didn't mean to kidnap someone. Another reason why I didn't want to take her out of the damn house.

All it took was someone bumping into her and a little stick and she could go down. There was nowhere in this godforsaken city that wasn't overrun with people.

"Take her out tomorrow, Quinn. That's an order."

I fisted my hand and pressed it against the glass. "Fine." I swallowed a growl. "Have you heard back from Carson about the glass?"

"Yeah, he's going to have it done while you guys are on tour. The house will be ready for their break in October."

"Good. Does he outsource the jobs?"

"No, Blake is as much of a pain in the ass as you are. He has secure teams that work on the houses. He understands the security issues, Quinn. We'll make sure the house is safe."

"I'm not worried about the glass. I'm worried about someone in the house who I don't know."

"I requested a special team. The same one that worked on Lindsey York's place out in the Canyon."

"That'll have to do. I'll do a sweep of the house when we get back before she's brought in."

"You're worse than I am, man. And Marcus says I'm a cynical bastard with a control problem."

"Yeah, well…no one's getting kidnapped on my watch."

"Let's keep it that way."

"Then I should keep her—"

"No. You need to do some recon out of that damn house."

I clenched my jaw so tight my head was starting to throb.

"Say it, Q."

"I'm taking her out tomorrow."

"Good. Send me the list from Patrick and I'll have Lucy dig into the names."

"Will do." At least that would be something. If there was dirt on anyone Lucy could find it. She was our resident hacker turned white hat. She was scary and amazing, and one of the few people I trusted to do research.

I hung up with my boss and took one step before coming to a halt again.

"No! You bastard!" Faith's voice rose and ended in a burst of giggles. I was pretty sure I'd never heard her giggle in all the days we'd been together. Laugh, sure—she was naturally light-hearted.

I left the office and followed the voices out into the dining room. There were two bowls of junk food between them—chips and something with the fake orange cheese that ended up on clothes and fingers like a radioactive cloud. Two bottles of wine were empty and a third was being uncorked as I walked in.

A child's game with manic-looking animals in primary colors was askew at the end of the table. In front of them was another game. Faith slapped a button gleefully and a geyser of black cards came at her.

"No! Come on." She gathered them with both hands until she had a mitt full of colorful cards. An alarming number of them were Wild Cards to boot. *Uno* on steroids. I remembered playing the game when I was a kid, but then it was just a tray that you flipped.

Now, not so much.

Owen had a similar handful of cards and his eyes were bloodshot with too much wine. He looked over Faith's shoulder and noticed me. "Oops. We're in trouble now, love."

She twisted around, the laughter in her eyes fading. "Here to ruin our fun, Warden?"

I smiled tightly. I really hated that name. I hated that I had to keep her cooped up when it was obvious she was one of the most alive people I knew. "Was just wondering if you wanted a pizza?"

She slapped her cards down. "Yeah?" She rushed over to a drawer near the fridge. "We've got three really good places."

"No."

She shut the drawer with a bang. "What do you mean, no?"

"I'm making pizza."

Her eyebrows shot up. "You're making pizza?"

I nodded. Last grocery order, I'd added a few things that were more in Faith's wheelhouse. We'd need to compromise on food, but at least I could do a few things to lessen her misery.

Her nose wrinkled up. "I don't want broccoli pizza or something gross like that."

I sighed. "Pepperoni and mushrooms sound good?"

Her eyes sparkled. "Now that's what I'm talking about." She crossed the room to me and dragged me into the kitchen. "I can help. We can help."

Owen came in with his glass of wine. "I could use the carbs. This one is trying to drink me under the table."

"Why don't you two go back to your game and I'll make a couple of pies, all right?"

"Yeah? You sure?" Owen asked. "I can actually do the pizza thing. I throw a frozen one in the oven all the time."

"I'm making it fresh."

He cupped his hand over the top of his glass, skull ring flashing on his middle finger. The rest of them were tattooed with letters so it spelled out, love with the skull as the o. Interesting look. "Oh, well then. We're getting fancy. Does that come with the bodyguard classes?"

"Frozen dinners get old, man."

"And that's why I usually go out to dinner every day." He took his glass. "C'mon, darling, we have a game to finish. I intend to win this round."

Faith came around the island. "Only if you happen to have low cards for the next five hands."

"Five?" He tipped his head back. "Can we switch to *Sorry*?"

She gathered the cards and started organizing them. I listened to them chatter on as I readied the dough and put the sauce together on the stovetop.

"Breadsticks are up," I called to the table.

Faith came running over and groaned. "Garlic-a-licious, you beautiful man." She snagged one out of the basket. "Hmm. I didn't even know I had these baskets."

I smiled down at her. "Your kitchen is as close to a chef's set up as I've ever seen outside of a restaurant."

She shrugged. "As I said, Tristan tricked it out. I think he used me as an excuse to buy toys to try out. He cooked for me for a week. It was fairly glorious." She snuck over to the sauce and dipped the end of her bread in.

"Hey!"

She popped it into her mouth. "What? You saw nothing." She broke off another and held it up to me. "Want?"

My mouth watered. And not for the damn breadstick. "I'm good."

"Come on. You're always denying yourself. It tastes so good. All buttery and perfect. Decadent and so bad for you." Her eyes were soft with too much wine and happiness.

Christ, she made me want.

She held it closer to my mouth.

"Faith."

She rolled her eyes. "Right. You said no. I forgot. It's your favorite word." She backed up and dunked it into the pot on the stove. "You're missing out."

I moved to the stove and swallowed a groan. Oregano and spices should have overpowered the space. Instead, her peach scent was the only thing I noticed. I reached around her to a ladle and the little bowl I'd readied for dunking.

She chewed, her lips shiny with butter. I held the bowl out for her. "Use this, huh?"

"Right. You know it's more fun to dunk in the pot, right?"

"You're going to get my sauce all greasy with the butter."

She dipped her finger into the bowl and licked sauce off her fingertip. "Wouldn't want that."

"Go feed your friend."

"We'll try not to fill up on the breadsticks." She twirled around, grabbing the basket on her way by. "I have appetizers," she said in her singsong way.

"Excellent," Owen said. "And I'm red by the way."

"I'm blue."

I listened to them trash talk each other over the game that was older than both of them combined. Oh, it was an updated version, but I was pretty sure my grandparents had played it. Or maybe that was *Parcheesi*.

Either way it was a comforting sound.

I could deal with that better than the music. Watching her hips sway and the bawdy, sultry voice that rolled out of such a tiny woman had nearly killed me. I kneaded the dough out a little too forcefully at the memory of her spinning around me earlier. So carefree and so defiant.

The fact that I wanted to snatch her up and wrap those distractingly bare legs around my waist was the mother of all bad ideas. Heightened situations and forced proximity were the gateway to serious trouble.

I wasn't her type—never would be her type. If it wasn't for the fact that I had to be in her space, she'd never give me a second thought. Hell, she wasn't my ideal either. She was brash and bucked at even the idea of rules. There was no safe corner in her world.

It was purely a physical response to her.

I could ignore physical needs.

I'd been ignoring them for the last year, ever since I'd enjoyed a mutually beneficial hour of stress relief with a woman after a charity ball. It had been a one-day thing where Aidan had needed extra security personnel. Since I'd been between jobs and knew the layout of the Kennedy Center, I'd been a logical choice.

There'd been some chatter about a possible sniper and I'd been using that particular woman's balcony seats as a lookout. Being on that kind of high alert for hours, then not having any action had resulted in a one-night stand with an heiress from some Fortune 500 company. She liked the idea of danger, and I'd been alone too long.

It had been sexual release, and that was it. Neither of us had wanted anything more than that moment and had parted ways with a, "Have a nice life". Then I'd taken the ambassador job and had been too focused on deciphering the ins and outs of D.C. to think about getting involved with anyone.

I wasn't exactly the flirting kind, and usually attracted women who found my serious nature an attribute. The problem with that was I ended up with women who were just as serious about their careers as I was. Add in the fact that there was little time for socializing when my calendar was full of political functions, as well as an active family to watch out for, and in the end, relationships had always landed on the bottom of the list.

Little moments like this, when I couldn't ignore the pull of intangibles like chemistry, were the times I wondered how long I could do this job without making another mistake.

I loaded the two pizzas into the oven and closed the door a little too hard. Faith turned in her seat and gave me a look over the rim of her wine glass.

If it wasn't Noah asking me for this favor, I would have requested a reassignment.

Not only because Faith was a wild card in so many different respects, but because having any sort of emotions in this job was detrimental to the safety of the client.

I stabbed the timer app on my phone and wished for a beer. Fuck, it was going to be a long night.

13

KEYS

I ROLLED OVER AND BURIED MY HEAD UNDER MY PILLOW. WHAT THE hell was that banging? And why did my mouth taste like I'd made out with a clove of garlic?

"Up and at 'em!"

"Fuck off!" I muttered into my mattress.

"You want to get out of this place, then shake your ass, Faith."

I flipped back my pillow. "What did you say?"

"We're going out."

I rolled off the side of my bed and stumbled. "Oh, fuck. No more wine." I weaved my way to the door and swung it open. "What? Leaving? Really?"

Quinn stood in the doorway, his standard cargo pants and Henley in place. "You keep ragging on about being stuck in here. So, we're going out."

I pushed my hair out of my face. "Awesome. I'll be ready in ten." I blinked up at him. "Wait. Is Owen still here?"

"Negative."

"Did you wake him up just as rudely?"

He pursed his lips. "I may have opened the blinds in your guest room before he went to bed last night."

"You're a cruel, cruel man."

"Did I not tell you to back off on the wine at two this morning?"

"It was way too late at that point, Warden."

"It's never too late to put the glass down. Get ready." He walked down the hall to the stairs. "And brush your teeth. Twice."

I slapped my hand over my mouth. "Hateful," I muttered and shut my door. Afraid that he would change his mind about actually leaving, I raced into my bathroom and took a five-minute shower. I would have skipped a shampoo except there was garlic coming out of every pore and it had traveled into my hair.

Holy mercy, that boy put garlic in everything. It had tasted amazing, but good thing I hadn't been kissing anyone last night.

A quick flash of Quinn pressing his lips together when I'd tried to lure him into tasting my breadstick came out of nowhere.

There were times when he was the most closed-off man on the planet. I had no freaking clue what he was thinking about ninety-five percent of the time. Then there were the other moments.

The dangerous moments, when he seemed to be on the verge of... something. I didn't know if it was shaking me, shooting me, or...other.

I didn't really want to think too much about the other.

The *other* played tag with me in dreams. As I was running away from someone, then running to him. Obviously it was because he was guarding me. Every woman had fantasies about a strong, virile man playing hero to her damsel in distress. Even friends who were the most independent people I knew had one or two fantasies that included a rescue.

When it came to Devon, my best friend, they were usually of the handcuff variety. But she was the exception to many rules. One of the reasons I loved her dearly. And missed her even more.

I didn't want to worry her while she was out of the country. I was going to catch hell for it, but I didn't want to ruin her trip. She'd been saving for years to backpack her way around Ireland. My little drama would still be here when she got home.

We'd actually coordinated our schedules so we had a few days together before my tour started up again. Tuesday. Just a few more days under the warden's rule and then I'd have Devon in my corner. Two feisty women against one man was more way more fun.

Until then, I had to deal with him on my own.

I quickly parted my hair and did two messy half-braids so my wavy hair wouldn't run wild. I didn't have time to dry it properly. Not if I wanted to make sure Quinn definitely didn't change his mind.

I slipped on a few rings because I felt naked without them, my favorite hoop earrings, and a trio of necklaces. After a quick dash of blush, gloss, and mascara so I didn't look like a teenager next to Mr. Silver Temples, I ran for my closet.

"Faith! Is this your idea of ten minutes?"

What? Was he honestly so literal? A girl's ten minutes was not actually ten minutes, for fuck's sake. "Two minutes," I hollered through the door. I dropped my robe and struggled into my bra. Dammit, my skin was still damp.

I snapped the strap into place and dragged on a Clash T-shirt, my favorite jeans, and my red Chucks. My lightweight leather jacket finished the look. I might have to be quick, but shit, I still could look cute. The cameras were always around.

Especially now.

I was halfway down the hall when I turned back around for a pair of sunglasses. Just in case the paparazzi really were out en masse, I didn't need to look like a deer caught in headlights. It was bad enough I'd made headlines at Hunter's wedding.

It was supposed to be his day—Kennedy's day.

Instead, everyone was talking about how I'd almost gotten... what? Kidnapped? Drugged? Murdered?

No one knew.

I took a deep breath as I got to the bottom of the stairs.

No one really knew.

I'd been trying so hard to believe that it was just a fluke. But what if it wasn't? I clutched the wall as I paused on the second-to-last stair. I wasn't going to let fear rule me, dammit. I lifted my chin and took the last few steps.

"What are we waiting for?" I put on my shades and headed for the door.

"Hold up."

I held up my arms. "Right. You first. Age before beauty."

He slid his hand behind his back and I heard the slide of his gun into his holster. What had I expected? That he wasn't going to carry a weapon? I knew he had a gun. I'd seen his shoulder holster the first day he'd come into my house.

But not this? Not at the base of his spine.

That was new.

He pulled down a button-down denim shirt over his faded gray Henley. He wore black cargos today. All of it made him look tanner, more unapproachable, and way more badass.

I swallowed as he put mirrored aviators on.

Why did he have to be so attractive? I could handle a paunchy ex-cop, or even a lantern-jaw marine-looking dude, but not an Alex O'Loughlin stunt double. The wrongness was beyond wrong.

He held the door for me, and shadowed me out the door. His hand was light on the small of my back as he looked around and led me to a sleek black BMW. He opened the door for me and waited as I swung my legs in.

"Buckle up."

"I'm not seven."

"You're right. If you were seven you'd be riding in the back." He shut the door before I could say anything else.

I clicked the buckle and fussed with the shoulder strap. Always choking the short people. He got in and the car instantly felt smaller. His long fingers checked gauges and settings, then he tucked his phone into the cup holder as the Bluetooth engaged.

"Welcome, Quinn. Do you have a destination?"

My eyebrows shot up? "It talks?"

He grinned at me. "Bulletproof too." Then he tapped the screen and cleared the menu, slapping the shifter into reverse. His driving was smooth and sure. He followed all the traffic laws—sort of. He drove defensively in a way that I'd never seen. And I'd been navigating California highways all my driving life.

Instead of being stuck in traffic jams, he seemed to know side streets I'd never heard of. He was always scanning his line of sight, his jaw tight with concentration.

"Where are we going?"

"I called your manager and checked if you had anything scheduled this week."

"I thought we cancelled all the personal appearances."

"Ms. West did, but I think we figured out a way to show everyone you're doing well. Diffuse some of the newspaper accounts, and give you a few hours reprieve from the house. Ms. West seemed to think it was a good idea too."

"Ms. West. Indie would freak if she heard you call her that."

"She's going to meet us at Mochachello's on Sunset."

I was pretty sure my jaw was somewhere on the floor. "Mochachello's? Really?" It was only my favorite coffeehouse. They specialized in creating hot chocolate-coffee hybrids that were to die for.

He nodded. "It's small, intimate, and I can cover all the egress points. You can soak up some atmosphere and I can make sure you're safe."

I pulled out my phone.

"What are you doing?"

"Texting Indie."

He nodded. "That's fine."

"Gee thanks."

"Just don't go blasting this around social media. I don't want it to become too big of a deal."

"Then how are people going to know I'm doing okay?"

"Indie's leaking it to a few select fan blogs. There will be some chatter, but we'll keep it to a minimum. If you want to do some Tweeting or Instagraming, or whatever when we're there, that's fine. By then we'll be on a clock to get out anyway."

"How long is my furlough?"

"Very funny, Faith."

My lips twitched. I thought it was funny. I scrunched down in my seat and spoke with Indie for a few minutes. For the first time in days, my mood was actually lifting.

This was going to be great.

14

QUINN

I WAS IN HELL.

How many females could actually fill the booths and bar stools in one little freaking place? The walls were chalkboards with art from local artists with a timer at the edge of each one.

True pieces of flash art.

It was about the only interesting part of the damn place. They ruined coffee with chocolate and caramels and all sorts of flavors. I had to tell the waitress three times to just put coffee in a mug and hand it to me. No extras. Not even sugar.

But Faith was in her element. Her smile was huge and her laughter rang through the room. Even people who hadn't realized she was famous couldn't help but notice her. She practically shone like a beacon.

It was fascinating and horrifying from a job standpoint.

How was I supposed to keep her incognito when we went on her tour? She was a natural entertainer with a gift of being fun and quippy and a laughter that drew people to her like a siren song.

I know I was already in danger of crashing into the rocks for her.

Fuck.

I was getting as fanciful as she was.

Not good.

My phone buzzed at my hip. I checked it briefly and groaned. I was set up to receive any and all alerts from her media accounts. It wasn't like I hadn't given her permission to do it, but I'd hoped she would avoid telegraphing her whereabouts our first time out.

A fancy coffee filled the screen and the edge of the menu. At least she didn't tag the place outright. But it seemed like the entire area flocked to this establishment for their froufrou coffee.

She had her second huge mug of coffee-laced hot chocolate in front of her with mountains of marshmallows and whipped cream. Who the hell needed both?

She was going to be zooming on sugar and caffeine for the rest of the damn day. I'd probably get another medley of songs as my afternoon treat.

Fucking wonderful.

I stood against the wall, three feet from her. An octopus and a ship were in an epic battle in DayGlo orange and purple over my shoulder. And across from me was a startlingly lifelike mermaid on a craggy rock.

Fitting.

Sirens and mermaids were pretty much the same thing.

A murmur of voices ramped up, and I stepped forward away from the wall.

Faith smiled at two children who came up to the table.

"Your rings are pretty."

"Why thank you." She held her hand out to show off a half dozen sparkles on her fingers.

"I'm sorry." A woman rushed to the table and I moved behind Faith. She had a short cap of blonde hair and a harried look on her face. I relaxed slightly as she led the children away from the table with more apologies.

Faith waved to the youngest girl with wispy pigtails in her almost nonexistent hair.

She dropped her other hand and waved me back.

When two more women came forward, I stiffened.

"Keys? Faith Keystone?"

She smiled warmly again and pushed her sunglasses up. "You got me."

"I can't believe it's you."

Faith waved her hand to encompass the room. "Who doesn't like chocolate and coffee?"

Me.

I'd never loved my sunglasses more than today. It was getting harder and harder not to roll my eyes at the incessant chatter about spice this, and dark-chocolate-sea-salt-fantastical-blend-with-a-hint-of-coffee that. Seriously. These people wouldn't know a decent cup of coffee if it was poured over their heads.

The three of them raved over their favorite drinks for a few minutes. Faith got each girl to talk through the stutters with kindness until they were all laughing like old friends.

She was kind of amazing.

The light conversation faded to the back of my mind as I watched the room—until one of the girls asked a question that made my ears perk up.

"We read such awful stuff on the internet about you. We're so glad you're all right. How could anyone be so uncool?"

Faith sipped her drink without answering. She gave her a noncommittal hum instead of actually going into detail.

Good girl.

"You're not canceling the tour, are you?"

Heaven forbid.

I knew from a business standpoint there was no way to do that, but the logistics of the next two months were giving me an eye-twitch.

"Absolutely not. You know nothing keeps me down for long."

The woman closest to Indie clutched her purse to her chest. "No. I remember when you broke your arm during the 'Rusted Armor' video. You were back on the piano before the cast came off."

Faith laughed. "It was only the wrist. My fingers worked fine."

The other girl clutched her phone in her hand. "Would you sign this?" She popped her phone out of the case and flipped it over. "I can get a clear case to show it off tomorrow."

"Really?" Faith's smile was a damn ray of light. Seeing her out and about with people made it even more apparent that she was miserable being shut away. "That's so sweet."

I stepped close again, watching hands and purses to make sure nothing else was going on. When her hand dropped to wave me off again, I ignored her. She got more insistent until her fingers brushed between my knees and I stiffened.

I opened my mouth to warn them to back off, but the girls looked up at me and instantly shrank away.

Guess the sunglasses only hid so much.

Faith nailed me with a dirty look over her shoulder. But the smile was back on her face when she faced the girls again. "Sorry. My boyfriend gets a little protective."

I blinked.

Boyfriend?

Indie quickly covered her mouth with a napkin, but I still heard the snort of laughter.

Well, that was one way to explain my presence. I had no problem letting people know I was a bodyguard, but this actually would work a little easier. No one would question me being around her if they thought we were involved.

I moved up until my thighs brushed the back of her chair. I tried for a genial grin, but the fans nearly tripped over themselves to get out of there.

When we were alone again, she craned her neck to stare up at me. "Must you be so menacing?"

I lifted one brow. "Yes."

"Incredible."

"Wrap it up. We've been here for an hour more than I'm comfortable with."

"We just got here."

"We've been here for eighty-eight minutes."

Indie grinned at Faith. "Is he always like this?"

"He's actually nice today," Faith muttered.

"I'll endeavor to make up for it tonight."

Indie leaned in. "Is there something I should know?"

"No," we both said.

Indie pushed back her battered straw cowboy hat. "Oh, yeah…tour next week is going to be anything but boring."

I waved to the girl behind the counter. "Could we have a to-go cup?"

"Sure thing," she called back.

"You suck, Warden." Faith muttered.

I leaned down until my lips were close to her ear. "Is that what you'd call your boyfriend?"

She turned her head until her cheek brushed mine. "You couldn't handle me *or* my nicknames," she said on a low voice.

The urge to say "try me" was burning a hole in my tongue, but there were some things you just couldn't take back. I stood up to my full height, and spotted another crowd of people heading our way.

"Time to go."

She spotted the same group, but instead of arguing, she actually nodded. "All right. Lead the way."

I pulled the chair out for her and dumped her cup into the to-go glass unceremoniously.

"Way to ruin a drink."

"Just mixing it thoroughly. Wouldn't want the caramel and choco-late to settle on the bottom now, would we?" I handed her the cup.

"I sense mocking."

"Now where would you get that idea?"

"Definitely mocking." She quickened her step. "Better than brooding," she said with a shrug.

I was never going to understand this woman. I led both women out of the cafe and deposited Indie at her car. It took another five minutes of me playing lookout for them to say their goodbyes.

But the fans were intent on seeing Faith, and found the side street we'd parked on.

"All right, time's up."

Faith's growl face started until she saw the ten people at the end of the street heading for us. "Guess they figured out the picture."

"Ya think?"

"Rude."

I hustled her down to the BMW. "Get in the car, Faith."

"Bye," she yelled back to Indie.

The older woman was standing at her Jeep with her hands on her hips. "I'll see you Sunday night."

Finally, I shut the door after her and rounded the car.

When the first hand landed on the window, I spun the tires. Three girls in their twenties reared back and they all held up their phones for a picture.

I fucking hated dealing with famous people.

Hated.

15

KEYS

The drive home was silent. Partly because my heart had been lodged in my throat for the first ten minutes of the drive. Defensive Driving 101 with your instructor, Quinn Alexander.

Holy crap.

He weaved in and out of traffic and on and off ramps on the highway until we ended up on a back road that I didn't even know about and I'd lived in the Silver Lake area of LA for the last five years.

We pulled into my driveway, only this time instead of parking there, he opened the garage and pulled in. Evidently my time with the outside air was over.

My fingers were sore from clutching my cup the entire ride home. The contents were stone cold, and I was exhausted. I should be climbing the rafters with sugar and caffeine, but all I could think about was my couch.

I'd enjoyed the interaction with the fans, and having the sound of life around me for a few hours, but I'd also been on guard the entire time. I didn't like that feeling.

Even when we'd had our first taste of fame, I hadn't been so unnerved in public. I'd lived for it—off of it. I juiced myself on the dynamic of strangers and people who loved our music.

Now, all I could imagine was turning around to see *her*. The faceless woman who looked so much like me that I couldn't differentiate us.

I jumped when Quinn opened the door.

"You all right?"

"Fine," I said and pushed by him to go into the mudroom from the garage. I pulled my headphones out of my purse as we walked through the hallway to the dining room. I pushed the earbuds into my ears and found my sleep playlist.

It didn't matter that it was barely two in the afternoon.

I wanted to check out.

I didn't want to think about the woman who'd forced Quinn Alexander into my life. I didn't want to think about anything.

I went straight for the stairs, ignoring Quinn calling for me. I didn't have it in me to spar with him right now. I was afraid that I'd actually do something stupid like scream at him until I was crying.

And I didn't want him to see me like that.

See the weakness that I hated.

I stripped out of my clothes and tugged on boxers and a sleep tank. Then I crawled into bed and zoned out.

I don't know how long I slept, but the sun had set when I rolled over the first time.

"Faith."

"Go away, Warden."

"You haven't eaten today."

"I don't care." I flipped the pillow over my head. Maybe I could sleep the rest of the time before the tour started.

It was better than being bored.

So much better than fighting the weird pull I had when Quinn was in my space. It had to be annoyance.

I'd never really actively disliked anyone. Okay, that wasn't completely right. I'd really hated Hunter's first fiancée, but I didn't have to live with her. I had to see Quinn all the time.

And I was tired. My phone had died long ago, but I went under the blissful wave of sleep again before the silence got to me.

The sun was shining into my room when I got the next dose of rudus interruptus.

He opened the door this time.

"Enough of this crap, Faith."

I rolled over onto my belly. "What do you care? I'm quiet, right? No music, no games, no TV." My voice was slightly slurred from the mattress conforming to my cheek.

"And it's been glorious. Now it's time for you to get up."

"Are we going somewhere?"

"No."

"Then, sleep. All of the sleeping."

He snatched my sheet and blanket off the bed. I was pretty sure my boxers had twisted sometime in the night and I was probably flashing him half a cheek, but I couldn't find it in me to care.

He yanked me by the ankle and I kicked out.

"Dammit, Warden. Can't I enjoy some solitary?"

He flipped me over. His eyes were bloodshot and there were dark bruises at the corners of his eyes. "You've had enough solitary."

"What's the big deal? So I slept a day away."

"Two."

"What?" I licked my lips and cringed. God, I was thirsty.

"Two days, Faith. I tried to come in yesterday, but you wouldn't move. You're moving now. I'm not going to let you get sick because you're throwing a temper tantrum."

"Oh, you haven't seen one of those."

He dragged me to the edge of the bed and tucked his shoulder into my middle.

"What the hell are—" I yelped as he tossed me over his shoulder. "Quinn!" He didn't stop, even when I kicked my feet and I fell a precarious two inches. He banded his arm across the backs of my thighs and opened the shower stall door.

He turned the water on cold and stepped in with me. I pounded on his back and shoulders, my ankle smacking into the tile before he finally let me down.

"What is wrong with you?"

"Time to snap out of it." He looked down at me, his eyelashes starred with water, and his super short hair falling forward from the deluge from the rain hood in my shower.

I grit my teeth against the shock of the cold and shivered. "I hate you."

"I know." He slowly turned the taps until it was warm water flowing over us. "I know this sucks. I know you're miserable and feeling out of control."

I crossed my arms over my chest, finally awake and with it enough to realize just how thin my shirt was.

He pushed my hair out of my face and cupped my head. "Hiding isn't going to work. But you know what will?"

My nipples tightened under my arms and I couldn't stop the shivers. Not because of the cold. I just couldn't have him this close to me. I couldn't deal with this on top of everything else.

I looked down and that was so much worse.

He was wearing workout shorts and a T-shirt. Both of them molded to his body in ways that I really didn't want to see. Because they were going to burn themselves on my retinas.

God.

I shut my eyes and fisted my hands, but it was too late. The outline of his abdominal muscles, the bulge under his shorts was still there behind my eyelids. I opened my eyes again because I was a masochist and the bulge was definitely different.

A ridge formed against his upper thigh.

Danger.

My internal jukebox went on alert and "End of Me" started playing at full volume. The curse of my world being music meant that songs embedded themselves into my DNA whether I wanted to deal with them or not.

Why did it have to be him?

I looked up at him. Anything not to notice that bulge that made my mouth water and my fingers itch. He seemed to be waiting for me to answer a question.

Had he asked one?

"What?" I asked and hoped it would cover me.

"I'm going to keep you safe. I promise."

"That's what you think this is about?"

He pressed his lips together and finally seemed to notice we were way too close. He tried to take a step back, but I gripped his shirt. "Faith," he said on a voice that was so low that it was almost indiscernible with the beating water.

"I hate this. I hate having you control every move in my life, but I don't have any doubt you can protect me, Quinn."

He looked down, his hands slipping away from my hair.

I pushed him back into the tile and his eyes locked with mine again. "My problem is distrusting everyone. I don't like that feeling. I don't like that there are so many holes in my memory that I can't trust my own judgment right now."

"That's why I'm here."

"It's not something you can control and fix." He clenched his jaw and that little muscle jumped again. The urge to climb up and flick my tongue over that distracting spot was new. I wasn't sure I liked it. In fact, it was about as confusing as the rest of my life right now.

His heart was slamming under my hand and he kept looking at my mouth.

Oh God. The song was so damn loud again.

He was so wrong for me. The timing for this was absolute crap.

His hands were fisted against the tile, and every muscle was flexed. So intense. I wanted to taste him. To see what all that repression tasted like. Would it be as sinful as I imagined?

He lifted his chin and looked away from me.

I sighed and took a step back. "It's a shitty situation that I have to deal with. I'm sorry I scared you."

"You pissed me off."

I felt the smile coming, and valiantly tried to beat it back. "Right. Pissed you off. Got it."

He slicked back his hair and his blue eyes blazed. "Be downstairs in ten minutes. You're eating, and drinking a fucking gallon of water."

"Yes, Warden."

He swung the door open and snapped a towel off the rack before his wet feet slapped their way out of my bathroom. I wiggled out of my wet clothes and tried like hell to ignore my aching breasts.

And I sure as hell didn't have an ache way lower.

Nope.

Hell no.

I tipped my head up to the stream of water. Maybe that would drown out the "liar, liar, pants on fire" refrain lighting up my internal jukebox like it was a Vegas slot machine.

16

QUINN

I METHODICALLY CHOPPED TOMATOES FOR THE SALAD. MY COCK WAS still as hard as the handle of the chef's knife, but at least my jaw had unlocked.

What the hell had I been thinking, dragging her into that shower?

I hadn't been thinking, that was the problem.

All I could think about was budging her out of that comatose state. I never would have pegged her as the hide-under-the-covers type, but then again, I was wrong more than I was right when it came to this woman.

She laughed when I was sure she was going to cry, she screamed at me despite the fact that I outweighed her by at least a hundred pounds and had tactical training. She didn't respect a damn thing about my job or the fact that I was working overtime to keep her safe.

And I wanted to lift her against the nearest flat surface and fuck her until I was blind. Until her screams ended in groans, and I could breathe around the ball of insanity living in my chest.

Not good.

For the first time since this hellish job started, I couldn't wait for her tour to start. At least then we'd both be busy dealing with her schedule. Between practices, soundchecks, and promotional inter-views, she'd be out of my hair.

So I couldn't pull hers.

I slammed the side of my fist against the marble countertop.

Christ, pull it together, man.

I'd had this whole chemistry thing under control until I'd gotten her wet. Fuck. My life had become the second circle of hell. Lust sitting on my shoulders with no outlet.

Rule one—don't fuck the client.

It was a fairly simple rule, and one that I'd never had trouble following. I may not like the Hollywood-esque jobs, but I'd been assigned to a few over the years. I'd even had to babysit a nymphoma-niac actress when I was first out of the Rangers.

I hadn't been even slightly interested.

This woman had to be the one to test all of my resolves. This woman who brought men to their knees without even trying. And not because she even meant to. I'd watched Noah around her that first night. He may have said their relationship was similar to brother and sister, but there was a fierce protectiveness that could have slipped into romance with the smallest provocation.

The other night with Owen...again, the friendship role, but I could see the glints of interest in the other man's eyes. If she had given him the green light, he'd have been all over her.

Both men respected the fact that she wasn't interested, but men didn't look at the friend zone in the same way as women. It was gener-ally a clear and simple line that could be walked over. If you liked a woman enough to be friends, there was very little needed to change it into a romance unless there was absolutely no chemistry involved.

Hell, two of my lovers in my twenties had started as friends.

Mutual careers and my status as a Ranger had killed the relation-ships, instead of real problems with the women. But then again, I hadn't been so far gone about anyone that I'd tried to make it work either.

But none of that mattered.

Because the line in front of Faith was more like a tripwire. And I'd be the one getting a limb blown off—and not the fun way.

"Smells awesome. I could eat a cow."

I looked up from my cutting board and had to swallow a groan. Had to be the white cutoffs. Second circle of hell making sure that I was going to be tortured with the never-ending hard-on today.

I pulled my Henley down over my zipper and prayed for divine intervention.

"How about a chicken?"

"I suppose a chicken would do."

"Good. I made buffalo grilled chicken, cheese rolls and a salad."

"Wow, you really were worried about me. Cheese? Doesn't that increase cholesterol?"

"Just take the basket to the table."

She peeked under the napkin and made this low groan that was the sole reason I would have my zipper imprint on the underside of my dick.

I followed her with the chicken, salad, and her preferred dressing tucked under my arm.

She took two of the largest pieces of chicken and attacked them with an appetite that would do an inmate proud. "I'd marry you for the cheese bread alone."

"Good to know."

"I'm a simple girl, with simple needs." She finished off her large glass of water and took her glass to the kitchen. I expected her to come back with a glass of soda, but she surprised me with another glass of water.

I doubted that my healthier eating was actually rubbing off on her, but at least she was being smart and rehydrating. Instead of discussing the shower incident, she was scrolling through her phone and texting between bites.

I was happy with the silence. We ate, and during cleanup she piped one of her crazy playlists through the speakers. She wiggled her hips as she scrubbed the grill pan I'd used.

The song flipped over to another full of brass and a happy beat. Through the chorus, she bumped her hip against mine. Her throaty voice purred out the lyrics about modern love.

She swung around until we were back to back, her hips still moving. I couldn't help but laugh down at her. She grabbed the bottle brush and used it as a microphone. She spun the pan in her other hand and set it into the drying rack.

After a low dip, she came up and kicked the dishwasher door closed. She threw the brush back into the sink. I reached in to put it on the drying hook, but she grabbed my soapy hand and dragged me into a box step.

Delighted when I could keep time with the music, she laughed and wrapped her arms around my neck. The lyrics spoke of modern love not being good enough, that you needed connection.

My hips followed hers regardless of the stern lecture I'd given myself earlier. The next song was equally jumpy. I recognized this singer's voice. It was the same song that she'd played on the piano.

She had some questionable taste in music, but I found myself humming along to this guy more than once.

"You like Frank?"

"Who?"

She dropped her forehead against my arm. "You kill me. Do you never listen to music?"

I shrugged. "Not a lot of time for it in my line of work, remember?"

"Music is elemental. Frank Turner—this guy," she pointed to the air, "is a genius. He writes sad songs, happy songs, drunk songs, recovery songs—all of the biggest emotions."

"So, you like him?"

"Little bit."

I twisted my fingers into the belt loops of her shorts as the next song slowed. We swayed slightly. I didn't know exactly what we were doing, but I didn't have it in me to push her away just yet.

Dancing was sex with your clothes on. And the closest I was going to get to touching this woman. So, I let myself dance to the sultry croon of the song. She rested her cheek against my arm.

I let the music in, I let the softness of her skin in, and the summer scent of her seeped inside my chest. The song was full of sad guitars and a slow beat that spoke about a man's regrets.

I needed to pull away from her, but I couldn't.

It wasn't the whiskey that was killing me either. The singer of the song had it more than correct on so many levels. It was a woman.

It was Faith.

When she turned her face into my neck, I couldn't swallow the groan this time. Her fingers slipped through the short hairs at the nape of my neck. "Faith."

"Don't put on your warden voice yet." She brushed her nose along my breastbone, her breath warm on my skin. "I'm just borrowing you for a moment. I need to hold on to someone."

And I was good enough for that.

The silky softness of her skin above her cutoffs burned my fingertips. Want strangled me like a noose, but I'd be her stand-in for now.

Because I couldn't walk away yet.

We danced like that for another two songs before she slowly dropped her arms. She rested her hand on my chest, her eyes a little sad. "Thanks."

I nodded.

"I think I'm going to go upstairs and write for a bit. I haven't been able to since the..." She trailed off. "Well, you know. There's a logjam in my head. I need to get it out."

I understood that tenfold.

"Sure. I've got some reports to look over."

"Okay. Night, Warden."

"Goodnight, Faith."

She scooped her phone off the kitchen island and went upstairs without looking back once.

I gripped the edge of the island and wished I was a different man for one moment. A man who would chase her upstairs and show her that I wasn't just a stand-in. That I could hold her, touch her, and hopefully make those sad eyes happy for at least a moment in time.

I swore and headed into the office.

Work. I needed work to center me again.

Hours later, I surfaced from the pages of data I'd gotten back from Aidan. There were a number of questionable people in Patrick's red file, but no one that fit the criteria of Faith's attacker.

I didn't have much to go on for a profile, but none of them felt right. I'd learned to trust my gut as much as the black-and-white files in this line of work. My gut had saved my ass, and my clients' asses, more than once.

I closed my laptop, then checked the lights and locks as I always did before going to bed. She actually had a decent security set-up, but it would be stronger once the Carson glass was installed while we were on tour.

Faith's room was quiet, though I did hear her humming as she moved around. It was an oddly comforting sound. I'd lived in silence for so long, it was an adjustment to be living with someone who couldn't bear the idea of it.

I took another shower, hoping the hot water would blast out the kinks in my shoulders and neck. I rested my forehead against the tile as she played her piano. The tones were sad and haunting, her voice almost hesitant.

I couldn't make out the lyrics, but I didn't need them.

I braced my arm over my head and willed my dick to behave. I twisted the tap to cold. I was tired of being a slave to the misdirected blood flow, for fuck's sake.

Through gritted teeth, I finished the shower and dragged on a pair of boxer briefs. Normally I wore workout shorts and a shirt to bed in case I needed to be ready to move, but all the fight was sucked out of me tonight.

Her voice chased me into dreams. My defenses were down, and memories of the wet heat of Georgia overlapped the night jasmine and lemon scent of her house.

Faith's sad eyes morphed into Lissa's.

And her voice became Lissa's screams.

The pervasive acrid tang under the humidity. Sulfur burning my nostrils, soot clogging my lungs as I crawled to her. The searing pain of the rebar piercing my shoulder. Pinning me to the floor, Lissa just out of reach.

Her silence.

My forever screams.

17

KEYS

My fingers ached from the number of times I'd followed the song to the end of the keyboard and back, chasing the chords around the high notes and back to the middle.

The song was still pure chaos. I finally found the right mix of notes and held the damper pedal to let it resonate and fade. I lifted my arms above my head to work out the kinks.

I was just about to play the chords again, when I noticed a male voice.

Looks like my warden had finally seen fit to come to bed.

I glanced at the clock above my upright. Two in the morning. I should probably give it a rest. He was probably yelling for me to do just that.

"No."

My fingers curled into my palms, and I leaned back on my bench. That was a moan this time.

My mouth tipped up. "Hot dreams, Warden?"

I stood and crept to the wall between us. The shift of cotton over skin came through, but what I thought was a moan of pleasure ended in a guttural cry. Before I could think clearly, I was out my door and through his.

"Lissa!"

He bowed up off the bed, and for a moment, I was afraid I'd crashed in on a really potent sex dream. The twist of jealousy that stabbed me left me unbalanced, but in the shaft of light from the hallway I noticed the beads of sweat on his brow. His temples were soaked and his neck gleamed.

Nightmare.

Not a sexy dream.

"Quinn." I pitched my voice so it was lower and more authoritative. The one I used to break up Bats and Hunter when they got in one of their fights.

Nothing.

All the muscles in his arms tensed as he writhed.

"Lissa, no."

I tried his name again, but he was too far gone. The anguish in her name clutched me by the throat. I reached for him instinctively and screamed out when he reared off the bed with wild eyes.

"Quinn!"

He twisted my arms behind me and pressed me face-first into the mattress. One hand on my neck, one making a bar through my arms. He straddled my thighs and clamped my legs together. I was completely immobilized.

Fear kicked hard.

PTSD?

Would he kill me even before he woke up?

"Warden!" I yelled into the sheets.

"Faith?" His voice softened. "Oh, God." The pressure on my neck eased and he released my arms. "I'm sorry." He crawled off of me, but not before I felt the full press of his rigid cock along my ass.

I rolled to the other side of the bed, my breathing as fast as his.

"Jesus, Faith. What were you thinking?"

"You were yelling. I didn't know what was going on." I could barely hear around the roaring of my heart. Had it relocated itself to between my ears? Or was that between my thighs?

Sweet hell.

"So you come running in here? What if someone had been in here? You could have gotten killed." He fisted his hands into his hair until it stood up in spikes.

"Excuse me if I was worried. Next time I'll let you scream yourself hoarse."

"Good," he shouted.

The light from the hallway highlighted his naked chest. There wasn't an ounce of flab on the man. Corded muscles flowed down his neck and shoulders to his arms. He had a tattoo down his ribs. I couldn't make it out in the shadows, but I knew it wasn't English.

Latin?

He paced away from me and into the bathroom. The water ran hard in the sink. I should have slunk away. Gone back to my room. Anything but follow him in there.

He met my gaze in the mirror, water dripping from his nose and chin as he hovered over the sink.

"I'm sorry," I whispered.

He closed his eyes, dropping his chin to further break the contact. There was a small LED nightlight beside the door, tossing his back muscles into sharply defined shadows. His hips tapered to a tight butt under the boxer briefs he was wearing.

They hugged him like a second skin, accentuating the endless miles of muscle. I had no idea what he did to keep in shape. I never saw him working out, but I knew he did something in his room every day.

I'd caught light footsteps in the early hours of the morning. Mostly because I hadn't been to sleep yet, instead of up early with the damn birds like he was.

Nothing about his body was inviting. His entire body was strained with anger, or embarrassment, or probably a mix of the two. And yet I wanted to step forward and rest my hand on his back, to ease the stress flowing through him.

"Not a good idea," he said to the floor, then walked back into the bedroom.

I followed him. Had he known I wanted to help? Did he not want me to ask questions? They fairly screamed in my head. He knew everything about me from whatever files he had, whatever research he was always doing, but I knew nothing about him.

"Who's Lissa?"

If it was possible, his shoulders tightened even more. "Not a topic open for discussion."

"Your wife?" I asked.

"Faith," he said in a warning tone.

"Your girlfriend?"

He held onto the doorknob. "Go to bed, Faith."

The cool light from the hallway emphasized his eight-pack, the arrow of shadow that led from his hips to below his underwear. I swallowed at the semi-hard shaft that followed those lines of sin.

My mouth was dry.

He never spoke about his life, his family, his anything. He could have a wife out there. Which made everything about this wrong. I had to know it wasn't just me.

"Lover?"

The muscle in his jaw jumped.

My stomach ached with the deep breaths I couldn't take. I curled my arms around my middle. "Sister?" Though that felt wrong. It had been a different sort of anguish in his throat.

He grabbed me by the wrist and dragged me toward the door. I slapped my free hand along the doorjamb.

He crowded behind me, angling me against the wall beside the door. His cock dug into my hip, as his mouth brushed my ear. "Dead," he said harshly.

I shivered. So much pain in that one word, and yet devoid of any real information.

"I'm not like the men that you wrap around your finger."

I flinched. "I don't do—"

"I see it with everyone that comes into your airspace. They'd do anything to see you smile, they want you to notice them, they want you to let them in."

Confusion dented the riot of emotions strumming through me. My nipples were pushing against the coolness of the wall, my shoulders and thighs burning where he pressed in on me. My mouth was dry and I was terrified that my thighs were anything but.

"I'm not one of those men. I don't want to let anyone in. My body wants you. My cock is screaming to bury itself into your sweet, perfect body, but I can usually ignore those needs. Do you know why?"

My heart was definitely between my thighs now. Breathing was a necessity, but I couldn't seem to gather oxygen into my lungs.

He brought his hand around my hip, his fingertips sliding into the frayed edges of my shorts along my inner thigh.

"Because we make sure to keep boundaries. In the dark, the boundaries get fuzzy."

I drew in a hiccupping breath as his scruffy chin dragged over my neck.

Were those his lips?

His tongue swirled over my pulse before his teeth caged the rioting vein. The tiny spark of pain dragged a moan out of me. His fingers slid deeper until we groaned in a duet.

Wet didn't even cover it. My entire body was a taut piano wire ready to be plucked. I was pretty sure it would only take one tiny flick.

My fingers dug into his outer thigh, as he bypassed the edge of my panties and slid between my cleft. He didn't move, just stayed there, invading and waiting. Two fingers branding every swollen nerve. There was barely a pulse of movement before he retreated.

"So, you can't come in here, because I need those boundaries to keep you safe." He took one long breath, then stepped back.

I'd never felt so empty in my life.

I stumbled out the door and raced for my room, slamming the door behind me. I collapsed against the door and slid to the floor. I wrapped my arms around my shins and pressed my forehead to my knees.

Adrenaline, shock, anger, and loss warred inside of me.

My body was a live wire.

I needed to scream. I needed to come.

And I hated him for showing me there was that level of want living inside of me, only to take it away because of some white knight complex. I pushed off the floor and launched myself at my piano. I didn't care if it was nearly three in the morning.

I pounded out the cords I hadn't been able to find before. The song soared into the rafters and battered the windows of my room. The lyrics came out in a rush.

I dragged out blank music sheets and scrawled notes over the staff lines.

The name of the song emblazoned at the top in huge block letters: "Idiot".

18

QUINN

THE NEXT TWO DAYS WERE TORTURE. KEYS CAME OUT LONG ENOUGH to grab food, but only when I was in my office. She disappeared back upstairs and played the loudest, most head-pounding songs she could.

Every time I thought she was finally done, that her fingers had to be bleeding from pounding on that fucking piano, she kept on going.

And every night, I heard that same song.

The song she'd played after I'd forced myself to push her away.

The lyrics got bawdier with every day that passed until I was ready to take a sledgehammer her damn piano.

Her feelings on the subject were loud and clear.

I was an idiot.

I knew I'd made the right decision. Didn't stop the blue balls I'd had that whole night. Her maniacal music-playing had killed some of the lust I'd been harboring for the last two weeks. Unfortunately, I was pretty sure it would return as soon as I got the regular Faith back.

She could hold her mad like a champ though.

Jesus.

Tuesday morning, she came downstairs before noon and knocked on the door to the office.

"Come in."

She opened the door, her fingers gripping the doorknob so hard that her knuckles were white. "We need to go pick up Devon."

I frowned. "And you're just telling me now?"

"She was supposed to have a ride, but there's a rally in the city."

"She'll have to find another way."

She put her hands on her hips. "No. She can't get a cab in this craziness. You're just going to have to use your super ninja driving skills and get me to LAX."

I had no time for recon to even figure out what the rally was.

"I figured we could grab dinner while we were out."

"Absolutely not."

"Look. I get it, bodyguard duty is paramount, but once we're on tour, you're going to have to ease up. You're just going to have to use your skills and your brain because there's no way you can keep me in a box once we're on the road." She started pulling the door shut. "Her flight comes in at seven. Practice. It's good for you."

"Faith—" She shut the damn door in my face. I tipped my head back. "Fuck," I growled and pulled up a Google page to figure out just what kind of clusterfuck I was driving into.

Two hours later we were backing down the drive and heading for the highway. At least she'd warned me about the rally. And yes, it was worse than even I'd feared.

I couldn't wait until the freaking election was over. I was tired of political agendas when I'd lived in DC, but now it was everywhere as November approached.

LAX was an absolute nightmare, and the only info I got out of Faith was that her flight had been delayed. So that meant we were going to be waiting at the observation area longer. More time for something to happen.

"I want to meet her inside."

"Enjoy wanting. We can pick her up near her gate."

"I haven't seen her in two months, Warden."

I ground my molars together. Back to warden. My fucking

favorite. "You sprung this on me with no warning, you're lucky I didn't hire a car service to pick her up."

Only because I hadn't had time. I'd tried, but it had been too tight of a time frame. Which Faith knew, which is why she didn't tell me until last minute. It took over an hour to get to the airport.

Because it had been a rough few days—and she was right, we were going to be in the wild soon—I took it as a sign to deal with our new reality. I pulled into the short-term parking structure to wait out the delay. She was grinning into her phone as her fingers flew over the keys.

"Her flight's in?"

"Yes. She's making her way through customs."

"Great," I muttered.

A twenty-something who had been in Ireland for weeks going through customs. That was going to go fast. Sure.

At least it was a Tuesday, and not a weekend. I was saved from making small talk with Faith thanks to her complete absorption in talking to her friend via text.

"The airport is the worst for reception." She held up her phone. "I keep getting double texts back. Stupid hiccups."

"You probably need to update your cell towers."

She slanted me an incredulous look. "Does that actually work?"

"Yes, it actually does."

"Huh. I'll be damned. I thought it was something they said to shut people up about their plan."

Half an hour later a leggy redhead came sprinting across the parking garage looking like an ad from Eastern Mountain Sports. From her well worn hikers to the tall backpack listing to the left, she looked like she'd seen the world.

Faith went for her door and I slapped the override locks.

"What the hell? You're not going to let me go hug my friend?"

"Are you delusional? We're in a parking garage that isn't safe on a good day, let alone with your current background."

She collapsed back against her seat. "You suck."

"I know." I got out, ducking my head back down to give her a stern look. "Do not make me regret this."

"Did I mention I hate you?"

"Daily." I slammed the door. "Hi. You must be Devon."

She tilted her head, her smudged green eyes tired but friendly. "Guilty. And you must be the warden."

"I see she filled you in."

"Barely. I expect a full report on the long drive home."

"I'm sure Faith will handle that."

Her auburn brows shot up and a huge smile split her face. She tucked her tongue behind her front teeth. "Faith. This is interesting already."

She was a redheaded version of Faith. I should just shoot myself now and get it over with. Then I'd be dead and I couldn't feel guilty if Noah had to find someone else to do the job.

It would almost be worth it.

"May I take your bag?"

She gave a husky laugh. "Yes, you may." She shrugged off her pack and shoved it at me. "If I get in the car, can I hug her?"

"You can do whatever you want with her in the confines of the car."

Her laugh got even darker and bawdier. "You probably shouldn't say that."

She was probably right. I popped the trunk and stowed her gear.

Devon opened the back door. "Get over here, you slut!"

I rounded the car to my side again in time to see Faith reclining the seat and climbing into the back. The two women were talking so high and fast that I was pretty sure only dogs could hear them.

Faith had her arms around Devon's neck and they busted into more of the suggestive giggles that were usually at my expense.

"Ladies, seatbelts please."

"Oh my God, he is the warden." Devon sat forward between the seats. "Do you have handcuffs?"

"Dev," Faith said on a laugh.

"What? Does he have a big stick too? Have you played with his baton? Do you drop the soap every night? I know I would."

"Are we done with the prison metaphors?" I asked.

Devon flicked her tongue over her eye tooth, perma-grin still in place. "Not hardly."

I met Faith's gaze in the rearview mirror. She arched one eyebrow and gave me a smile that promised retribution. It was going to be a very long drive.

The next hour included a singalong of Journey's *Greatest Hits* in its entirety, twenty questions that I refused to even entertain answering, and a litany of food trucks that Devon wanted to find now that she was back in the States. The only good part of the entire ride was the last part of their conversation.

We ended up stopping at a food truck outside of Silver Lake to have fish tacos. I passed on tacos of unknown origin, and found the farthest picnic table in the quad to let the girls eat in peace. They each sat on the table and wound their legs together in this weird pretzel formation as they plowed through five tacos each.

I scanned the handful of people around as dusk settled. I started to get itchy as the foot traffic increased. There were a number of bars in the area, as well as eateries, which equaled far too many variables, especially with limited visibility.

"Time to go, girls."

"I'm so tired of being stuck in that house." Faith collapsed against the table.

"We can stop and get wine. I miss a good Moscato. There's only so much Guinness and Harp that a woman can drink."

"Speak for yourself," I muttered.

"You're a woman?" Devon's eyes widened and snapped to Faith. "That explains so much."

I walked into that one.

"Up. We have plenty of wine at the house."

Faith sat up. "Since when? Owen tried to drink me dry."

"I called in an order."

"Is that where we keep getting food from? I thought it was a food fairy."

Roth Defense had a Los Angeles branch and I used one of the couriers we trusted to pick up food. The kid had a crush on Faith, probably why I didn't allow him to see her.

And definitely why I didn't tell her about him. She'd have him inside, making lunch and playing checkers or something.

"I got three of all the kinds I saw in your wine fridge."

"Will you look at this guy?" Devon waggled her eyebrows. "We should keep him."

"You keep him."

"Only if he has handcuffs and a healthy baton."

I held an arm out toward the car. "Okay. Time to go."

Both girls laughed, but they didn't give me any more trouble.

They both piled into the backseat again. The conversation calmed to more of a play-by-play of Devon's trip and my shoulders relaxed the closer we got to the house.

I pulled into the garage and gathered up Devon's gear from the trunk. Thankfully, Faith stayed in the backseat. Probably because they were too busy talking, but it gave me enough time to check the security.

I'd done a scan on my phone using her cameras while they'd been eating, but I liked to be the first through the door. I held the door open and they loaded out arm in arm.

Devon went right to the wine fridge, grabbed a bottle of white, and two glasses. Faith made sure to give me a wide berth.

I'd had her to myself for ten days, and having her ignore me for the last three had stung more than I thought it would. I missed my solitary time. When I'd worked for the ambassador, I had plenty of hours down in my apartment off the main house.

He hadn't been a huge security risk. It had been more of a hands-on assignment when he went into DC for meetings and parties.

Faith was much different. She filled the room and couldn't be ignored no matter how hard I tried. I left the girls to continue their catch up and logged into the main system in the office.

I frowned at the package I saw on the porch in the camera. That hadn't been there before we'd left. And it was rare for the mail to come that late. Not unheard of, but rare.

"Faith," I called out.

"Yes, Warden?" she hollered back.

"Have you been shopping?"

She peeked around the corner from the great room into the dining room. "No, why?"

"You have a package."

She shrugged. "I get them all the time."

I frowned. "You haven't since I've been here."

"No, which is kinda rare actually. I usually get a box once a month. What's today?"

"Thirtieth, duh?" Devon elbowed her. "Actually that's about the time you get them. End of the month."

"And you didn't see fit to inform me that you get a package every month?" Frustration sharpened my voice.

"I'm a little famous, Quinn. I get packages."

"Why do they know where you live?"

"People figure it out. Google Earth has pretty much killed any and all privacy when it comes to the paparazzi figuring out where I live. That and paying off the DMV."

"Remember that guy who came right up to the door of our old apartment?" Devon asked.

"Right? He was harmless, but man was he bold."

The bands between my shoulder blades were tight again. This is why I didn't like to deal with famous people. *Damn you, Noah.* "I don't want to know."

Faith shrugged. "I've been getting a box from this fan for…wow. Probably five years now. I wonder what he got me this time."

"You know it's a man?"

She tipped her head and chewed the inside of her cheek. "No. I just assumed. Some of them are a little off-color."

"Oh, and your sense of humor is white as the snow?" Devon said with a snort.

"That's true."

"And you had these boxes checked out?" I asked.

Faith sighed. "Before this all happened my life was very boring. Actually, these packages have been some of the most entertaining of my rock star life."

I frowned. "Stay there." I went to the front door and looked around. The box was small and unadorned, save for her address on a sticker and the postage marker from New York City.

Part of me wanted to have it x-rayed. The other, more insidious part of me wondered if the person who had been focused on Faith had been around a lot longer than any of us thought.

I unclipped my utility knife off my belt and flicked out the blade. I shook the box, then sliced open the packing tape. A small leather-bound novel was inside and a single sheet of paper.

"You don't find love, it finds you. It's got a little bit to do with destiny, fate, and what's written in the stars."

"You're killing me, Quinn."

I spun on my heels and stood. "Get back inside."

She tipped her head back and stomped down the hall. Christ, that woman was going to be the death of me. I folded the box to check the post office mark. It wouldn't lead anywhere. The person who sent it probably dropped the box in one of a thousand boxes around the city.

I took the sheet of paper and novel inside, reengaging the security system.

I met the girls in the dining room. "It's time for you to tell me a bit about this guy." I read the spine. "Anais Nin?"

"Really?" Faith snatched the book, then opened to the title page. "Wow. First library edition." She smoothed her palm over the leather. "Frances outdid himself this time."

"Frances? I thought you didn't know who it was."

She shrugged. "We call him Frances the Fan. Gets a little weird to call him 'unknown'."

"The weird part is that you don't know who it is."

"This isn't the weird stuff. Believe me. You should see the sack I get from Ripper Records."

"Oh, yeah. Remember the guy who sent you a video diary from every show on the first tour?" Devon sipped her wine. "Though that was sort of sweet."

"Yeah, I Skyped a thank you to him for that one."

"You spoke to him?" My head was reeling.

"Sure. You might have a suspicious mind, but I just see them as fans." She frowned, her voice lowering. "Just because one of them went loopy, I can't automatically assume everyone is out to get me."

She couldn't, perhaps. But I damn well could—and would. It was my job, and I was excellent at it. Even if she thought I was doing it a little too well.

At least she would be safe.

"Same as Frances," she continued, though she seemed more subdued than she'd been a moment ago. Maybe she was finally beginning to second-guess her easy trust.

Not everyone was a friend. Far too many foes wore their faces.

"And you know that for certain," I said, but she seemed to be lost in her thoughts.

"His presents are always thoughtful. I can't believe he found the Anais Nin book though." She shook her head. "I mentioned that on a little tiny blog."

"Super fans!" Devon said, making Faith smile.

I really didn't like the sound of super fans. At all.

19

KEYS

"Okay, you need to explain to me how this all happened." Devon slugged me in the arm. "And why I didn't get a call right away."

"You were on—"

"If you tell me one more time I was on my trip, I'm going to do more than bruise your arm."

I rubbed my upper arm. "You're a brute."

"I can be much worse."

That was a whole lot of truth. Devon had been my best friend since high school and the girl might look like a lily white wood sprite, but she was actually more of a bloody-your-nose brawler.

I sighed. "I don't know what this is. It was so weird. I can't really remember what happened." I refilled my glass. "I think that's the worst part." And the part I hadn't really been able to tell anyone. "She was right in front of me and I can't even tell you what she looks like. Literally as close as you are."

Devon took a huge gulp of wine. "I don't like that at all. That she was actually able to touch you—to pull you in and walk you off like that."

I looked into the bottom of my glass. "Yeah. She literally roofied me. Who does that? The bigger question is, why would she?"

"Because she's a sick fuck, that's why." Dev poured more into my glass, then hers.

"We can be sisters." My fingers shook. That was a new memory.

"Of course we're sisters, dork."

"No. I just remembered her saying that. We can be sisters. I didn't remember that part before now."

"Okay, that's even worse. She's obviously delusional." Devon got up. "We need cookies. Like now."

"With wine?"

"Everything is good with wine." She dragged me up off the floor. "I need to bake before I drink five bottles of wine and have a heart attack thinking about this shit."

"Oatmeal chocolate chip?"

"Is there anything else?"

I laughed. "No."

"So, no sign of this psycho since the wedding?"

I tucked my phone into the docking station of the speakers I had in the kitchen and cued up an old Keith Urban album. "Not a single one."

"And yet you still have Warden Hotstuff prowling your house. Or is he prowling your bedroom?"

"No, he is not." The other night didn't count. Sort of. Okay, so he'd actually had his fingers inside of me for a split second. And okay, I'd been unable to sleep at the thought of said fingers filling me up like that.

Like at all.

I measured ingredients and lined them up for her.

Devon dumped oats into the KitchenAid, along with the wet ingredients. "You're lying."

"No, I'm not."

She gave me a look as she locked the mixer into place. A stare down that only Devon could do as the batter mixed.

"What?"

She turned it off and pushed off a clump of oats before turning it back on. She licked cookie dough from her thumb. "You're not telling me everything."

"Can't hear you."

"Yes, you can. Don't be that girl."

I slumped into the chair at the end of the kitchen island. "It was nothing." I picked a chocolate chip out of the cup.

"It was something if your cheek color is any indication. Did he slip you the big D? Did you call him Warden?"

"You are disgusting."

She fist-pumped. "He slipped you something though. Tongue?"

"No." Well, his tongue hadn't been in my mouth. Did the swipe along my neck count? I brushed my fingertips over the spot.

Devon came around and took the chocolate chips away from me. "Or maybe just your neck, Miss Hickey."

"What?" I slapped the spot.

She dragged me out of my chair and to the mirror in the dining room. "Right there."

I turned my head and gasped. "Oh, no he didn't. He freaking marked me."

"Now, I don't normally go for hickeys at this age, but right there? That's *the* spot. You know, the spot that makes girls do dumb things like make out with an Irish dude in the back of a bar after three Guinness's."

I blinked and turned to her. Devon wasn't exactly innocent, but she didn't normally sleep with strangers. "Oh, really?"

She winked. "The man had a way with the fiddle. And I definitely rosined his bow."

"Whore."

"Yes." Her green eyes sparkled with humor. "Oh, yes I was. And I sang 'Danny Boy' the whole night."

I laughed and pushed her back into the kitchen. "Was he worth more than a night?"

"Nah. He was exuberant though. At least there was that."

I shook my head and stole another chocolate chip.

She slapped my hand. "Those are for the cookies."

I pouted and sipped my wine.

"Just because I had a fling with a fiddler, doesn't mean you get to stop your story."

"There *is* no story. He's too Mr. Rules to have a story. It would be untoward for him to bang a client."

"Nice."

I shrugged and took a drink. "Maybe if I fucked the hell out of him then I'd stop thinking about it."

"So, you *are* thinking about it?"

"Dude. Seriously, look at him."

"He does have that rugged thing going on. And wow…eyes."

I frowned at her. "Just how much have you been looking at?"

"What? I'm an artist." She grinned. "I notice stuff. Things. Like his baton is probably impressive."

"And why would you say that?"

"Just to see what you'd do. So it is, huh?"

"I don't—it seems to be." From what I felt of it, digging into me. Sweet hell. I felt it all along my backside.

"Your face is on fire."

"I hate you."

"I hate *you*. Seamus dude was fun, but definitely not packing."

"You said he was exuberant."

"He made up for his shortcomings." She waggled her brows.

"Oh, that sucks."

"I said I sang 'Danny Boy'."

"Oh, so…"

"Dexterous hands and the tongue of a devil."

I laughed. "Oh, I missed you."

"But we're not talking about me and Seamus. I need details about the warden."

"I've thought about it. He's just got such a stick up his ass about rules." He'd been all up in my business then he'd just walked away. Walked away. *What the hell?*

I wasn't going to beg him to touch me, dammit.

"Rules don't have to be a bad thing. Especially if they come with handcuffs."

"You have a fetish."

"I kinda do." Devon pulled out cookie sheets and parchment paper. "Since Officer Rodriguez." She sighed. "Now that man had a baton."

I snorted. "Bad."

"I sort of didn't tell you that he put the cuffs back on me after he let us go."

"Devon. Were we even eighteen yet?"

She blew her bangs out of her eyes. "When did we almost get arrested? Senior year?"

"After the spring dance."

"You were eighteen. I was not."

"Did Officer Baton—er, Rodriguez—know?"

She slid the cookie sheets in and shut the oven door. "Hell no. I lied."

I shook my head. "A delinquent then, and now."

"You know it." She tossed her Cookie Monster oven mitt on the island. "Be right back. I need jammy pants and a quick shower."

I twisted around the timer. "You have thirteen minutes."

"I lived in a hostel for three months. I'll be back in ten."

I refilled my glass and started cleaning up. Devon was the only reason I made it through my senior year.

I hated high school. All I ever wanted to do was read my own books and listen to music. I snuck out every night to find seedy bars full of smoke and passion. I'd lost my virginity in the back of a van with a guitar case digging into my back, and a pair of cymbals keeping time with each of my boyfriend's less than stellar thrusts.

But he'd been passionate. About his music, his lyrics, how much he loved me, and ultimately drugs. I'd left Brody behind the day I found him sticking a needle in his arm. I might have a soft spot for the pot heads in my life, but anything involving a needle was my hard limit.

I'd never looked back. In retrospect I loved the idea of a passionate artist, more than I'd loved Brody. Instead of a gateway drug to the hard stuff, I'd figured out that nothing mattered more than music.

The next most important man in my life had been Owen Blackwell. I'd met him in a dive on Sunset—the Blue Rhino. God, what a dump.

But I'd been lured by his passion for music. Hammered was a band with big dreams and a rotating roster of drummers. Owen, Reed, and Hunter had the drive, but their sound was still a work in progress. Zach hadn't even been in the band yet. They were auditioning drummers when I wandered in. The relentless beat had dragged me in off the street.

The sound was heavier than I was usually into, but there'd been so much magic in the room. I'd dragged Devon in with me. We watched as drummer upon drummer had come in and been dismissed.

Owen had chatted us up on a break between auditions. He'd had the hots for Devon, and I was addicted to music. It didn't hurt that they were a bunch of guys in their twenties looking for hook ups.

Boys in bands had always been a weakness of mine, so we'd ended up partying with them until the bar opened, and then through the night. We were under age and full of ourselves, showing off for hot guys with more flirting power than sense.

And as the night wore on, and last call was coming to an end, I'd found the old upright backstage. I hadn't touched a piano since my lessons as a kid. But I had a good ear, and could pull songs apart— that inner jukebox finally came in handy.

It had just been sitting there, waiting for me to play. Out of key, and battered as a back alley boxer in Boston, but it had been glorious. And instead of finding a drummer, they'd asked me to join the band as their keyboardist.

And Keys had been born.

Funny how one moment in time had changed my life forever.

"Do I smell cookies?"

I turned to his voice, my arms dripping with suds in the sink. "Oatmeal chocolate chip."

He pressed his lips together and arched a brow. "Why would you ruin oatmeal raisin cookies like that?"

"You don't even know. But you will in...Hey, Siri. What's the timer say?"

"You have two minutes remaining."

"There you go."

"Cookie ruiner," he muttered.

I turned off the taps, then dried my hands. "So, the rules go for cookies too?"

"It's either chocolate chip, or oatmeal raisin. That's it."

I wiped off the KitchenAid mixer and pushed it back into the corner of the counter. "You, are a cookie snob."

He leaned against the kitchen island. "And proud of it."

"You'll see."

The vroom of a motorcycle cut off Keith Urban mid croon. I grabbed the Cookie Monster mitt and pulled the two trays out. The smell was enough to send me into an orgasmic moan.

I managed to control myself, but it was a close call. I used my little spatula and transferred one cookie to a plate and pushed it at him. "Try it."

"And burn my mouth?"

I rolled my eyes and broke off a piece and popped it into my mouth. "Perfect."

"Asbestos tongue."

I broke off another piece and blew on it then walked up to him. "Here."

He moved his head away. "I'm good."

"Come on, Warden. Try it, you might like it."

His nostrils flared and he did the jaw clench thing. Honestly, why was that so freaking hot?

I lifted the cookie to his lips. "Open up."

His eyebrow spiked, and his blue eyes heated. And somehow it had become about way more than a cookie. Finally, he opened his mouth. My fingers brushed his bottom lip and his lower teeth scraped my thumb.

He closed his eyes and a little moan rumbled in his chest.

Good grief.

His tongue swiped out and caught the bit of chocolate at the corner of his mouth. "I stand corrected."

I broke off a piece and slipped it into my mouth. Chocolate chips and vanilla with a hint of cinnamon. "More?"

His eyelashes cloaked his eyes as he looked down at me, but he opened his mouth again.

"It's a shame you're always denying yourself. See what you're missing?" I held it toward him, then redirected to my mouth.

He grabbed my wrist and dragged it up to his mouth. He nipped my fingertip as he took the bigger chunk of cookie. The smear of chocolate was bigger this time and he couldn't get it with one swipe of his tongue.

I stood on my tiptoes. "Missed a spot."

His chest rose and fell as I got closer, but he didn't move back. He didn't move forward either, but I was determined to see just what was here between us.

He watched me under a veil of lashes as I used the tip of my tongue to clean off his lower lip. The muscle jumped in his jaw as I went for another pass. A touch of stubble rasped my tongue and burned my lips. Chocolate gave way to warm, soft lips.

Softer than I'd imagined they would be. He seemed so hard everywhere.

I moved in until we were just touching. His lips parted and I breathed in as he breathed out. He flicked his tongue over my top lip. Barely a touch, not even a taste.

I couldn't look away. I wanted him to move in. I wanted him to take, dammit. Then I felt his fingertips at my belly. He lifted my shirt and drew circles across my midriff.

I drew in a breath and then he wasn't just standing there any longer. He brushed his nose along mine and angled our lips to whatever plan he seemed to have.

His hand slipped around my back and dragged me up against him.

20

QUINN

Turn back.

What the hell are you thinking?

That was the problem. I wasn't thinking. This maddening woman had been standing there with cookie crumbs on her perfect lips, just daring me to kiss her.

I should have been across the room and back in the office.

I should have been anywhere but here, in front of her, with her peach scent in my head, and chocolate lacing my tongue.

Her fingers went into my hair as she plastered her chest to mine. Or maybe I'd done the plastering. Whichever way it happened, I now had her mouthwatering breasts flattened against my chest and her tongue in my mouth.

I sucked on it. I couldn't seem to slow down to show her I wasn't a goddamn animal. I'd wanted her taste for far too long. Ever since my nightmare I'd thought of nothing else. I'd tried to scare her off with crude tactics, but instead I'd gone to bed with her scent on my fingers.

Fear and rage had been too close to the surface. I didn't want to want her. I didn't want to give her any ideas about us. There couldn't be an us.

And here I was again, making asinine decisions.

I tore my mouth away from her, both of our chests heaving for oxygen.

"Oh, no you don't." She gripped the back of my neck and dragged me down. "No way are you stopping now."

"Faith, we—"

She sealed her lips over mine and slid her tongue lightly along mine. I tried to back up. I really did, but then I just couldn't. I twisted my fingers into the belt loops of her jeans on either side of her hips, resisting the urge to simply rip them until her button popped and her zipper busted.

Because they weren't coming off intact if I didn't rein it in.

"I smell coo—whoa. Sorry!"

We broke apart and I fisted my hands in my hair.

Shit.

"Ah…I'll just come back." Devon twirled toward the stairs.

"No. I'm going. You guys catch up."

"Quinn—"

I strode out of the kitchen and down the hall to the office. I was a sack of shit. I should have said no. I should have walked out of the damn room as soon as she'd offered me up that fucking cookie.

"So stupid," I muttered to myself and swiped my hand down my face. My cock was as hard as a steel post. In fact, I could probably nail in the post with it.

"Get it together." I dragged in a breath and forced my shoulders to ease. I reached up and blew out a long breath as I got into position for the opening posture for my usual Tai Chi exercises.

It was the only thing that had put me back together after going through rehab eleven years ago. After the rebar had punctured my shoulder and pinned me to the floor.

The night I hadn't been able to get to Noah's wife in time.

I forced myself to move through the steps of the routine I'd done a million times.

My body was washed in sweat, and I'd done all thirty-seven of the advanced form movements. Each style flowed into another until my brain quieted, and my muscle memory kicked in.

The music from the other room, Faith's laughter, Faith's voice, the memory of her taste—all of it faded to the back of my mind. Where the memories lived, but didn't tear at me until there was nothing but screams.

Finally, I bowed my head and moved to the desk. There was work and duty waiting for me. Things I understood. Things I excelled at.

I answered emails, made a few requests from Lucy, our expert hacker, and monitored the security system. I made my final walk through for the night, and found Faith and Devon asleep on the sectional couch in the great room.

I should have woken them up.

I should have sent them to their beds.

I should have done a lot of things tonight.

Instead, I let them sleep and made an extra sweep around the perimeter of the house. I needed the air. The lemon trees and jasmine from the hill beyond her house was a far better scent to hang onto tonight.

By morning, I was more fully under control. I hadn't slept worth jack, but at least I could function.

Right now that's all I could ask for. I'd been trained to live without sleep. And I had a lot of planning to do for the next few months. I'd finally gotten schematics for all the venues they'd be going to through October.

There were a lot of them, and I hid myself away while the girls reacquainted themselves with each other for the rest of the week. There was a lot of laughter, a ridiculous level of board games, and I was more than happy to let Devon do some of the cooking.

If that meant I could hide away and ignore the fact that I went to bed aching for a woman I wasn't meant to have, and woke each morning cursing the same woman, then I was all for it.

Long calls with Aidan, Indie, and Lila Shawcross from Hammered's record label kept me busy. The logistics of a tour were a nightmare to begin with, add in the bonus stalker and everyone was on edge.

Except Faith.

She had a countdown going. I got the Post-It Notes on my door every morning. It was an effective dick deflater, that was for sure. The fact that we hadn't heard a single rumble from Faith's attacker had me even more on edge.

It was having the opposite effect on Faith. I'd overheard more than one conversation with Devon, letting me know she was more convinced than ever that it had been a fluke.

My gut said nothing about this was over.

Finally, it was the night before we were leaving. Devon and Faith had been cooking all day. We were having a picnic on the deck. At least she hadn't requested to leave the house, but I hated having her in the open like that.

There was no reason to believe her stalker wanted to kill her, but the fact that she'd used Ketamine to try to walk Faith off the property during Hunter's wedding didn't give me warm and fuzzy feelings about her attacker. However, Faith also didn't need to be stressed out every hour of the day.

It was my job to manage the stress, and keep her safe. Tomorrow was coming whether I wanted it to or not.

So I ate the early Labor Day feast that the girls put together. I manned the grill for burgers and brats, I enjoyed their banter at my expense, and I soaked up a perfect sunny day in Los Angeles.

And somehow I kept myself in check as Faith walked around in a bikini top with white stars over blue triangles of material that molded to her perfect breasts. And I almost ignored the fact that she wore red denim shorts that went an inch past her ass.

Devon wore the exact opposite ensemble, and while very attractive, she didn't make me wish for an ice bath to control my dick.

When the sun set, and the girls broke out s'mores fixings, I relaxed for the first time in weeks. It probably helped that Faith had put on a hoodie. I wasn't a saint, for fuck's sake.

I even had a beer while we sat around the fire pit.

"I'm heading to bed. I'm just buzzed enough to sleep instead of cry."

"Aww, Dev." Faith struggled out of her nest of blankets in her Adirondack chair. "You won't even notice I'm gone. You'll be too busy painting seventeen hours a day."

"I hope so." They hugged and Devon even dropped a kiss on my cheek. "Night Quinn. Take care of my girl."

"I will."

"I know it."

Faith pulled her chair over near me and curled back into her cocoon. "So, how's my itinerary look tomorrow?"

"Eight AM flight."

"Ugh." She tipped her head back. "At least we don't fly commercial."

I lifted my beer. "Can't say I mind the private jet."

"The tour bus got old by the third world tour. Especially when getting to some of the venues meant traveling on roads that a donkey wouldn't pass."

I grinned around the lip of my bottle. "Adventure, right?"

"Oh, it was an adventure when the axel broke on the twenty-eight-year-old bus in the middle of Brussels."

"How long did it take to get rescued?"

She laughed. "We were rescued by a bus full of nuns." Her teeth flashed in the firelight. "They taught us folk songs through the country side. Zach got his first set of bongos from Sister Mary Percy. I think I still have the picture somewhere."

"Definitely not a boring life."

"No. Why I love going to work every day."

That smile was the reason why I'd make sure nothing ever happened to her. Even if I went crazy in the process.

21

KEYS

I WOKE JUST AS THE SUN WAS CREEPING OVER THE HILLS. I'D BEEN SO excited about the thought of touring that I hadn't done my usual farewell to the house. I took a leisurely shower and made sure my bathroom was clean.

I went through my writing notebook on my patio. I was excited to share a few of the songs with the guys. A few others would remain just for me. I smoothed my fingers down the scribbled lyrics for "Idiot" with a smile.

My bags were packed. Tour clothes were much different than the clothes I wore around the house. Makeup, boots, blinged-out jeans, concert shirts, and dozens of pairs of Chucks were included. My lucky leather jacket, denim jacket, and vintage white denim jacket were packed for the various photo shoots I'd be required to attend.

My jewelry case was packed, and my three classic iPods were full of songs to get me through the long days of travel.

The last step was playing "Rain" on my piano. It was the first song I'd ever composed. No words, just music. The song was quiet and lovely. So different than the music I wrote with the guys. It was just for me.

Just for my house.

Just for the goodbyes.

When I closed the cover, I turned to find Quinn in the doorway. His eyes were a little sad, but he didn't say anything.

"Ready to go?"

"Just need your bags."

I grabbed the smaller ones, then patted his chest. "There you go, Hercules."

"Hercules, Warden, what's next?"

"Jeeves?"

"I left myself open for that one."

"Yeah, you did."

I flew down the stairs and dumped my bags in the hall, then jogged to Devon's room. I swung open her door without knocking. She was under her covers with her favorite quilt over her head. "I know you're awake."

"No."

I dropped onto her bed. "Yes."

"No. Then you can't leave."

I pulled the blanket off her head. Her bottom lip was already stuck out. "Don't do that."

"You did when I left for Ireland."

"Okay, that's true. I'm used to being the one doing the leaving."

"And it sucks." Devon threw her arms around me. "I'm going to miss you."

"I'll be back before you know it. Besides, you need to find us a rocking costume for the masquerade. Or, even better, make us one."

She sniffed. "I could do that." She pulled back and hugged her knees. "I have some really cool silks I could dye to make us masks."

"See. Now you're thinking. And you're far more talented at that stuff that I am. Maybe a freaky Harley Quinn costume. You know, from the movie."

"Oh, yeah. You can be Harley and I can be a manic Queen of Hearts."

"Awesome."

Devon clapped and dragged her sketchbook off her nightstand. "Project," she said in a sing-song voice.

"I expect photos of all drawings."

"Pinterest board," we said in unison and laughed.

I stood up. "I'll FaceTime with you when I get to Boston."

"You better. Take care of you."

"Take care of you," I said back. I left her to her pencils and mutterings. Devon was always better if she had a big project to fill her head. I blinked back a few tears and met Quinn in the hallway.

He'd already loaded my things and was flicking his keys in and out of his palm. "Good?"

"I'm good."

The ride to the private airport was much quicker than the one to LAX. Hunter was on the tarmac when we pulled up. Cujo, his Morkie terrier, was sticking out of his hoodie as he said goodbye to Kennedy. Since I didn't need to see kissing this early in the morning, I waved and headed into the plane.

Owen was curled into his favorite chair, already asleep. He was practically narcoleptic when it came to travel time. Zach had Lorraine, his favorite guitar, next to him on the couch, and a pile of music magazines. Wyatt was sitting in the oversized captain's chair at the front of the plane, his iPad open, headphones already in.

Bats came up the stairs, his eyes exhausted. "Hey Keys."

"Hiya Bats. Rough night?"

He grinned. "Saying goodbye to everyone."

"I bet."

He waggled his eyebrows and fluffed my hair as he went to the back of the jet. He stretched out on the couch opposite of Zach.

I didn't have one set place to sit on the plane. I was a restless flier. I decided to start out in one of the chairs. I patted Patrick as I walked by then waved at Saint, our tour chef.

The familiarity ignited the flame I'd been missing lately. I needed these people around me to keep sane, to feel alive.

Oh, that's a lie. He makes you feel alive.

I ignored that little voice. The warden made my skin feel alive, my hormones feel alive. It was just temporary.

It had to be temporary.

I heard a familiar yip and smiled.

Hunter climbed on and let Cujo free, who ran down the aisle to Indie.

"Control your toy," she said with an annoyed voice.

Hunter snapped his fingers and Cujo scampered back to him. He patted the top of the tiny dog's head. "She didn't mean it."

She stomped her battered cowboy boot. "I'm going to step on the stupid thing one of these days."

"He bounces back," Hunter said. "I do it all the time."

I scrunched down in my seat. "Come on, Cujo, you can sit with me." The dog leaped into my lap, then up my shirt to treat me to a tongue bath. I tried to push him away, but it was no use. "So, how was the honeymoon?"

Hunter dropped into a chair near me. "Amazing. Never thought a hut could be so glorious."

"Right. A hut."

He shrugged. "Yeah, it was two thousand square feet. Still was in the middle of nowhere." He held his hands up like a photo frame. "Water on all sides. So…still a hut."

"Had a lot of sex, huh?"

He dropped his arms. "Must you cheapen things?"

I giggled.

Hunter blew out a breath. "How are you?"

I looked down at Cujo, his blissed-out face utterly adorable as I scratched behind his ears. I knew Hunter didn't really care about anything other than stalker central news. "I'm good. Not a peep out of this idiot punk. I really think it was a one-time thing."

A shadow fell over the aisle. My attention shifted. Quinn filled the doorway. His gaze scanned the entire plane, all of the people that meant more to me than life, and landed on me all in the space of a few seconds.

I'd been living with him for weeks, knew the feel of him in the room, knew the moment a rule was coming my way. And still, my breath stalled as he walked toward me.

He'd changed.

He'd been in bodyguard mode when we left the house. Suit, crisp white dress shirt, aviators. He thought that made him fade into the background, but instead it always made him stand out to me. Because I knew his jacket was cut to hide his gun, I knew under that crisp cotton and no-nonsense wool was a lethal body that could immobilize someone in less time than it took to blink, and that dangerous side of him made my body come alive in ways I didn't want to face.

This Quinn might be worse.

Ancient jeans molded to his hips, thighs, and...I swallowed hard. Well, everywhere. Stress tears shown at the corners of his pockets, and knees. Not tears created by a designer. No, these were years of abuse and wear from Quinn.

I didn't even know he owned jeans.

The frayed bottoms of his jeans stretched over motorcycle boots.

Honestly?

My eyes scanned back up to make sure I hadn't had a stroke or episode or something. Nope, all that ripped denim glory was still there. An old belt that matched his battered boots was cinched at his lean hips, half hidden by a red T-shirt with faded letters spelling out *Ommegang*. He still wore a blazer, but that actually made it worse. Because there was still some of the Quinn I knew there.

At least if he was wearing an entirely new ensemble I could look at it like a costume. Now, I simply wondered if I knew him at all.

"What?"

I blinked. "Huh?"

Quinn stood in front of me. "Why are you looking at me like that?"

"Who are you?"

"Your boyfriend, remember? You're the one who said it. I was pretty sure a guy in a suit wouldn't fit that description."

"Right." *Wow, head in the game girl.* "I didn't even know you owned jeans."

He shrugged. "My parents run a horse farm up in Saratoga, New York."

"Another thing I didn't know." And now I was picturing him on a horse. I needed another shower.

"You all right?"

"Sure. Why wouldn't I be?"

"I'm going to talk to Patrick about the next few venues."

I resumed petting my wiggling seatmate. "Knock yourself out."

He slid an absent finger around Cujo's ears for a quick scratch before passing me by. No, my belly wasn't doing the Macarena because he was good with animals. Absolutely not.

Sweet baby Ray.

It was the jeans.

It had to be the jeans.

I glanced at Hunter and his lips twitched.

"Shut up."

"I didn't say anything."

I dug out my headphones as the captain gave us the head's up we were leaving in fifteen minutes. Cujo curled into the little spot between my hip and the side of my chair. He definitely had the right idea.

Lights out.

22

QUINN

WE WENT RIGHT FROM THE AIRPORT TO THE VENUE. THERE WAS NO show tonight, but the band wanted time to rehearse. New songs and some sort of addition to the stage. They'd had a band meeting during the last hour of the flight.

Patrick had requested some research help while we were at the amphitheater. With the sudden influx of issues thanks to Faith's stalker, Ripper Records was getting more diligent about security with their artists.

We sat at the sound board and poured over the names of people who had been offered up to head security.

Patrick ran a hand over his buzzed head. "I hate asking for help, but I don't trust the rental services we use for security anymore. Not even just because of the shit stain who tried to kidnap Keys, but the ticket sales alone warrant more security."

I nodded. "Agreed." I tapped the short list of names he had. "I've worked with Gabe Matthews before. He's my number one pick."

Patrick pulled out a stapled packet. His eyes raced over the background I pulled from Roth. "Yeah, he was one of my top two. I'll have him come in for an interview."

"Sounds good."

He tucked the sheaf of papers into his back pocket. "Backstage is a shitshow. This place may have changed its name, but it's still the Woods."

I raised a brow in question.

He shrugged. "I've been their security since the first tour. Hammered has been coming to this venue for ten years. Sells great tickets, but man, they don't put any money into the back of the house." He tapped the sound board. "Here, yes." He nodded at the stage and the huge setup of screens. "You can watch from space, for fuck's sake."

"I wasn't a big concert guy, but I think we were lucky to see a projector screen at SPAC."

Patrick laughed. "Saratoga? We'll be going there too."

I nodded. I'd remembered seeing it on the list of venues. At least I knew those stomping grounds. "Show me the back."

He nodded curtly. We walked down the main aisle. When the handful of venue security barely looked at us, I seethed. Lanyards and personnel should be checked every fucking time.

I kept a mental tally of each weakness. When I got to the side stage, I paused as Patrick spoke to Hunter.

"Hi."

I turned at Faith's voice. I was used to the girl that ran around in shorts and T-shirts, not this one. Her eyes were smudged with dark makeup making her blue eyes glow. A trio of crystals sparkled on the apple of her cheek, and her lips were slick with a frosty pink gloss. She wore purple plaid pants that hugged every goddamn curve and a short pink shirt with a purple skull across her distracting breasts. She sawed her fingers up and down a pair of improbably glittery suspenders.

She snapped a piece of gum. "You're staring."

"You're different."

She dug out a pack of gum from her pocket and folded another piece into her mouth. "I did a YouTube video for the fans. Want?" She held out a silver wrapped stick.

I wanted every fucking inch.

Because my mouth was dry, I accepted the gum. I was normally a spearmint guy, so the cinnamon bite on my tongue didn't do anything to cool me down.

Now all I could imagine was how I'd like to suck that taste off of her tongue.

Yeah, it was time to go backstage with Patrick. I was turning into a sex obsessed idiot. Part of me wondered if I got her out of my system, then maybe we could go back to normal.

That, however, was me thinking with the wrong part of my anatomy. If I had a taste of her, I was pretty sure the opposite would occur. I just needed to focus on my job and get through the next few days.

Once I figured out her rhythm then I could establish a schedule.

She tilted her head and looked up at me. "Are you craving cookies?"

I crossed my arms. "Pardon?"

She stepped forward, dropping her voice to a purr. "I'm suddenly craving cookies."

The stage was alive with technicians, roadies, and her fellow band members. There wasn't a quiet pocket to be found on the expansive design of ramps and lighting rigs, but still it felt like she was shouting.

Or maybe it was just my brain screaming, "Get out of there, idiot".

"We're not going there again. No cookies."

She snapped her gum. "I think you're craving my cookies again."

"We're not having this conversation."

"You didn't know that oatmeal chocolate chip was going to be your favorite, but now that you've had a taste…"

My gaze dropped to her mouth. I wanted to wipe off that glossy artifice and taste her. I didn't give a shit about cookies. I couldn't even pretend to play along with her winding euphemism. I wanted to drag her into a corner and lay her on one of the dozens of trunks littered around the space, peel off her pants, and see if her pussy matched her naked lips.

That's what I wanted.

She sighed. "You're back on salad, huh?"

"You do have the strangest way of asking me questions."

She went up on her tip toes and pitched her voice lower. "I didn't think you'd appreciate me actually spelling out the fact that I haven't stopped thinking about that kiss. That I'd still be kissing you until my freaking lips were chapped if we hadn't been interrupted."

I stuffed my hands in my pockets. "Five minutes more and I'd have been kissing you somewhere else, Faith."

She dropped back down onto her heels. "Oh."

"Yeah. I don't play games. I don't have a sweet side. You'd have gotten fucked."

Her lips parted and instead of horror, like I'd hoped to see, her pupils dilated.

Dammit.

I stepped back and walked around her. What the fuck was I supposed to say after that? I wasn't going to lie. I did want to sink into her until there was nothing left of us except sweat and spent flesh.

I didn't want her to romanticize what this was. It was pure chemistry and forced proximity. Any other time she would have dismissed me as an asshole who didn't fit in her world.

She didn't seem the type to give into the animal side of sex. She deserved a guy that treated her like gold, and would be there in the morning to make her breakfast for the next fifty years.

Faith Keystone wasn't one-night stand material.

"I told you it was a security nightmare back here."

I snapped back into my surroundings as Patrick's voice intruded. The narrow corridors had a dozen doorways leading into a labyrinth of closet sized rooms. Some were obviously set up for dressing rooms, others were storage, and still more should have been closed off and condemned.

There were tons of spaces to sneak off with a groupie, or, in my nightmares, places for a stalker to hide.

"Are all the venues like this?"

"Most of them," Patrick answered.

"Perfect," I growled.

Hunter's voice crackled over the speakers and bounced around the empty amphitheater. A few minutes later drums and guitars made it impossible to talk.

Patrick motioned for me to follow him out the side door. I didn't want to leave Faith alone, but if she wasn't safe on stage with her band, then when would she actually be safe?

I closed the heavy steel door and leaned on the brick side of the building. "Did you notice that we walked by seven security guards and no one asked to see our lanyards?"

Patrick frowned. He flicked his on his hip. "Mine was showing."

I dug mine out of my pocket. "Mine wasn't. They don't know me from Adam. Anyone could have walked in."

"They couldn't get through the park security."

"Sure they could. Walk in the middle of a group of roadies wearing black, they wouldn't have noticed a damn thing."

He opened his mouth to argue, then shut it. "No, I don't suppose so."

"I need to talk to the security manager. We need to have a little meeting before tomorrow night."

He dug out his phone. "You got it."

The rest of the afternoon consisted of me pulling apart the security measures that Hammered had in place. As far as I was concerned, there simply *was* no security.

A woman with curly blonde hair came down at the last half of rehearsal with a dozen people. I met her at the top of the pavilion. "And you are?"

She stopped. "Jess."

I glanced down at her lanyard. It had the album cover on it, with the words "fan club" scrawled under it. Anyone could have made it on a printer and used a laminating machine.

"I run Hammered's fan club." She whipped off her designer sunglasses and got into my space. "Look, I'm with the band. You need to back off. Who do you think you are?"

"Jess," Patrick called from behind me. "Hang on."

She put her hands on her hips. "We've got a fan club event today. What gives, Patrick?"

"Sorry, Quinn. I forgot to merge the fan club calendar with the tour schedule for you. We have a lot of these events."

Nightmare number eleven today. Fucking wonderful.

He scrubbed the heel of his palm over the back of his head. "Jessica Travers, meet Quinn Alexander, our new security coordinator."

"I don't care if he's the secret service. I've got twenty-five fan club people coming in to listen to rehearsal."

"No, you do not," I said. There was no way to vet that many people right now. Especially when the twelve who were behind her right now were women. And three of them looked like Faith clones.

Any one of them could be the stalker. They might just be fans, but I didn't know that. And there was no way I was taking any goddamn chances.

"I'm doing my job." Jess's voice rose. "I've been the coordinator for the Hammered fan club for three years now. I'm not some noob, here with a God complex."

"All right, chill out Jess."

"I'm not going to chill."

"Problem?" Hunter asked from the stage.

I turned around. Great. This so wasn't happening.

The dozen girls behind Jess started waving and jumping. Evidently I was getting an up close and personal introduction to fangirls in action. They screeched Hunter's name, as well as Reed's and Zach's since they were the only other two on stage.

I tried to stop the forward momentum, but the crowd of women ran around me like water. I had less than zero control. I ran after them and waved to the security to stop them.

"I need your badges, ladies."

Purple lanyards with the fan club symbol and a number were waved in my face.

Jess huffed. "I already checked them in. I know my job."

I crossed my arms. "Well, things are changing. We'll be having a meeting after rehearsal. Welcome to the new security enhancements, Miss Travers."

"We'll see." She brushed by me.

Patrick hung his head. "I'll talk to her. Her sense of entitlement has been…a sore spot with a lot of us."

"Well, if she needs some enlightenment to go with that, I shall provide it."

"I just bet you will. Things are definitely going to be changing."

"Indeed."

I climbed back up to the top of the pavilion to meet the next group of fan club members. I tried on a smile.

Let's try it with honey this time. "Welcome, ladies and gentleman."

23

KEYS

I wasn't going to let Quinn's little bomb ruin my first show. How he expected me not to follow that little slice of enlightenment up with a little q and a, I didn't know.

Of course that would require me getting a moment alone with him.

He made sure that didn't happen for the rest of our rehearsal.

Then he proceeded to explain his new style of security to the entire team—including roadies, techs, and staff. I was pretty sure Indie was apoplectic by the end of his list of rules.

I was used to his lists.

I didn't like the new list any more than the one at home, but I was fresh out of outrage. Bats, Hunter, and Indie had enough for the rest of us.

Jess, the head of our fan club, was still screeching three hours later during dinner. If Quinn came up to me right now and told me he was going to bring me back to the hotel and fuck me brainless, I would have said no.

I had a headache.

Okay, no. I would get over it—maybe.

But that would require him actually speaking to me, and he was in full-on avoidance mode. Instead, my babysitters included Indie, Patrick, and Owen.

By the time ten o'clock rolled around, I'd had enough companionship. Which wasn't like me at all. I'd been begging to get back on the road for the last two weeks, but everyone kept staring at me like I was going to have a breakdown.

I was done with people.

The band usually shared three suites on tour—two of us per suite. I shared mine with Owen most of the time, but now that I had Quinn in tow, we'd messed up the status quo.

Owen was pouting about having to play pass-the-roommate with the rest of the band. Bats was still acting weird, demanding a room to himself for this leg of the tour.

On stage, we were tighter than ever. The minute we put our instruments down—or in my case, stepped back from the keyboard—things seemed to get strange. Bats kept disappearing, his phone either at his ear, or fingers flying over the keys in rapid fire texts.

Hunter had dreamy eyes and was FaceTiming with his wife whenever possible. Wyatt was giving him shit about it, even though I was pretty sure the jealousy card was actually in play there. He wasn't used to sharing his best friend with a woman.

And because Bats was acting odd, the other half of the terror twins, Zach, was at loose ends.

Did I mention that I couldn't adult any more today?

I left Owen and Zach deep in discussion about the pros and cons of a Taylor acoustic versus a Gibson. Since I didn't care, it was easy enough to walk away.

I took a shower and de-staged myself. I loved dealing with fans, and usually ran point on most of the fan interactions, but now I had Quinn's rule book and hulking presence to contend with. He was definitely killing my tour buzz.

All I wanted to do was sleep off my mood and start over again tomorrow. The front door of the suite opened as I climbed into bed. My heart rate tripled.

"Faith?" I jumped when he knocked on my bedroom door.

I collapsed back on my pillows for a second. Holy cow, I needed to get a grip. There hadn't been a peep out of my attacker, but everyone was treating me as if the moment I was alone, I was doomed to be abducted.

I was starting to believe the damn hype.

"Yes, Warden?"

He cracked open the door. "You heading to bed?"

"It's been a long day."

His eyes swept over me and I pulled the sheet up to shield the instant response. It was getting ridiculous. I was going to need to wear my padded Vicky Secret bras if this kept up.

"Sorry I wasn't around tonight. Your tour schedule is far more complicated than I thought it was going to be."

I hugged a pillow in front of me. "Are you mentally compromised because of the chaos?"

He leaned against the doorjamb. "Very funny."

"Are you going to stroke out before the show starts tomorrow?"

His eyebrow arched in that Quinn way—sardonic and mildly amused. I kinda lived for that look. I was pathetic. "Patrick and I have devised a better schedule, and possibly hired a new head of security. Tomorrow will be better."

"Oh, boy. More rules, the guys will be ecstatic."

"Regardless of your unique situation, the band itself needs a better security setup. Hammered has coasted on luck for a long time."

I propped myself on my elbow, my fingers tangling with my still-damp hair. "We've had a few run-ins over the years, but nothing that required a huge security team."

He pinched the bridge of his nose and closed his eyes. "As I said, lucky."

"You're used to ambassadors and senators. We're just rockstars."

"You attract just as many unstable fans as the harmless ones. Patrick is good at keeping most of them at bay, but all it takes is one."

I understood where he was coming from, but I also hated the idea of living that way. We got where we were because of our openness with fans and the way we connected to people through our music. If we were looking for shadows and specters in every corner, wouldn't that ruin everything we'd created?

"I'm trying my best to look through your lenses, but I really don't like them."

He sighed. "I know you don't. It's one of the most beautiful parts of you, Faith. It's just not realistic."

A basic difference between us. I loved the fantasy. I *lived* the fantasy through my music, and through the magic on the stage. I wasn't sure I could live with his reality intruding on that.

"Well, it got me this far."

He flicked off the light switch on the wall. "I'll be here to keep it that way."

I slid under the covers. "Night, Warden."

"Night, Faith."

He shut the door. I reached for my headphones, but decided I wanted a little silence for once. I heard him moving around, the light click of his keyboard, and all the other sounds that demonstrated the way he filled the space.

At my house he'd been there, but separate. Here, it was like living with a man minus the benefits. My pulse spiked at the memory of his words.

I don't have a sweet side. You'd have gotten fucked.

That side of Quinn thrilled me as much as it scared the crap out of me. I may have had a thing for bad boy rockstars when I was a teenager, but I'd never really acted on it after Brody. I was too worried about playing music to want to jump into a relationship with someone in the business.

And as much as the media outlets had wanted to create romance in the band, it had never happened. The guys were my brothers, not lover material.

I'd had a fling with a photographer on our first tour, a summer romance with a guitar tech for one of our opening acts, and had almost fallen in love with the soundboard engineer for our second album. But in the end no man had ever captured my attention for more than a few months.

And none of them had ever made my pulse pound between my thighs without a helluva lot of foreplay and help from a toy or two. Why did it have to be this contrary man with all his rules that got me so wound up?

I reached for my iPod and headphones on the bedside table.

Screw silence.

I needed music-induced sleep.

Morning came with an evil amount of sunshine. But after my initial grouchiness, my mood lightened considerably. Today was our first show of this leg of the tour. I was starving for the stage, for my keys under my fingers, and the vibration of Wyatt's drums behind me.

I took a shower and dressed in street clothes for soundcheck. My costume trunk was already at the venue. I think I was going for a little vintage Gwen Stefani and her ska days tonight. I pulled my hair into tight twists along the side and sectioned off a Mohawk French braid down the center of my head.

I finished the look with liquid liner for my eyes and extreme red lips. Quinn was on the phone and his computer when I came into the main living space.

He glanced at me and gave me a distracted nod, then did a double-take. "I'll call you back," he said into his phone.

"Too Gwen?"

He frowned. "The woman from *The Voice*?"

I grinned. Look at Mr. Warden knowing something of pop culture. Maybe there was hope for him yet. "Impressive, but I was thinking more along the lines of her early No Doubt days." I knew he wasn't exactly a music guy, but I saw him trying to piece together the look. He was delightfully confused.

"Your stage look takes some getting used to."

"It's still me."

His gaze drifted to my jeans and Frank Turner shirt, then the little jaw tick happened again. "Ready to go?"

Interesting.

I wasn't sure what I thought about Mr. Repressed. I'm not sure if he was worse than the warden, or better. They both kept telling me *no* with a side of "It's for your own good".

Yeah, I pretty much disliked both.

"Absolutely. Saint promised our favorite start-the-tour meal."

He gathered his laptop and tucked it into his messenger bag. "Which is?"

"Family-style Italian."

"Before a show?"

The horror in his voice made me laugh. "Yes."

"That's like eating baked ziti and then going for a run."

I grabbed my phone off the charger station. "That's why we're going now and eating at two in the afternoon."

He shook his head. "If you say so."

We met Bats and Zach in the hallway. I grinned at them. "You jonesing for Saint's start-the-tour meal too?"

"You know it." Bats rubbed his rock-hard belly. "I'm not even going to bitch about how much cardio I'm going to have to do to make up for it."

I linked my arm through his. "Yes, you will."

"You're right."

Zach ran by us and walked backward with Lorraine strapped to his back. "Is it wrong that I dreamed about Saint's garlic bread last night?"

"You should have been dreaming about the woman I heard you banging through the wall, son."

I punched Bats. "Rude."

"Why were you listening? Needed the extra help for your hand?" Zach asked.

"I didn't have a choice. You brought home a howler." Bats made a crude gesture. "Or she had to fake it really loud to make you feel better."

I held up a hand. "All right, all right. You're both pretty."

"No, they aren't. Why you lyin'?" Wyatt called from the end of the hall. He leaned against the wall near the elevator.

"You only look good because you pay a seamstress, Giorgio."

Wyatt straightened. "If you bought your suits with me, then maybe you'd have better women surrounding you, Reed."

Laughter fell off. I resisted the urge to sigh. Wyatt had to go there. We couldn't have one good day without drama about this particular subject. Bats wouldn't talk about his relationship with Hunter's ex-fiancée. He wouldn't define it, nor would he discuss any aspect of why Victoria Sheer was still in our lives.

She was a viper. A beautiful one, but a snake nonetheless.

But it was a bone of contention between Wyatt and Bats. Hunter had let it go, deciding to trust his friend. Wyatt only saw disloyalty. And for him, that was the worst offense.

I was hoping since we were all laughing that maybe, just maybe we could start off this leg of the tour with a clean slate.

Evidently not.

I hung back, choosing to stand with Quinn instead of walking into a fight.

But in a surprising turn of events, Bats grinned. "I'm an equal opportunity bachelor. I don't discriminate." He turned and spread his arms along the bar at the back of the elevator. "It's going to be a very good show today."

I smiled back at him. "I think you're right." I turned and met Quinn's frown. "Come on, Warden. It's a good day to be a good day."

"That remains to be seen."

"Not even you can dim my fabulous mood." I pulled out my phone and opened up SnapChat. "Hey guys, we're getting ready to rock your face off tonight. Any requests, hit us up in Twitterlandia or use hashtag HammeredX and I'll be checking all over." I panned around the elevator. "Say hi, everyone."

"Hi everyone," all the males said in unison. Well, except Quinn. I skipped him thanks to the death stare.

"It's a good day to be a good day," I said again.

I was determined to believe it.

24

KEYS

"Why did I eat that much?"

"Because you have no willpower." Hunter dropped onto the couch beside me. "Just like the rest of us."

"So much cheese. Glorious cheese." Cheese that was going to make me pop the top button on my tight white jeans tonight. Ugh.

Garlic scented the air and a celebrational bottle of wine had been consumed, leaving me sleepy and content. I'd raid the ginseng-laced tea I drank before soundcheck to rev myself up, but for now I was just happy to have all my guys around me.

Indie and Patrick were checking over the guest list. Quinn was on the phone, pacing the length of the cafeteria area. His gaze would stray to where I was sitting every few minutes, but otherwise he stayed out of my airspace.

I was happily surrounded by my band. Bats and Zach were piled into a saggy loveseat across from me and Hunter. Owen was on a folding chair curled over his acoustic, strumming softly. And Wyatt was in a lotus pose on his pre-concert stretch mat.

A perfect moment.

Hunter twirled a pen through his fingers. "What's the vote for opener?"

"Cathedral," Bats and Zach said in unison.

"Me three," I said.

"Wyatt?"

"Works for me. I'd like to start the night out by splitting some eardrums."

Owen stuck out his tongue and made the "rock on" sign.

Hunter started writing in his slashing block print. "All of us in agreement? I think that's a fucking first."

"I've got a good feeling about tonight," I said.

"I'll take that good feeling and raise you with a fuck yeah," Hunter said and kept on scribbling.

Twenty minutes later, we had a setlist and a plan. We all went our separate ways to perform our little rituals. Wyatt and his yoga, Hunter and his voice warmup in the shower, Bats and Zach took a copy of the setlist and went to pick through their trunk of guitars.

Me?

I sat with Owen and slapped my thighs with the opening beat of our favorite warm-up song.

It wasn't exactly easy to play "Barracuda" on an acoustic, but we did it every time. It was the perfect way to get my voice working. And it also decimated the lethargy that had settled into my bones with the food fest.

It didn't suck that Quinn's gaze locked with mine as I sang about getting down on my knees. Nancy and Ann had a bit of a different definition of the song at the time of writing it, I was pretty sure.

But the flash of heat in Quinn's eyes was well worth a little extra growl in my voice. I ignored Owen's knowing smirk. I was climbing the walls in more ways than one.

I stood and jogged to the room I used to get ready. Owen finished with a super strummy version of "Faith" as I laughed and closed myself in.

The next hour was a lesson in frustration and vibrating nerves.

The amphitheater was filling up, and the sun was finally setting. We didn't have an opening act this leg of the tour. Hunter liked starting the show as the sun was setting. The night sounds blended with our instruments pounding into the night.

"Cathedrals" blasted into the sold-out crowd. Zach and Bats dueled with Wyatt's drums, I pounded on my keyboard, my head back and bliss filling up my chest as Hunter came down to the stage screaming from the top ramp.

All the bullshit I'd dealt with for the last few weeks melted away as the music took me out of reality and transported me into the song. My element. The place where nothing else mattered.

We went right into our bar song, "The Cure". The crowd shouted back the lyrics to us. Arms up, feet pounding, voices filling the sky.

I didn't know how much I needed my music, my people, my men. My back was coated in sweat thanks to lights strobing over me, under my keyboards, and behind me. We came to the midpoint of the show where we slowed things down.

It was just me on the stage, purple and pink lights cutting the night. A dozen screens moved around above me. I could see myself from every angle.

It always freaked me out to watch myself play.

My white jeans and ripped white shirt glowed in the unforgiving lights. My fingers were slick with sweat but found the keys unerringly. Screams of my name, of the band's name, and the ethereal shine of lighters filled my heart.

I started the next song. The lyrics to "Crossing My Line" blanketed the crowd in a hush. When the chorus came up, Bats and Zach sauntered out on either side of me. The fans screamed and sang along in a sweet crash of voices that brought a wash of tears to my eyes.

Some nights were perfect.

Some nights were shit.

And then some nights transcended both. In the middle of the bridge, Wyatt's pounding rhythm built, Owen's bass vibrated, and Hunter's voice resonated with mine.

We did a stripped down version of "Nailed" and rebuilt the frenzy of the show with another step up in intensity. Hunter stood on Wyatt's drum kit, bashing his high hats as he opened up "Pounded" a capella style that drove the crowd insane.

He prowled the stage as Bats and Zach crisscrossed behind him in a frenzied wash of blurred fingers. The Terror Twins shone as they played so hard and fast that I had to race to keep up.

My arms ached and my muscles trembled as I raced up and down the piano on my left, and the harpsichord on my right. The two instruments shouldn't work together so seamlessly. The twisted carnival flavor with the pounding chop of piano spun out until I lost my breath.

I climbed onto my baby grand piano as the crowd went nuts. My piano teacher would be offended on behalf of all piano makers, but the fans loved it.

I could barely breathe as I draped myself along the top. I stretched my arms over my head and arched my back. When the fans screamed louder, I turned my head and arched even higher.

Screams turned to catcalls as I flipped over onto my belly and swung my feet as I propped my head up with my hands.

Bats switched from "Pulse" into "Foxy Lady". I laughed and popped onto my knees and played it up for the crowd. The whole band joined in. I crawled to the front end of my piano and played from the top.

The crowd lost their mind.

Improv was our favorite part of the show. I was laughing my way through the ass-backwards playing of the song when I caught Quinn watching me from the side of the stage.

I was hanging over the piano, my girls way more on display than usual. Jaw tight, he'd fisted his hands on my upright piano stashed on the side stage.

I imagined myself pinned to the keyboard, his hands on either side of me. I wanted his teeth on my neck again. He'd suck on my pulse point until I did more than moan. Until I was wrapped around him, my hips mimicking each pull.

Breath gone again, I had to turn away.

Zach had flowed from "Foxy Lady" into "Little Wing" for a Jimi double play for the crowd. I slid off the baby grand and played the high end of the harpsichord to flavor the guitar-rich song.

I could still feel Quinn's eyes on my back.

My skin buzzed with the need to melt off the stage and find him. To pull him into me to ride the dark edges of the show. When the house lights went down, my lungs felt too big for my chest and my thighs vibrated.

Roadies rushed out to switch out my pianos for the next number. I had three minutes to switch out my shirt and suck down a Vitamin Water.

What I did?

Ripped off my shirt and pushed Quinn into the folds of the curtains that blocked the crowd from seeing our side stage. He didn't say a word, didn't pretend to not want me.

His fingers twisted into the tail of my braid and yanked my head back. His mouth was hot on mine, his tongue tangy from a spearmint Altoid that was almost always rattling around his molars when he was stressed.

He lifted me off my feet and I wound my legs around his hips. "Fuck yes," I said against his shoulder.

He flipped up my bra, staring at me as he sucked the tip deep into his mouth. Who needed to breathe? Not me. I was good right here in this moment for the rest of my life.

Okay, maybe I wanted to get him inside me at the same time, and maybe I wanted to come so bad my brain burned for it. But right now, his lips were on me, and his rage had transferred to me.

I dug my fingers into his shoulders and clamped down on his hips until he groaned. He moved his mouth to the cup of my bra and dragged it back over my breast. His fingers would leave bruises on my hips, but I didn't care.

Sweet fuck, I wanted those love bruises everywhere.

25

QUINN

My dick was so hard I was positive I was going to go insane. Music was her thing. She was obsessed with it on a level that I couldn't understand, but here...now? Watching her pour herself into the song and the crowd?

I got it.

Lust and the driving need to protect her coalesced into a dangerous need to possess every molecule of passion I watched unfold on that stage. I'd been able to slot her into the untouchable client role for weeks now.

Not all the way.

But I'd been able to mostly resist her.

Until now.

The word *no* hadn't been even a glimmer in my mind when she locked her gaze on me. Hell, I might have walked right on to that stage and fucked her on the piano if my training hadn't kicked in.

But then she came at me.

And it had been all over. Madness had locked onto me like a sidewinder missile. No way around it, no evasive maneuver to be found. If I hadn't heard three people shouting her name from the side-lines, I'd have been inside her until we were both spent.

The haze dissipated. Our timing was beyond wrong to the point of hilarity. I wanted to tell her that we'd pick it up after the show. I wanted to promise her that I'd hold her down until she was boneless from a twenty-four-hour orgasm.

In a perfect world, I could have all of that. But that wasn't our world.

I covered her breast and lowered her to the ground.

Here and now I was her guard, and her escort. I wasn't her lover. I didn't have that right.

She saw it in my eyes. I wanted to deny it. I was sure I'd never wanted anything so goddamn bad in all my life.

"Damn you, Warden."

Duty.

Loyalty.

None of those were synonymous with *fuck the client until she was unconscious.*

I shut my eyes and took a step back. When I opened them again, she was gone. The stage was alive with green and gold lights and she was on a pedestal with an upright piano similar to the one she played at home.

The mini stage rose and spun slowly as she crowded over the keys. She wore a jet black tank with straps up the back and criss-crossing her front, molding her flesh like I wanted to do with my hands—with my mouth.

Hunter sang and the guitars howled.

The crowd ate it up.

The higher she climbed, the farther she traveled from me in so many ways.

I couldn't watch any more. Not if I wanted to pretend I could keep it together for the rest of the night. The list of VIPs needed to be reviewed again, I needed to do a perimeter check for my own sanity, and a check in with Lucy at Roth Defense—also for my mental wellbeing.

Those were the items on my list, not pinning Faith Keystone to the nearest available surface.

I stalked backstage, barking orders at the on-site security. The band was moving into the encore in ten minutes and I had to be ready for them to come off stage.

I channeled my frustration into the people working under me. Right now I didn't care if they thought I was a grade-A asshole. I just needed to get her out of my head.

The roar of the crowd and elated laughter followed me down into the dressing rooms. Exhaustion and elation laced everyone's voice. She was safe. She was surrounded by her people.

Nothing to worry about.

Nothing that I needed to intrude on.

I busied myself with my list. I caught her gaze a few times as she worked the room. Owen stayed at her side, and while jealousy pricked at me when I saw how easy she was with him, I tried to ignore it.

I didn't have any right to be jealous.

There was nothing between them but friendship, but there was a closeness that I'd never seen between a man and a woman that didn't end in a relationship.

Though the woman in question was Faith.

And she couldn't be defined in any general sense anyway. Like this was going to be any different?

She flitted in and out of circles of people. She was friendly and sweet with some, borderline outrageous with others. The only thing that stayed the same with everyone was the quick and genuine smiles that instantly happened when she was in their space.

"Oh, is that how it goes?"

I turned to the voice behind me. Indie was leaning on one of the bar top tables that had been scattered through the afterparty space. She used a finger to push back her ever-present straw hat.

"It's my job to watch her."

She smirked. "Not like that it's not."

I really didn't have an answer to that, so I said nothing. I doublechecked my belt holster, making sure my blazer covered it. The room was getting more crowded, and I didn't like this many people between me and my client.

Between me and Faith.

I moved through the crowd, my skin prickling when a cluster of women circled her. Playing the boyfriend card wasn't out of the question. Not now. Not here with hundreds of people I didn't know. Double what was originally planned.

"Faith."

She reacted to my voice, but didn't turn away from the people she was talking to. She did reach behind her, her fingertips brushing my thigh to let me know she was fine. She was relaxed and at ease.

I tried to take my cues from her, tried to let myself settle, but it wasn't going happen until I got her out of there.

And obviously she had no intention of leaving.

I'd kept her in the ivory tower for weeks. She wasn't made for it. This was her element. Not necessarily the limelight, but she needed people. She'd never be happy to hide away in the quiet.

Never happy with a man like you.

I shook that off and settled my hand on her hip. Not even a ripple in the conversation. She just kept on talking as her skin burned under my palm. Didn't she ever wear a damn shirt that went past her belt?

I tried to tune into what she was so animated about, but all I could focus on was her ass brushing across the front of my jeans. My fingers curled into her belt loop and her breathing changed.

"Are you guys going to be in town for the show?"

Faith's nails grazed my thigh. "What?"

"We've got a show in Denver at the end of the year. Can you guys make it?"

"Yeah, definitely. I'd love to."

The girl talking to her had jet black hair streaming over her shoulders and down her back. Her obsidian dark eyes flashed at me, then down at Faith. "Bring tall, dark, and delicious."

Faith's nails went from a light scrape to bite. "Want to go to Brooklyn Dawn's show with me, W—Quinn?"

I stifled a groan. Right now, she had to go with almost slipping? With the name that had taunted for days, and brought me back into myself. I tried to step back, but the tips of her fingers grazed my cock. "Wherever you want to go, babe."

She dragged in a breath that ended in a laugh. "See why I keep him around?"

The blond with the dark-haired woman laughed. She was startlingly beautiful. The kind that made headlines for more than just ticket sales. I hadn't even noticed her until Faith made me click in.

Fucking dangerous as hell.

What else wasn't I paying attention to?

Her ass swayed across my thighs, inciting more anger. "Would you excuse us for a second?"

The blond grinned. "Sure."

"Oh." Faith shot a glance over her shoulder at me before smiling at the girls. "All right. I'll catch you two later?"

The brunette nodded, her gaze raking down my body. "Definitely."

Faith's voice deepened. "Behave, James. He's mine."

My grip increased. I wasn't—not really—but right then, I wanted to be. Right then, I wasn't sure how I could turn it off.

I slid my hand from her hip to lock with her fingers, dragging her across the room to the darkened hallway.

"What the hell, Warden?"

"We need to have a conversation."

"If you wanted me in a dark room, all you had to do was ask."

"This isn't a game."

She whirled on me, causing me to take a step back into one of the trunks. "I know it's not. But if you don't stop staring at me like that…"

I gripped the trunk. "It's my job to stare at you."

"I'm used to you watching me, Warden. There's even a little bit of a buzz under it that I've acclimated to. That's not what you've been doing since we got here." She moved in until she straddled my leg, and she gripped my side. "Then on the side stage. When you touched me."

"That shouldn't have happened."

"It's going to keep happening. You know why?"

I refused to answer, even though I knew she was going to keep talking. I pushed her away, and she came back at me, her nails slipping over my belt buckle into the front of my jeans to anchor me in front of her. "Faith," I said in a low voice.

"That's why. Right there. That voice." She put pressure on heel of her hand as her other hand tugged at my tucked T-shirt until she got under the material. "Because neither one of us can resist this."

"I can resist."

"Why?"

"Because that's not what I'm here for. I'm here to watch and protect. I don't fuck clients."

"I'm not just a client."

"Yes, you are."

Her blue eyes blazed. "Liar."

"Chemistry. Lust."

"Somehow I don't think you'd really give into that if you didn't want to."

"Believe me. If I could turn this off, I would."

A flash of something in her eyes made me wish I could take that back. I don't know if it was hurt, or hate, or something even more incendiary. She flipped out the tail of my belt from the buckle and I stilled her hands. "Touch me, Warden. Take this all away and then maybe, just maybe we can concentrate again."

"If I touch you, I'll never stop," I growled. I hated the truth in that statement, but there it was.

She tugged at my belt. "Thank God."

I pushed away from the trunk, into the dark. The crash of notes made me curse.

"It can take it."

"It's your piano."

"My harpsichord." She went up on her toes and nipped my chin. "Sturdy."

"Christ," I said and looked over my shoulder. We were alone. The party was still going on. Music carried down the hallway and the laughter reminded me there were people close.

But not *that* close.

She tugged my zipper down and I pushed her hands away, spinning her around to face the large, curved instrument. "That is not how this is going to happen. Not right now."

Her hand reached back to my thighs. "I want it to happen here. I don't mind our first time to be in the shadows." She cupped my shaft. "I just need it to be now. I can't wait any longer."

No way was I going to be able to handle her touching me right now. "My way then." I slid my arm along her elbows, pinning her shoulders back. Her breath stalled as her head rested on my chest. Her moan made my dick pulse behind my half-undone zipper. A shaft of light highlighted her high, upturned breasts and the nipples pushing against her shirt.

I'd tasted them tonight. Salt and peaches over silk.

I moved forward and nudged her body into the curved side of the piano. I lowered my head until my lips were at her ear. "Just how sturdy is this thing?"

"As sturdy as I am, Warden."

26

KEYS

My back arched at the angle. He towered over me, his breath a brand on my neck. This was what I wanted. I hadn't known it. I'd never known sex could be this exciting.

Adrenaline from the stage I'd used and fucked through before. This was different. The taste of this kind of intoxication couldn't be duplicated with anyone but Quinn. That scared me as much as it thrilled me. Part of me didn't want to know these kinds of feelings existed.

Part of me wished that I could stay ignorant and happy with the status quo of my life.

But the part of me that strained against his touch, that ached for the danger of his huge, hard body—that was the part of me that had never been more alive.

The part that I could never, ever put back in a box.

His teeth grazed along my pulse.

"Mercy."

Was that my voice? It was broken and husky.

"There isn't any mercy to be had tonight, Faith."

I shivered at the low tone of his voice. It wasn't the clipped Quinn

I knew. It was darker, almost angry. His grip was harsh, almost too much—just on the verge of causing fear.

With his free hand, he coasted down to my jeans, digging between my legs until the seam of the denim rubbed over my swollen folds. He was relentless, the friction driving me higher quicker than I thought possible.

"I need you with me." He ground his cock along my ass. "I've been like this for hours." He sucked at my neck. "Fuck, I've been like this for days."

I bucked against his touch. My low groan only made him move faster. I was as immobilized as the night he'd pinned me to the bed. He held me there, on the edge of the fastest orgasm of my life, and then he just stopped.

"Fuck," I growled and rolled my hips. "I need…"

"What?" His voice was at my ear again. "I said I needed you to catch up, not go over."

I kicked at him and he laughed.

Fucking *laughed*.

"I want your nail marks on my back." He nosed my shirt out of the way and nipped my collarbone. "I want them in my flanks when I fuck you."

I whimpered. "Yes."

Holy crap, yes. Everything about his touch made me want to rip into him. I wanted to leave marks too.

How did he know?

"But right now…" He twisted my arms up until they were folded against my back. "Now, I need you to just take me. Round two you can do what you want to me."

Then he pressed me down onto the piano cover, my cheek flush with the pillowed material. I stretched up onto my tiptoes at the angle. I wasn't tall enough for this. He seemed to realize that, but instead of correcting the situation, he boosted me up and released the snap of my jeans.

"Quinn."

"Do you want me to stop?"

"God, no."

"Good, then hold on to me with your legs." He dragged his teeth down the dip of my lower spine and peeled away my jeans.

"What are—Oh, God."

He held both arms with one hand, bracketing my wrists. With his other hand, he drew his thumb down the seam of my ass to my slit. "Fuck. So fucking wet."

Exposed and splayed on my belly, I couldn't move if I wanted to. But then his mouth was there and the idea of moving melted into the shadows.

His tongue was relentless as he filled me. He sucked and slid along every fold. The sounds. It was like I was another person. That couldn't be me, writhing under his strokes. He slid his thumb inside me and pulsed in time with his tongue.

There was no beginning, no end, no rhyme and no reason. There was only him and his mouth and my inability to deny him. He let go of my arms and I flailed to pull away, to crawl over the piano to get away from the insanity drowning me.

He dragged me back and rolled me over onto my back. His eyes were shiny black in the low light as he draped my knee over his shoulder and spread me open. He licked me until I sobbed out his name.

His hand slid up my chest to my throat and over my mouth. I dug my teeth into his palm, but he didn't stop, didn't relent. He sucked and stroked my clit until there was no light left, no sweet little sparkles of a shiny orgasm.

No, this was a maelstrom of pain, pleasure, and finally, a boneless release.

He dragged me off the piano and the fabric cover slid with me on to the floor. But not me. No, I was safe in his arms.

No.

No, *safe* wasn't the word.

He rounded to the front of my harpsichord to the bench and sat down with me. I ripped at his belt, at his zipper, at the cotton of his shorts until there was skin.

Hard, hot, skin. The flared head of his shaft was so tight that he hissed when I swirled my fingers around it. "Faith."

I shook off the jeans that were dangling from my ankle. My other shoe clattered to the floor. I wasn't really sure when I lost the first one. It didn't matter. My only goal was to get on top of him, to get him inside me.

"Wallet," he growled.

I moved so he could dig into his pocket. His wallet flipped onto the top of my harpsichord and then there was the crinkle of plastic and the snap of rubber.

Thank God.

"Inside, inside, inside," I chanted. I fisted my hand around his base and he hissed. "Now."

He gripped my hips and pulled me down on top of him. I arched, suddenly not so certain I could survive this. I tried to back off of him. Hard, huge, full.

So freaking full.

He slipped farther inside me, his eyes fierce. "Okay?"

"Okay," I gasped. Every nerve was alive and firing as I tilted forward and took all of him. "So okay."

He gripped the cover of the keys and rocked me. The impact of the bumpers getting shifted resonated inside me like an extra vibration. "Fuck." His lips crashed into mine, scraping over my lower lip as he seated himself again and again. "So fucking tight and perfect," he said against my mouth.

I tucked my face into his shoulder, curled my arms around his neck, and held on as he lifted his hips up and drove into me again and again. I should have been able to control the angles and the depth, but I was lost to his overwhelming force.

I couldn't deny him.

I couldn't do anything but hold on and roll my hips in time with his deep strokes.

He hollowed me out and owned every part of me.

I leaned back enough to press my forehead to his, then dug my fingers into his shoulders, slipping down into the collar of his shirt to get to skin.

He groaned into my mouth, his fingers racing up my back to pull me down on him. Harder, harder. My name was a broken curse.

His cock pulsed inside me as I grasped his shoulders and clenched around him instinctively. I wanted all of him tattooed against the inside of me where no one could ever take this feeling away.

Trembling, I held on as he slowed and finally stilled. But he didn't leave me. He was still inside me even as the world had surely shattered around us.

His arms fell away first. I immediately missed the bite of his grip on my hips. Like he couldn't handle the idea I'd get away.

"Trying to compartmentalize me, Warden?"

"Dammit, Faith."

My body tingled at the warning and frustration in his voice. "Is it the *Warden* thing that has you pissed off, or the fact that you just fucked the stuffing out of me?"

He stood, but instead of allowing him to unseat me, I clamped my knees on his hips and seized his shoulders. His eyes flashed in the limited light. "This isn't a fucking game."

I wrapped my legs around him and had to bite back a moan as he lost his footing and slammed me into the harpsichord. He was still inside me and still semi-hard, which was kind of amazing actually. Did they give them extra doses of testosterone in Ranger school?

They certainly hadn't skimped on what he was packing. Front or back.

His jaw was so tight that I could see the vein throbbing in his temple, even in the dark. I didn't want this to be weird.

It was going to be weird regardless. No one could have that kind of sex and not want to regroup, myself included. But I also knew that if I didn't handle this right, it would turn back the clock to the first day we met.

The reserved Quinn without humor. I liked the little bits of sarcasm that had started bleeding through.

I didn't want to lose that.

I tipped my hips so he had no choice but to pay attention to me. And *all* of him was paying attention—and growing.

"You promised me a round two."

He closed his eyes as our bodies started moving together. We had a rhythm of our own, a beat that would never come from an instrument. I didn't want to let that go. I didn't want him to push it into a box.

I slid my fingers up to the nape of his neck as he finally held on to my hips again. "This isn't round two," I said.

Saying nothing, he dug his fingers into my ass.

"You only get one ride on my piano, buddy."

The puff of air along my neck eased the nerves building inside me.

"Was that a laugh?" I asked.

"No."

"Yes, it was."

"I don't laugh."

"Liar."

He pinned me to the elongated cover. My harpsichord was a two level keyboard so my ass actually fit right in that space. However, it wasn't meant for the kind of action this man could provide.

Damn those thrusting hips.

"This can't be what we're about, Faith. No matter how much I want to be inside you." He groaned and ground us ever closer. "How good this feels—"

"If you say it's just sex, I'll boot you across the room right now." Just the idea of him withdrawing made my heart sink.

"You're more than just a fuck. Even if I was that kind of guy, I couldn't be with you."

The stark truth in his voice and eyes kicked my heart rate up until I could barely hear around it.

"I'm also here to protect you."

"Nothing's happened," I muttered. Frustration with him and with this entire situation, as well as the fear that was always just a step away, made my voice louder than I intended.

"I can't have this conversation with you clamped around my cock. I can't think when you're this close to me, let alone when I'm balls deep inside you."

"Maybe that's the problem." I didn't like that my voice was so hesitant, but I was riding on way too many different emotions right now.

"One of us has to be clear headed about this." His hands came up to cup my face. "You're Noah's."

Startled, I blinked. "What? No, I'm not."

He shook his head, his jaw flexing. "No." He growled. "Christ, I can't." His eyes were hooded as he kept instinctively moving inside me.

I dragged in a ragged breath. "You can't be talking about someone else when you're inside me, Quinn."

"Not like that or I'd never have touched you." He touched his forehead to mine as he glided in and out of me. The unhurried pace fractured my resolve to talk this out.

He coasted down my shoulder to my breast and cupped it, plucking at the nipple that was poking through my bra and shirt. His hands weren't gentle. I liked that he couldn't seem to stop touching me. I liked that he wasn't soft and sweet.

His focus shifted to where we were joined. "Fuck." When his gaze lifted to me, it was bleak. "Nothing can happen to you."

"It won't." I met his firm lips and softened for him. Waited for him to unclench and kiss me. I was pretty sure I'd been waiting him out for what felt like forever. I hooked my arm around his shoulder and took each stroke, felt the tremor of the dampers undulating along the strings of my harpsichord under me, and my own skin that felt too tight.

He tore his mouth away and buried it into my shoulder as his hips flexed and the friction pushed me out of my head. I gasped as the release blindsided me. I'd been so focused on him and trying to figure him out that my body's reaction dropped like a curtain.

Nothing but Quinn filling me up.

His breath fusing with my skin, his fingers branding me again.

"It won't," I said again as I held on.

27

QUINN

FUCK.

Fuck.

Fuck.

I withdrew. I had to. A pale shaft of light highlighted the red marks on her hips and her swollen, battered slit.

I'd done that. I couldn't even lie to myself about trying to be gentle. I'd fucking lost it.

Wet from me, from us. From both of us coming our damn brains out. That soft pink place was where I wanted to be back inside right now.

Fuck.

"Stop it."

My gaze dropped to the floor. To the twisted puddle of the piano cover and her rumpled jeans—her shoes scattered.

My mind equally scattered.

She hopped off her piano—harpsichord, whatever—and wobbled.

I steadied her, and got an armful of nail gouges for my trouble. I drew in a sharp breath through my nose.

"Stop it. Do *not* regret this, Quinn Alexander."

How could I?

I should. God knows I should be calling my boss and reassigning someone to her immediately. But there was no way I'd walk away. No fucking way.

At this point it wasn't even because Noah asked me to take care of her. I *couldn't* walk away from her. Not just because my dick was as compromised as my morals, but because the moment I'd slipped inside of her, she'd become mine. No question, no way to avoid it.

I was so beyond fucked.

A door banged open and laughter echoed down the hall.

"Get dressed." I turned away from her and took care of the condom. I grabbed a rag from one of the trunks and rolled the condom inside, tucking it away into my jeans pocket before I zipped up.

"Crap," she muttered and snapped out her jeans. "Where the hell did my underwear go?"

I dug out my phone and used my torch app. "Here." I picked them up, but instead of handing them over, I jammed them into my blazer pocket.

Her eyebrows snapped together. "Those are mine."

"They were on the dirty floor. You really gonna put them on?"

"No, of course not." She wiggled into her jeans and zipped them up with a wince.

Was she reminded of the seam that I'd used to get her off the first time, or the fact that she was still soaking wet from my touch?

I wanted to dig my hands into her jeans and see.

Wow. I was so far gone, I was actually heading into Neanderthal territory.

She twisted her fingers under her shirt and did this shimmy thing and her breasts settled back into the cups of her bra. I didn't even remember pulling at it.

I didn't remember much of anything. Just the feel of her under my hands, on my cock, the searing heat of her as I slammed inside of her again and again.

Those were the things that were clear.

Not things like the piano cover hitting the floor, or that her instrument hadn't been meant for such an...energetic session.

More importantly, I hadn't watched the doors.

I'd been so insane for her that I came into a dark room without checking it out just so I could finally breathe around the wanting of her.

Yeah, none of this was in the good category. And still I couldn't regret it. Not with her.

I grabbed her hand and dragged her behind me as I checked my gun to make sure it was secure. All I needed to do was drop it like some fresh recruit walking into basic training.

"Warden, hold up."

She hopped while she pulled on her other shoe then collided into my back. She jerked back when her fingers brushed my holster. I held on tight and moved down to the west wing where the dressing rooms were.

I backed her into the wall, caging her in as a group of people walked down a parallel hallway, Indie and Owen chatting about some of the people who had shown up backstage. Naturally, it had to be Indie.

I turned the doorknob to get out of the line of fire, but it was locked. Of course it was. I couldn't duck out, I just had to hope they wouldn't notice us.

Her breath was hot on my chest and she smelled of me, with that underlying trace of peaches. Always the goddamn peaches.

Her fingers fisted into the hem of my shirt as the voices faded.

I was damned in every way, but there was one thing I couldn't lie about. I brushed my lips against her temple. "I'm not sorry." I took her hand and led her out of the back, and back into the light of the party.

I glanced down at her. Her lipstick was gone, her lips a raw pink from my kisses. More like clashes of intent between us—but kisses nonetheless. My stubble had created hatch marks on her neck and the collar of her shirt was stretched—again, from me.

As we entered the room, I looked around for Patrick. He was at the back door, arms crossed, shoulders busting at the seams of his jacket. I gave him the signal for leaving. He nodded so I steered Faith to the side door where I'd stashed the car for an easy escape.

She was quiet for once, and I took full advantage. I loaded her into the car and rounded to the driver side, turning toward the city and our hotel. Mansfield was in the middle of nowhere, and traffic was nonexistent at this time of night.

I turned into the parking garage under the hotel and pulled into one of the last of the available spots.

She still hadn't said a word. As much as I'd enjoyed the silence, I knew it probably wasn't a good sign.

"Ready?"

"Hmm?" She looked up from her knotted fingers. "Yes, of course."

I assessed the garage and hustled her to the elevators. Most of the parking spots were filled thanks to how late it was. People were back from whatever touristy thing they'd done, or possibly even the Hammered show she'd played.

In the quiet, her heels clicked loudly on the cement. She walked fast, matching my longer pace with ease. When we got into the elevator, she moved into my space. Not leaning, but definitely touching me.

Again, I was afraid I was missing some subtle clue, but for the life of me I couldn't figure out what her angle was. When the doors opened, she waited beside me, then followed me out of the elevator.

I unearthed the keycard from my wallet as we got nearer to the room. A door opened across from us, and Zach peeked out. "Did you see Reed?"

I frowned. "I didn't notice him at the party."

"Pain in my ass," he muttered and slammed the door.

I looked down at Faith. "Is that…"

She shrugged. "Usual for them."

"Hmm. Should I worry?"

She shook her head. "Bats disappears a lot lately. We're not his keeper. As long as he shows up for soundcheck and the concert, we've been giving him some space."

I held the door open for her and trailed her into our suite. She lay her hand on my torso, her fingertips absently drifting down the line of my abs. "I need a shower."

I nodded. "Okay."

She reached into my blazer pocket. "I'll take these back now."

I covered her hand, staring her down.

"Is there a fetish I should know about?" Her lips tipped up at one corner. "You're not going to raid my drawers, right?"

"I'm only interested in the ones that smell like you."

She pressed her lips together, her gaze dropping to my mouth. "Not sure what to say about that one."

"That's worrisome. You always have something to say."

Her eyes were heavy. "Someone may have tired me out. Not to mention that I had a very kickass show tonight."

"Get some rest. You get to do it all over again tomorrow."

She smiled brilliantly this time. "Yes, I do."

"Goodnight, Faith."

"Night, Warden."

I should be appreciative that she wasn't pressing for something else. Like round two—well, I guess technically round three, if it came to that. But she walked to her room and closed the door.

Out of sorts, and restless as hell, I checked my messages.

Aidan's resident hacker guru, Lucy, was no closer to finding anything. In fact, her emails were worded rather strongly in the negative column. A voicemail flag was showing on my phone.

Noah.

Did the universe know or something? Fate watching with a maniacal laugh?

"You better be taking care of that bottle of sunshine. She's probably giving you hell. The girl does not like rules. She may rail against the idea of structure, but she's not stupid. Keep her in the loop and she won't give you any trouble. I'll check in next week."

I threw my phone on the desk and collapsed back in the chair. "Fuck."

No amount of Tai Chi was going to get me out of this one. I checked the room over and plugged my phone in to charge. Her room was silent—not even any music going.

I strode into my bathroom and cranked the shower to boiling.

I needed to get her scent off me so I could sleep. The bar of soap wasn't too feminine. I flipped over the box. Cucumber. Why the hell was that a scent? Whatever it was, it wasn't peaches. I soaped up my shaft and the hair above. The places that were alive with her.

I tipped my head back, let the steam roll through my lungs, and clear my head. I dried off and tugged on a pair of boxer briefs. I couldn't handle clothes tonight—my skin was still going haywire from Faith. It had been nearly a year since I'd touched a woman. No wonder I'd nearly dislocated her shoulders in reaction.

I dropped on to my belly, my dick already twitching at the memory.

Endlessly beautiful and so out of my damn league.

I shoved my hands under a pillow and slowly unknotted each muscle in my arms, shoulders, back. I was trained to survive on little sleep, but I was also conditioned to sleep when I could.

And right now, I had to shut it off or I'd be a fucking basketcase tomorrow. I stared at the small clock beside my bed. Hell, it was already tomorrow.

Two in the damn morning.

I don't know when I drifted off, but my body came alive and alert at the same time.

"Warden?"

I rolled onto my back. A filmy gray wash of pre-dawn light filled the room. "What's wrong?"

"Nothing. I just didn't want to come in and risk another pinning."

I dropped my arm over my face. "What are you doing, Faith?"

The sheet rustled and my bed dipped.

"I'm here for round two."

"Jesus."

"The second one on the harpsichord didn't count since you never actually pulled out of me."

I groaned as her fingers slid up into the hem of my underwear. They were a tight fit to keep the line of my suits, but it didn't seem to matter to her. Her head disappeared under the sheet and her hot breath fanned my cock.

Her nails scored lightly over the tops of my thighs as she moved her lips along my shaft.

I pushed away my sheet. Her hair was tousled around her scrubbed clean face. She wasn't wearing seduction wear. Just a white tank and tiny yellow and blue striped panties that hugged her ass. An ass that was currently arched out of the blankets.

She was going to kill me.

I pushed her hair out of her face as she moved up my hip. She paused and redirected her efforts to my ribs. She'd been right there, her breath over my cock, and now she was moving away. I should have stopped her before, but now I could add frustration and morning-wood-denial to the day.

Her lips brushed over the skin of my tattoo. She followed each letter with the tip of her nail. "What does it mean?"

I beat down the urge to groan as she tangled her legs with mine and lay against my side. "Ranger thing."

"Latin, I'm guessing?" She swiped her thumb along my stomach.

"Loosely translated, 'of their own accord'." Because we were always first in for the most dangerous missions. I'd been a paratrooper for a lot of years. So many missions included me getting dropped in the middle of chaos.

Of course my troop, the 75, caused more chaos than we were ever dropped into. I'd gotten the tattoo with a bunch of men on a night out. Most of the guys went for large tats on their arms and down their backs. I always knew I'd need to go out and find another career. Constant killing and danger would either kill me, or kill my spirit.

But finally, it had been Lissa who made the decision for me. And the rebar in my shoulder. And the acrid smoke and screams that scarred more than just my shoulder.

She stacked her hands on my chest. "Where'd you go?"

"Doesn't matter."

"Does it have to do with Lissa?"

"Not really." I shrugged. "Some." I tucked her hair around her ear. "She doesn't belong here."

She slid one hand up higher to where my heart thudded harder with each touch. "Is she in here?"

I dragged her up higher until her knees straddled my chest. "Not like you think. I was never in love with Lissa."

She propped her hands on either side of my head. "But you loved her."

I cupped her face. "Faith, I didn't love her like that. She was Noah's."

She frowned. "Noah's what?"

"Noah's who." Resigned, I rolled up to a seated position and circled my arms around her waist. "His wife."

She tried to climb out of my arms, but I held her tight. "His what?"

"His wife," I said again.

"You saying it again isn't going to make it any less shocking. He's never mentioned a wife."

"He met her back when we were Rangers together."

She nodded. "I know. I've seen pictures of you with Noah in the middle of the desert. I don't know how you guys ever managed to parachute with so much on."

"Training."

"You say it like it wasn't awful."

"It was awful. Dangerous and grueling work. It mattered, though. And when we had down time, we didn't really know how to be with anyone else other than our troop."

She trailed her nails through the hair on my chest. She frowned at the little scars that marred my pecs. Little silvery burn scars that never quite faded.

Nothing like my back.

I didn't hide them, but I didn't discuss them either. Why I felt the need to do it with her, I wasn't sure. "Burns," I said softly. "There was a fire on the base." I laughed harshly. "So many jumps to my name. So many times that I'd been in the middle of a firefight—not a scratch."

Her nails dug in and climbed to my shoulders.

"Noah was out on a jump. He was part of a specialized team." I didn't need to scare her with the details, nor could I tell her much of them. Especially about Noah. Even I didn't know what happened on half of his missions. "There are a lot of individualized teams within the unit. Lissa hated when he was gone without me there to have his back. So, I stayed in their guest room when she got really bad. I knew how to distract her."

Her fingers coasted higher along the nape of my neck into the short hairs there. Her eyebrows snapped down.

"Not that kind of distraction. She was Noah's. Sweet and funny, but also the most innocent woman I ever knew. She honestly couldn't handle when Noah was on a job. It's a tough life, and being a Ranger's wife is probably right up there with being a SEAL's wife."

She would have either had a breakdown, or divorced him. Intellectually, I knew that, but it didn't change the fact that I'd watched her die. I hadn't been able to help her.

I'd let Noah down.

One hand slid back down to where the scars on my chest. "The fire?"

I sighed. "Base housing. Think townhouse, but not quite as nice."

"Nice to know our soldiers are so safe."

"Budgets, the never-ending struggle. One of the main reasons so many of us go into the private sector." I drew little circles on her lower back as the memories snuck in. "I woke to smoke. Thick and disorientating, but my training kicked in and I went on the offense. Get everyone out. I went looking for Lissa. The hallway was in flames—they said it was an electrical fire. There were no sirens, no help coming. I had to go get her."

I couldn't leave her behind. It wasn't an option. Self-preservation was an afterthought in my line of work.

"I got her out of their bedroom and into the living room, but there were flames every which way I turned. The load-bearing wall came down on us. I was pinned by a steel rod into the floor. I couldn't get up. I couldn't get to her." The flames and the heat—so much heat and noise.

Her cool hands came up to cup my face. "Hey."

"I couldn't save her."

"You know it's not your fault, right?"

"Yeah. Doesn't make her any less dead. Didn't make me any less alive because the wall actually saved me."

There were no screams from Lissa in my nightmares. The screams were mine. She'd already been gone before the flames had done their horrifying damage.

Faith wrapped her arms around my neck and gripped my back. Her eyes were damp with tears for me. She frowned, and her touch went across my shoulder.

She scooted around me and gasped.

"Faith, I'm fine. Maybe not fine enough to parachute anymore, but I'm fit and able to do my job."

She punched my arm. "I don't care about that. I know you can shoot your damn gun."

I laughed. God, I hadn't thought I'd ever be able to laugh with memories of Lissa lodged in my brain. "You've never seen me shoot my gun."

"If Noah trusts you to shoot, I know you can shoot. He was a sniper, for God's sake. He wouldn't let just anyone take care of me."

I swiped my hand over my hair. "You know he's a sniper?"

"I figured it out." She dashed away tears. "He wasn't exactly happy about it, but he didn't deny it. He won't give us any details—

Hunter either. I just know that I wouldn't want to be on his bad side."

"Truth." I pulled her around in front of me again. She knelt between my legs, her hair wild and her eyes bright. "Now that you know my ugly little secret, can you see why this isn't a good idea?"

"Why? Because you'll worry about me? Would it change if we weren't sleeping together? Would it magically make everything better if you put me back into that box you had me in before?"

"Yes, dammit."

"No." She linked her arms around my neck. "This thing between us? It's going to be here whether you try to deny it or not. I don't want to pretend I don't want you." She brushed her cheek against my dark scruff. "I've never felt like this before."

"Dammit, Faith."

She scraped her teeth down my earlobe. "Let it go, Warden. This is happening."

I gripped the hair at the base of her neck, dragging her mouth to mine. "What if I don't want it to?" I asked against her lips.

"Why lie right to my face?" Her fingers coasted down my belly to my dick. She palmed my shaft and swiped her thumb over the head. "All it takes is one touch."

"I've had hard-ons before."

She pushed me back on the bed, then stripped down my underwear. Before I could nudge her away, she had me in her mouth. She looked up at me as she bobbed her head down, taking me deeper with every sucking stroke of her mouth and hand.

My fingers twisted into her hair. She took more of me and I bucked my hips involuntarily. "Faith."

She hollowed out her cheeks as she sucked her way to the end of my cock and swirled her tongue around the head. She did it again, finally releasing me with a greedy hum. "It's not just about making you hard. It's your eyes as you watch me." She twisted and pulled at me until my damn eyes were ready to cross. "In the shadows, I felt it. Here, in the light, I have proof of it."

I slapped the mattress as she sucked me deep. I couldn't guarantee that I could control myself if I grabbed her hair again. The need to bury myself inside her mouth, inside her pussy—it didn't matter. Both were equally brutal.

I reached over my head for the headboard, for the pillow—anything to hold onto.

She knelt between my legs, hovering over my cock while she sucked me in. She didn't let up, didn't allow me to even breathe.

"Faith."

She hummed around my shaft and tongued under my head. I didn't want to come in her mouth. I wanted her up and over me, taking me deep, but she wasn't having any of it.

I released one of my hands and pulled her hair. She peeked from the curls and bangs that had fallen forward, watching me go insane.

She wasn't stopping until she had what she wanted.

Me.

My cum.

I gripped her hair and growled out her name, letting her have what she wanted. Like I was ever going to be able to deny her. Her nails scraped over my belly as she swallowed me down.

My chest heaved, and my brain quieted. I dragged her up my sweat-slickened body and buried my face into her neck. "You might have to wait for payback."

"I'm looking forward to it."

"Smug shit."

She made this humming little purr of a laugh and dragged the sheet up. "Tired shit."

I brushed her hair back. "We have a few hours."

She settled herself along my side and tangled her legs with mine. "Good. Maybe by the time I wake up, you'll have found some strength for another round."

28

KEYS

WELL, WE DIDN'T GET TO START ANOTHER ROUND. A 911 TEXT CAME through and we ended up with an emergency band meeting. Reed hadn't come back the night before, and we were about an hour away from soundcheck.

Still no Bats.

Quinn and I slipped into the room to find Wyatt pacing the living room and Hunter on the phone.

I sat next to Owen on the couch. "What's going on?"

"I don't give a shit that you're understaffed. There should be video from the SUV."

My eyebrows shot up at Hunter's sharp tone.

"What video?"

"I had dash cams added to all your vehicles," Quinn said.

I spun around. "You what?"

He crossed his feet at the ankles as he stood against the wall near the door. "Don't give me that outraged face. You guys are at your most vulnerable in the car."

I swung my gaze to Indie. "You knew this?"

She pushed her hat off and scrubbed her nails through her white-blonde hair. "It's my job to get you from one venue to another. If I can get more eyes on you idiots, all the better. And look, I still lost one of you."

I slumped down into the cushions. I should have known about the extra security things. Not even because I was currently banging my bodyguard, but he should have told me.

I aimed my rage at Quinn, but before I could blast him, he shook his head slightly. His face was stony, and his gaze uncompromising. I so wasn't winning *that* conversation.

Sighing, I rested my cheek on Owen's leather jacket. I hadn't been paying attention to Bats. He'd been moody since the drop of our new album. Even by Reed standards, he'd been combative.

Wyatt's thumbs were flying over his phone. His auburn hair was usually perfectly styled and neat. Now it stuck up in crazy curls. He shucked his suit jacket and rolled up the cuffs of his dress shirt as he switched from texting to speaking quietly into his cell.

Zach sat on the other side of me, Lorraine cradled in his arms.

I patted his hand. "When did you see him?"

"He doesn't talk to me anymore, Keys. He stalked off the stage after the encore and I haven't seen him since."

Gabe Matthews, our new head of security, came in with an iPad in his hand. "I found him."

Indie rushed over to him. "Where?"

"He just called for a car. I sent Patrick."

"Good, maybe he'll beat some sense into him," Hunter growled.

"I'd prefer to do it," Wyatt said with a low, flat voice. With his sleeves rolled back and powerful forearms flexed, he didn't look like his usual elegant self. He was more the brawler race car driver I'd known years ago.

None of us had been in a hurry for that side of him to re-emerge. Leave it to Bats to cause it.

"No one's beating on anyone." Owen stood. "We don't even know what happened yet."

"*She* happened," Wyatt snarled.

I sighed. "Here we go."

Wyatt's fists clenched. "No one wants to talk about it, but we all know that bottom feeder has been all over him. Her career's headed for C-level fame and she's doing anything to save it."

Hunter held up a hand. "Vic's in New York doing some show for Netflix."

"She was." Wyatt folded his arms. "She was at the concert last night."

"Awesome," I muttered. I'd been in my own world last night. Even on stage, I'd been so focused on the songs and...well, Quinn. There hadn't been much room for anything else.

"And you didn't say anything?" Zach asked as he crossed to Wyatt.

"Hunter wants to trust him. I'm trying like hell to do that, but every time I do, he pulls some bullshit like this. And he won't explain a goddamn thing."

"Would you?" Hunter threw his phone on the end table. "Would you be so excited to have one of us dig into why you were seeing a chick?"

"Not a problem." Wyatt tipped his head down as he crowded into Hunter. "I'm a one-and-done guy."

"Jesus." Hunter held up a hand. "Fucking Bats," he muttered as he strode out of the room.

Indie looked up from her little powwow with Gabe. "All right, guys, get ready. Cars roll out in ten."

We all stood. Quinn held the door for me and followed me into the hall. We were quiet until we got inside our suite.

"What was that about?" Quinn dipped his fingers into his pocket and jangled coins.

"You did some research on us, right? And I told you about Victoria."

"Hunter's ex, now Reed's current?"

"He says no, but I don't know what to believe. He won't give us a reason why she's always hanging around. Just pulls this 'it's my business' BS."

He moved to the desk. "Victoria Shaw?"

"Sheer."

His fingers paused over the keys. "The actress?"

I shook my head. "Seriously, why do all the guys fawn over this chick?"

"I didn't say I did."

I dropped onto the couch. "Sure."

"Not the kind of blond I'm interested in."

"Smooth, Warden."

"Just speaking truth. I logged into work and pulled her credit. Wyatt's correct. She's struggling. She just tried to get a three-million-dollar loan and was denied."

I rushed over to him. "How the hell do you know that?"

"Told you I pulled her credit report."

"Just like that?" I peeked over his shoulder. "That fast?"

"Any bargain basement PI can do that, Faith."

I put up my hands. "Excuse me. You're all of the awesome. My very own bodacious, badass bodyguard."

"Appreciate the alliteration."

I crossed my arms and cocked my hip. "Makes my girl parts tingle when you throw around big words."

When his face closed off, I was afraid I'd gone over some invisible line. Work mode equaled no teasing?

He pulled me in front of him and jerked my ass against his front, then wound his arm around my shoulders. "You enjoy a loquacious man, Miss Keystone?"

I tried not to shiver. Really. But I didn't think I'd ever heard Quinn use a teasing tone.

"I'm far more likely to manipulate an engagement of force, than to use erudite language."

"That was a whole lot of wrong." My voice sounded way too breathy.

He lowered his mouth to the skin between my shoulder and neck and gave it a playful nip. "Time to go."

I turned in his arms and went up on my toes. He stared down at me, but didn't move in for a kiss. I was shocked that he'd initiated any contact, actually. I tugged on his lower lip, watching him watch me as I flicked my tongue between his lips.

He bent his knees and curled his arms around me, lifting me off the floor. His kiss was hot, consuming, and rough. Every inch of my mouth was invaded. I was pretty sure his fingerprints were now branded on my skin.

Then he put me down, turned me around, and smacked me on the ass. "Time to work."

I spun around. "Who are you?"

"Keep on moving, Faith."

I tried to stuff down my smile as I grabbed my Go-Bag and left the room. It was going to be a very good day.

And I was right. The show was amazing. Bats and Wyatt were raging at each other, but used it on stage to bump up the songs to a whole new level of intense.

The crowd fed off the energy and gave it back to us. We ended up doing two encores. Indie didn't even yell at us when we went beyond the park's curfew.

Bats disappeared after the show—again. But this time, Gabe had Patrick shadowing him. Whether that would become a problem remained to be seen. Since Bats was playing Houdini, I couldn't get away. Unfortunately for me, it seemed like Quinn was going to be dragged into that end of security as well.

I felt his eyes on me as I made the rounds. The first night had been the big VIP party, this afterparty was more like our general touring deal. A few friends, some people that Ripper Records had on a list to entertain, and a handful of special fan club winners.

Things were getting back to normal, and the memories of the night of the wedding were getting further and further away. I was actually starting to believe that maybe it really was a one-time thing.

But part of me wanted to thank her, that awful woman who had spawned all of this. That terror had brought me a happiness I'd never known I was missing.

Quinn would never have been in my life without *her*.

I met his gaze across the room. He was deep in conversation with Gabe, but he'd paused to make sure I was good. Odd to be thankful for something so scary.

But I was.

I didn't want to let him go. With the threats lessening, and my life slipping back into pattern, I wondered just how long I'd be able to keep him with me. Just how long could I ask him to protect me when there was no threat?

And what the hell was I going to do when he wasn't around anymore?

29

QUINN

WE DESCENDED INTO A LULL. NOTHING SEEMED TO BE GOING ON except what was becoming our normal. Faith was flourishing. I was drowning in rehearsals, her shows, more endless hours spent listening to a cacophony of instruments.

I was gaining an appreciation for the amount of work she did— what her band did. I was even learning to enjoy some of her lessons in genre music. Nights were spent racing to touch every part of her. Desperation seemed to chase us into the morning, and an eerie stasis filled the daytime.

I didn't watch her every move anymore. I actually started building on the plans for security measures for the band with Gabe. It gave me a purpose and helped to keep me sharp. She didn't need me at all.

It was humbling to know that, but it was also one of the reasons she filled my head far more than she should. She didn't need me, but for some goddamn reason, she wanted me.

She lit up when she saw me, and she opened me up in ways I'd thought were long dead. I'd decided years ago that I didn't need anyone long-term. My line of work as a Ranger had initiated that decision, and working security perpetuated it.

Now, I didn't know what the hell to think.

And for the first time, I was taking things day by day. It was terrifying, and thrilling. Until the night I couldn't find her.

My training locked down the outward panic. On the inside, I was losing my mind.

I checked in with Owen first. "Have you seen Faith?"

He was sprawled in one of the battered couches that seemed to always be in the backstage venues. A slightly scary and yet objectively gorgeous brunette was curled under his arm. "Nah, mate. She was on the phone with Foxy Murphy last I knew."

I frowned. She usually spoke to Devon during the day. I heard many a confusing conversation between them when they had one of their video chats. They spoke in a completely different language sometimes. "Thanks."

He sat up. "Do you want me to help look for her?"

The girl next to him had laser beams for eyes. And they were aimed at me, set on destroy. "I'm good."

I made my way through the party. I checked the side rooms, and then finally went to find Indie.

"Have you seen Faith?"

"Aww, crap."

My chest tightened at the look on her face. "Tell me you know something."

Indie sighed. "I knew things had been too damn quiet. These freaking kids are going to give me an ulcer and a heart attack in the same week."

"Why, what else happened?"

She pointed to the corner. "Everyone's favorite princess arrived ten minutes ago."

I gazed over my shoulder. Victoria Sheer was holding court. She'd crashed a few of their shows over the last few weeks. And each time it was more of a spectacle than the last. If I hadn't been on a Faith seeking mission, I would have noticed.

As usual, I had tunnel vision when it came to her.

"Everything good there?"

She shrugged. "I'll probably have to sit on Wyatt so he doesn't do something stupid like toss her out the window."

I tried to push down the panic. I didn't want to infect anyone else, but I couldn't really concentrate on Indie's problem. "Is there somewhere Faith would escape to?"

There'd been no indication that she was overly restless, but when it came to Faith, it was usually something impulsive that pulled her away. And it was the impulsive part of her I couldn't pinpoint.

The one thing about us that was fundamentally different.

Indie tipped her hat back. "Well, we're in the city. That's always a danger."

I frowned. "How so?"

"Has she been playing any new music at the hotel?"

"All her music is new to me."

Indie snorted. "Truth. But has she been playing something incessantly?"

I cracked my knuckles. "There is one song that's been playing so much that even I'm getting to know the lyrics."

She snapped her fingers. "What is it?"

My molars clicked together. "I don't sing."

Indie pulled out her phone and typed then started flicking through screens. "A show on the west end. Probably too far. I don't think she'd go out of the way for that one. Maybe for Griffin House, but not this derivative douche."

"English, Indie."

She started tapping again. "Okay, these three places are my best guess."

My phone buzzed. I pulled it out and looked at her text. "The Gull, Sin City Mage, and Maggie's? Are these bars?"

"With live music."

"Oh, for fuck's sake."

She flashed a tight smile. "Welcome to my life. Keys used to sneak out after shows all the time to go see live music in the area."

"Why didn't I know about this?" There was suddenly a dull throb in my temple. It had been awhile since that particular reaction was attributed to Faith. "What the fuck was she thinking?"

"She's not. She's a junkie, and she's been missing her fix."

And now she was out there unprotected. Exactly the time someone that was watching her would wait for.

Goddammit.

"Patrick," I shouted on my way out of the room.

"Yeah?" He jogged to meet me. "Problem?"

"Notice someone gone?"

He frowned, looked around as if counting heads, then his brows shot up. "Oh, fuck."

"Yeah, she gave us all the slip." I pulled out my phone. "I'm forwarding you three places. You go for The Gull. See if she's there. Check in with me if you find her, or if you don't."

He nodded. "Got it."

We split up, and I headed for the back where the trucks were. They were packing up to go to Michigan on the overnight. I just had to hope they hadn't put my BMW on the tow hitch yet.

Gabe met me in the parking lot. "I had your car pulled around."

I fisted my hand around my phone. "I didn't want you to leave the band unattended."

He shrugged. "They're fine. I've been talking to Indie and I checked out the three places Keys usually goes to. Maggie's is closed down for a violation. I'd go to Sin City Mage."

"Thanks." I nodded to one of the drivers as he pulled up and hopped out. "I'll check in when I find her."

"Good luck."

I slid into the car. The Beemer was outfitted for stealth, speed, and bullets. Right now, I needed the speed. I didn't give two fucks if she was pissed at me. I was going to freaking kill her.

I slammed it into gear, my tires chirping as they grabbed asphalt. I used the dash to find the address for the bar. It was in the heart of

Chicago, on a street that had as many drug dealers as pimps. I'd lived here for a few years after I'd gotten out of the service.

"Jesus, woman." I activated my traffic app and looked for the back way into the area. Would she take a cab in? A car? I prayed that she'd be smart enough to use one our drivers, but if she was trying to sneak off, I doubted it.

I held down my call button. "Call Lucy."

"Calling Lucy."

"Yo. What's up, sexy?"

"I need you to pull Faith's credit cards. Her Paypal, find out if she's got an Uber."

"Uh oh. Did you lose your charge, Q?"

"Just do it, Lu."

"Touchy." I heard her fingers flying over her keys. I just hoped that crazy keyboard of hers actually pulled up info I could use.

"She has an Uber. She called for one, but turned the dude away."

"Destination?"

"Maggie's. Downtown."

I sighed. "Yeah. Place shut down unexpectedly."

"I just got a card hit though. Looks like she used it for a cab. Please hold." Her fingers clacked again, then she whistled. "Your girl has expensive taste."

"What did she do?"

"Bottle of wine. Three of them actually."

"Great. Sin City—"

Lucy interrupted. "Mage? Yep. Looks like a cool place. Oh, man. Halsey's there tonight. I'm officially jealous."

"Dammit," I muttered. That was definitely the name of one of the bands I saw on her iPod. I punched it and swung past the underpass and skipped over two streets. "Thanks, Lucy. I owe you."

"That was an easy one. You saved me a call anyway. I got an SOS from Devon on those packages Keys gets monthly. They squicked her roommate out a bit. Enough that when I press her from some details, she painted a much different picture than what you mentioned in your report."

"Dammit."

"Q instincts on point again."

My gut clenched. "I prefer not to be right."

"According to Dev, Keys always downplays them. On a hunch, I made a call to Ripper Records HQ and had them pull her fan mail. Those little plain boxes with no return address? Yeah, way too many are littered in her archives, and all from different post offices in New York City."

"They keep them?" I was surprised.

"Yeah, they crate them up for the fan club crew to go through. But there's been a backlog yadda yadda—so it's just been stockpiling. I'm having them sent to me."

"Aidan doesn't pay you enough."

"Tell him that."

"I will." Lucy was more than just a hacker. She was our best defense when it came to research and finding needles in stacks of needles. "Let me know what you find."

"Oh, there's more."

I downshifted and swallowed a curse.

"She got one today."

That explained the call with Devon tonight. Why the hell hadn't Faith talked to me about it? And why would she go out on her own with that kind of knowledge?

"Is she sure it's the same sender? Faith usually gets one at the end of the month."

"I scanned in the labels from both boxes. Generic as hell, but I'd put my money on the same printer. Nothing we could go to the cops with, of course, but enough to put my Spidey sense on alert."

Mine too.

"But the box was a little bigger this time. Devon took pictures. I gotta say, I'm creeped out. I'm sending them to your phone."

"Give me the high points and I'll look at them when I lock Faith down."

"That sounds like a fun night."

"Lu."

"All right, all right. Don't get your cargos in a bunch." Her fingers clacked on the keys some more. "So, they have a setlist every night, right?"

"Yeah."

"Well, this box has one from every concert. There's notes scribbled on them critiquing the show."

"Like a tour diary?"

"Creepier."

Not only did this person read the tiniest interview, but now he or she thought they could make notes? "Can't they get that on the internet or fan boards?"

"Yeah, but the thing is these aren't just pictures printed out from someone's Instagram account. These are the actual ones from each show. They have rips on them and footprints from being taped on the floor."

My blood chilled. "How many?"

"Every one this tour."

My fingers ached from the force of my grip on the wheel. "Since I've been with her?"

"No. Since the new album. Even the small shows."

"Son of a bitch." I took an alley pass-through and ended up a block away from the bar. "I'm almost at the club. Send me everything you have. Faith and I are going to have a conversation."

"Will do. Don't be too hard on her, Q. You can get used to a lot of strange when you're a rockstar. Fans can equal crazy, but for the most part they're harmless."

"Doesn't sound very harmless."

"No." She sighed. "I'll send you what I have, and check back in when I get through the rest of her mail."

"Thanks."

"Lucy out."

I downshifted as the building with a neon purple sign came into view. I curbed it up onto the sidewalk and threw it in park. I got out and locked the vehicle.

There was a bouncer at the door. He pointed at the car. "Not happenin', man."

I flashed him a fifty. "Think we could possibly do this the easy way tonight?"

He glanced at my holster and stood up taller. "Cop?"

I shook my head. "Security."

Discreetly, he showed me the .45 in his belt holster. "We're not going to have a problem, are we?"

"Nope. Just need to pick up my client."

"Taking a troublemaker out of my club?"

I sighed as I heard laughter pumping out the door. "Probably your favorite customer."

He pulled at his bottom lip. "Aww, you not takin' blondie, are you?"

My heart sank. I held my hand at shoulder height. "Yay high, light eyes, head-to-toe purple?"

"Yeah, yeah." His white teeth flashed from wide lips. "She hired out one of the bouncers to sit with her. Said she probably would have some company. You company?"

"I'm the company."

He took the fifty. "Welcome."

I rolled my eyes. "Thanks."

The bar was small and unique. The walls were papered with comics and overlapping graffiti, and the stage was intimate and smoky. Moody blue lights strobed in time to the watery, Far Eastern flavor of the music. A petite girl with blue and pale blond hair hung off a microphone stand, swaying to the music.

Beside her was the woman I knew better than anyone past or present.

Faith had tied her T-shirt under her breasts and a light sheen of sweat beaded up on her midriff. A flash of gold glittered at her waist and her fingers. She leaned into the other girl, their shoulders touching, as Faith gripped a microphone stand as well.

She knew all the lyrics to the song. The same one I'd heard running on a loop for the last three days. The sultry voice of Halsey mixed with Faith's surprisingly husky voice.

It was a dreamy, dark piece full of pain and the echoes of a manic episode. Her eyes were closed as she wailed with the young girl beside her. The younger artist had stars in her eyes.

For Faith.

Because this woman drew people in like she was their own private reserve of candy. The girl wound her arms around Faith's waist and they sung into the same mic.

When the song ended, Faith hugged her back and they both hopped around in a circle. "Thanks for letting me sing."

"Anytime. Faith Keystone, people!"

The small room clapped and called for more, but Faith shook her head and jumped off the stage. She shook hands and hugged strangers.

My blood heated with every exchange. I moved to make sure I would be in her line of sight. When she got to the edge of the crowd, she finally saw me.

"Hello, Warden."

"Dammit, Faith."

She pressed her finger against my lips and shoved me into the crush of people dancing beyond the tables around the stage.

I braceleted her wrist and pulled her hand away from my mouth. "This isn't happening."

"It's already done. I needed this." She twisted her fingers into my shirt and swayed against me. "I made sure I was safe."

I lowered my mouth to her ear. "You weren't with me, so you weren't safe."

"You'll hurt Ray Ray's feelings." She twisted in my arms, her ass swaying back and forth across my thighs and zipper. She waved at a truly huge guy with obsidian skin. He waved back at her, his ivory teeth glowing out of the dark.

I turned her back around and swallowed a groan as she slid her knee between my legs. She crouched low, her short nails grazing my thighs, then over my growing erection and finally over my belly. She walked around me as the song grew more heated.

The music spoke of a man coming for the woman. That he'd never let her go. I tried to push out the lyrics, to ignore the beat that echoed a long slow fuck, and definitely struggled not to notice her far from subtle seduction.

Most of all, I didn't want her to think this was okay.

I gripped her hips, my fingers digging into her ass until she was flush with me. "I need you safe."

"I am safe. You came for me. I knew you would."

I moved one hand up to the back of her sweaty hair and gripped a handful. "Anyone could have followed you. That ex-football jock could knock some heads if the room got rowdy, but that's not the kind of trouble you need to watch out for."

"I'm dying in that hotel room. I need this. I need to go out and soak up music and people."

"Ask me," I growled.

"What would the answer have been?"

"Fuck, no."

"Exactly. I made an executive decision."

"You made a selfish decision."

She flinched. "That's right. I've been holed up for over a month. I can't stay in a box, Quinn. I just can't."

"So you slip away? What if something happened to you?" I shook her. "If someone took you from—" *Me*. If someone took her from me, I'd raze a city block to get her. "Goddammit, not on my watch."

Her eyes flashed. "I was smart. I was safe."

"No one will keep you safe like I do." I dragged her against me. My grip softened in her hair until I simply cupped the back of her head. Until my heart stopped raging and my pulse eased back into a regular rhythm.

All that shit Lucy told me was burning my damn brain. I had no proof it was the same person who tried to take her before. I just had a gut feeling and enough fear to choke off any hope that stubbornly tried to rear its head that maybe the boxes didn't have a damn thing to do with the woman at the wedding.

The hope was due to Faith's influence, no doubt.

She looped her arms around my waist, her fingers slipping under my shirt to get to flesh. I lifted her up on to her toes and crushed her mouth with mine. I needed her taste, her warmth, her peach-drenched skin.

After a moment, I hustled her out of the bar into the cool September air. The bouncer waved at us. "Sorry to see you go, Blondie. You're just what the Mage needs. You come back anytime."

"Thanks, Walter."

"Your man, eh, he's a bit intense for us. But maybe we make an exception for our little Keys."

She grinned. "Hear that?"

I clamped my hand along the back of her neck and urged her along. "I hear it."

The bouncer gave me a once over, but spoke to Faith. "You okay with this guy?"

My shoulders tightened. "I'm her security."

"Is that what the kids are calling it these days?" Walter asked.

Faith gave him a cheeky grin. "He doesn't like when I break the rules."

"Thank you, Walter," I said with gritted teeth. I led her to the car and opened the passenger side door. When she swung her legs in, I reached in and pulled the belt across her chest.

"I can do that, you know."

As I slid my hand across her naked midsection, my thumb brushed the line of her bra. The fact that she was making light of this fueled my anger all over again. "I'm going to need you to shut up right now so I don't yell at you any further."

She cupped my jaw. "And here I thought we were going to fuck it out."

"Oh, you can count on that."

She lifted an eyebrow. "What if I'm not in the mood for make-up sex?"

"Who says we're making up?"

30

KEYS

He slammed the door, and I winced. I'd known that this little venture was going to bite me on the butt. It had been worth it, though. The songs, the music, the atmosphere—those were the things that got me through the grueling parts of touring.

And my body was buzzing with the anger coming off Quinn in waves. He only wanted to keep my safe. I also knew he would find me. Though finding the car wildly parked up on the curb worried me a little.

I'd seen Quinn angry before, but this was a bit different. When he got in and slammed the car into gear, I held on. I was getting used to the BMW. It rode way low to the ground and cornered like we were on an invisible track that only he seemed to know. I always felt safe and a little out of control at the same time.

I drew in a slow breath. When he got like this, my system went haywire. He was definitely one of the most intensely dominant men I'd ever been with. Okay, he was *the* most intense. No one was like Quinn.

From the bone-jarring sex, to the liquid gray dawn when his

defenses were down, I thought I'd seen all of the different sides of him. Right now, I wasn't so sure.

I reached for his hand on the shifter, but he shook me off. "You really don't want to touch me right now."

"Because you're angry with me?"

Jaw click thingie in progress. Yeah, mad didn't cover it. His jaw was so tight that I could actually see the vein pulsing in his temple.

I shifted restlessly in my seat. I was way too keyed up, and the caveman tactics should have simmered me down.

Not so much.

Two shots of adrenaline and I couldn't settle. One at our show, and the other on that tiny stage. I didn't get behind the mic very often. I was happy in the back on my keyboards, but Halsey's lyrics had been buzzing under my skin all week.

I should have asked Quinn to take me to the little hole in the wall. I just couldn't take the chance that he'd have said no. It was better to beg forgiveness than ask for permission.

I was pretty sure Indie was going to stamp that on my wardrobe trunk. I was always disappearing on her. The lure to explore was always there. Add in the shine of live music and I couldn't resist.

I'd tried to, but there hadn't been a single incident. I was so tired of putting my life on hold.

I looked out the window as Chicago passed me by. We took the Quinn route home. Back streets, side alleys, on and off the highways, but this time he seemed to be taking longer than usual. We skipped past our exit and turned off into a residential area. I frowned as he pulled up to a brownstone.

"Where are we?"

"My place."

"What?" I scrambled out of the car after him. Well, that made sense why he knew the streets so well, but then again he always seemed to have an innate sense of direction that I so didn't have.

He glanced down the block and held his arm out. "Inside." He dug out his phone and typed furiously. He shoved his phone back in his pocket and went to a keypad at the door. The door buzzed and opened. He held open the door for me, and I rushed through.

The hallway smelled of beeswax and lemons. I followed him up the stairs, my fingers trailing over the silky, polished banister. When we got to the top, he twisted a rosette in the upper right corner of the old door and the fleur de lis came off. He took a key out of it and replaced the small wooden piece.

"Did you tell people where we are?"

"Yeah, I contacted the security team."

I took in the room. Tall windows were unadorned, leaving shadows and moonlight to make a grid pattern over the hardwood floors. He walked through the dining room and finally turned on a light in the kitchen.

The house felt empty. Everything was pristine, and the lemon and beeswax scent carried into the living space. He came back into the room with a bottle of wine and two glasses.

"So, we're going from hate fuck to romance?"

"No."

"Just *no*?"

"We need to have a talk."

I crossed my arms, cupping my elbows against the chill. "Why did we need to come here?" My heels clicked on the hardwood as I paced in front of the fireplace.

"I needed a secure place to take you."

"And the hotel isn't?"

He reached under the shade of a lamp and snapped it on. "It's fine. I just can't have eyes and ears on us right now."

I swallowed. "Because you're going to kill me and bury the body in the basement?"

His eyebrow rose. "Tempting."

"Funny."

He poured half a glass and downed it in two gulps. I was pretty sure the only time I'd ever seen him drink had been at our going away dinner with Devon. He filled the glass this time, then mine, and stalked up and down the long room.

I reached for my glass and took a sip. It was much bolder than what I was used to. Good, just a lot richer. I sat on the couch and waited him out.

Patience wasn't exactly my strong suit, but I had a feeling keeping my mouth shut was definitely a good game plan. He didn't talk, just kept pacing. "Okay, you're officially freaking me out."

He finished the second glass and put it down. "Tell me, Miss Keystone, what do you think we're doing?"

My eyebrows shot up. *Miss Keystone?* "We're working together —sort of."

What the hell were we to each other? I ached for his touch, reached for him in the night, in the morning. Even now with the anger lighting him up like a storm in the desert, I wanted to touch him. I wanted the burn coming off him in waves.

"Right. I think my role may have gotten lost in this relationship. You seem to think that my rules are subject to interpretation."

My heart stalled. "I've been following them."

"Really? Tonight?"

"It was just—well, one time."

"That's all it takes. Just one time."

"There hasn't been one peep out of this psycho. She probably crawled back into whatever hole she was in before."

"Because that's how kidnappers work?" His hands were at his sides, not clenched. Still, the little hairs on my neck were freaking the hell out. "You know this how?"

I stood. "Wouldn't she have done something by now?"

"What if she's been doing something this whole time?"

"Like what?"

He crossed his arms. "You don't think it's crazy you get a package from a fan every month?"

"Not you too. You've made Devon all paranoid now. Did she put you up to this?"

Quinn spun his phone onto the coffee table in front of me. "It starts with little things. A book you spoke about, a handmade scrapbook, a shirt you mentioned in an interview, a ring that made her think of you."

"I don't know if they're from a *her*. The packages are never signed."

He tapped the home button on his phone and slid it in front of me. "How about this?"

I frowned and picked up his cell. There were a bunch of images in a gallery. I opened one. "It's a setlist. So what? We throw them out into the crowd after shows. People like them as keepsakes of the concert." I handed him back the phone.

"Look closer."

I sighed and opened another file. Then another. The date was scrawled across the top, as was the venue. "Seattle, Spokane, Boise, Billings… These are in order."

"Notice anything else?"

"That your screen is absurdly small."

"Magnify it, Faith."

My hand shook a little, but I tapped on the picture. My name was in the corner. Smudges of ink and dirt from taping it on the floor, but it was the perfect block letters in the margin with notes and arrows that dried my mouth. I opened them one by one. Every single one had notes about improving a song, changing one out, demands for longer solos.

I placed the phone on the desk.

"You don't think this is a bit over the line?"

I stood up. Nerves jangled under my skin and a sheen of sweat popped up on the back of my neck. "Of course it is, but it's not a threat."

His light blue eyes flashed. "I'd call it intent."

I swallowed. "If you brought it to a cop, what would they do?"

"Nothing. Because the boxes come from mail centers all over Manhattan. They're unmarked and unsigned."

I brushed by him to stand in front of the fireplace.

He came up behind me and settled his hands on my shoulders. "I know you want to believe the best in people, but not everyone is harmless."

I lifted my eyes to meet his in the mirror. "Devon tried to show me these, but I put her off. Before you took over my life, I barely paid attention to the packages. I swear, I have like five of them in my closet unopened."

His nostrils flared.

"I just didn't think—"

"No, you didn't." He turned me around to face him. "I know you believe it's paranoia talking, but I really think this is the same person. It's what my gut says."

"You can't know that." My voice was little more than a whisper. I could barely hear myself above the heartbeat thundering in my ears.

"I don't. I just know that following my gut has saved me more times than I can count. I'm not going to ignore this, not when it comes to you. I need more proof, and I'm going to find this woman, but I need you to help me. I can't do my job if you're undermining the operation because you're bored."

I winced. "It sounds so awful when you say it like that."

His voice was cool and almost detached. Almost. But I heard the rage simmering in the quiet. "You think I like being the bad guy? But you pay me to look at the shadows and the ugly parts of this world."

My father *paid* him. My chest constricted. Mustn't forget that he was with me because he had to be.

So much truth in one evening.

The notes and presents from my fan had always been sweet. I'd even thanked him or her on our YouTube channel and showed off some of the items.

I closed my eyes.

Had I deepened the focus?

"This is my fault."

"Absolutely not." He cupped my face. "But that sweet nature of yours can make people believe anything is possible."

I sniffed and pulled out my phone. "I didn't even think about it. I used to do video blogs all the time. Little things to thank the fans. We've been so busy I haven't been able to do them much lately." I kept scrolling and finally found it. "Here. My Secret Admirer." I pushed my cell into his hand and crossed the room to pick up my wine again.

I tipped back the glass and swallowed all of it, refilling my glass as my chirpy voice laughed through a video, gushing about the gifts I'd received so far.

Had I inadvertently made this person believe they were even more important?

"I'm sending this to Lucy to look at. Maybe she can check out the code and see who's visited the site. A repeat offender that can't stop watching it, maybe."

"Yeah, maybe." I wandered to the window and watched the trees sway in the light breeze. Right now, I actually missed my back patio, and my lemon trees—even if glass had just as much fear attached to it as anything else these days. I never knew who was watching anymore.

If this super fan had been to all my shows lately, had she been watching me other times of the day?

Had she seen me with Quinn?

Would she hurt him?

I pressed my forehead to the cool window.

"Faith?"

I took a step back. "Yeah, yeah. I know. Get away from the glass."

He came up behind me, his eyes so dark and intense. "No, actually you're safe here. My house was one of the prototypes for the Carson glass I told you about."

"The same stuff that's getting installed at my house soon?"

"The same."

I shuddered. Safe. Not on display. I'd never really worried about it before. I'd spent most of my adult life in the spotlight—it had always been my normal. But it felt different now. Shadows felt darker, and the lights felt intrusive. I was able to ignore most of my current reality on stage, but now that she might be at every show, I wasn't sure how I was going to handle it.

He slid an arm around me and caught my hand, bringing it up to the glass. He spread his fingers between mine so we both touched the coolness. "I know I scared you tonight."

His warm skin seeped into mine. I didn't realize just how cold I'd been until now. "Guess we're even. I probably scared the hell out of you by disappearing."

"Understatement." His other arm looped around my hip, his thumb brushing over my belly chain.

I rolled my head against his chest. "I hate this, Quinn."

"I know, babe."

I couldn't stop a smile. He used my name almost exclusively. He didn't seem to be a nickname person like I was. But every once in awhile that one slipped out. Usually when he wasn't quite awake. "Can we have that make-up sex now?"

"What if I'm still mad at you?"

I covered his hand on my hip and slid it up to my breast. "Be mad later. Touch me now."

He flipped the cup of my bra up and plucked at my nipple. The window was like a mirror with the night behind it and the soft light at our backs. "I'm not sure I have gentle in me yet."

I groaned as I watched the pink flush to a darker rose with every tug. His hand was large and tanned with little silvery scars hatching his fingers in odd little spots. A man's hand. No part of him was soft.

But I didn't want the soft, or the sweet. Not really.

I just wanted him.

He watched us in the glass, his eyes hooded as he took my other hand and put it against the window. "Keep them there, Faith."

I shivered at his dominant tone. The fact that this voice could piss me off and turn me on was wrong on a number of levels. He left the bra flipped up, and my shirt shoved up against my neck. He dragged his lips and stubbled chin along my ribs to my spine and followed the dip to my ass as he crouched behind me.

He traced the chain around my belly with his middle finger from each hand, then came back to the middle, under my navel, and flicked open the three buttons of my hip-hugging jeans.

His breath fanned along the cleft of my ass as he pulled them and my thong down and off.

"I can smell the stage on you." He nudged my legs apart and licked my inner thigh just under the curve of my ass.

I swallowed hard.

He smoothed his palm over each cheek and opened me with his thumbs. "Peaches and Faith."

My breathing was shallow. My thighs shook as I waited for him to touch me. My pulse filled my brain, my heart was trying to leap out of my chest. He was crouched behind me, silent, waiting.

"Quinn."

I was going mad.

I stared at myself in the window. Lost. Wild. Trembling on the edge of something I was too afraid to name.

A light, cool breeze kissed my overheated skin.

Breath.

His.

On me.

My fingertips went white around my lilac nail polish.

Then finally there was his mouth. His tongue as harsh as sandpaper on my oversensitive skin. He went deeper, touched everything, and sipped.

No—he drank.

God, I was so wet. My face flushed red at the way my body reacted. I flooded his mouth, heard the groans as he teased and tormented. He drew his knuckle through my slick folds to my clit and circled endlessly, patiently, and relentlessly.

My thigh shook as everything inside me clenched and released. We were alone, there was no one across the hall, no one on the other side of us. Thank fuck because I could hear the screams above the roar in my head.

That couldn't be good for the neighbors.

And I didn't care.

I dropped my face between my outstretched arms as I raised my hips to get away from his greedy mouth. I couldn't take any more. Every atom felt as if it was going to fly apart. He didn't stop. His tongue and fingers wrought damage. The kind I enjoyed even as I knew I might not survive it.

Finally he stood, his chin damp as he stared at me in the glass. He reached around me and yanked me back against him, driving two fingers into me as he jerked at his pants.

"Hurry." I took one hand off the glass and he growled into my ear. I put my palm back on the cool window with a moan.

I moaned again when his fingers retreated. *No.* I needed him inside me. The telltale crinkle flooded my blood with euphoria.

Yes. Yes, inside me.

I must have said it out loud because his voice rang in my ears. "Fuck, yes."

Then he lifted me on my toes with the force of his thrust. I was so ready for him. I wanted this Quinn. The one that was a little too harsh, missing the gentle entirely.

"Harder," I said.

He slammed into me and my teeth rattled. So full. So much Quinn. So much mine.

He drew my hands together on the window, lacing his fingers in between until we were twisted. His other arm held me steady, his fingertips circling, ever circling as he destroyed me.

Branded me from the inside out.

My nails dug into his fingers, into my own, my muscles clenched as I sobbed out his name.

My forehead fell forward on our tangled fingers as I took each stroke. He was so much taller than me and the angle was tough on him, but he didn't relent. I reached onto my toes as much as I could until my calves cramped and my spine buzzed for mercy.

I didn't want it, though.

God, I didn't want mercy. I'd never felt this alive.

Finally he drew back and spun me around, wrapping my legs around him as he walked us toward the fireplace and the leather bench in front of it.

"We have a thing for benches."

He laughed, his teeth and tongue scraping over my neck. He sat down with me astride him, fully seated inside me. "Oh, wow." I rolled my hips and the veins in his neck bulged.

There.

He gritted his teeth and plunged deeper. Distraction threatened to take me under, back to the mindless place where I took and took. It was so easy to fall into that blackness of pleasure and let my body just ride his storm.

I wanted to be his storm.

I wanted to watch him go blind. Because of this. Because of *us.*

I tipped my hips forward. I cried out at how deep he was, how he filled every empty place inside of me. Places I didn't know were there. I curled my arms around his neck, slid my fingers into his hair and rode him.

Staring into his eyes as I took him again and again.

I watched him lose it, his icy blue gaze so fierce as he tried to hold out. He grasped my hips as he pulsed inside of me. The groan wrenched out of him as I squeezed around him. As I watched him come for me.

So beautifully savage.

So much mine.

31

QUINN

"MERCY. UNCLE. ALL OF THE WHITE FLAGS."

I grinned as she crawled away from me on the bed. I'd rented out my house for so long I couldn't remember the last time I'd slept in this bed.

Of course, we really hadn't done any sleeping.

I dragged her back under me and slipped my hand between the mattress and her slick thighs. Wet from me, wet from us, and so very wet from the string of orgasms I'd dragged out of her.

Still, it wasn't enough.

I'd hoped that if I made her scream my name all night I could get the burning insanity out of my chest.

Sex I could do. I was good at figuring out what pleased a woman and going after it like a tactical mission. I knew exactly what to do for Faith. Watching her break for me was addictive.

Breaking for her...yeah. Not so much.

I'd made my mission for the rest of the night to leave her in a trembling heap. Maybe then she'd think twice about ditching me for a fucking concert.

I rolled us both to the side and dragged the head of my cock along her pussy. I looked down at us, her skin rose pink and swollen as she took me inside of her. I groaned, rolling my hips until my shaft scraped along her walls and I felt her quake.

I drew my fingers down where we were joined. So fucking wet for me.

She reached up between us and anchored her hand in my hair. I stroked up and down her body. Belly to breast and up to her neck, then back around. I couldn't stop touching her.

I couldn't let go.

Finally all the times I'd denied myself to watch her go over had been one too many. She rolled into a ball, trapping my hand against her. As if that would stop me. I was high off the number of times she'd waffled between Warden and my name as I stroked her clit and thrust inside of her.

She wrapped herself around my arm as I curled around her and finally let go. I buried my head into the back of her damp neck and breathed through the searing release. She fisted around me, her cries finally turning to hiccupping shudders.

I held onto her, gentled my touch and kissed her neck, her jaw, her mouth. When I slid out of her, she twisted in my arms, her face in my neck, her body still tight.

I stroked her back until she unfurled, until I heard her breathing ease and finally until she drifted off.

I was so very fucked. I knew I was too close to her, but I couldn't find the distance I needed. I wasn't sure I'd ever be able to find it. That scared me most of all.

What if I wasn't enough to protect her?

That last gift she'd received went beyond fan adulation. Profiling courses had been offered as part of the training with Aidan's team. How to spot a threat and devise a way to protect our client was one thing, but there were a number of stalking cases that Roth Defense took care of in their bodyguard unit.

I didn't generally work those. My specialty was long term defense for dignitaries, and the elite rich. They often required my tactical background. I had no real defense for the psychology of obsession.

Especially when each clue seemed to point closer to someone whose focus went way beyond addiction and adoration. The fan going to every show told me she or he didn't have a regular day job, but she or he also had the fiscal ability to travel and pay for tickets.

I'd seen the prices for Hammered's tickets. Not exactly on the cheap end of the spectrum. Sure, they could pay for the bargain lawn seats at the outdoor venues, but that wouldn't get them near the front of the house where the setlists were.

Especially since eighty percent of the physical copies had been labeled *Keys*. Worrisome didn't cover it.

I held on to her as the night turned to the pearl gray of morning. I hated to wake her, but we needed to get back to the hotel and get ready to leave for the next city.

The next few weeks would consist of arrowing toward New York and my old stomping grounds. I managed to go home for most holidays, but an impromptu visit home was tempting.

Faith would need to be with me.

The idea of her meeting my folks was a little nerve-racking. Especially since I had no way to turn off my feelings around her, and my mother was a damn hawk.

She'd figure it out.

But if I was in the area and I didn't go home—well, there was no way I'd be forgiven. Ever.

It was going to be a rough few weeks.

Faith seemed to understand that she was going to be on a short leash, but I knew she wasn't going to make it easy.

Why would it be easy anyway?

I pressed a kiss to her forehead and massaged the base of her skull.

She groaned into my neck. "No."

"Time to go. There's going to be hell to catch when we get back."

She sighed. "I already have five angry texts on my phone from last night."

"Your people care about you."

"I know. I have learned my lesson. Mostly."

I propped myself on my elbow. "All the way."

"There will be whining."

"I figured."

She wrinkled her nose at me. "Those shows are how I broke the monotony of touring."

"Guess I'll just have to find other ways to do that."

She dragged her sheet up and sat cross-legged. "I'll be holding you to that."

"Why don't you make me playlists then. Your...what do you call it? Jukebox brain?"

Faith grinned. The pure happiness in her face, was like a punch to the solar plexus. "I get to play teacher?"

I rolled out of bed and stood. "Don't get so excited."

"Oh, no. This is awesome. I shall school you by genre." She rolled onto her knees, holding the sheet over her breasts as she inched across the bed. She reached up and put her hands on my chest, her eyes sparkling as the sheet slipped.

I groaned and lowered myself to her level. She curled her arms around my neck, giggling when I extricated her from the sheet and into my arms. "Shower."

"Wait. Need my iPod." She made grabby hands for her bag.

What did I get myself into?

The shower consisted of three songs from Metallica and a dissertation about the difference between mullet-rock and heavy metal. I had to admit her way of explaining things was hilarious.

"Have you thought of doing a podcast with this stuff?"

Her blue eyes got wider. "You think anyone would care?"

"You made me care. I had no idea Lemmy from Motorhead was so very important to metal."

"Yes, but you're humoring me to keep me *and* you sane."

I tucked a towel closed at my hip. "Don't forget the want-to-keep-you-naked thing."

"Can't forget that." She fluffed her hair with a towel.

"Honestly, a podcast or something similar would keep you from getting bored."

"You're correct." She went onto her toes and kissed me. "Such a smart guy sometimes."

It was probably the best thing I'd ever come up with.

She threw herself into the idea wholeheartedly. By the time we returned to the hotel, she had a schedule of recordings and about twenty people who had already agreed to do a vidchat with her.

She was mildly terrifying in her ability to get people to do what she asked.

Myself included.

She sat up as we passed a strip mall on our way back to the hotel. "Can we just—"

"No."

She sighed. "I need a notebook. Just the drugstore right there. No big. See?"

I pulled in. "Only because it seems to be empty."

"That's because it's six in the morning, but yay for twenty-four hour drugstores."

I opened my door and went around to her side of the car. I hustled her inside. She made a beeline for the candy.

"Faith."

"It's on the way to the office stuff." She plucked a bag of Starbursts off the shelf as well as a bag of peanut M&M's. She jogged down the end of the aisle to the back of the store. I lengthened my stride as she snatched up two notebooks and a package of pens in pinks and purples.

She spun around, her arms full. "Okay. Ready."

There was no way to take them from her without upending the pile, so I led her to the front with my hand at her back. She dumped her loot on the counter and chatted happily with the woman checking her out.

Five minutes later, we were in the car and she was happily scribbling in her large block print. She was so engrossed that she didn't notice as we arrived at the hotel.

"Faith."

"Can you just leave me in the car?"

"No."

"Meh." She stuffed her pens and the rest back into her bag, but left the smaller notebook out.

"You have to pay attention to your surroundings."

She looked up from writing and walking, her eyes unfocused. She was already gone into some other dimension where music ruled her brain. "Right." She closed the notebook and held it against her chest. "Let's go."

I honestly wished I'd had the idea sooner. Talk about making my life easier.

We got on to the elevator and back up to our floor. Indie and Patrick were running herd on the rest of the band.

The door to her room shut behind her as she stood in the hall with her hands on her hips. "Faith Elizabeth Keystone."

Faith hunched her shoulders. "She's more intimidating than my mother," she said out of the side of her mouth.

"She's fairly terrifying."

"That's why she's our den mother. Don't tell her I said that."

I schooled my features as Indie stalked down the hall, dragging her suitcase behind her.

She stopped in from of Faith. "What the hell were you thinking?" Then she looked up at me. "And you—not bringing her back last night? What the hell kind of bodyguard are you?"

I tried to swallow down the idea that I was being scolded by a woman who was a foot shorter than me and weighed in at just over a hundred pounds. "I took her to a safe location, ma'am."

She dropped her voice. "I know you two are more than bodyguard and client, but honestly, if you pull this shit again, you won't have to worry about this crazy fan. I'll kill you myself. Got it?"

"Understood."

She pushed by us. "We leave in ten. If you're not in the Escalades, your ass will have to find your own way to Maryland."

"See?" Faith looked up at me. "And you think you're scary."

"I heard that!"

"I love you, Indie," Faith called after her.

"Love me on the plane, Keys." She got on the elevator and stared down the hallway at us. "I already had to chew through a sleeve of Tums because of you two," she said before the doors closed.

I cleared my throat. "We should get our bags."

"Yeah. Good idea."

32

KEYS

THE NEXT FEW WEEKS WERE A WHIRLWIND. WE TOURED UP THE EAST Coast and there wasn't a peep out of my would-be stalker. The podcast was a success. I'd tapped every source I had in Ripper Records.

Jazz Duffy had spent the last week with me doing a nightly hangout online. We broke the internet twice. Our podcast was lighting up YouTube and iTunes. We even added it to our band site as a new feature.

It was honestly the only thing that kept me from going insane. I tried to get Quinn to take me out to a few shows on our days off—anything to kill the monotony, but he was holding firm.

He didn't want to take any chances. The warden was in full effect. He was constantly on the computer or his phone. His eyes were tired, and his mood was mercurial at best.

Every time I caught him talking to Lucy, I knew it was going to be one of the nights I left him alone. Their hacker wonder girl was getting just as frustrated as Quinn. She couldn't find a digital footprint anywhere for the packages. And I hadn't gotten one yet for the end of September. We were already into the first week of October.

Each night we came together in a clash of sweat and soul-bleeding passion. The more impatient and frustrated he was, the more times he looked for me in the night. I had a feeling tonight would leave me in an exhausted heap by morning.

I couldn't say I minded it, but I couldn't get him to talk anything through. He said it was because he didn't have news to share, but I had a feeling it was more than that.

I rolled across the bed, flicking through my phone to find anything to entertain me. Another night trapped in the hotel room, waiting for Quinn to finally close his computer.

Owen and Zach had escaped to an amusement park since we were outside of New Jersey. We had two days in the refurbished Giants stadium. The only problem was we had a night off in between.

Everyone was gone, doing something fun and I was under hotel arrest. I rolled onto my stomach and flipped open my laptop. I tabbed through our YouTube comments and answered a few questions, ignored the trolls, and created a poll on our Facebook page.

The watery clunk of a Skype call notification made me perk up. I hit the accept button and grinned as Devon's face filled the screen. "What's up, slut?"

"Hi, Dev." I smiled automatically at her greeting, then glanced up at the time stamp. Even by Pacific time standards, it was way past her bedtime. "What are you doing up so late?" Devon was one of those freaks who actually liked the daytime.

"Let me ask you a question."

I rolled onto my side, propping my head up with my hand. "Okay. Shoot."

"First of all—does Quinn's boss grow these bodyguard dudes especially fine or something?"

I laughed. "Not that I'm aware of."

"Well, you know I'm kinda the way station for these guys. Like they cut their teeth on little ole me."

A prick of guilt settled between my shoulders. "I know you've had a lot of different guys in the house. I'm sorry about that."

She shook her head. "Oh, no—it's awesome. As I said, the eyecandy is obscene. Like the guy who's staying with me this week? Holy Thor. The dude is huge and built like a god."

"Did you get him to sit for a sketch?"

"No. But good plan." Her green eyes sparkled. "I like it."

I snickered.

"Okay, so then I kinda forgot to get the mail this week. I was hip-deep in this huge triptych painting of the Cliffs of Moor."

"Can I see?"

"When it's done."

Disappointment cut deep. Damn artist. "Meh. You suck."

"No, I believe it's you who sucks. Are you bored or something? Figure you're going to drive me crazy with catalogs? You're killing a lot of trees."

"What the hell are you talking about?" I swung my feet up as I rolled onto my stomach.

Devon reached off camera. "What the hell is this?" She fanned out a dozen catalogs in front of the lens. She peeked around the thick electronics catalog with a quirked eyebrow. "Since when did you even know what to do with a motherboard, let alone how to build one from scratch?" She flipped through them. "And man, do you really need toys like this?" She held up a leather bondage magazine.

"I did not order those." I leaned forward. "Is that a gimp mask?"

"Yeah. It's scary. There's stuff in this magazine that actually makes me want to burn it. Like bonfire-on-the-deck burn it."

"I swear I didn't do that." A tickle of unease grew in my stomach. "Did you get anything else from Frances the fan?"

"Actually, no. Which is weird since it's already the third."

"One sec." I rolled off the bed and padded to the door. "Warden?"

He looked over his shoulder. "I'm in the middle—" He stood up. "What happened?"

I nibbled on my lower lip. "It might be nothing."

"Trust your instincts."

I went back into our bedroom and came back with my laptop. I set it on his desk. "Dev? Is your Roth guy there?"

"Yeah." Her eyes went from playful to hesitant. "Well, crap." She sat up and crossed her legs.

I gave Quinn a quick recap, with a few extra embellishments from Devon, and his jaw tightened with every word. "Devon, can you—"

"Already on it." She disappeared from the screen.

"How many days has this been happening?"

I shrugged. "Devon slipped into artist mode, but since it's the third, I'd bet money they started right around the end of the month."

He picked up his phone and I lost him to Aidan, Lucy, and some other tech person who was forever mining my sites for some elusive data that I didn't understand.

Yet again, I was officially tossed out of the loop.

The rest of the night was lost to hacker talk and speculation. The latest part of the investigation involved checking the labels on the magazines to figure out if they were requested online or by some other service.

It seemed to be a mix of different ways. Some right in store—like the scary dominatrix stuff—and some through regular mailing list signups on websites. It caused a flurry of actions for the next few days.

I focused on the shows and tried to keep a lid on the hope that something was actually happening to end this friggin' nightmare. But as with everything else, it seemed to be a dead end.

We had ten dates left on the tour and the first blast of cool night air was putting a damper on the lawn tickets for the Saratoga, New York show. But New Yorkers were a hearty bunch.

Personally, I was ready for a parka. I rubbed my hands together and held them over the radiator in our room. Quinn was checking the rear of the hotel. We'd decided to stay in downtown Saratoga in one of the older mansions that had been converted to a hotel.

Quinn was being really weird. Distracted, and spending even more time on his phone than usual. Usually he didn't care when I listened in about what was going on with the stalker, but he kept shooing me away.

I was ready to kick his ass.

I peeked out the window at the busy main street. People were walking around in hoodies and lightweight jackets. There was so much greenery around even in October. Huge oak trees that weren't quite changed over, dogs on leashes everywhere, and shop owners even had water stations out for them. The town actually looked like a postcard.

I turned a the knock on the door.

"Keys?"

I crossed to open the door. Owen stood in the doorway, decked out in denim, leather, and his bling. "What are you doing here? I thought you were going to the Racino for some concert."

"Aye. Fuckin' Gin Blossoms. I didn't even know they were still together."

I grinned. "That'll probably be fun."

"Right? I wish you were coming. I miss my concert buddy."

I let him in. "I know. Believe me, I'm jonesing so hard."

"Quinn sent me up to get you. We're having dinner in the dining hall. They put together some spread for us." He waggled his eyebrows. "Evidently this is kind of their off season. Horse racing or some shit."

I frowned. "Yeah. Quinn mentioned something about that. I think his folks might live around here."

"Huh. That's why he seemed to know everything about the area. I never know if it's just because he's playing super-bodyguard or if he actually has been to these places."

I crossed my arms and tucked my cold fingers into the warm pockets I'd made. "Tell me about it."

"Are you wearing that?"

I looked down at my jeans and *Supernatural* sweatshirt. "Is dinner formal?"

"Everyone's all fancy." He shot his French cuffs. "See? Fancy."

I rolled my eyes. "Give me five."

I didn't do fancy. I ducked into the bathroom and put on some quick makeup, exchanged my sweatshirt for an Aerosmith T-shirt, red flannel, and my heavy leather jacket. I swapped out my Chucks for a pair of black knee-high boots with a wedge.

"Better?"

"Damn, girl. I wish all women got ready like you did. Especially with those results." He whistled.

I punched him in the arm. "Behave."

He draped his arm over my shoulder. "Where's the fun in that?"

I was so tired of being safe. And even more tired of not having fun. Maybe the band getting together for dinner would put me in a better mood.

We met Wyatt and Hunter in the hall. "Guess it must be some spread tonight if we even got you to stick around, Wyatt."

"I'm escaping to the speedway, actually. I didn't realize they had one near here." He'd swapped out his suit for dark jeans and a thermal shirt and heavy flannel.

"Guess we're all going to be busy tonight," I said. I left out the "except me" so no one would feel sorry for me.

We walked down the staircase to what used to be a grand ballroom. The floors gleamed, and sconces were lit. There was a banquet table set up and the rest of the crew and band were settled in. I looked around for Quinn, but didn't see him.

I raided the plate of rolls and dished up a bowl of stew from the huge iron pot. I wandered over to the table and picked at it as everyone laughed and talked around me. The hostess of the hotel was bustling around, completely charmed by my guys.

I knew they were hoping for special treatment and food—con artists all of them.

"Faith."

I turned, a crusty wedge of bread halfway to my mouth. I dropped it into the gravy. Whoa. I put down my bowl and picked up my napkin. Wasn't sure if I'd need it for the food or drool.

Quinn stood at the edge of the dining room in heavy cargos with a wide belt with a chain wallet. He wore thick motorcycle boots and a heavy leather jacket that made his wide shoulders look even more massive. He wore a gray thermal shirt under the jacket with a silver chain winking from his neck.

Yeah, it was definitely drool.

I stood up. "Wow."

He held up his hand, a black helmet outstretched to me. "Want to go for a ride?"

"Holy crap, yes." I crossed the room and snatched the helmet from him. "Is this what I think it is?"

"Thought I'd show you around. You've been cooped up for weeks."

I grabbed him by the heavily zippered lapels of his jacket and dragged him down to kiss him. "We're going out?"

He nodded. "We're going out."

I looked over my shoulder and saw the thumbs up from Owen. I grinned at him and did a little dance around in a circle.

33

QUINN

I CLASPED HER HAND IN MINE, AND DREW HER OUT THE BACK DOOR. My nerves quadrupled in my chest. Taking her to my folks' farm, and then to a concert seemed like a huge gamble. I'd had her on complete lockdown for weeks. Nothing. Not even anything to go on with the crazy array of catalogs that had started coming to her house.

They made me uneasy, but I didn't know if they were something to truly worry about. I couldn't figure out this elusive stalker's game. I was convinced it was the same woman that had tried to take Faith at Hunter's wedding. I had shit for proof, but it just seemed way too coincidental.

But tonight, I just needed to let us be us.

I didn't know what was going to happen after the tour. I wouldn't leave her side, but I couldn't keep up this double life crap either. She was far too important to me for that.

Important enough that I was going to show her where I came from.

Her mouth dropped open when she saw my bike. "Are you kidding me?"

"I had one of the hands drive it in from my folks' place."

"You keep this at your parents' farm?"

I shrugged. "Not really something I can take with me when I'm living on the estates of my clients. Nor do I really have time to ride." I pulled her in front of me and took the helmet. "But I think we need some fun. I don't know if meeting my parents is fun or not, but if you wa—"

"Yes." I set it on her head and pushed down. Her blue eyes were huge. "All the way yes. I gotta see where you come from."

"It's not that impressive." I cinched her chin-strap.

"Don't care."

I flipped her visor down. "Here we go." I got on the bike and kicked up the stand. I put on my helmet and groaned when she slid on behind me. "Been on a bike before?"

"Oh, yeah. Plenty." I didn't like the idea of her on the back of anyone else's bike, but when she hugged my middle I let it go. "Fast. Go very fast."

I pulled onto the main drag and went north. The lanes narrowed to two, and the wind pulled at me. I hit the throttle and we tore down the winding roads.

She screeched behind me and held on. I heard her laugh and it was one of the sweetest sounds I've ever heard. She laughed so easily that it was very apparent when she wasn't happy. And I knew the last few weeks had been hard to bear.

The sun slipped behind the hills as we came upon my parents' farm. The horses were being led in before dark, but I'd timed it so she could at least see them from afar.

Her nails dug into my belly as we slowed and puttered to a stop at the main barn.

She tore off her helmet and her huge blue eyes were dazzled. "What was that about not impressive?"

I took her helmet with a laugh. "By Saratoga standards, we're small potatoes." I waved to the hands corralling the quarter horses.

"This is awesome." She turned around, her gaze eating up everything.

I took her hand. "We don't have much time to stay."

"Aww, why?" Her eyebrows lowered. "We don't have to be back right away. This is probably the safest place ever."

"You're right. So, I should kill the surprise."

"This isn't my surprise?"

"Nope."

Her grin spread. "Now, I'm even more intrigued."

I followed the path to the main house and up the stairs. I'd only given my mother a few hours' head start. When I opened the door, I took in a deep breath. "Bless her. I figured she'd cook my favorite if I mentioned I was coming in."

She tipped her head sniffing the air. "Are those peaches?"

"My mom makes the best peach cobbler ever."

"Quinn?"

I took a deep breath and brought Faith through the kitchen door. "Hi, Ma."

"Oh, it's been so long." She rushed over to me and folded me into her arms. She smelled like the outdoors and violets, just like always. "You did not warn me there was company." She looked around the house. "I could murder you."

I grinned. "I didn't want you to go to any trouble."

"You don't bring girls home."

Faith wound her arm into mine. "Yeah well, he didn't give me any warning that I was going to meet his mom." She held her hand out. "We're even. I'm Faith Keystone."

"What a pretty name. Ellis!" She called over her shoulder. Then turned back to Faith. "I'm Maggie Alexander."

"Cripes, Magz. I'm in the living room, not the barn." My dad came into the room. His weathered face stretched with a smile. "Q Ball."

Faith looked up at me. "Q Ball?"

I gave my dad a look. "Thanks, Dad."

He shrugged and hauled me in for a hug. "I can't help it if you decided it was a good idea to play pool shark with the ranch hands."

My dad looked down at Faith. "He swindled all of them. They came to the farm and held him down, shaved his head. It was dead of winter and he was white as hell."

Her lips quirked up. "Q Ball indeed."

"Now that we got the embarrassing stories out of the way. Faith, this is my dad, Ellis."

"Pleased to meet a pretty girl." My dad took her hand and settled her at the table. "Now, we need to know all about you."

I tried not to sink into the floorboards as my parents threw me under the bus left and right. At least my sister was overseas or she'd be doing it far worse. I did get peach cobbler out of the deal, so the night was only mildly horrifying.

Faith was completely enchanted.

While my father was telling her more embarrassing stories, I cleared the table and went into the kitchen to help clean up. My mother was elbows deep in suds when I came in with another stack.

"She's amazing, Quinn."

My chest tightened. "Yeah. She really is."

She scrubbed a plate and spared me a glance. "Is she the girl you've been protecting?"

I slipped the pile of dishes into the sink and lightly pushed my mom to the side. "You can dry."

"I'll take it. I always have to dishes," she said with a smile and picked up a towel.

"She's Noah's friend."

My mom frowned. "What kind of friend?"

"Ma. I'm not dumb enough to go there."

"Not again?"

"You know it wasn't like that with Lissa."

"Your sister was convinced there was some torrid affair going on there."

I frowned. "God, no."

"But there is with this girl?"

I sighed. "Affair isn't the right word."

"Okay, what would you call it?"

"Terrifying." I hadn't meant to say that. It just sort of popped out of my mouth.

She tipped her head back and laughed. "Oh, took you long enough."

"This isn't good. Being involved with a client is bad enough, but…" *Being in love with her was far, far worse.*

Fuck.

So much worse.

"It was bound to happen sometime. You don't get to see anyone besides clients."

"Yeah, well, it's very ill advised. Aidan's going to skin me alive. And Noah? Christ—pardon, Mom."

She inclined her head. "It's all right."

"This girl is family to Noah. I can't let anything happen to her." I cleared my throat. "Not like last time."

"That wasn't your fault, and you know it."

I fished around for another plate and scrubbed it until it squeaked. "I know. I just can't get clear of it." I gripped the side of the sink. I woke every night in a cold sweat, reaching for her. I had to be inside her and around her just to remind myself she was safe and there with me.

The end of the tour was barreling at us like a runaway train, and I was no closer to an answer about anything. How I was going to protect her? How I was going to figure out who this phantom girl was? And more importantly, how the hell I was going to tell Faith how I felt?

My mom gripped my arm. "It's scary to love someone even when it's just a normal relationship. I was the same with your father. I didn't know if I wanted to spend my life on a horse farm in the middle of nowhere. The first year we got married we had the worst winter in the northeast. We lost three of our horses, and almost lost the whole damn place."

I looked down at her. "I didn't know that."

"Of course not. It was our problem to deal with long before you and your sister came along. The important part of that story is that we all have tough times. Maybe this is yours."

I frowned. "She's pretty headstrong."

"Good. You won't roll over her like a freaking bulldozer."

"Gee thanks."

"You're a very forthright young man."

"Is that the nice way of saying pigheaded and stubborn?"

Her eyes crinkled at the corners. "Don't forget blunt."

I laughed and kissed her temple. "Thanks, Ma. I don't know how the hell I'm going to figure this out, but I'm glad I stopped in to talk."

"Me too." She set a plate into the cabinet. "You'll make me very pretty grand babies."

"Oh, God." I didn't really want to go there. I couldn't go there.

"Can I help?"

I spun around to find Faith in the doorway. How long had she been there? I cleared my throat and took the last plate out of the suds and rinsed it. "All done. Besides, we have to get going to the concert."

"Concert?"

The way she lit up would never get old. She was excited about every damn thing. "My bad, didn't I mention we were going to a show tonight?"

Her eyes widened. "Are we going with guys to Gin Blossoms?"

"No."

"Oh." She nibbled on her bottom lip. "Who are we going to see?" She came further into the room when I didn't answer. "Who?" She dug into my ribs and I couldn't defend myself.

"Hey!"

My mother laughed as Faith dragged me away from the sink and shook me. "Tell me!"

"It's a surprise."

She glanced at my mom. "Your son is a masochist."

"You got him to willingly go to a concert. That's more than his sister could do."

"My sister likes terrible music. At least Faith has eclectic taste." I usually liked every third band, but she didn't need to know that.

Faith squinted at me. "When are we leaving?"

I laughed. "I guess we're going now."

"I mean..." Faith turned to my mother. "I'm having a great time. We could totally skip the concert."

If I didn't love her before, I would have after that statement. I hooked my arm around her neck and dragged her into my chest. "We'll come back and see them again."

Faith beamed up at me. "That sounds like an awesome plan."

34

KEYS

I HUGGED QUINN AS WE MOTORED DOWN PITCH BLACK ROADS. WERE there even street lights in this town? The narrow beam from his bike was the only thing that cut through the miles and miles of nothing.

Finally we crested a hill and the whole area changed. A streetlight, a few dozen stores, and an old bar came into view. I couldn't make out the marquis, but felt his bike throttle down as he slowed.

The parking lot was full and a folksy beat streamed out of the doors. I took off my helmet before we even parked. A raucous crash of a piano and voices made my heart race. "No. No way." I climbed off and ran a few steps before Quinn snagged my arm and hauled me back. "Hey!"

"We still have rules. You stick by me, no exceptions. I don't care if he plays every single favorite song of yours ever that you just have to get up the near the stage. Do. Not. Care."

I tugged at him. Warden in full effect, but I couldn't care. Not now. Not here with this perfect surprise. "Let's go. Let's go." My brain whirled with happiness. Of all the things he could ever have done for me—*this*. This was the one that made my heart absolutely swell. "Frank Turner!"

"Yeah, I saw something on one of your Twitter feeds. He was doing some impromptu show to raise money for a friend of his."

"And you bought tickets?"

"Yes. Absurdly expensive tickets. Especially when we are in backwater Glens Falls for this."

"Quinn." *I love you madly.*

Hmm.

Well, this probably wasn't the time for that. At all.

"You are so getting laid tonight."

He laughed. "Babe, I get laid every night."

"Yes, you do. Mostly because you're a beast who cannot be sated." And I absolutely loved that about him.

He laughed. "You say the damnedest shit."

I jumped up and down and curled my arms around his neck. "Gah! Frank Fucking Turner!"

"Good surprise?"

I wrapped my legs around his hips. "The best!"

He swung me back onto my feet. "Then let's get in there."

I nodded and dragged him forward. We had to give our names at the door, and then we were in. Frank's upright piano was jammed into the corner of the small stage. He was standing, his long form bent over the keys with the box microphone swinging in front of him as he screamed out the lyrics to "A Love Worth Keeping".

The crowd was a mix of fans and people that were obviously other artists, or friends. There was a decidedly anxious crush of people near the front that were singing along. The rest raised their glasses for certain songs.

I knew every one. I sang at the top of my lungs and leaned back on my guy as the most perfect of moments was mine. The night wore on and Frank played deep cuts, bar songs, singalongs, and ballads.

The drinks were plentiful and the stories amazing.

Did I mention the drinks were plentiful? There were a lot of United Kingdom boys in attendance. The first rumblings of a quarrel made its way to us. Quinn curled me closer and headed for the fringes of the room.

"Stay with me. Things are—crap."

The swing of an arm and a body blundered through the crowd of people. That's all it took. A chain reaction blazed through the bar. Drunk men and women in a small space were always a volatile mix. It was one of the most exciting things about a small venue.

Fingers gripped my arm and slid down to my hand. I frowned and swung around. A flash of blond hair and huge blue eyes swam into my vision. I shook my head.

The woman slipped a glove off and tucked it into her pocket.

Quinn.

Had I yelled it?

My mouth suddenly felt dry as dust and the room twirled. I heard him in the distance. The group of people near me passed me around like a doll. Round and round, the room spun like the teacups at an amusement park.

Spinning.

So much spinning.

The woman.

Focus, Faith.

Quinn.

I screamed his name.

At least I hoped I did.

"I've got you, Keys."

I pushed at the soft hands on mine. Those weren't his hands. Not Quinn's hands. He didn't call me Keys. I was Faith. His Faith.

Faith, mine.

That's what he said in the middle of the night with his face buried in my neck.

Quinn.

The singsong voice was at my ear. "Finally, I've got you. I've been waiting so long."

35

QUINN

"FAITH!"

I pushed through the dense crush of people and ducked as a fist came at my face. I shoulder-blocked and plowed the huge guy back a few feet. I searched the crowd for her blond crown of hair.

My blood pressure drowned out the music as my head pounded.

The singer was slamming on the piano keys and frowning. He stopped the song in the middle. "Okay, guys. I like a good brawl as much as anyone, but I want all the money to go to Richie, not the bar because of you miscreants." He held up a bottle of Coke. "Give me a sing, not a punch."

The carnival tones of the song and the sway of the crowd calmed.

I still couldn't see her.

"Faith!"

A woman looked over her shoulder. Huge blue eyes made up just like Faith's. High cheekbones and bow lips, even the same fringe of bangs. Not my Faith, though. Not at all.

Then I saw another blond bobbing and weaving behind her.

"Stop!" I pushed through the crowd, then lost sight of them. Panic drowned out sense and I bashed through the people. They pushed me back and a guy that was about six-five swung at me.

"I. Don't. Have. Time. For. This." I used my fists for each word and punctuated it with a hit. I took out four people before I got to the edges of the room.

Fuck.

Which way? I ran down the narrow hallway to a kitchen. A woman looked up with a cigarette dangling from her lips. "This is my kitchen, dammit. Stay out of it."

"Did two women come through here?" My gaze darted to every corner. No place to hide.

"Yes. A drunk girl and her friend."

My gaze focused and stilled on the old woman. "What?"

"You find 'em, you tell 'em they're out."

I swallowed down fire in my throat as bile rose. *No. No. No.* "Which way?"

The woman pointed at the back.

I ran through the door and down another set of stairs. A hatchback was pulling away as I came out, my gun in my hands before I even remembered unholstering it.

I had a second to make a decision.

It could have been a stranger. Just someone leaving.

I aimed for the tire and fired. Instead of stopping, the car fishtailed and careened for the back roads. I took off after it, but even on a flat tire, she was going to outrun me.

"Fuck."

I doubled back into the crowd of people that had escaped to the parking lot during the brawl. I needed a car, a truck—something. A guy was standing beside a large truck, laughing with his friends. I didn't think. I didn't pause. I held my gun to his face. "I need your truck."

The guy held his hands up. Shock whitened his skin as he stumbled back a step. "Whoa."

"I'll bring it back." I waved the gun at him. "Move."

"Fuck. What the fuck?" the guy spluttered.

I hit the gas as I was closing the door. Gravel spit from the tires as I roared up the dirt road. I gunned the engine and took off after the lights bouncing in the distance.

Thank God for backwater guys with stupidly big trucks. I ate up the distance between myself and the vehicle and rammed the bumper. The car careened off the shoulder, then righted itself.

I slammed into it again. "Pull over," I yelled out the window.

She took a left and I rammed her again. Her axel caved in on itself and the car slid down the embankment. I slammed the truck into park and leapt out.

"No! She's mine." Her face was warped in the spiderweb-cracked glass. Blood streamed from her nose.

"Not yours." I skidded down the dusty shoulder and into the gravel and garbage strewn ditch. I coughed as exhaust clouded the air.

The woman inside the car crawled over the backseat, her arms around Faith. My girl's head was at a scary angle. *Please, God let her be okay.*

Panic and nerves lit her eyes. So damn blue—almost the same color as Faith's. They could have been sisters for fuck's sake. "She's mine, don't you understand? No one loves her like I do. No one could ever love her like I do. No one."

I shoved my gun into the small of my back and held my hands up. "Please. Please don't do this."

Faith was slumped in the woman's arms. Her eyes opened, but she didn't seem to be aware of her surroundings. Faith pushed at the woman, but her hands just fell away—useless.

Fear clutched my chest. I didn't know what to do. Was she dying? Was she drugged? The car was tilted down, and they were both wedged against the back door on the passenger side. I was looking down on them from the shoulder of the road. I wrenched open the door.

"Get back!" The girl screamed.

"Okay, okay."

I stepped away from the open door. "Just come out. You don't want anything to happen to her, right?" I glanced at Faith, but had to look away. Pale. So, pale and her face was unnaturally slack from whatever she'd given her. "She doesn't look very good."

The woman stroked Faith's hair. "Why does everyone think they know what's best for her? Only I do. Only me."

"Then help her." It killed me to say it, but Faith's color was getting worse as we stood there. Sirens wailed in the distance and so did the girl. The girl who looked so much like Faith that my stomach churned.

"Just step away." She held up a glove in a baggie. "If you don't, I'll use this on me and her."

Everything quieted inside me. My vision sharpened, and my senses cleared. Panic wasn't going to help me here. "What is that?"

"It just makes her more sedate." She shook out the glove. "It's just to make her quiet. But I can use more. I can make us both quiet and we can always be together." She looked down at Faith, her intent clear. "If I can't have her."

I reached behind me and gripped my gun. I didn't think. Didn't pause. Didn't do anything but react.

Her or Faith.

It would always be Faith.

I fired.

The girl's face was shocked and she seemed to fall in slow motion. I didn't wait. I dragged them both out of the car, flinging the baggie out into the street.

The woman fell in an awkward heap. It might be cold and callous, but I couldn't concentrate on anything but Faith.

"Faith. Stay with me, Faith. Stay. I love you, you hear me?" I dragged her against me. Her eyes were glassy, and blood was splattered across her neck. I wiped at it to make sure it wasn't hers.

Two patrol cars pulled in, blocking the road and the truck. Blue and red lights flashed against her pale cheeks.

"I need help." My voice didn't sound loud enough, so I said it again.

"Sir. Sir, put down your weapon."

I dropped my gun and held on to her. "Just help her, please."

She gripped my shirt.

I met her heavy eyes. "Help's here, babe. Help's here."

She was breathing.

She was alive.

36

KEYS

Noah rushed through the door to my hospital room. "We've got to stop meeting this way, Keys."

"Where have you been?" I struggled to sit up. "I've been calling you for hours."

He held up a hand. "I got here as quickly as I could."

"They won't let me see him." I ran a shaking hand through my hair. I'd been in this damn hospital for two freaking days. I didn't remember the first one. They had me pumped so full of drugs to counteract what that woman had given me that I had no recollection of the day or even the time in the car.

Or that Quinn had killed for me.

My lips trembled and a sob threatened to jump out of my chest. I'd been successfully tamping it down, but now that Noah was here, I wasn't sure I could hold on any longer.

"I'm on my way to the jail right after I see you. I figured you were going to bust out of this place if I didn't check in."

I swallowed the lump in my throat, but a bubble of hysteria escaped. "You would be correct."

He sat next to me on the bed, his eyes tracking over the IV in my arm. "Have the cops been in to talk to you?"

"For a few minutes. The doctor chased them out again which is why Quinn is still in that friggin' jail cell."

He covered my hand. "Okay. It's all right. I'm here to fix it."

I sat back and closed my eyes. My head still felt like I was on a seriously bad acid trip. And considering I'd done absolutely zero drugs in my life, I was so not okay with this feeling. Who would do this to themselves on purpose?

"She stole from me again," I whispered. That was one of the worst things about it. Each time this woman had tried to kidnap me, she had used something that scrambled my memories.

I'd been absolutely useless.

At her mercy.

Tears leaked out the sides of my eyes. I dashed them away.

"Ah, sweetheart."

I hated tears. I tried to swallow them back, but I was just so tired and worried. "If she stole Quinn from me too…" My voice was thick with them now. I cleared my throat and growled. "I'm going to dig her up and kill her again."

He patted my hand. "Well, she's not in the ground yet, but I love when you're fierce."

I laughed through a half sob. "You suck."

"Thank God," Hunter said as he rushed in.

I sniffed and blinked away the rest of my tears. I didn't want my guys to see me fall apart. They were all worried about me as it was.

He hugged his brother. "I didn't think you were ever going to get here."

"I'm getting tired of coming to see this one in a hospital." Noah tugged at my braid.

"Yeah, well, this better be the last of it. No more crazed fans, all right?" Hunter gripped my hand.

I squeezed back. "No. No more."

The woman who still didn't have a name. Even dead, she was still a mystery. How could someone have no name? I couldn't even wrap my brain around that bit of insanity.

I pulled the IV out of my arm with a wince and tossed it over my shoulder. I gripped Noah's wrist. "You have to take me to him."

"Hold on." His eyes widened. "Jesus."

"No, I will not hold on. I've been in this fucking room for two days. I need to see him."

"I'll get him. His parents are working on bail."

"He was protecting me! He shouldn't even be in there."

"He's fine. I talked to Quinn's father. He's going a little nuts because he can't see you, but otherwise he's fine."

That statement was the very definition of a whitewash. I knew Quinn. "A little nuts" was more like climbing the walls. And if the cops had taken him in, there was a good reason. And that reason was me.

I fisted my fingers into his jacket. "I need to see him. Find a way to get me over there or I'm going to raise so much hell—"

"Are you trying to extend your stay?" Noah asked me.

"I'm fine."

"Your pupils are the size of dimes. Nothing about you is *fine*."

"I'm not going to be fine until I see him."

The nurse bustled in. "Miss Keystone, you have to sit back."

"I'm checking myself out." I swung my legs off the bed and tried to stand up. My knees didn't really work. They sort of dissolved.

Noah caught me and swung me up into his arms. "All right, tiger. Back in bed with you."

"No. I just need to get my feet under me." I tried again and stood on my feet this time. "See?" The room swam a little, but I was determined. "Someone find me a shirt. This thing is a little too revealing for the jail."

"She is in no condition to leave yet." The nurse crossed the room. "We can't allow it."

"I can check myself out." I sat on the chair next to my bed and started pulling on my jeans. I looked up at the nurse. "Right?"

She frowned. "I can't advise it."

Noah raked his hands through his hair. "Keys, I'll go get him out of there. I promise."

"I need to do this." I blinked away tears. "He killed someone for me. He saved me."

Noah crouched down in front of me and clutched my hands. "I know."

"Now, I need to go get him out of that cell and back where he belongs."

"His job is done," Noah said quietly. "You're safe."

My chest tightened. "This isn't about his job. It hasn't been about the job for a long time." I wasn't ready to say it before. I wasn't ready to believe, but I was now.

He was mine, and I was his.

End of story.

Actually, more like beginning of the story. *Our* story.

Noah's gaze crashed into mine. "Well, it's about time."

I laughed and brushed my nose with the back of my hand. No sobbing. Action now—cry later. "I love him. So, you need to take me to him *right now*."

The nurse stalked out, muttering about finding a doctor.

They could tackle me at the damn door if they wanted, but I was getting out of there. I grabbed my boots, and wished for my Chucks. Not sure I was three-inch-platform-wedge worthy.

"What the hell are you doing?" Indie scowled at me from the doorway, holding my go-bag.

I gripped the top of one boot and tried to get the zipper down. "I'm staging a coup?"

"I think you mean jailbreak," Noah said from the side of his mouth.

"Whatever. I'm blowing this pop stand to get my man."

Indie's chin dropped to her chest. "Save me from melodramatic rockstars." She stalked in and dropped my bag on my bed. "All right, how about these?" She pulled out my black Converse sneakers.

I stood and only weaved a little bit. "Oh my God, bless you."

"I don't think you're quite catwalk-worthy."

I glanced down at Indie's ever present four-inch-heeled boots. "Only one of us gets to be fabulous today."

She grinned up from under the shadows of her hat. "Damn right." She snapped out my Elvis *Jailhouse Rock* shirt. "Thought it was fitting."

I laughed for the first time in what felt like forever. "I love you."

"Yeah, well, I'm just glad you're okay. Now, we have a moody warden to save, huh?"

"Damn right."

Indie helped me into the bathroom. My hair was a wreck, but a high ponytail would just have to do. She stood behind me in the mirror and reached around to pinch my cheeks.

"Hey."

"You look pale as death, girl. I don't think blusher is appropriate, so old school it is."

I winced as she pinched again, but at least there was some blood flow going on.

"You look like you hung out in a pot tent for twelve hours."

My eyes did look way too huge, but I didn't have time to worry about that. I needed to get to Quinn and fix this mess. I reached into my bag and found the sunglasses I used when I was getting attacked by flashbulbs.

"There we go. Rockstar chic."

"Oh yeah. Not obvious at all." Indie rolled her eyes. "All right." She turned me around and fluffed my bangs, then straightened my shoulders. "Fair warning, you scare me like that again, I quit."

"You can't quit." I curled my arms around her neck. "You're my hero."

She pushed me away. "Asshole."

I grinned and followed her out the door.

Noah was pacing, his attention on his phone.

"Ready."

He looked up. His gaze drifted over my face before he squinted. "Better. Not great, but better."

"The ego, she soars around you, pal."

He put a hand at the small of my back and led me toward the door. "You do realize Q's going to have my ass when he sees you. Keep the shit to a minimum, huh?"

I'd deal with a grouchy Quinn later. I just needed to see him. Now. Now times one hundred. All this was my fault. If I'd listened to him before, maybe none of this would have happened. Maybe he wouldn't have more blood on his hands.

The nurse was waiting with a clipboard and a wheelchair. "At least sign this."

I scribbled on the bottom of the paper and handed it back to her.

"Get in the chair."

"I don't need that."

Noah crossed his arms. He was as immovable as Quinn, for God's sake.

I sighed and dropped into the chair. "Fine."

He spun the chair around and headed down the hall. "That wasn't so hard."

I gripped the arms as he picked up his pace and we zoomed by my band in the waiting room.

Owen leaped out of his seat. "Keys!"

"I'll see you guys at the hotel."

He ran after us. "Where are you going?"

"I gotta go get Quinn."

Owen slowed to a stop and slapped his leg. "Dammit, girl."

I couldn't worry about him right now. I'd explain everything to my friends after I made sure Quinn was okay. Noah slapped a button on the wall and the doors opened into the lobby. The hospital was more like an extended clinic. We reached the front doors and I jumped out as soon as we crossed the threshold. The sun was long gone. October had snatched the longer days and brought a crispness to the air.

He hustled me to his SUV and we took off into town. Noah gave me a quick rundown on why there was no movement on Quinn's arraignment. Quinn and his family were Saratoga-based, so the Glens Falls police department didn't give a crap who he was. And again, they knew nothing of Roth Defense, nor did they feel the need for any special treatment.

Especially when Quinn had been less than cooperative when they'd tried to take me away from him.

My heart ached as we pulled into the small parking lot. "This is where he is?"

"Yeah. You can imagine the lack of staff at this time of day on a Saturday. The cops are more worried about the kids partying than getting him set up with a judge."

I fisted my hands as I walked in. The reception area was empty. I looked around and finally heard someone behind a desk. "Hello?"

"Can I help you?" A woman came out in jeans and a uniform shirt. She had a tired face, and flat brown eyes.

"Hi. My name is Faith Keystone." At her continued blank look, I kept going. "I was involved in the shooting."

Noah came up behind me. "You have a man here by the name of Quinn Alexander?"

"Oh, him."

I twisted my fingers together. "Can we see him?"

"Faith?"

I turned toward a female voice. "Maggie?" Quinn's mother's face was drawn, but she was clear-eyed. And from her expression, I knew I looked even worse than I thought. I weaved a little, but walked to her on my own steam. "Hi. I'm so sorry." *No waterworks. No waterworks.* "Is he okay?"

"He's fine, honey. He just needs a shower and possibly a fifth of whiskey."

I laughed. "I don't think I've ever seen him drink more than wine or the occasional beer."

"Then you be careful around him when he's with his dad." She hugged me tight and smoothed her hand down my ponytail. "He's been asking about you."

"Yeah?" I sniffed back the tears that kept threatening. "I've been so worried."

"Faith? What the hell are you doing here?"

I broke away from Quinn's mom. He stood in the middle of the dreary hallway. His clothes had seen better days. His folks must have brought a new shirt for him, but there was a stain of red on his arm and rusty streaks on his jeans.

I swallowed. "I'm here to rescue you."

He frowned. "You should be in the hospital."

My lips trembled. I'd really needed to hear that gruff voice. "Nice to see you too, Warden."

He closed his eyes and I saw his fingers shake before he fisted them.

No way I could resist that. I ran to him and threw my arms around him. He was so stiff, his shoulders and arms like granite. "I'm here. I'm okay. I swear I'm okay."

He dropped his forehead to my shoulder. "Faith."

I looped my arms around his waist and put my nose right into the middle of his chest—savoring his warmth and the scent of fabric softener and the underlying hint of mint that always clung to him.

Home.

Quinn.

Mine.

Finally, his arms came around my shoulders. He crushed me to him. "They took you from me. Never again, you hear me?" He gripped my ponytail. "Never again."

I couldn't stop the grin against his shirt—or the tears. Damn him. I wiggled until I could get my face away from his chest. I peered up at him. "Never?"

"Never." He snatched the sunglasses off my face, then frowned. "How high are you?"

I laughed. "Those are hearts in my eyes, buddy. You're ruining my buzz."

His frown deepened, then he looked over my shoulder. "You let her out of the hospital like this?"

Noah held up his hands. "She required an audience with her beau."

"You're an asshole."

Noah folded his arms. "Is that any way to talk to your best friend? The hero who brought your girl to you?"

Quinn looked down at me. "I was on my way to see you."

I curled myself into his side and pressed my cheek against his chest. "I saved you a trip."

"You should still be in bed."

"How about you tuck me in?" I batted my eyelashes at him.

He pressed his forehead to mine. "You drive me fucking nuts."

"The feeling is entirely mutual."

I love you.

I love you to a stupid degree.

The words were a logjam in my head.

I wanted to tell him, but all of a sudden, the hallway exploded with people.

So much for our big romantic moment.

The detectives who had come to my room wanted a statement, then there was more paperwork. I was put in a room with a table and four chairs. The detectives wanted to speak to me alone, but Quinn was an immovable wall.

Even now, when I didn't need a bodyguard anymore, he was still standing sentinel beside me.

Finally, the detectives decided it was easier to let Quinn stay. There were endless questions about the incident that I couldn't answer because I had been incoherent at the time. All I remembered was the music, the laughter, Quinn holding me, then the fight broke out and a face that could have been mine had materialized in front of me.

A face that was finally burned into my memory.

"She was me," I whispered.

"No, she wasn't." Quinn's hand cupped my shoulder as he crouched beside me. "She was a very sick woman who somehow got focused on you."

"A little more than that, I'm afraid." The detective scratched his buzzed short hair. He pulled a large bag marked *evidence* out of a manila envelope and placed the sealed bag in front of me.

I swallowed at the photo of her identification. It had my name on it.

Quinn sat down next to me at the table. With shaking hands, I shook the bag of cards they'd assembled. Her license and even her insurance had been under my name.

I blinked up at the officer. "How?"

"All it takes is getting a hold of your social security number."

"But..." I pushed the cards through the bag until I came to the license again. My address. I looked at Quinn.

"That's why we couldn't find anything on her."

"Because she was trying to be me. To *become* me."

The detective pulled out another bag. This one was smaller and contained a cell phone. "From what we can tell, she cloned your phone. I wish it was hard to do, but a little know-how and a Google search make it a lot easier than you think."

Quinn's fingers fisted and he slid his hand under the table. "Your cell problems."

I swallowed. "The weird double texts I got."

He nodded. "I should have picked up on it. She was using your own cell to track you. Everywhere you were, that geotracker that's in most cells—talk about a damn homing beacon."

I sat back in the chair and curled my arms over my stomach. "All my conversations..."

His fingers curled over my knee. "It's over."

I nodded numbly. "Right. Over."

The detectives spoke to Quinn a little more, but the charges were finally dropped in light of the evidence. I signed where I was supposed to sign and we were sent on our way.

Quinn led me to Noah's car. "We're going to stay at my folks place tonight. All right? Your parents are there with my mom."

I nodded. "Okay."

He helped me into the backseat and snapped my belt. "Faith."

I stared at my hands as they blurred.

"Faith."

I blinked furiously before I looked up at him.

"You're going to be fine."

I tried to put on a smile. I had a feeling it was pretty much a fail, considering the look in his eyes. "I'm already fine."

He cupped my face, his thumb tracing my cheek. He leaned in and pressed a light kiss to my mouth, then shut the door and got into the passenger seat.

The ride to his house was eternal. I was a mixture of numb and broken. The gentle rocking from the uneven roads and then the highway lulled me into a light doze. They guys were speaking in low voices—low enough that I couldn't really make out what they were saying.

I tipped my forehead toward the glass. I didn't really care.

It was over. I just wasn't sure how over.

The door opening snapped me back into the truck and into the moment again. I blinked up at Quinn. "Hi."

His blue eyes were tired and red-rimmed. "Ready for the circus?"

I shook my head.

"Your band is here, your parents, your sister—the whole kit and caboodle."

I unclipped my belt and stepped onto the gravel driveway. "Oh, God." I twisted my fingers into his.

He kissed my temple. "You have a lot of people who love you, Faith."

"I know."

He led me up the stairs, but I jerked him back before we got to the porch. I turned back around and went toward the horse barn.

"Where are you going?"

The gravel wavered a little under my feet, but I was determined to get a few things off my chest. I couldn't do this with all my friends, my family, and the hugeness of the emotions waiting for me. The worry and the coddling I couldn't avoid no matter what. "I'm not ready for this. I can't face all of them."

He grasped my shoulders and dragged me back against him. "I'll be with you every step of the way."

"Will you?" I moved away from him and cupped my elbows. The navy stained wood of the barn got very watery. I tipped my head back, but it was no use.

"Of course I will. I wouldn't leave you like this."

Not like this. "But tomorrow?"

"No. Not tomorrow."

"Next week?" I ducked my head and dashed away the tears I'd been trying to hide.

He took two long strides to me and turned me toward him. He framed my face, his fingers sliding into my hair. "I said never, didn't I?" He brushed away my tears with his thumbs.

I gripped his wrists. "I'm not your job anymore."

"No, you're my life." He lowered his head until our foreheads touched, then his lips were on mine. Not the crushing kisses that fried my blood. Just firm and solid, warm and real. "My whole life," he said against my mouth.

Relief and love pushed away the numbness. I gripped the front of his shirt and slid my hands under the cotton to find flesh. *Mine.* The rough slide of hair along my palms stabilized me. He wasn't going anywhere.

He was mine.

I grinned up at him. "Oh man, are you in trouble."

He laughed. "So much."

I gave him a watery laugh. His red-rimmed eyes blurred a little. I wasn't sure if it was my vision or his eyes. I went up on my toes. "I love you."

His eyes crinkled at the corners and a rare smile split his face. "Yeah, I can live with that."

I pulled his hair. "That's it?"

His brows snapped together. "What?"

I pulled harder.

"I said you were my whole life. Jeez." He leaned down until our lips lined up again. "You want the words?"

I lifted my knee. "You're going to be walking funny if you don't spit them out."

He gripped my leg and wrapped it around his hips, then hiked me the rest of the way up until I had my arms around his neck. "I love you, Faith. All the way, hearts and flowers and diamond rings, babe."

"I expect a better proposal in the near future, but I'll go with *yes* to all the above."

He kissed me in that wild, wonderfully pushy way of his. I locked my ankles around his back and held on.

"Faith Elizabeth Keystone, you get in this house!"

I winced and hunched my shoulders at my mother's voice. "I guess we have to face our family."

He gripped my ass. "In a minute."

I grinned against his mouth. "I can work with that."

EPILOGUE

KEYS

Halloween Night

"What are you doing in there?" I paced the carpeted floor outside our hotel room. It was the tenth annual Hammered masquerade and my fiancé wouldn't come out of the damn room.

I looked down at the filigreed band on my finger with the surprising sparklers. Instead of one big diamond, my guy had surprised me with a ring I would never have to take off on stage.

I think he kinda had a thing about the whole *mine* deal.

He'd stamp it on my forehead if he could.

The fact that I was the same didn't seem to bother him. We were planning a quickie December wedding while we were on hiatus, but our mothers weren't making it easy. Oh, they loved us. No worries there. It was more that the guest list kept growing.

If they kept it up, the Hammered jet was going to be more like a pickup bus for families across the nation.

I slapped the door. "Dammit, Warden. Get your hot little ass out here. What are you doing in there?" He was probably dressed up like a SWAT team dude or something. That kind of gear was in his damn closet.

Actually, it was more like vests and jeans these days, which happened to be the current uniform for the Hammered security team that Quinn had revamped. I still said it was a gross misuse of his talents, but he was happy.

And I liked him being around me even if he was Mr. Rules and Regulations about everything. But we didn't have to worry about our phones being cloned or obsessive fans getting up into our business. So there was that.

"No. I changed my mind. I'm not dressing up," he said from behind the door.

"We don't have time for that crap. We have to be downstairs in ten minutes to start the costume contest."

"I can change in ten minutes."

Owen closed the door to his room next door. "What's the hold up?"

My eyebrows shot up. "Hello, Hook."

"Ya like?" He turned to show off his brocade vest and long black jacket. His bright blue eyes were smudged with guy-liner and he wore a black silk shirt open way too wide.

"Quite the man-pelt you have going on there. Manscape a little, maybe?"

Owen squinted at me. "I'll have you know that women love my hairy chest."

I nodded sagely. "I'm sure they do."

"Bah, what do you know, Claire?"

I grinned. "I knew making you watch Outlander would pay off." I flattened my hand down my historical dress. I'd originally thought I wanted to be Harley Quinn for the holiday, but the growl from my guy had made me re-think the outfit. Especially since he ripped the costume getting it off me when I tried it on for him. Ah, well. I kinda liked the girl thing sometimes. The dress gave me hips for days and the bustle was kind of cool, even if I did keep bumping into things. I wasn't used to taking up so much space. At least the bustier hiked up the girls in a serious way. "Like?"

"Aye, Sassenach."

I stuck out my tongue. "Stick with the Irish."

He laid his hand on his chest. "You wound me. Besides, the Scots are beasts. We're lovers at heart, full of song."

I laughed. "Is that how it works?"

"Yes." Owen frowned. "Where's the warden?"

"He won't come out."

"Come on, mate." Owen raised his voice. "It's just a costume ball." He glanced at me. "Did you try to make him dress up like Jamie?"

"No." I tried. And failed.

"I'll come out when he's gone."

"You know everyone is going to see you eventually, right?" Owen asked.

"Go!" Quinn thundered through the door.

I laughed. "Okay. Go, Hook. I'll take care of this."

"Is he gone?" Quinn asked a moment later.

Owen peeked from around the corner and held up a finger to his lips. I waved him away. He pointed his hook hand at me and made a rude gesture.

"He's gone."

"I don't believe you."

"Quinn!"

"If you laugh, I'm wearing my dignitary dinner suit instead."

"Oh, the horrors." Quinn looked damn fine in a suit, but now I was very intrigued.

The door opened a crack. "Seriously. I thought this would be funny, but now I just feel dumb."

"Get out..." My words trailed off as he opened it a bit farther. "Wow."

He started to shut the door. "Nope."

I slapped my hand on the jamb. "Oh, no way. You're so coming out here." Good thing I had this ridiculous dress holding down my girls. My chest flushed right up my neck. "Wow."

His hands fisted at his sides. Black leather pants hugged his hips and thighs right down to a generous cut over his motorcycle boots. He wore a thick belt with a mouthwatering buckle and a tight Megadeth T-shirt that I was pretty sure was actually his. He had on his motor-cycle jacket and a single silver necklace that I'd seen tucked away under his shirt a few times. Tonight, the Celtic cross was plainly visible.

His eyes, though. Those silvery-blue eyes were smudged with black liner.

Holy shit. My bodyguard had dressed up like a hot rockstar.

I dragged him out the door. "Did I mention wow?"

"I look dumb," he growled. Then his eyes tracked over my chest, down my dress, and then back up to the hair bundled on top of my head. "You, however, are ridiculously gorgeous."

"Why, thank you." I pressed my hand to the super tight bodice. "I can't breathe, but the dress is awesome. And my almost-husband is delicious."

"Your sister did the eye thing."

I laughed. "I wondered about that."

He gave me another once-over. This time, not so hungry.

"What?"

"Can you move in that thing? What happens if someone tried to grab you?"

I rolled my eyes. "Quinn, this is a party and our mystery girl is long gone."

"Do you realize how many people are on your orange list? I put five on the red list just this week."

I reached up and cupped his jaw. "Quinn. Repeat after me: 'My girl isn't stupid and has the hottest bodyguard next to her at all times.'"

"I'm not saying that."

"You think I'm stupid?"

"No." His eyebrows snapped down. "You're far from dumb, but this party has a million—"

I moved my hand over his mouth. "You can't keep me in a bubble." He mumbled under my hand. I let him go. "What?"

"I can keep you in bed."

I grinned up at him. "Yes, you've tried that for the last two weeks. And we can revisit that sequence of events again," I looked down at his rippled abs under the concert shirt, "right after the party. Or maybe if we sneak into one of the other ballrooms…" I tapped his stubbled chin. "Actually, I think there's a library."

"That's an escape plan I can get on board with. Speaking of, you know where all the—"

"Yes! Yes, I know where all the exits are. Now come downstairs so I can show you off."

He frowned and crooked his arm for me to take it. "If I see one picture of me on the band Instagram account, I'm going to punish you."

"Promise?"

I might just have to make that little threat from my bodyguard come true.

*Turn the page for a sneak peek at **MANIPULATED**, book three in our HAMMERED series, available now!*

MANIPULATED

Chapter 1
Callie

A BOUDOIR PHOTOGRAPHER AND HER LOUD, IMPATIENT, INSANELY *beautiful younger sister walk into a bar...*

Nope, scratch that, we were walking into a bedroom. *My* bedroom. The boudoir photographer's. Or that was what I'd been once. Truthfully, I'm no longer one, at least if getting paid for a job is the litmus test for actually having it. I suppose I could be called an active hobbyist who was trying to get back to her former glory. Right now, I worked as a hostess at a martini bar and photographed landscapes and occasionally children for pay. Very occasionally. I'd debated getting into weddings—because weddings were where it was at in the money-soaked venues of Los Angeles—but that wasn't my passion.

No, my passion was plumping up boobs while I frantically snapped to get the right shot as my luscious sister splayed across my queen bed and complained it was too small.

"How can it be too small? You're five-foot nothing."

"I know, but I feel like I'm not getting the extension I need." Ava stretched her legs toward my headboard, thereby completely ruining my shot.

"You don't need extension right now. Just plump your boobs again. I'm getting a shadow. And cross your legs at the ankle."

She smirked and did the honors with her truly enviable rack before daintily crossing her ankles and inching up on her hip so her ass was properly displayed in the way I'd instructed earlier. "Aww, and here I so enjoyed having you feel me up."

I sighed and moved back to adjust my ice light. Not that my sister needed a ton of light to look gorgeous. Basically, Ava breathing outshined half the women in LA. But it was heading toward evening, and I was losing the natural light in spite of the reflector I'd set up near the window to bounce the available sunshine toward Ava.

We'd probably have to suspend this session soon until later in the week. In a studio, working with artificial light was typical. In my small bedroom, I needed the daylight to offset my equipment. I simply didn't have the storage room in my apartment to keep all the supplies I would need to outfit a real studio.

But someday. Someday I would.

"What was that sigh for? Is my butt floss showing crackage?" Ava reached back to adjust her gorgeous lacy lavender panties.

She wasn't wearing a G-string, but her lingerie was definitely… edgy. Edgier than anything I would wear, but then again, I was a wuss. Though I'd once had an account with all the major lingerie shops, from La Perla to several fancy stores in Europe, I hadn't typically bought things for myself. I'd started buying lingerie for my prop trunks at sixteen, and stopped shortly after my marriage at almost twenty.

God, I'd been a baby then. A baby who'd gotten married. And look how that had turned out.

Now I was twenty-nine, semi-newly divorced—well, I was a year-and-a-half past my divorce, but I damn sure was still navigating my way—and trying to pick up the pieces of the career I'd abandoned before it had ever really taken off.

"No, your ass is perfect. It's just the light is proving problematic." I adjusted the light again and checked out Ava through my viewfinder. Her cap of tousled orange hair tumbled over one eye, and she posed effortlessly, bracing the fingers of one hand on her shoulder to offer the perfect angle for her cleavage. Her butt was gorgeous too. Hell, every part of her was.

I wasn't jealous. Much.

She'd done a little modeling as a teen for print, since she was way too short for runway, and she'd been one of my first victims to use for practice taking photos. Not that I'd started off with boudoir photos. I'd done the usual kids and faces for years, as soon as my small hands could hold my first Nikon. Eventually, I'd gotten braver. It had started with my best friend Raven in high school flopping on my bed. Her shirt had fallen down her shoulder, revealing a magenta bra strap. Something about the pose had made me grab my camera, and by the end of the session, she'd been down to her bra and panties. By the time my mom had opened my bedroom door two hours later, Raven had been sprawled on her back with a pillow between her legs and I'd been on a step stool above her, shooting pictures from every angle.

For about three months after that, my mom had asked me daily if "there was anything I needed to get off my chest." Mainly, that I liked them. Chests, that is. Ones belonging to females.

She hadn't truly believed me when I said I was simply capturing art until my wedding day to Steven. Maybe she still had some lingering doubts, I don't know. My dating record of late probably wasn't assuaging her concerns.

I had no dating record since my marriage had ended, and I liked it that way. Besides, that was what vibrators were for. Also for efficiency in power consumption, thanks to rechargeables.

"Whose fault is that? You were the one out shooting reptiles until most of the day bled away."

I wasn't about to explain to her the importance of my bearded dragon shoot. It paid actual cash money, therefore it was important to my current financial picture.

True, I hadn't gotten into photography to do close-ups of amphibians for the grand opening circular for a pet store, but faces were faces. I just hoped I didn't have nightmares about this particular bunch wearing tiny strapless bras and panties.

"I had work, Av. I couldn't pass it up. You know how hard it is for me to get jobs nowadays. The market has changed."

Ava broke pose and glared up at me, flattening her hands on the bed. "No, sis, you changed. It's always been hard to get ahead in the cutthroat world of LA, especially if your job touches fashion in even the most minute way. But you used to be hungry. Now? Now you're practically starving to death and you still are content to break off a corner of the cookie." Ava shook her head. "Seriously, stop waiting for permission. Bite in the center, baby, or don't bite at all."

I started to peek out from behind the safety of my camera, then caught a glimpse of my sister in the viewfinder. The anger and frustration on her face transformed her porcelain skin, making it glow from within. Her green eyes sparkled like wet grass in the morning sun.

"That's it," I said excitedly. "Don't move. Stay just like that."

Moving quickly, I swept around every side of the bed, capturing her from every angle. High, low, in front, behind. Ava sighed dramatically but she didn't move. She knew when I was on the warpath for a shot.

"You look incredible. Damn, those calves." I cocked my head and decided to quickly swap lenses. "Seriously hot. Spin class is so working for you."

"I don't do spin class for my calves. Try my ass. Wait, no, don't try my ass. I'm not on some *Flowers in The Attic* trip. Just hurry up and finish so we can discuss something important."

I braced my camera on my hip and frowned. "This is important. I thought you said you wanted new sexy shots for your website."

"A sexy profile shot? Sure." Ava broke pose entirely and climbed off the bed to grab my camera. I let her, but I immediately started chewing on my ragged thumbnail. That sucker cost a lot, and I didn't exactly have the funds to replace my equipment if she dropped it and scratched a lens. "But I'm a blogger and esteemed magazine writer. You really think I should have my tits on display on—holy shit, my tits are amazing!"

I snorted. "Modesty, thy name is Ava."

"No, no, it's you. You have all these mad skills, and the world doesn't know about them yet. Just me. But that's going to change." She set my camera down on the bed and gripped my shoulders. "Tonight is the start."

Dividing my attention between my sister and my precariously balanced camera, I frowned. "Tonight is the night I watch *Jason Meets Buffy Meets Freddie* and eat caramel popcorn and congratulate myself for being smart enough not to go down into the basement unarmed when I hear a noise."

"You don't have a basement."

"I know that. I'm just saying if I did."

Ava rolled over me without blinking a starry blue eyelash. "And if you heard a noise, you'd call the police and probably numb your own arm off digging through all your clothes and crap to get to the Taser in your closet."

"Props," I said primly. "That crap, as you call it, are props for my shoots."

"Whatever. I'm just saying you don't need the subtle lesson from those gore porn movies you watch and besides, that can't be a real movie title, can it?"

I shrugged. "What do you care? It's only gore porn." I made air quotes and she rolled her eyes at me.

"C'mon, you know you love Halloween. We should do something fun to celebrate it. More fun than watching canned cr—movies on TV," she amended.

Already, I was suspicious. My sister's idea of fun and mine rarely jived. "Like what?"

"Like going to an incredible party at the Houdini Estate."

I eased out of my sister's hold and picked up my camera. After tucking it away safely in its case, I turned to pack the rest of my equipment. "I'm not in a party mood, sorry. I've been working all day."

"Exactly why you need a party. Besides, you said if I let you take some boudoir shots for your portfolio, you'd do something for me." Ava grabbed my comfortable well-worn floral robe and pulled it on, then grimaced. "Is this what you wear before bed? No wonder you can't get laid."

"Can't is not the same as won't."

"Pfft."

"If it's a party, why do you need me there? You always have a date. Probably because you shun floral robes," I said under my breath, folding one of my lights. I didn't have a studio, or even much of a dedicated working space in my cramped apartment, so I slid the light into the narrow area behind the headboard.

"I don't have a date tonight. I'm doing the solo thang. I thought we could have a sisterly night together."

Our sisterly nights together were few and far between, since we enjoyed absolutely none of the same things. She loved to shop; I loved to sip coffee and people watch. She watched rom coms and foreign films with subtitles and lots of crying; I watched horror movies and action flicks. Her idea of party wear was digging out a tiny little sequined flapper dress from the back of my closet that showed approximately six miles of bare leg; mine was not.

While I watched, she dropped the floral robe and shimmied into the dress. "I knew it would fit," she said triumphantly, spinning to view her reflection in one of the many mirrors I had around the apartment. They were all different sizes and shapes, and I collected them both as props for my shoots and because they created the illusion of space.

Ava had commented more than a few times that she'd like to bring whatever guy she was dating over for a night of fun in front of them, but I wasn't about to leave my sister alone with a man, half a dozen antique mirrors and photographic equipment. She'd probably end up as an internet star in under a month, either accidentally or intentionally.

"You look great." I moved up beside her in the mirror, focusing on my sister to avoid the inevitable comparisons I'd make in my head. "Tiny little waist," I added as she turned this way and that, examining herself from all angles.

"You think?"

"I do. It just needs something." Angling my head, I went back to rummage through one of my trunks. With the space problem in my apartment, I also used them as seating. Not that I had a lot of guests as a rule. Mostly just my sister and a couple of girlfriends, since the bulk of our family lived back east.

My lack-of-a-date thing extended even to having male friends. I'd avoided the species as a whole since my divorce, probably due to my attorney's insistence "we get to know each other better" as soon as the ink was signed. While he had his hand on my knee and his tongue in my ear.

After I kneed my lawyer due south of his belt buckle, I'd steered clear of anyone with a penis and a charming smile. They tended to lead to bad things for me.

I drew out a pair of elbow-length black silk gloves and passed them to my sister before moving to my jewelry case. I went right to the costume drawer and tugged out a long strand of fake pearls that could be knotted just below where Ava's ample cleavage strained against the dress, drawing the eye.

Not that she needed any help there, but hell, might as well highlight your assets.

I only realized I'd spoken aloud when Ava sighed. "That applies to yourself too, you know. In case you've forgotten. Your assets gotta be feeling mighty neglected lately."

Saying nothing, I looped the necklace over her head and adjusted it to fit the image in my mind. She'd already put on the gloves and waited while I fussed with her jewelry, and then her hair. All it needed was a quick tousle with some gel and she was in fine flapper style.

"Now, shoes." I knew exactly which pair I wanted and retrieved the slinky black heels from the closet in a snap. Luckily, our feet were close to the same size, and I had a range of clothes sizes in my closet and in my trunks for shoots. Even after I'd stopped taking boudoir photos, I'd haunted thrift shops and lingerie sales out of habit. You never knew when you would happen upon the exact right thing.

On Ava, everything was right.

"Wait." She took the shoes but she didn't slip them on. Biting her lip, she studied her reflection. "Got any hooker hose? Fishnets," she explained when my eyes widened.

"Oh yeah. Thigh highs."

"Perfect."

I pulled out an unopened package and tossed it to her, then busied myself studying my orange and black moons and bats Halloween manicure in lieu of watching her tug the hose up her legs in her effortlessly sexy way. Men never flummoxed my sister. She chewed them up, savored them, and then forgot them before she got indigestion.

Once, I'd been concerned about her inability to settle down with one man. Now I was jealous. Because yes, I had needs just like everyone else, and one could only hibernate for so long before they started waving the little white flag of defeat.

I hadn't reached that point yet, but parties were definitely a no-fly zone in case my expiration date on celibacy came up before I was ready to acknowledge it.

She finished fussing with the hose and slid her feet into the shoes, making a bit of a face. So mine were a wee bit smaller than hers. She could crimp her toes. They matched the outfit perfectly.

"Hmm. You do have a way with this stuff." She rubbed a hand over her hip before turning toward me with a bright smile. "Now let's do you."

"Uh-uh." I shrank back and gripped the bedpost. "I told you, movie and couch for me tonight. I have a backache from shooting all day." To add veracity to the story, I dug my knuckle into the slightly sore knots near my spine.

"Yeah, and you know what is better for aches and pains than anything? I'll give you a hint. It begins with o and ends with m."

"No. I self-assist there."

She laughed. "Yeah, well, don't we all, and however you choose to do your deal is your decision. But I actually wasn't referring to that particular o and m combination, you dirty hussy."

My face flamed hot. Damn pale skin, always turning traitor on me. "Then what do you mean?"

"Optimism." She sounded out the word like she was a kindergarten teacher and I was her clueless student. "Something you're in desperate need of, and it doesn't come with batteries. You have to power it all on your own. So I figure one way to start you back down the road to being my annoyingly perky older sister again is to get you working on things that utilize your talents."

I waved a hand at the bed. "Wasn't that what I was just doing? You know I'm trying to get back to boudoir photography, but it's not an overnight thing."

"No, but you're good at other kinds of photography too."

Yay, maybe there were more pets in my future. Though I couldn't imagine any being at a Halloween party at the Houdini Estate, but you could never be sure. Rich people tended to be eccentric. Maybe someone had smuggled in a big cat or two.

Or a peacock. I'd actually photographed one of those before at the house of a Hollywood starlet, back before I'd completely given up on my "filthy little sideline" as Steven had once referred to it. Nothing like having the support of your husband.

Ex-husband, I reminded myself. Over and done.

I crossed my arms and attempted to look stern. "Such as?"

"Turns out I might just need a photog myself." Ava grabbed my arm and hustled me over to my closet. "Let's find you a sexy costume to wear, and then I'll tell you all about your opportunity of a lifetime."

Chapter 2
Owen

My rings scraped against the wooden banister as I hurried down the stairs to the party, humming to myself. I paused on the first flight and uncapped the flask of whisky I'd tucked into my costume's inside liner. God bless pirates and their gear.

Her laughter still rang in my ears, and witnessing the cartoon hearts filling Faith's eyes was always a double-edged sword. It was my favorite sight after all. Too bad the hearts were for a different man.

I hadn't meant to fall for my best friend. I hadn't even realized I'd done it really. Not until she'd turned those huge blue eyes on someone else.

Faith "Keys" Keystone was the linchpin in our band of idiots. She kept the fun blooming, the heart beating, the wildness at bay when we got too stupid for words. She kept us moving forward in so many damn ways.

I think we were all a little bit in love with our favorite sparrow. The problem was I'd done the unthinkable. I'd fallen past the entranced into the pit of despair. Loving a woman who would never be mine.

And I hadn't even known to fight for it until Quinn had arrived on the scene. I'd never had to worry about Keys being interested in anyone else. She'd had a few flings over the years, but she always seemed impervious to the sins of the flesh.

Unlike me of course.

I'd plowed my way through a bevy of beauties for more years than I could count. My Irish accent was a lure that not many women could resist. And I admit I played it up most times. I'd lived in America for the better part of twenty years. Immigrant parents relocating to find the American dream. The whole deal. They were hard-working Irish people who understood my need for song. My brethren loved their music, but for my da and ma it was meant for the pubs and parties, funerals and weddings.

It wasn't for a job.

And they surely didn't understand the circus that I lived, breathed, and loved with all of my big bleeding heart.

But Keys did.

We'd bonded over similar pairs of parents.

And an undying love of games. I admit some of my games had a much more sexual flavor than the ones I played with my once innocent Faith.

But seeing her hurt at Hunter's wedding had woken me up, and by then it had already been too late. The moment Quinn—her then bodyguard, now fiancé—had come into the picture she'd been lost to me. Not that she'd ever been close to mine anyway.

I took another swig from my flask and put it away. I cracked my knuckles and let the party vibes fill up my chest. Maybe, just maybe I could push out the heartsick parts and refill it with a bit of the Halloween horny.

Those bits I understood.

And the colorful wind of women in the party downstairs was a great place to start. The band had started the charity Halloween benefit five years ago. It had grown in size every year, and now boasted attendance by three hundred of the wealthiest rockstars and artists in the world.

Brocade ball gowns dominated the party this year thanks to the Houdini theme as well as the resurgence of historical interest thanks to television shows like *Outlander* and my personal favorite, *Another Period*. One used drama, one used humor.

I smiled as I caught a fetching redhead in full Lillian Bellacourt gear. Even the ridiculous fox stole around her neck from the show. She was a lass who could make me forget about lost loves.

I was almost sure of it.

At the bottom of the stairs, I quickly backed up a few steps as Reed Mason, the guitarist in my band, came careening around the corner in hot pursuit of...someone.

I peered down the hallway that lead to the huge front door. Sure enough, the Grecian Whore herself was running across the wide Spanish tiles. Victoria Sheer, the bane of our existence, was of course wearing a white toga and gold winking from her wrists and ankles. "Dammit, Bats."

He spun around, jogging backwards. He bumped into a sexy devil in black and red, and an angel who immediately twined her arms around his shoulders. "I'm trying, Owen."

"Try harder, mate."

Reed growled and extricated himself without even a fake smile. He pushed his way through the crowd. The front door was wide open with two men dressed as gladiators checking invitations at the door. He chased Victoria out the door and into the gardens.

Bloody chancer. None of us knew what the fuck Reed was doing with her and he wouldn't talk to any of us about why he'd let that viper back into our lives. It had been bad enough when she'd been engaged to Hunter a few years ago.

We'd literally had a party the day they broke things off.

And now she was back, like the taxman with a list of grievances. Trouble was, we were all paying.

I shook off those dark thoughts and turned back to the crowd. The party was in full swing and still more guests were drifting in, but I'd lost sight of the lovely Lillian, dammit.

"Captain Blackwell, permission for a kiss?"

My face split into an instant smile as I looked down. "Anything for you Kenny, m'love." I swooped her back in a bend and buried my face in her neck.

She screeched out a laugh. "Let me up."

"I'm the only one who gets to dip my wife, Hook."

I grinned up from Kennedy Jordan's very pretty neck at Hunter Jordan, one of my best mates in all the world. He also happened to be the lead singer in my band. "Aye but she makes a lovely bit of executive pink. I might just kidnap her." I swung her up and twirled her about.

Kennedy laughed and kicked up her pink skyscraper heel.

I frowned. Her look was very familiar, but I couldn't place her costume. Especially with the blond wig. "And who might you be?"

She curtsied with a little grin. "Elle Woods at your service."

I laughed, glancing from her to Hunter. "Movie?"

"Oh, Owen. We'll have to add a few movies onto the bus."

I fiddled with my hook. "Well, don't keep me in suspense."

She flipped her hair over her shoulder. "*Legally Blonde* of course."

"And why would I know a chick flick?"

"Right there is why you don't get enough callbacks for a second date."

My eyebrow rose. "Is that why? I thought it was because I stole away in the night to get to my ship before they could trap me."

She rolled her eyes. "Some girl is going to change your mind when you least expect it."

I forced my grin to stay on my face. The one I wanted was no longer available. I beefed up my pirate voice. "Aye, but the fun of the chase will keep my bed warm until then." I gave her a sweeping bow and nodded to Hunter in full Dominic Toretto gear. "You keep Dom here out of trouble."

Hunter swiped his hand over his newly shorn hair. "Go get your own wench." He pulled Kennedy into his side. "We're going to find a car to debauch later, right?"

Kenny flushed and punched him in the ribs. "Maybe."

"Just make sure he's not too fast or too furious."

Hunter groaned. "Awful."

I laughed. "Yeah it was." I swiveled to take in the room. I lifted a hand to wave at Wyatt. He tipped up a bottle of beer and gave me a salute. He didn't put much effort into his outfit, opting to wear what he'd worn in his old Formula 1 racing days.

Didn't stop the ladies from draping themselves all over him. Then again the ginger just had to walk in the room. He was usually a head taller than most. Now clad in white, red, and black with the top unzipped as if he'd just jumped out of his car, he was at the center of attention along the bar.

"Looks like everyone's getting along."

Hunter's jaw flexed. "Mostly."

I sighed. I was hoping he'd missed that. "Saw Victoria, then?"

Kenny laced her fingers with his. Hunter looked down at her and gave her a half smile. "Sorry."

"It's fine. I saw her making a scene earlier. I don't even know about what. A tray of glasses hit the tile though. Much green punch."

"Viper," I muttered.

Hunter's rueful smile tipped up into a flashing grin. "Good word."

"I saw Bats chasing her out the front."

"Good," Hunter muttered. "Maybe he took her the hell home."

"I hope not."

We both raised our brows at Kenny. "Beg pardon?" I asked.

"You guys have a photo op in front of the Houdini box. Our hour is at ten o'clock." She nodded to the huge glass box replica of the one Houdini had used in one of his many illusions. Right now it was a flurry of green with bills flying around in an cyclone.

A blond that I vaguely recognized was standing on the top of the stairwell to drop in a wad of cash. She flashed a wide smile at the crowd as it was sucked in and added to the purple hued storm. Purple numbers spun like a Vegas slot machine. A cackling screech flooded out and the goal total went up by ten thousand dollars.

"Who thought that up?" I asked.

Kenny beamed. "Keys."

My stomach lurched. Of course it was Faith. She loved the dramatic way of making the donation into a fun game. One of the reasons I loved her. She got that ridiculous Game Show Network side of me.

"Sounds like her."

"Your envelope is ready to drop in whenever you want."

"Is that right?" I snagged a drink from a pretty waitress dressed in all black with a skeleton printed on every luscious inch of her. I grinned in thanks and sipped the frothy purple punch as she spun and smiled invitingly at me.

When I gathered my wits again, I laughed and shrugged at Kenny's deadpan face. "What?"

"Shameless."

I scratched my neck with my hook. "As if there was any doubt."

Kenny rolled her eyes. "So go up there and put it in would you?"

"Must get my picture taken, right?" I frowned. "I donated with my banker, love."

Kenny's smile widened again, obviously pleased with herself. "A little inventive Monopoly money. Can't have that kind of cash available. At least not with Quinn around. He nearly had a heart attack when I wanted to use real money."

"He is a careful one."

"You say it like that's a bad thing."

I swallowed down the green that had been flowing out my throat with too much whiskey and bubbles. "Someone has to keep us in line, right?"

"Damn right."

I turned to the deep voice of the man in question. A red flush marched up his neck, but Quinn Alexander stared me down. I sucked back a guffaw of laughter. His makeup was as heavily smudged as if Nikki Sixx had taken a hand to his eyes. The bloody bastard could rock the leathers though.

Fucker.

He certainly had the surly rock god look down, though when it came to Quinn it was just his natural state of being. Surly that is. And honestly, I just didn't get it, because Keys was such a patch of sunshine.

But then Quinn glanced down at her, and his face softened. He ran a proprietary hand down her back as she curled into him.

And that was my cue. No way could I continue to watch that. A little too fresh on the personal pummeling thank you very little. I caught an angel in the crowd and let her lead me into the throng of people.

"Don't forget to check in with the Houdini box!" Kennedy yelled after me.

I turned and waggled my eyebrows at her. "Yes, Ma."

She gave me a very unladylike gesture. Obviously she'd been spending far too much time with us animals.

I flitted from angel to devil, and then finally to Sinderella, who definitely deserved the alternate spelling. My Disney movies never included *that* kind of dress.

Finally, I climbed the stairs to the cage with the lights bleeding purple and white from the bottom. Delightfully wicked skulls covered the banister railings at the bottom and top of the stairs. I trailed my fingers over the winding purple lights as I climbed.

I nodded to one of my label mates, Gray Duffy, who was lifting his wife to the cash box. The ever adorable Jazz Duffy was dressed as Tinkerbell. She was dumping her bit of money into the glittering Houdini box.

"This is freaking awesome," she said with a grin over her shoulder. Her eyes widened when she saw me. "Let me down!"

"Finish dumping the money in," Gray said patiently.

"Oh, right." Jazz stuffed in the rest of her money, then wiggled.

I laughed.

"All right. Lord, woman."

She narrowed her eyes at Gray.

"You know that doesn't really work when your eyes are more glitter than anything else."

"The evil eye always works, buddy." She hopped down and rushed over to me.

"I guess I can't call you Purple Pixie tonight, hey?"

"Green Pixie thank you very much." She laid a gentle hand at my shoulder and brushed a kiss over my cheek. "That was for the hand drawn art you sent me for the kids shirts we've been designing."

I hugged her close. "How could I resist?" Jazz had been working on baby lines for food and clothing with her bandmate's wife, Harper McCoy. When she'd asked me to draw "something Irish" for her, I'd been happy to comply.

I had a stash of Irish knots for rings and it had been easy enough to doodle one up for her. Sitting on a plane or a bus with a bunch of animals left me plenty of time to sketch in my lyric book.

Keys had started coloring on the plane, and because wherever Keys was I tended to follow, I'd ended up playing with the manly colors to appease her.

She'd grown tired of the fad, but it had stuck for me.

Gray stepped off the stool and brushed his hands on his...skinny jeans? That didn't seem like him. He tugged at a wig and I snickered. "How's it hanging, Mick?"

Gray gave me a Mick Jagger snarl and draped an arm around Jazz's shoulder. "Nice to see you again, Blackwell. Quite the party."

I shrugged. "We like Halloween." I turned to the room at large. Twirling dancers, a handful of photographers that Kennedy had vetted, and a whole lot of alcohol-induced frivolity seemed to be a key factor to our annual charity Halloween party.

My gaze locked on a woman with high waisted black pants and a white shirt who had just arrived. Her black hair was coiled in the old pinup style. She gripped a professional camera, but she was too occupied talking to the woman at her side to focus on any points of interest.

I wasn't sure why she'd stood out to me. Maybe it was that she was the exact opposite of the overdone and glammed-up women in the room, or perhaps it was the way she was so involved in her conversation with her friend. Or maybe sister, as they were both stunning.

Men approached her, but she didn't seem to notice.

Jazz snapped her fingers in front of my face. "Hello in there."

I blinked. "Sorry."

Jazz looked down into the crowd. "Some saucy wench catch your eye, Hook?"

I laughed. "Many have tried to tonight. Before I let one debauch me, I have to do the money thing."

Her huge blue eyes sparkled. "You're too stinkin' adorable."

"Not nearly as adorable as you, love." I looked over my shoulder again, but the woman was gone. I gave my complete attention to Jazz and Gray, clasping each of their hands. "I saw many bills flying around in there. We appreciate the donation."

Jazz shrugged. "For kids or animals, I'm always in."

"If Hunter and Kenny had their way it would always be animals, but we went for kids this year." I winked before climbing the stairs to the woman with the clipboard.

I glanced down to say my goodbyes but Jazz and Gray were already snuggled up against each other, intimate laughter drifting up to me. I pushed down the twinge of something that felt way too much like jealousy. A perpetual state for me tonight, evidently.

I turned my smile on the delicious belly dancer. "So, you're the one who gets to give me a stack of play money to put into the box, then?"

She smiled. "And a very generous stack it is, Mr. Blackwell." Her voice was a purr. And for a moment I utterly forgot about the green-eyed monster that had been climbing up to nest in my chest.

I much preferred this.

Flirting and attraction were far easier to navigate.

"Then maybe you'll need to help me out." I scratched my neck with my hook. "I could use a hand."

She nibbled on her lower lip, then put down her clipboard. "I can do that."

"Much obliged." I bowed low. And as expected she giggled and moved closer.

I'd keep laughing and smiling until the green monster was snuffed out. No matter how long it took.

Chapter 3

Callie

"Opportunity of a lifetime, huh?" I slid a glance at my sister as we passed the gladiators blocking entry to the wide front doors of the Houdini Estate. "Does that include getting patted down by guys wearing fake tin?"

"It's real tin, lady." One of the gladiators thumped his breast plate and I rolled my eyes as Ava adjusted the press pass around her neck. She'd had it displayed before walking in, of course, but it had blocked some of her cleavage. Somehow she'd managed to drape it just below her twin peaks of glory.

Her pass covered us both. She'd been granted clearance by her friend Keys in the band Hammered, who were some of the featured attendees of tonight's soiree for charity. The article she was there to write about the fabulousness of this shindig needed photos, after all, and her normal photographer was out with laryngitis. Besides, photos were my business, right? So what if I hadn't covered a party this huge since…oh, ever. It was all good. At least according to Ava.

From lizards to my sister's boobs to inebriated rockstars, all in one day. My world was getting more fascinating by the nanosecond.

"Your wig is crooked." Finished fussing with her pass, my sister stepped to me and inched up on her heels to adjust my newly dark hair.

It was coiled and poufed in front in the classic pinup style, but I couldn't stop toying with it. Normally, I braided my hair back for work. Instead I had fussy curls and the length swinging down my spine. I hated having hair on my neck. Playing dress up, I loved. At least I used to.

Pre-Steve. Even early Steve, back when we'd had fun together. Mid-Steve had been tolerable. Late-Steve? Absolutely sucked, so I was years removed from partying or even socializing much. I barely remembered the steps anymore.

Anyway, this wasn't for play. Tonight was a job. Working after the day I'd put in was hard enough, especially since I had a double shift at the bar tomorrow. The bar was what paid my rent and allowed me to afford equipment, so I couldn't sleep in and make up for what I would surely lose tonight. Add in working when I didn't feel appropriately dressed...

Admit it. You don't feel capable, period. You might grumble about reptiles, but that wasn't above your head. Schmoozing with rockstars, though? Miles up and climbing.

"You're shaking."

"What?" I hid my nerves behind the glare I aimed at my sister. "Of course I'm not. I'm just not as steady on these heels. It's been a while."

Ava grabbed my hand and dragged me across the Spanish tiles to the corner beside a large potted plant in a golden urn. So much gold here. It dripped from the chandeliers, the banisters, even the curtains. The feel was glamorous and ritzy, and the old me craved to be let loose, camera in hand.

And alone. I really wished I was all alone, left to safely explore.

"This isn't any big deal, Cal. I swear. I know it seems intimidating, and this is a fancy place, but hello, we weren't exactly raised like paupers."

"It's not the place." I closed my eyes. "I just don't know how to do this anymore. How to smile and flit around as if I belong in this world. I don't anymore."

"Says who? Look at you. You're fucking gorgeous. You have a killer body, and amazing eyes, and you're smart and funny and a million other positive things that would totally disrupt our sister balancing act if I told you every one of them. But even if I don't say them out loud, I still know them." She tugged on a long loose curl and made me smile. "I still have the best big sister in the whole world, and everyone is still jealous of me."

I snorted. "Sure they are. Can you give me a little of what you're smoking?"

"No, but I can slip you some of what I'm drinking." She opened up her tiny purse and pulled out a notebook. At least I thought it was a notebook until she discreetly flipped open the top of the spine. "Straight tequila," she whispered conspiratorially, tossing some back and wiping her mouth. She offered me some and I shook my head. I needed every one of my faculties to get through tonight.

"You know they have an open bar here, right?"

"Sure. But I also know how to get things off on the right foot. You're not the only one who needs to soften the edges, Bettie. Now fix your blouse. Your bikini is showing."

I glanced down at the white shirt I'd tied off over my midriff, hearing Ava's voice in my head all over again.

"Bettie Page rocked a bikini like no one's business. It's a costume, not the real you. Just lose the shirt. Show off that smokin' body you work your ass off for on the elliptical."

But I wasn't losing the shirt, and I wasn't getting loaded, and I was going to have a great time and take some incredible shots. Maybe if I was really lucky, the horror movie fest would still be playing on TV when I got home. I didn't have DVR like the rest of the free world. No nonessentials in the budget of Calliope Templeton, the original drudge.

"Here." I handed her my camera bags and waited until she had a good hold on them before tightening the tie of my shirt. I fluffed my hair, straightened my shoulders and took a deep breath—and realized I had to pee.

Lovely. The nervous tinkling had begun.

"Do you have any idea where the bathroom might be?"

Ava huffed. "Already? Didn't you grow out of that when you were like seven?"

"It's a natural function." I grabbed back my camera bags. "You know what? Never mind. I'll find the bathroom myself."

I heard my sister call after me, but I was on a mission. I rushed up the wide sweeping staircase to the second level, dodging and weaving around an assortment of partygoers. I ducked around an angel, a fox, a pilot and two Donald Trumps before I'd made it halfway up the stairs.

But I pressed on, hoping I'd find a moment's solitude if not the ladies' room. I really needed that too, though perhaps one would lead to the other. Surely it would be quieter upstairs. Already the spookily themed music coming from unseen speakers was becoming fainter. This was a more private space, not meant for such frivolity.

Even if part of me sincerely wished I was having fun too.

At the top of the stairs, I turned left, following the patterned tiles to a circular space at one end. The door to the room was open, and the windows were bell-shaped, curving out so that the man who stood at one, glass in hand, his hair gilded by moonlight, was outlined in sharp relief. Instead of singing along to "Monster Mash", he was belting out his own raucous tune, singing lyrics in another language. Gaelic, if my ear was correct. His costume wasn't unique—I'd seen more than one man wearing a brocade jacket and with a hook for a hand.

None of them looked like him, or had an accent like that. His voice was like whiskey, rich and drugging, winding through my veins like a chaser.

You want fun, baby? Right there. Climb on and take a ride.

While I waged my internal debate—that really wasn't one at all, because c'mon, as if I'd summon the nerve to speak to someone like him—he opened one of the balcony doors and stepped out. The balcony seemed narrow enough that he might have been suspended in air. A gleam of blue reflected off the glass in his hand, and when I took a deep breath, I picked up the slightest tinge of chlorine on the breeze.

He was staring down at the pool, and I was staring at him.

Before I could check the impulse, I slung the strap of one of my bags over my shoulder and dug out my camera. I didn't fuss with lenses or apertures. There wasn't time. I just needed to capture on film the image that would live behind my eyes once I closed them tonight.

As quickly as possible, I clicked the button. I couldn't resist angling to the right to try to get in a bit more of him, but then he was turning back to the door, and my need to pee changed from a desire to an urgent need.

Like the coward I was, I fled, shoving my camera back into my bag as I ran. And stumbled right into the bathroom that was one door away.

Once I was safely inside, I locked the door and pressed my hands to the cool porcelain sink. The straps of my bags slid down my arms and for once, I was too rattled to care.

What if he'd seen me?

Of course, I was a photographer, with a press pass. I had a legitimate excuse. But it didn't feel legitimate to be hanging out in shadowy rooms, taking illicit snaps of a man I didn't know.

He could be anything. An actor. A politician. A lawyer, like Steven.

A rockstar.

Shuddering, I set aside my equipment and took care of business. Then I washed up, carefully splashing a little water on my neck to bring down my temperature. Time to cool my jets. I was there to do a job. Ava had invited me to take pictures of the event to accompany her article for *Music Life,* and a big part of that article would revolve around the musician types in attendance. If the guy I'd taken sneak photos of was a rocker, well, then I'd gotten my first great shots of the night in already.

I dried off my hands and grabbed my bag to unearth my camera. Were the shots great? Hard to imagine they wouldn't be with that subject. They might be dark, but I could do some touchups in Photoshop. Besides, I liked the moody surroundings. They fit him. Isolated by choice, ruminating over the events of the night and the people below him, frolicking in the pool. Solitary, sexy beast of a man.

Swallowing hard, I flicked through the pictures I'd taken. They'd need some work, but not as much. He was as glorious in this view as he'd been in the flesh. Tall, well-built, that silky dark hair spilling every which way. Inky black and thick, the kind meant for a woman's hands.

My hand trembled around my camera. Christ, what was wrong with me? He wasn't for me.

Just a guy at a party. Just a subject who probably had more women in his life than weeks of the year. He seemed that type.

"Fucking famous," I muttered. "I know you are. You're no attorney. You're someone who prowls around for salivating females."

Hearing myself, I cast a quick glance at the door. There were voices too close outside. People probably needed to use the bathroom. How rude was I being?

Just another minute more.

I clicked a couple buttons and emailed the best of the photos to myself. Then I pulled out my phone and used the picture to do a reverse image search on Google.

Surprise, surprise, the man I'd lusted after—in a purely professional sense, of course—had pages and pages of hits.

"Owen Blackwell, bassist of Hammered," I murmured, amused at myself. At life.

Of all the men I could have spotted first at this party, I'd lasered in on one of my targets. I wasn't a newb. I'd done research on the artists who would be at the shindig once Ava had told me who I'd be photographing, but I hadn't had long in the car to scroll through everyone. Ava had mentioned Oblivion, so I'd started there. Then I'd moved on to Hammered. I'd flipped through bios on each of the band members but Keys and Owen. I hadn't even seen a picture of either yet, but Ava had told me enough about her pal Keys to fill in some of the details.

Owen, however, was a mystery.

I started to scroll through the pages of hits. Where to begin? The guy seemed to be a mega star. His whole band was. But I wasn't interested in finding out stuff about Hammered right now. I wanted to know the pertinent details about Owen Blackwell. Where he was from, what his music sounded like.

If he was single.

Nope, not going there. Ah, what hurt would it do to look? No one would know.

I bit my lip and pulled up his Wikipedia entry, scanning through info about his modest upbringings. Ireland. Damn. Didn't that just fit? I skimmed through his preferred bass guitars, the garage bands he'd played with before meeting up with Hunter Jordan, the lead singer of Hammered.

A loud knock sounded at the bathroom door. "Hey, gotta go. You almost done in there?" The voice belonged to a very pissed-off female.

While I didn't blame her, I was on a mission. "Yeah, yeah, just a second."

I scrolled on, not stopping until I reached the personal life section, where it named a few famous types he'd dated over the years. Nothing for long, no one serious. At least if Wikipedia knew what it was talking about. So he might very well be single right now, or what passed for single with rockstars anyway.

And it matters why?

The knocking became more insistent. "Listen, lady, there's a line forming out here."

"Yeah, yeah, sorry, almost done, I swear." I went back to the list of hits and went to another article about a stalker going after Keys. A picture of Keys and a couple of her bandmates was included with the piece, and Owen was standing off to the side, his gaze all for Keys.

I knew that expression. Worry, yes, but I would've bet my Nikon that there was more there than friendship. I made my life trying to get people to emote on camera, so I had a good idea what I was looking at.

Had they been an item? I didn't see it in Wikipedia, but maybe they'd missed something. Perhaps it had been on the down low. Or maybe it was one of those unrequited things. Thoughtfully, I chewed on my thumbnail. One-night stand gone wrong? Friends with benefits?

"Lady, if you don't open this door right now, I'm coming in there. My boyfriend will pick this lock," Pissed-Off Woman threatened, punctuating her words with sharp raps of her fists.

I sighed. Whatever the deal was with Owen and Keys, I wouldn't

320 CARI QUINN & TARYN ELLIOTT

be finding it out right now. If there even was one. Besides, I had a job to do, and it wasn't searching for gossip that was none of my business.

Like he was none of my business, even if my suddenly raging libido didn't seem to care.

"That's it, lady, we're coming in!" The screech outside the door broke off as I turned the knob with one hand and grabbed my camera stuff with the other.

I smiled at the woman and her giant of a boyfriend, my heart racing at the now winding line of people behind them waiting to use the facilities.

Man, when I got inexplicably horny, people paid the price.

Sorry, everyone.

"My apologies," I said to the woman. "Don't eat the cream puffs." I pushed past her and weaved through the grumbling partygoers until I made it to the stairs and safety.

Once I'd made it down them, I slipped into the laughing crowd, winding through an assortment of spooky and sexy creatures in search of my sister. I could text her, of course, and I probably would soon if I couldn't locate her. But first, maybe I'd get the lay of the land from behind the lens.

Where I was always most comfortable.

I slung one bag over my shoulder and took out my Nikon, going with a lens more suited for panoramic shots. Later, I'd go for more intimate.

My finger never stopped clicking the shutter as I moved through the crowd. A couple times, I was so focused on the wide angle shot I was going for that I nearly tripped over my own feet. Or someone else's feet, usually ones that were dancing.

More than a couple guys tried to get my attention. I wasn't sure if it was because of me or the camera I wielded. A lot of fame junkies liked to chat up the photogs in hopes of getting more favorably photographed. I simply smiled and kept right on going.

Hours seemed to pass while I circled and shot, circled and shot. As I went, I swapped one lens for another, changing the aperture depending on the intimacy of the picture I was going for. In a stroke of pure luck, I walked right into Mick Jagger and Tinkerbell, and my surprise at the costume combo led to my meeting Gray Duffy and his wife, Jazz, two of the members of Oblivion. Once I'd taken a few fun close-ups of them, they introduced me to some of the other musicians in attendance. Hunter Jordan and his new wife, Kennedy, were both extremely gracious. Even better, they were insanely photogenic.

I probably took ten pictures just of them.

Once I told them I was a cat lover, they all but offered to drive me over to their rescue of choice, Love 'n Paws. That my apartment didn't allow pets seemed to be of no consequence.

I liked them immediately.

Next up I met Zach Kane and Reed Mason, the guitarists for Hammered. They were best friends with entirely different vibes. Zach had a zany sense of humor, but he seemed pretty low-key. Not so much for Reed, who was known as Bats, which made sense when I snapped a shot of him parading around while doing lewd—and admittedly amusing—things to a beer can.

After that, I was introduced to the band's drummer, Wyatt. Holy crap, he was tall. I squinted and cocked my head, trying to place where I'd seen him before when he put me out of my misery and told me he'd used to race Formula 1.

"Wild Man Wyatt," I exclaimed, my eyes going wide. "No fucking way." I flushed at his grin. "Pardon."

"Pardon? Oh God, you're cute." He gripped my elbow and steered me toward a waiter who offered us both glasses of purple punch in fancy glasses. "Would you like a drink?" he asked me, and I found myself nodding in spite of my reticence.

I'd been working for hours already, and the party was nearing its peak if not about to slide past it. Might as well take a load off. A small one, because I had hours of work yet.

"Sure. Thank you." I took a small sip of the punch and popped my eyes wide. "Wow, that's strong."

Wyatt laughed at me and sipped his own without blinking. "So let me guess. You're a good girl who rarely drinks while on the job." He inclined his chin at the camera hanging around my neck. "Is that how you know who I am? Did your work take you across the pond?"

"I wish." I took another tentative sip. "I've never traveled much. Born-and-bred Californian."

"You're a photographer who doesn't travel much? How does that happen?" Smoothly, he took my camera bags off my shoulder as they slipped down yet again. "What's your name, by the way?" he asked before I could question the move. "Seems rather one-sided for you to know me and I don't have the same pleasure."

"Callie," I replied automatically, leaning toward him to safely tuck away my camera into its bag. I zipped it up securely and eased back. "Callie Templeton."

Immediately, one of his ginger brows rose. "Sister to the beautiful Ava?"

I tried not to wince. Ava was beautiful, and I adored my sister. But it was hard not to feel like an old, tired shoe sometimes in comparison. "The one and only. You know her?"

"Met her tonight when she was palling around with Keys."

Keys. The woman the sexy, mysterious Owen had been looking at like she was a big juicy steak and he hadn't eaten in a lifetime or two.

Stop reading between the lines. Didn't Steve accuse you of that often enough?

"Keys and Owen, are they a thing?" I asked, as casually as possible. Just to see if I was right, of course. I didn't really care. It wasn't as if I even knew the guy.

Though I still needed to take his picture before I could go to sleep tonight. Face to face, eye to eye. No more hiding in doorways to snap him in secret.

His and Keys.

Wyatt laughed. "You're kidding, right? She's with Quinn."

I remembered that name vaguely from my super quick stealth recon mission in the bathroom. "Her bodyguard, right? From when that stalker…" I trailed off as a shadow passed over Wyatt's face and he nodded grimly.

"Yes. He saved her life."

"Quite a setup for romance," I mused, shoving down the resulting tickle of envy.

First, I'd wondered if Owen and Keys were a thing, now I was pondering her thing with her bodyguard. And one thing didn't preclude another thing, but I wasn't about to ask Wyatt if Keys and Owen had ever been together.

Again, not my business. This was just a job. I didn't know these people. Hell, I didn't even listen to their music.

Couldn't have picked their songs out of a lineup on the radio.

My preferred era was the nineties, with some eighties thrown in for good measure. I definitely wasn't up on current music. Especially not rock. I tended to prefer pop and R&B. Softer songs meant for easy listening.

No screaming for me, thanks.

I didn't know if Hammered's music was of the screaming variety. I had no clue. Ava said they were good, and judging from her taste, I'd made an unflattering guesstimate of their sound. Not like me. Usually I was more open-minded.

A tiny bit anyway.

There must be something about the air in this place. I was coming to snap judgments and feeling all kinds of things that I hadn't felt in forever.

Lust. Jealousy. Lust.

Oh, and did I mention lust? So much that I might just make cardboard cutouts of the pictures I'd taken of Owen and do bad things to them later when I was alone?

Okay, I wasn't that bad. And it wasn't like there was a shortage of handsome men in this place, not the least of which was standing right in front of me.

"Hudson Wyatt," I said, trying to remember what I'd read about him earlier. Somehow I hadn't put together his past and present in my sister's car, but it had slammed right into focus once I'd met him in the flesh. "Drummer for Hammered, former race car driver. Successful one at that. Now effortless camera-bag juggler." I nodded at the bags of mine he still held as if they were weightless. "Is there anything you can't do well?"

The corner of his full lips ticked up, his smirk partially hidden by his scruff. Just the right amount. Not too much or too little. "Oh, I'm sure there are a few things. But I do have my skills."

From the way his blue-green eyes were sparkling, I had a good idea of the skills he was referring to. And I flushed. Like an adolescent.

Charming, Callie, almost thirty and you absolutely have no idea how to flirt.

Oh, I had once. So long ago the same rules probably still didn't apply.

"I wasn't coming on to you," I said quickly, gulping down more punch when his knowing smile grew. "I just was trying to make conversation."

"Oh, I know. No sparks here whatsoever, are there?" He said it more than a little sadly, and I found myself smiling back. "Shame, too, because you're easily one of the most beautiful women here tonight."

"She is, isn't she? I've been trying to get up the nerve to say that all night, but now that you've done it for me, hi there."

I blinked at the so-not-suave guy in *Miami Vice*-wear who slid between us like a knife between two slices of bread. Except he did it extremely awkwardly, shoving his way in without paying any mind to the bags of my equipment on Wyatt's hip or the fact that I had a glass of punch in my hand.

A glass of punch that was now splattered on my white shirt, and quickly seeping through to the bikini beneath.

Fuck, that was cold on my overheated skin. My nipples felt like mini ice picks.

Oh lookie there. *Miami Vice* guy had already noticed their current condition. If he noticed any harder, he'd probably pop a blood vessel.

Defensively, I set down my glass on the closest table and crossed my arms over my breasts. If I could have, I would have covered my entire body to hide it from his prying eyes. "What the hell, dude?"

"Oh, I'm sorry. I'm a little clumsy sometimes." Don-Johnson's-worst-nightmare's too-white teeth gleamed as he again dropped his gaze to my dripping chest. "Guess that means you'll have to lose the shirt, hmm?"

I didn't think. Embarrassment and discomfort and flat-out irritation welled up inside me and I lifted my fist, intending to plant it right in the faux ladykiller's cleft chin.

Halfway up, someone caught my hand. And it wasn't Wyatt, who seemed perplexed by the recent events.

Definitely wasn't leering dude.

Warm fingers and a calloused palm closed around my hand. Tightly. Possessively. Heat traveled up my arm, setting off a trail of heat like gasoline lit by a match.

My eyes connected with Owen's. And I'm almost positive I died seventy-two times in quick succession, only to be reborn in the same mortified state as I'd departed this mortal coil.

"Not the best idea, love." That voice. That accent. God. Who needed panties?

I already had to lose the shirt. Might as well go full monty and strip all the way down and beg him to take me.

I'm sure he wouldn't mind. Annoyed punch-embalmed Bettie Pages were always a hot ticket on the open market.

"You're going to want to apologize to the lady," Owen said to Don's black sheep fifth cousin. "Now."

The guy spluttered until Wyatt stepped forward and lifted an eyebrow. "Now."

"I'm sorry," he mumbled. "I just saw you a couple times tonight, and you were so pretty, and these blasted rockstars get all the babes."

Before I'd picked my lower lip off the floor at being called a babe,

Don Not-son decided that the better part of valor was to abandon the field before he got his ass kicked.

He wasn't wrong. Owen still had hold of my hand, but I'd been about to introduce the jerk's groin to my size-nine chunky heels.

"You can let me go now," I said reluctantly to the guy I'd been mentally stalking all night. I couldn't quite meet his gaze again, in case he had an innate horndog detector.

I was probably beeping in every way known to man. Or woman. He was probably laughing at me on the inside.

But he didn't seem to be. In fact, his smoky blue eyes seemed to smolder into mine as if we were the only two people who existed on the planet. And his fingers tightened around mine, clasping firmly as he brought my hand to his mouth.

"Oh no, love, I don't think so. Not just yet. What's your name?"

I shifted to grab my drink off the table. After taking a quick gulp, I started to answer in my usual way. My name, after all, wasn't a multiple-choice question. But then I glanced back toward where Wyatt had been, and he wasn't there anymore. He'd set my camera bags on the small settee nearby and vanished.

Which meant I was totally on my own, without anyone near me who knew any better to tell me I was making a mistake by telling Owen the first lie that popped into my mind.

"Bettie," I murmured, pressing my glass into his hand so that he would finally let me go. Once he had, I undid my sopping shirt. My timing was suspect even in my own head, but I couldn't claim to be disappointed when his focus dropped to what I'd just revealed.

Amazing how different my reaction was between him and Miami Viceless.

Owen's reaction was different too, though. Instantly, he raised his gaze to mine. He wasn't looking to cop a cheap glance. He was staring right into my eyes and gripping my glass when all I wanted was for him to be holding my hand again.

Stupid. I was so stupid. He must have fifty girlfriends.

He could even have Keys. Or have had her. And who was I to compete there?

Not that I wanted to. It was just the punch making me dizzy. So what if I'd been similarly dizzy when it came to this man all night long?

Fevers always passed, and Halloween always ended.

I just had to keep my head about me long enough to get through the night without any lasting scars. I had enough already.

Swallowing hard, I bent to pick up my camera bags. And heard him inhale sharply.

"Bettie, is it? Bettie, I'm Owen Blackwell. And I think you're going to have to either have a drink with me, dance with me or marry me and have my babies." His heavily rimmed, seductive blue eyes simmered into mine as I turned back to stare. "Your pick, love."

NOW AVAILABLE!
Manipulated

Have you read all the books in our Hammered Series? Each book can be read as a standalone, but to enjoy the series the way we intended, this is the reading order.

Manaconda #1
Manhandled #2
Manipulated #3

Coming October 3, 2017
Manster #4

Would you like to try MORE rockstars? Try our fun series, WILDER ROCK with our first book, ROCKSTAR DADDY. A title under our other pen name, TARYN QUINN.

Rockstar Daddy
Kellan

Fucking blizzard.

Again.

Why was I even surprised?

I was the jackass who had grown up on the outskirts of Turnbull, New York, snow capital of the northeast, and had escaped to sunny LA only to return.

Voluntarily.

No one had held a gun to my head or shackled my wrists. Nope, I'd strapped my surfboard to the roof of my SUV and made the trek home to buy property on the very edge of town. Outside of town, truth be told. Because the icy tundra in the city proper—ha ha—wasn't enough for me. Might as well build a damn shack with my own two hands and surround it with pine trees and solitude.

So much freaking solitude.

True, it was just my vacation home. Cue more laughter. My place to escape from the rigors of being a famous rockstar.

At least the rockstar part was right. In my head if nowhere else. The famous? Working on that. Wilder Mind's first single was due to drop just after the holidays, and our manager, Lila Crandall, was prepping us for the big time. A lot of that was smoke and mirrors designed to build us up into being the showmen we weren't quite yet, but under her bluster, there was a kernel of truth.

Wilder Mind was poised to take on the world.

Me? I was poised to chop some wood so I could hole up in my cabin and spend New Year's Eve soaking up the silence.

No other company. No other voices. Especially no incessant interview questions or even the shrill scream of fans. Not that we'd dealt with much of that yet. Only a taste. A hint of things to come if we were lucky enough to make it big.

In the meantime, it would be just me and my old Taylor acoustic, a roaring fire, and a case of Coors.

Hey, I never said I had highbrow tastes. So sue me.

Blowing out a breath, I heaved the ax through the chilly air, savoring the pleasant burn in my muscles. I was chopping way more wood than I'd need for a weekend at the cabin. If I was lucky, I'd make it back to Turnbull a few times over the winter. With the single dropping, we'd be branching out. Spreading out to do shows some distance from LA, which meant all the press that went with that. I'd be talking myself hoarse before I was expected to go up and bleed out onstage for the price of a ticket.

That was my role. My *new* role. The one I'd craved since I was a kid with a cheap thrift store guitar, a joint in my back pocket, and the requisite amount of teenage angst that made me think I could be a great songwriter.

Now I was getting my shot, and the battered composition notebook I'd been lugging around for years—first in backpacks, then in briefcases during my brief stint working at Ripper Records—was definitely getting a workout.

Just like my arms. I slammed the axe into the snowpack and threw back my head. Shit. The chill seared my lungs, yanking out my breath in icy puffs. And I still wasn't smart enough to go inside.

Nope, I kept splitting logs, continuing until the overcast afternoon turned into dusk. The foggy dark hung in ribbons of mist around my forest, and I didn't stop until the distant cry of a lonely coyote made me think maybe it was time for that fire.

We didn't get a lot of coyotes out this way, but we had some. In this much dense forestation, you got quite the range of creatures. Even the occasional black bear. My mom had told stories about one coming up to the back door and rattling the knob of her folks' old ramshackle place, but I had to think that was bullshit.

Maybe I just hoped it. If a frigging bear couldn't just break down a door, fuck the rest of us who rued being so goddamn polite all the time.

Still, much as I lobbied for the rights of bears and coyotes, I wasn't stupid enough to be whaling on logs after dark. Not when I had a twelve-pack and a hot shower waiting for my sore ass.

"Getting soft," I muttered after stowing the axe and piling up the wood to haul inside.

I grunted as I made my way around the side of the cabin in the knee-deep snow, part of a cord of wood in my arms. Obviously, I needed to hit the gym harder before Wilder Mind went out on tour. My body freaking hurt. I was covered in sweat. Probably looked like a frigging maniac with snow sticking to my beardy face.

I jumped around night after night onstage in closet-sized clubs and bars, but I wasn't as hardy as when I'd lived in good old Turnbull full-time. Back when I'd worked on cars and picked up odd construction jobs to get by.

It had been blind luck and a dose of small town friendliness that had even gotten my ass out to LA. Lila's mom and pop ran the local orchard, and my mom had gotten to talking to Lila's mother one day about how I didn't want to be stuck working construction for the rest of my life. One thing led to another and under six months later, I'd been on a place out to LA to meet with Donovan Lewis, the head of the record label Lila worked for. We hit it off and though I didn't know shit about selling anything that didn't come in a bucket or wrapped in cellophane, I'd ended up as an account rep.

Representing artists. Me. The guy who'd barely graduated high school but could schmooze a quart a milk out of a cow. Or so my mom had claimed to Lila's mother.

Because a way with cows surely meant a way with egotistical, often drugged out musicians. Right.

Somehow it had worked though. Lila said I had a knack. Donovan had given me raises. A bunch of them, in short succession. The mogul some jokingly referred to as Lord Lewis didn't shortchange his talent, and he'd seen something in me. I owed him and Lila a shit-ton of gratitude. First, for hiring me to represent some of their musical acts, and then for trusting me to front a band.

The band part I had more familiarity with. I'd been stroking an acoustic long before I'd stroked my first girl. Let's just say I'd done my share of touching both, and leave it at that.

One more thing about Turnbull? They had some damn fine women, but it was hard to see them clearly under all the layers of outerwear when it snowed for what felt like half the freaking year. I preferred California women anyway. They seemed more good-natured as a rule. Maybe all the sunshine and hot temperatures put them in a better mood.

And goddammit, I loved me a woman in a bikini.

When I reached the front of my property and heard the squeal of tires, I didn't react fast enough. Put the image of a half-naked, tanned woman in the mind of a man who'd nearly frozen his nuts off and who wouldn't miss a car fishtailing off the road?

Right into my ditch.

Tires spun, spewing up snow and dirt and tiny rocks, and a horn went off about sixteen times. And I stared, my wood in my arms. Shocked as hell that anyone had even come down this practically deserted road in the first place, never mind took the curve way too fast and gone ass up in the ditch.

The chick was now attempting to shimmy her way out of the driver's side window. Painfully. With no shortage of groans and screeches and noises no adult female should ever make.

Since she was moving—and frantically at that—I had to figure she couldn't be too badly injured. Still, she could have done harm to herself she'd yet to realize.

With more than a small sigh, I set down the wood on the short set of steps to the cabin, brushed off my hands on the thighs of my jeans, and trudged down the snowy hill to where the squealing damsel's car was lodged.

She turned her neck and gave me the biggest, brightest smile I'd ever seen. I was a little taken aback, since she was half in and half out of a window and her car was fucked up, if not totaled. It appeared to be an older model under the snow and grime, and an accident like hers could screw up the frame. If that happened, the vehicle was shot.

Not that she seemed worried overmuch.

"Hi!" she called over the rushing wind, her voice as cheerful as her expression. "Thank God for you."

I didn't know how to respond to that, so I came around the ditch and eyed her lopsided car. "Yep, well and truly stuck."

She blinked at me from under the pink fringe of a stocking cap. "It's just a little fender bender."

"Oh yeah? Then why are you climbing out of the window?"

She wiggled. "Because the door won't open."

"Seems a bit worse than a fender bender to me." I came around the driver's side, hooked my hands under her armpits in her heavy down coat, and simply plucked her out of the car.

Only afterward did I think of possible internal injuries. Though what possible injury could've allowed her to jump and dance around now that she'd been freed, I did not know.

The other thing I noticed about her right away? She was dressed as if she was in competition with the Michelin man, except her bulk was made out of layers. Many layers. She had earmuffs under her hat to go with her bulky scarf, huge coat, ski pants—likely layered over thermals—and some serious freaking boots with enough snaps and ties to secure a horse.

And yet she was still jumping around, blowing on her gloved fingers, and laughing like a crazy person.

"Whoa, that was nuts. I seriously feared for my life. I saw Jesus and heard angels and all that stuff." She frowned at her car with its likely bent axel. "I paid extra for the best snow tires. I still skidded. That seems like a warranty violation. Don't you think?"

What I thought was this chick was going to talk my head off.

"The forecast predicted two feet today. Typical lake effect. Are you not from around here?" Though it was hard to believe someone from a warmer climate would've been that well-prepared, but maybe. They did tend to have thinner blood than us hardy northern types.

Though what the hell was I saying? I was a California boy now too.

Happily.

I'd never actually heard someone roll their eyes at me before, but her disgust was palpable. "Hello, look at me. Do I seem unprepared for this weather? If anything, I *over*prepared. In my trunk, I have a spare battery kit, a First-Aid kit, a tire repair kit and—"

"Lady, I got it. You're prepared. You just spun out. It happens."

She propped her hands on her hips. Or at least where I figured her hips would be. Hard to tell with her coat.

"Very pragmatic of you, buddy, but now what? I'm stuck and I need to get to Mrs. Pringles' before she goes to New Year's Eve mass. This is her first year without her husband, and she puts on a brave face, but she and Joe were so in love. It was sweet to see, really. And if I can't get there before mass, then I'll have to wait until she gets back, or worse yet, go join her in the church, which would be okay except I kind of got ex-communicated last year."

I wiped away the flakes collecting on my face. I would've hoped my expression coupled with how I looked might've intimidated her— big, burly, bearded—but if anything fazed this one, it wasn't me glaring at her during her endless monologue.

"I'm sure I'll regret asking this, but why, exactly, do you need to go to grandmother's house?"

She brushed snow off the arms of her coat. It was coming down faster than she could efficiently whisk it away. "Oh, she's not my grandmother—"

"That was a joke, Red." I gestured toward her attire. Red and pink everything, which didn't go together but somehow seemed to suit her. "You also have a car instead of a basket, but let me mix a metaphor or two."

"Ah. Big bad wolf, is it then? Sorry, you don't seem to fit." She marched toward me and grasped the side of my pants. "Wile E. Coyote sweats aren't exactly scary, tough guy."

"Don't touch," I growled and that made her step back and cock her head, much like a puppy. Instead of a floppy ear, she had the bouncy pouf on top of her hat. "I can't just touch you."

She seemed to think about that. It was getting darker, and the snowflakes falling between us were coming faster and harder. But if I wasn't mistaken, she was pondering that comment as if I'd just said the most important thing she'd ever heard.

"No," she said after a moment. "I guess you can't. You shouldn't. Just because Derek ran off with Trini isn't a reason for me to let strange men touch me. Especially ones wearing sweatpants."

"What's wrong with sweatpants?"

The most ridiculous thing about this whole conversation? I didn't *want* to touch her. I was almost sure. So what if it had been a while for me? That was by choice. God knows I had women throwing themselves at me front, back and center, and it only promised to get worse as things took off with the single. I'd backed off the fuck-and-duck game simply because I'd gotten bored.

I was tired of fake women cloaked in pretenses who just wanted me for my fame. As much as I exploited my growing fame to get any damn thing I wanted.

Never said I wasn't a fucked-up bastard, now did I?

"There's nothing wrong with them, per se. They're just not fashionable."

Although my face felt as if it was freezing into place, I cocked a brow. "Oh, and that eye-searing combo you have on is? You practically have on a snowsuit. Like a child."

Her cheeks reddened. I don't know how I could tell the difference considering she'd been awful damn pink from the wind to start with, but somehow, I knew I'd gotten to her. "I'm not a child. I'm a grown woman who likes to be prepared."

"Huh." I crossed my arms and jutted my chin toward her car. "So how's that working out for you?"

She stepped forward, kicking up snow with her gigantic boots. Then she let her gaze wander down the front of me and let out a little *harrumph*. "And you know what else? Statistics say that eighty-eight-point-six of grown men who wear sweatpants are either still living in their mother's basements or they're serial killers."

Deliberately, I moved into her space, dwarfing her with my size. And yet again, she did not back down. "Those are some odds, Red. Are you feeling lucky?"

WANT MORE?
Visit www.tarynquinn.com for more info!

FOUND IN OBLIVION

A ROCKSTAR SERIES

Bedded Bliss #1

Triple Trouble #2

Dirty Duet #3

Lost Lyric #4

Coming August 4, 2017

Perfect Pitch #5

IF YOU'D LIKE MORE INFORMATION ABOUT THE SERIES & EXTRAS,

PLEASE VISIT WWW.ROCKERREADS.COM.

HAMMERED

A ROCKSTAR ROMANTIC COMEDY SERIES

Manaconda #1

Manhandled #2

Manipulated #3

Coming October 3, 2017

Manster #4

IF YOU'D LIKE MORE INFORMATION ABOUT THE SERIES & EXTRAS,

PLEASE VISIT WWW.ROCKERREADS.COM.

LOST IN OBLIVION

USA TODAY BESTSELLING ROCKSTAR SERIES

IF YOU'D LIKE MORE INFO, PLEASE VISIT WWW.ROCKERREADS.COM.

LOST IN OBLIVION

USA TODAY BESTSELLING ROCKSTAR SERIES

SEDUCED

Music kept them going. Now it might tear them apart…

Guitarist Nick Crandall has one focus in his life—Oblivion, the band he started with his closest friends, lead singer Simon Kagan and bassist Deacon McCoy. After losing their drummer to rehab, they take on two members, one of them female. A YouTube video gone viral later, Oblivion is heading to the top faster than they ever dreamed. If the band doesn't break up—and hearts don't get broken—before they manage to sign their first recording contract.

ROCKED

Music saved him, but now it's keeping him from the only woman he craves...

Hot nights with a naughty, inventive rockstar are one thing, but more isn't on the playlist. Until Deacon's dream with his best friends starts turning into a nightmare, and Harper begins to see the real man behind the façade. Except Harper has her own dreams to chase, even if what she's started with Deacon might be the most important one of all.

ROCK, RATTLE & ROLL

Loving in fast forward...

A beachfront cottage, hours of alone time, and plenty of skin on skin action is just what the rockstar ordered. Until the future once again comes much quicker than Deacon and Harper expected, threatening to crumble not only their perfect honeymoon but also their brand new marriage.

TWISTED

Sometimes the knight in shining armor needs to be saved himself...

Being the rhythm guitarist in one of the country's hottest bands with his best friend Jazz is Gray Duffy's dream come true. Now that they're making music together, the time is right for Jazz to make a move toward the man she loves. If the secret he's keeping doesn't destroy them—and their band.

UNTWISTED

Falling in love was easy...figuring out the rhythm of being a couple, not so much.

Now that they've pressed play, life is going way too fast for Gray Duffy and Jazz Edwards. A super hot video has boosted their band Oblivion's popularity even higher, and suddenly Gray and Jazz are the reigning prince and princess of rock. But as their private wedding ceremony in their treasured place approaches, they realize they can't go forward without facing their roots.

DESTROYED

Only one woman has ever refused him…and she's the only one he wants.

Now that he's beyond successful with Oblivion, lead singer Simon Kagan is enjoying his all-access pass to the groupie train. But from the moment he met Margo Reece, he knew the classy, buttoned-up violinist was different. After an amazing night in the studio, he's finally connected with someone on a deeper level—only to have her walk away without a backward glance. Except maybe Margo is ready to take a walk on the wild side…or even fall in love with the one man she was never supposed to. If it's not already too late.

CONSUMED

Is it better to burn out or fade away…

Oblivion lead singer Simon Kagan is used to being in the spotlight, but not because of the epic ending to Oblivion's last show. That unforgettable night rocked the band in more ways than one, and now the journey back seems almost impossible. The only bright spot is Margo. As long as she never realizes the man she fell for no longer exists, maybe he won't lose everything that matters due to just one all-consuming night.

SHATTERED

He's shattered…and she's the only woman who can help him pick up the pieces.

Nick Crandall has everything he ever thought he wanted, but it doesn't stop his dream from shattering, right before his eyes.Until the person he least expects pulls him back from the brink. Ripper Records exec Lila Shawcross isn't about to let a hot-headed, hard-bodied lead guitarist wreck her orderly existence or dilute her focus from managing the band. Except Nick is determined to possess her…and what Nick wants, Nick gets.

FUSED

They're shattered...and he's the only one who can fuse them back together.

From the pinnacle of success to the depths of despair, Oblivion has been through it all. Nick Crandall is the only one who can begin to put the pieces back together after the most catastrophic night of his life. That includes making a stand to win back the woman he needs. His only choice is to fight hard and dirty for what—and who—he loves.

OWNED

Music kept them going. Now it's torn them apart...

Guitarist Nick Crandall lost the most important thing in his life—his band—just as he was falling in love. A year after going on hiatus, Oblivion is returning to the studio and he's about to ask the woman he loves to marry him. Simon has spent the past year trying to find his way back to the thing that sustained him in his darkest hours, then grew to be his biggest demon. With Margo's help, he's ready to admit it's showtime. It's do or die, one more time.

IF YOU'D LIKE MORE INFORMATION ABOUT THE SERIES & EXTRAS, PLEASE VISIT WWW.ROCKERREADS.COM.

ABOUT THE AUTHORS

USA Today bestselling author *Cari Quinn* likes music and men, so she figured why not write about both? When she's not writing, she's screaming at men's college basketball games on TV, playing her music too loud or causing trouble. Sometimes simultaneously.

USA Today bestselling author *Taryn Elliott* is obsessed with rock stars, men, and her unending playlists—maximizing these things seemed like a very good idea. When she's not writing, she's losing hours to hot men on TV, and/or a graphic design project. Multitasking is her middle name.

They decided to combine forces and found that hey...this writing deal is even more awesome when you collaborate with your best friend.

And so **the Oblivion World** was born.

You can find more information about them on www.rockerreads.com.

www.ingramcontent.com/pod-product-compliance
Lightning Source LLC
Chambersburg PA
CBHW061321200626
46813CB00016B/2312